MARK OF THE SHADOW

MARK OF THE SHADOW

WICKED HUNTERS
BOOK ONE

J. L. JACKOLA

ALSO BY J. L. JACKOLA

FANTASY ROMANCE

Unbound Prophecy Universe

Unbound Prophecy Series

Ascension

Descent

Surfacing

Submerged

Riven

Adrift

Unbound Kingdom

Severed Kingdom

Cursed Kingdom

Prophesied Kingdom

Unbound Kingdom (the trilogy omnibus)

Unbound Prophecy Sequels

Orlaina

Wicked Hues Universe

Wicked Hues Series

The Forgotten Hues of Skye

The Coveted Hues of Skye

The Shattered Shades of Crimson

CONTEMPORARY ROMANCE

Paper Memories Series

Paper Flowers

Paper Horses

Standalones

The Wishing Thread

Library of Congress Control Number: 2024909287

Paperback ISBN 978-1-960784-41-4
Hardback ISBN 978-1-960784-42-1
Electronic ISBN 978-1-960784-43-8

Distributed by Tivshe Publishing
Printed in the United States of America

Cover design by Dawn Bookcover Designs
Map design by Worldwyrm

Visit www.jljackola.com

AUTHOR'S NOTE
TRIGGER WARNINGS

Mark of the Shadow is the first book in my Wicked Hunters duet. Please be aware that it contains content that may not be suitable for all readers, including explicit sexual scenes, an aggressive & unapologetic mmc, language, and violence.

NILIKE

SNEPORE
WISTIRE

CHAPTER 1

CALLUM

The streets were busy, and the morning sun glared off the glass buildings and the chrome of the cars. I wiped my eyes against the brightness that irritated them. My preference was to work at night, in the shadows, but my mark was more active in the day, and I wanted to observe her before I made the kill. I knew it was twisted, but after centuries of hunting, I liked to break up the monotony. Getting inside the heads of my marks added a level to my hunt that kept me satisfied.

"Have you spotted your mark yet, Callum?" Gerrand's voice came through my earpiece.

One would think with our unique abilities, we'd have a more sophisticated method of communication. I shook my head and scanned the active sidewalk below, my heightened vision allowing me to see even the smallest details. This was my first scouting of her, but I'd know her when I saw her. My instinct would draw me to her. The description Gerrand had given me provided little, except she was a tall brunette. Considering the number of brunettes walking by, that wasn't the most helpful information.

"No, I—"

A brunette turned the corner, tall and fuller-figured than the petite blonde she walked with. She held a cup of coffee in one hand and a phone in the other while she talked animatedly to her companion. Coffee sloshed over the tiny lip in her lid, but she took no notice. Her blue eyes were bright in the sunlight. There was a strange tightness in my chest when her eyes looked my way, as though she could see me hidden on the rooftop in the shadows. Within seconds, she turned away, and the breath flooded back into my chest. I hadn't realized it had been stuck, my body forgetting how to breathe.

"Callum?" Gerrand said.

I ignored him, my eyes trailing her, taking in the sway of her hips and the way her jeans sculpted perfectly to the voluptuous ass below them. Her leather jacket hid most of her upper body, but slipped around her chest enough to accent the ample breasts below. She wore her hair in a ponytail that followed the movement of her steps, swinging back and forth over her back. I watched as she chatted to the doorman of the building to the left of me, my eyes staring at the door long after it had closed behind her and stolen her from my view.

Sitting back, I tried to grasp what had come over me. I wiped my hand over my face, noting the slight shake in it. Never had I been so intrigued by a mark. Never had I found one so tempting. To even contemplate touching one in any way but extermination risked punishment, and I wanted to touch every inch of this one.

"Callum, what in the gods' name is going on with you?" Gerrand sounded pissed, and I knew I needed to answer him or risk his wrath. He was my commander, at least for the next few months. He'd been grooming me to take over for years, and the mantle of leader of the Shadows was falling on my shoulder. I wasn't sure how I felt about it. I preferred to be active, hunting marks and adding to my kill count.

"I'm fine," I answered finally. "Just spotted her."

"Did you take her out?"

"No, it's too busy here. She's a simple hit, but I'm concerned about what she knows. I want to do a little extra with this one, play a little."

I waited to see if he'd be suspicious. I should have followed her home and killed her while she slept, but my reaction to her intrigued me.

"Play? We don't play with our marks, Callum." Gerrand's tone was gruff, but I heard the questioning. I never deviated from the plan. Sure, I made it fun, scouting out marks and following them to get into their heads for a day or two, but I never involved myself with them. I hunted, I killed, and I left my marks for dead. The only thing I ever did that rubbed the others the wrong way and irritated our gods was to leave a calling card. My calling card—a pair of black wings. It lent a bit of mystery, added some fun to the monotony of the hunt, and gave credence to the mythology that was the Shadows.

The mortals needed to know we existed, no matter that they'd let us fade from their history, letting knowledge of us morph to a myth that now held little credence. We'd let them, taking to the shadows, hiding from their consciousness until we had become only the things of bedtime stories. I hated it. We were the hunters, the ones who kept their streets clean of demons and creatures who infiltrated their lives. We and our enemies, the Torch, were the only things keeping this world safe, even though we remained at war with the Torch. They hunted for the Galere gods, existing in the enemy realm, and vying for our marks. They were constantly getting underfoot and in our way, stealing our kills for their gods.

"Callum. You know what you need to do. I cut you slack with most things, but this mark needs to die quickly. No leaving your clues, no watching her like you do. Quick and efficient."

I wiped my hand over my face, those blue eyes returning to my mind. "If she really knows too much, then I need to find out what exactly she knows."

"It's your fault she knows anything. If you weren't leaving a trail behind for the police and nosy reporters like her, she wouldn't know anything."

"That's bullshit. So they see my symbol—"

"She knows who you are. You play in the mortal world too much, Callum. She's on to you, and she's become a liability."

I did like to play in the mortal world. They fascinated me with their ingenuity, their toys, and their lifestyles. I preferred to live among them rather than with my kind and had even built a persona, one that lived in the world's underbelly. It had its advantages and made finding my marks easier because I knew the terrain and their ways. This part of the world had been my territory long enough to build wealth and a reputation, and now I was leaving clues. Clues my mark had noticed. She was smart, the only one to figure me out, which intrigued me even more.

"I need a few days. Let me lure her in. She's been hunting me down through her contacts, trying to meet with me. Let me bring her into my nest and find out how much she knows and who she's shared with. It will ensure there are no more liabilities out there who need to be dealt with. That should satisfy the gods. I promise I'll discard the persona, maybe start a new one—"

"No, you relinquish your life in the mortal world and return to us. You will be commander of the Shadows soon; your place is here. No more playing with the mortals. No more pretending you're something you're not. You are a Shadow. That's my compromise. Give up your rebellious ways or kill the mark today."

Damn, he'd cornered me. I had no choice but to agree if I wanted to get closer to her. "Fine. I'll return to the fold once this mark is dead, and I have her information."

"Three days, Callum. If she's not dead in three days, I send Trias to kill her."

I gritted my teeth. Trias was my junior, but he'd been making his way up the ranks, determined to take over the Shadows and push me aside. Gerrand knew what he was up to, as did I, but he also knew I detested the way Trias worked. He was messy and violent to an extreme, and if he didn't rein himself in, he'd expose us all. It would satisfy the Torch to no end, but it would bring unwanted attention to us, more than just one curious reporter.

Rolling my neck, I answered, "Agreed. Three days."

"Don't let me down. Whatever's up your ass today, remove it quickly so I don't have to deal with Trias' smug face."

He hung up, and I ripped the earpiece out, squeezing it in my hand until it shattered.

Three days wasn't enough time. "It's longer than you ever take, Callum," I told myself. I should have walked away, given the mark to Trias, or just killed her like I'd been told to, but I didn't. Instead, I picked up my phone and made the call to put her right where I wanted her—in my hands.

CHAPTER 2
HARMONY

You're late." Matt slammed the paper down on my desk, startling me so that I jumped in my typical unladylike fashion, spilling coffee all over my desk.

"I'm not late, and you owe me a coffee," I complained, yanking a handful of napkins from my desk to clean up the mess.

"You're ten minutes late."

I glared at him. "Since when do you care?"

Matt and I had known each other for ten years. In that time, we'd developed enough of a love-hate relationship to allow me the leeway to talk back to him, even if he was my boss.

"Since your story had to be scrapped, I had to scramble to find a replacement."

"You scrapped my story?" I balled the napkins as my aggravation increased and tossed them into my trash bin with an exaggerated force. Gaping at him, I crossed my arms and waited for his explanation.

He pulled a handful of printed pages from behind him and smacked them down on the desk on top of the others. "What were you thinking, Harmony? I can't print this."

I snatched the pages from him, seeing the title of my story at the top. "It's a good story."

"Are you mad? Has someone been slipping something into your coffee? Accusing Callum Montrose of the string of unsolved murders over the past ten years?"

"The killer leaves a mark on each victim, Matt. It's the same as Callum's tattoo."

He pinched the bridge of his nose, a sign that I was driving him close to pulling the bottle of vodka he kept hidden in his desk drawer out early.

"It's Callum Montrose, Harmony. I print something like this, and my head rolls, followed by yours. You can't go around making stuff up."

I dug around in my desk drawer and pulled out the picture of the city's most reclusive, eligible bachelor, Callum Montrose. There were barely any pictures out there, but this one caught his profile—the wavy black hair so thick it screamed for a woman's hands to run through it, the chiseled jawline, and the shoulders that looked strong enough to bring down a door. There was a reason women melted even at the mention of him, glancing over the fact that he lived in the shadows. No one knew for certain where his money had come from. There were rumors he'd inherited it, others that he'd built his fortune in real estate before settling here. Whatever the source, everyone knew he had his hands in almost every part of the town.

"Can't you just imagine clinging to those broad shoulders," Mia cooed from behind me. "And those arms, I bet they'd feel good wrapped around you. I wonder if he likes to grip your neck…he looks like a choker." Matt and I were staring at her. "What? You can't tell me you haven't imagined it, Harm. And even you, Boss. That man is eye candy worthy of being your man crush."

"Do you have a reason for being part of this conversation, Mia?" he asked.

"Just providing my input."

"Take your two cents back to your desk. I believe you have an article about popular lipstick shades to write."

She slinked away, grumbling about how her technical writing skills were being wasted on lipstick and mascara.

"What does a picture of Callum have to do with this blasphemous piece you presented to me?"

"His tattoo." I pointed to the marking on his arm that showed below his short-sleeved shirt. "See. A pair of black wings."

Matt picked up the picture and squinted at it, tipping it from side to side. "Seriously? That's what you're risking both our careers on? This grainy picture? I can barely see the bottom of the tattoo, and calling those two spots of black a pair of wings is stretching it. There's no substance to that suggestion."

"I'm serious, Matt. He's involved."

"Look, Harmony. You're a talented journalist, one of the best we have. And there's a reason I put your stories on the front page. But this," he picked up the pages and crumpled them, "is nothing more than speculation. Callum Montrose, murder, and Shadows." He said the last word hushed, looking around as he brought himself closer to me. "The Shadows are a myth. They're not real and writing a piece that associates one of the most powerful men in the city with them is career suicide."

"I'm on to something—"

"You'll be on to lipstick shades with Mia if you don't drop it."

He walked away before I could come back with any further arguments. The buzz of a text on my phone dragged my eyes away from watching him shut himself in his office.

"Dammit," I muttered, flopping back into my chair and grabbing my phone.

I have what you need.

The cryptic text from Slate had me jumping to my feet. I stared at the phone as the dots danced, indicating another message was coming. My heart was pounding with anticipation.

Meet me at the bar in 10.

There was no reason to respond; Slate knew I'd be there. I ran to Matt's office, barging in without knocking. He almost dropped his flask into his coffee.

"Harm—"

"My contact came through. I think I've got the interview."

His eyes went wide before his lips thinned.

"Don't even think of talking me out of this, Matt. I've been working on this for months. I'm leaving to see what the offer is."

"Shit, Harmony. This could be dangerous, especially with the snooping you've been doing."

"I know, but it's something no other reporter has gotten to do. I'll text you when I know what the offer is."

Not giving him time to talk me out of it, I rushed from the office, snatched my purse from my desk, and bolted.

WHEN I WAS A CHILD, I was awkward and alone. I drifted from foster home to foster home, never fitting in until Slate Dimetri walked up to me on the playground and claimed me as his friend. There was nothing remotely awkward about Slate. He was confident, smug—some might say—and he ruled the school. He would go on to rule the town, becoming the most powerful man in the city. Callum Montrose may have given him a run for his money, but the city had been Slate's long before Callum emerged.

Through his rise to the top of the crime syndicate, Slate never wavered in his friendship with me. And I never judged the path he'd chosen. While I'd earned scholarships to the local university, he was carving his place as a man to be feared. Making sure he didn't miss my graduation, every birthday, and every event in my life because that's what family does, or so he would tell me.

Few knew about my relationship with Slate. It was better that way. He wanted to keep me safe, and I wanted to keep my career separate from his lifestyle, wanting no chance that someone would use my tie to him to take him down. Not that such a thing was possible; he owned everyone in town by the time we were eighteen, and now at thirty-three, the city was his.

"If it isn't the prettiest girl in town," he announced when I entered the bar.

"You're obliged to say that, Slate," I answered, giving a nod to Frank, his bartender. There were few Slate let close enough to know about our friendship, and those included his henchmen whose loyalty to Slate was unwavering and Frank, who had worked with him since the beginning.

"I'll always say that, Harm." Slate gave me a kiss and drew me in for a bear hug that about broke my ribs. "Because it's true. You're my girl, so you are the prettiest."

Rubbing my ribs, I replied, "First, I'm not a girl. Second, I haven't been your girl for a long time, remember?"

"Oh, I remember, Harm. Still the best lips in the province, ain't no one who comes close to blowing me like you did."

I elbowed him, trying to hide my blush. As I'd blossomed in high school, Slate's attention to me had shifted, and my attraction to him had grown. There was no denying he was hot. His dirty blonde hair swept in waves that rested on his forehead to highlight thoughtful brown eyes, the kind that could go from warm and loving to terrifying within seconds. He'd started adding tattoos to his toned muscles the minute his mother gave him the okay, and by the time we'd graduated, they covered most of him. He was hot in a sexy, dangerous boy way, and I'd fallen hard for him. We'd fallen hard for each other until we realized we were too volatile together.

Loving Slate came with risks, and he wanted me nowhere near those risks. By the time I was a junior in college, we'd concluded that we made better friends. Four years of living on the edge with him and juggling life in the real world had been too much, jeopardizing my mental health and his patience, putting the bond we had on the line. We'd turned our back on our attraction to each other until the unbreakable friendship we'd had as children returned. Now we lived a comfortable life that resembled more siblings than lovers, with the occasional reference to my sexual prowess thrown in. Not that I'd been some sexy bombshell. I'd been an inexperienced teenager who had handed her virginity to a boy who brought out the vixen buried deep below. Because sex with Slate had been the best I'd had—rough, demanding, intense, mind-blowing sex.

Shaking the thought of his taste and the way he'd enjoyed fucking my mouth while ripping strands of my hair out in his tight grip, I pushed past him and took a seat at the bar. "I thought it was the swallowing you liked best, Slate."

Frank groaned, and I heard a few chuckles from Slate's two henchmen.

"Shit, that I did." He hopped on the bar seat next to me. "You know, she once deep-throated me so good I blacked out. Fuck, I've never come so hard."

Frank's mouth was hanging open.

"Been a long time, Harm. You want to go down on me for old time's sake? You owe me after hounding me for the past few months."

I never used my relationship with Slate to advance my career, keeping him separate, but I'd called in a favor. I knew he had connections with Callum Montrose. He'd dropped his name a few times over dinner with his family, and as entrenched as Slate was in the goings on in this city, there was no way he didn't know how to contact Callum. I'd been begging him to get me in with Callum, even for a few minutes to talk to him. So far, I'd gotten nothing but silence.

"What would your mother say if she heard you asking me that?"

He gave a loud belly laugh. "She'd be planning the wedding before my cum finished dripping down your chin. You know how heartbroken she was when we broke up. That woman has judged every girl I've had since against you."

"There's no judging against Harmony, Slate," Frank said, dropping two shot glasses in front of us and filling them with vodka.

"I highly doubt that," I mumbled. There were plenty of women with whom I couldn't compete. While I wasn't shy about my body, embracing the fact that my figure was fuller than others and that my hips and thighs didn't take well to skinny jeans, I knew I wasn't cover-model material. I took what the gods had given me and flaunted it. My fuller figure gave me tits that others paid for and a waist made for grabbing in the throes of passion. I loved my body, and it came out in a sexual confidence that intimidated other women and quieter men. Not that I cared; I didn't want a soft man. I liked it hard and dirty, and I wanted to be fucked that way.

I picked the shot glass up and, with a raise of my brow at Frank, I asked, "A bit early for shots, isn't it?"

Slate pushed my hand closer to my mouth. "Drink it. You'll need it after what I'm about to tell you."

I eyed him before downing my shot. Wiping my mouth with the back of my hand, I waited for him to down his.

"See, that's what I love about you, Harm. You chugged that

thing without even flinching. Any other girl would have gagged, but then again, you've never been a gagger."

The laughter that filled the room made me wish I had another full shot so I could toss it at Slate.

"I bet that new girl…what's her name? Brandy? Mandy?… isn't a gagger," I teased back.

"Mindy, and yes, she is. Fuck, I can't last long with all the noise she makes. It gets me so hot I'm coming in minutes."

"That's just gross."

"That's hot, but not as hot as hitting the back of your pretty throat." He reached out and wrapped his hand around my throat, moving it down my neck. The move would have had me soaked if it wasn't Slate. Although I couldn't deny the clench in my thighs; it had been too long since I'd had sex. If we weren't such good friends, I would have gladly fucked him just for the excitement. I hadn't found a man who matched his level of aggression and the mix of commanding ferocity he had.

"Enough, you two," Frank muttered. "Somebody's gonna have to jerk me off if you two don't stop, and Harmony, you're too much like my little sister to make you do that, so it'll have to be one of these wankers."

"Little sister you have wet dreams about," Slate teased.

"Fuck, who wouldn't? Now either fuck each other and let us watch or get down to business."

Slate dropped his hand, leaned over, and kissed my cheek. "Not gonna happen, Frank. Harmony is too much woman for me to handle."

And he was too much man, but he wasn't mine. I knew that deep down. There was someone out there for me, my soulmate, but Slate wasn't that man. And I wasn't that woman for him. I doubted there was a woman who could keep up with him. Mindy didn't seem like she would last. She wasn't his type either, too meek for Slate. He needed someone who could handle herself, and she didn't look like she could handle basic math.

"What do you have for me, Slate?"

"Besides a raging hard-on—" I punched him in the abs. "Fine," he said, rubbing his stomach. "Montrose agreed to meet you."

My mouth dropped to the floor. Callum Montrose wanted to meet with me. Holy shit. My stomach flipped.

"He'll let me interview him?" I wasn't sure why my voice sounded so childlike.

"Yes, but on his terms. And Harm, I don't know that I like his terms."

The room grew tense. Slate was in business mode now—no more teasing or flirting. This was the side of him that kept people under his control.

"What are the terms?"

"This guy is dangerous, Harm."

"What are the terms, Slate?"

He sighed, motioning Frank to pour him another shot. "You're to go to him for the weekend. Leave today, no phones, no electronics. You go alone, follow the instructions exactly as directed, and you do not tell anyone. I don't like this Harmony. No one knows this guy."

My stomach knotted, and I clutched my hands together, hoping Slate didn't notice how they were now trembling. "You know him," I said, trying to sound like those instructions hadn't sent every nerve in my body on edge.

"No, I don't. I've seen him in passing, which is all anyone seems to do. No one knows anything about him." He leaned closer to him, worry creased around his eyes. "He's dangerous, Harm. He has his hands in the same things I do. The only reason I let him keep that position is because he's untraceable. I can't find him to threaten him, and I can't find him to kill him. Not that I would. I know when to pick my enemies, and that's why I do business with him."

"Then you know him."

"No, I do business with him. He has my number, and I have his. It's not a traceable number; trust me, I've tried. He reaches out to me and not the other way around. That's why I haven't been able to do more than mention you in passing a few times."

"I'm sure he's fine. I deal with you."

"You know me, Harm. We're family, and we've known each other our whole lives. This man you don't know, and I have no way of ensuring he won't lure you somewhere and kill you. That terrifies me."

I rubbed my arms, trying to remove the chill that had settled into my bones.

"Don't do this, Harm." It wasn't a request; it was a demand.

"I have to do this—"

"Why? For some story? Some theory you have? What if your theory is correct? What if this guy is responsible for the string of murders over the past ten years? If he really is associated with the Shadow? What will you do?" The word Shadow fell so softly from his lips that I barely heard it. No one talked about the Shadow; they were a legend that brought death and misery. Hunters for the Errant gods, a myth with no credence but one everyone feared as much as the gods themselves.

I swallowed uncomfortably, not sure what to do. Every part of me screamed that I needed to talk to Callum, that I needed to meet him. I didn't know how to explain it, other than some instinct that told me he was more than he seemed. Some desire that was driving me to find out who Callum Montrose was.

"I can't explain it. I need to meet him. It's like something driving me that needs to do this, Slate. No matter the risk." And that was the truth. I couldn't deny that I was risking my life if he really was the killer or worse, if he was a Shadow. But something was nudging me, drawing me to this man, and I needed to know why.

Slate took his second shot and sat back on his stool, eyeing me. "You're stubborn to a fault, you know that, right?"

"So I've been told."

"Fuck, Harmony. I can't protect you if I let you go through with this. There's no way I'm going against Callum Montrose." And that was saying a lot, considering how powerful Slate was.

"I know. Now tell me what he wants."

He studied me as if waiting for me to change my mind. When I didn't, he rubbed his face.

"You're to go home and pack. A car will pick you up at exactly four. Take only your phone. He'll text you instructions as the journey continues. When you're told to leave your phone, you leave it, or he leaves you stranded with no way back."

That pounding in my heart increased tenfold. "Pack for what?"

"You're going away for the weekend. He said to bring clothes for a warm climate."

"Warm?" I mouthed, remembering how cold it had been when I'd walked into the bar since the province was in the winter season.

"Warm." He leaned closer to me. "Are you sure you want to do this?"

I nodded, unsure of where my voice had gone.

"Damn. You sure I can't convince you to give me one last blow job before you head to your death?"

I smacked at him, but he grabbed my hand. "I'm serious, Harm."

"About the blow job?"

His laugh eased the tightness in my chest. "No, of course not. About Montrose. The guy is an unknown element, and I don't like unknowns. That's the reason I've kept on his good side."

16

"Keep your enemies closer?"

"Exactly. And Callum Montrose is an enemy nobody wants."

As I left Slate's, his words ricocheted through my head. Callum was an unknown element, an enemy nobody wanted, and I was about to walk right into his hands. Pulling my coat tighter around me, I wondered if it was the chill on the wind that had me shaking or the fear that meeting Callum Montrose would change my life forever.

CHAPTER 3
CALLUM

The knife hit the demon in the center of its bulbous head, causing it to emit a squeal that nearly shattered my eardrums. Gerrand lifted his hand and threw another, this one hitting with a death blow. The demon exploded, its guts turning to ash before they met the air.

"You test your position within our ranks, and that makes the Goddess leery, Callum," he said, picking his knives up and returning to where I stood. Without turning, he threw one over his shoulder that met its target dead center, the second demon disintegrating within seconds.

"Are you done?" I asked, crossing my arms.

"With the demons or you?"

"Both."

"The demons, yes. Those were the last two captured today. You, no."

He waved his hand in the air as bits of demon ash drifted toward us. He got a strange pleasure from executing them. I supposed it was the same pleasure I took in killing my marks and capturing the demons as they escaped their host. It was a shame we couldn't catch the damned things before they entered a host, feeding from its soul until it was no more than an empty vessel. The camouflage hid them from the gods and gave them a playground from which to feast. Shadow and Torch were the only ones with the power to identify and capture them. We had an entire unit dedicated to locating them, just as we did to killing the host bodies and capturing the little shits.

"The woman needs to die."

"And she will. I want to find out what she knows, Gerrand. If the gods want her dead—"

"The Goddess wants her dead," he said, the creases around his eyes deepening.

Shit, if the Goddess wanted her dead, it was serious. When the Goddess demanded we kill a mark, which was rare, there was nothing but a swift, calculated death that was inescapable.

I moved closer to Gerrand. "The Goddess?"

"Yes, this came directly from Harperia."

The Goddess, Harperia, ruled the six gods and goddesses who sat at her side, overseeing the world from our realm, The Blight. While she and her cohorts reigned in The Blight, Farinthion, her enemy, reigned in The Sect.

Demons were one thing, kills that our unit, the Shadow, had the autonomy to keep in check. When a god chose a mark, there was no demon to blame. The mortal was to blame. Whether it was blasphemy, a total disregard for the life the gods had blessed them with, or some other severe blight against the gods, it didn't matter. We followed the order without question.

If Harperia wanted Harmony Decker dead, the woman had done more than stick her nose where she shouldn't have. She'd discovered something the Goddess didn't want known. That fact piqued my curiosity even more and did nothing to dissuade my desire to toy with her.

"Even more reason for me to interrogate her."

Gerrand flipped his knife in his hand, the blade landing in his palm and slicing through with the impact. He didn't flinch. Shadows didn't acknowledge pain; our training conditioned us to ignore it. The wound healed in a matter of seconds.

"You're not usually the torturing type, Callum."

"I don't need to torture her to get answers."

He raised his brow and stepped closer to me, his intense glare meant to challenge me. I didn't budge. Gerrand didn't frighten me; nothing did, which was why I was in line to succeed him and not any of the others.

"We don't play with our kills. She's not a demon, Callum. She's a liability that the Goddess wants dead."

"And she'll be dead once I find out what more she knows." I didn't know why I was so adamant about keeping her alive for a few more days. Or why I'd already devised a plan to ensure I got close to her, close enough to touch her, even though it went against everything I was. Shadow law forbade such a thing. Touching a mark in any way but a lethal one was instant expulsion and death…but I wanted to touch her. I wanted to feel her flesh against mine and hear her screams of ecstasy as she came undone in my arms.

Gerrand studied me, and I worried that he'd read my thoughts. Thoughts I was wrestling with because they were wrong. That those thoughts were even in my head should have made me give the kill to someone else, to walk away from her, but I couldn't bring myself to. Her image invaded my mind each time I imagined turning away. "And you expect me to tell the Goddess that she doesn't know what this woman knows? That she doesn't know with all her power why this woman is such a liability to us?"

"No, I expect you to tell Harperia that I want to ensure our secrets are safe. That the mark hasn't shared them with anyone else. If she has, I'll kill them as well. Now, I'm expecting company and need to prepare for my guest."

"You promise me she'll be dead?" he asked, his brow creased.

"Yes." But I heard the mistruth in my words, the instinct that coiled in my gut telling me I wouldn't do it. That I would risk my life to save Harmony Decker, even though I had no idea why except this driving need to do so. A need that was building in me with every passing minute, along with that need to have her in my grasp. As if not doing so would be the biggest mistake of my life.

WHEN I LEFT GERRAND, a feeling of betrayal sank into my soul. He was risking his neck by letting me defy the order for an immediate hit on my mark. But he trusted me, and I was about to throw that trust out the window for a woman I'd only ever seen once.

As I checked over my compound, ensuring everything was in place for her arrival, I questioned my sanity. Maybe this woman was more than she seemed, and she'd somehow placed a spell on me when she'd looked my way. I'd heard that other gods and goddesses sometimes visited the worlds of their brothers and sisters. Maybe she wasn't a mortal, but a goddess who had escaped her world. There'd been one a few years back who had run from her world and hidden here for a brief time before the gods had discovered her presence. She'd caused an unsettled feeling among the Shadows; strange anomalies had occurred throughout the world, disturbances in the weather, and fractures in the land. The Goddess had chased her out. Hearing that story had opened my eyes to the idea that there were other worlds beyond ours. The gods who ruled those worlds could never inhabit another god's world, or that world would collapse from the unbalance.

The gods were a mystery, and I considered myself privileged to be as close as I was to them. The mortals didn't know what went on outside of their sheltered lives.

Wiping my hands down my face, I muttered, "Shit, Callum, what are you doing?"

This was madness, suicide even. I'd lose everything I'd built and fought for if I allowed myself to get close to this mark, to even touch her. I rolled my neck, thinking I needed to change my mind, that I would wait for her to arrive, then kill her like the Goddess had ordered. The thought turned my stomach as I pictured her dead body, those gorgeous blue eyes staring back at me, lifeless and empty. And I knew I wouldn't do it, not immediately…maybe never.

Placing the bag on the bed, I cursed myself again, unsure as to why I'd invited her here. Or why I expected her to wear the black bikini I'd bought her. The one with the tiny pieces of material and thin strings. Just the thought of her in it had me hard, and I cursed again. What the fuck was I thinking? I grabbed the bag but stopped myself because I wanted to see her body. If I couldn't touch it, I wanted to see it.

"Fuck, if you see it, there's no way you won't touch it," I told myself. It had been a while since I'd let myself find pleasure in mortal flesh. I'd yet to find a mortal who met my force, and the Shadows I'd had may have met it, but they rarely tempted me a second time. There was no one who matched me, and I wouldn't settle for someone who didn't. I wanted a woman who could take what I brought and give me back an equal share of aggression and intensity.

I adjusted my hard-on, thinking that Harmony Decker looked

like a woman who would be my match. One who would break me like no other had come close to doing.

My phone buzzed again. She was almost here. Anticipation shivered through me, along with a sense that this was the first step toward my doom and there was no going back. Everything I was, everything I stood for, was on the line and I was crossing it. I left the package behind in the guest room, making my way through the open house that led to the paradise beyond, content to await the woman who held my fate in her hands as much as I held hers in mine.

CHAPTER 4
HARMONY

S hit, shit, shit," I mumbled as I hurriedly threw clothes into my suitcase. "Pack warm, he says." I held up the one pair of shorts I owned, contemplating them before I threw them on the floor and shoved my jeans into the bag. Closing the lid quickly, I chastised myself for never traveling outside the province. We had such a short warm season that it wasn't worth buying shorts or sandals.

Rummaging through my closet, I pulled out a white tank top and switched my heavy sweater out for it, ignoring the black bra that showed below the material. I checked myself in the mirror, fluffing my hair, irritated that I couldn't make the ponytail line disappear from having my hair up earlier. As I threw on lip gloss, a text came in from an unknown number.

There's a car outside your building. Give the driver your bag and get in.

Nothing else, just a succinct command and the deep sexy voice I attributed to it as I read it. I couldn't help but imagine the power behind that voice. Looking over myself once more and content that I looked sexy but not desperate, I grabbed my suitcase and phone and headed out of my apartment.

My boots clicked down the hall, the thick wedge heels elongating my calves. I wasn't sure why I was trying to look sexy. This was a business meeting, but I kept envisioning Callum Montrose's profile and how those muscled arms would feel wrapped around me as I rode him. And damn, would I ride him if given the chance.

No, you wouldn't. This is business, and he's likely a killer, you idiot.

A man in a driver's uniform interrupted my internal scolding, taking my bag and gesturing for me to get in the car. No words of greeting came in response to my "hello," just a hand gesture to the door. I'd need to have a talk with Callum about how unwelcoming his employees were. After his head emerged from between my legs.

Fuck! What is wrong with me?

I scraped my hand through my hair as the driver pulled away. I should have taken Slate's offer and gotten laid before I made this trip, even if it would have been a mistake. There was no way, after going months without sex, that I should be heading to some undisclosed location with a man as hot as Callum Montrose. Or as mysterious, eligible, and wealthy as he was. This was a disaster waiting to happen. Of course, that was assuming he was into girls like me.

Stop it, Harmony.

I hated when I got in my head and doubted my curves weren't as sexy as other women's. It was rare; Slate had convinced me early on that my figure was one men wanted, and he'd never let me doubt that it wasn't. My confidence resulted from years of his attention, the way he'd parade me by his side, never even glancing at another girl when we'd been together. Even after we'd broken up, he'd make a point of keeping his attention only on me, and I loved him for it. I knew I wouldn't be the woman I was today if Slate hadn't encouraged me.

Sitting up straighter in my seat, I flipped my dark brown hair from my shoulder and pursed my lips, catching the driver's eyes on me as the streets passed. I gave him a wink and adjusted my tank top to dip a little closer to the rim of my bra. He smirked and looked back at the road.

Callum Montrose didn't know what was coming his way. Whether he wanted a sexy, confident woman to contend with or not, he was getting one. But he was going to answer my questions before I let him play. I chuckled to myself, thinking of how I'd work him for answers before I worked him for my pleasure.

"You're a deviant, Harmony," I muttered. I was delusional, too. Maybe I'd read too many smutty books, my overactive imagination setting up a scene where the irresistible hot man suddenly lost all restraint for the woman who showed up to interview him.

WHAT I THOUGHT WOULD BE a quick trip lasted all night. After several car changes, I found myself on a private plane, snacking on cheese and wine until my tired eyes got the best of me and I fell asleep. I woke, my hair plastered to the drool on my face, only to be ushered to another car. After three more car changes and a gut-churning trip on a small fishing boat that looked anything but regulation—not that I noticed as I was heaving my cheese and wine over the side of it—the boat captain unceremoniously dropped me off on a beach. The man, who didn't understand a word I was saying, tossed my luggage on the sand, jumped back on his boat, and raced away.

He'd pointed to the trees behind me, gesturing for me to walk before he'd left me stranded. I was speechless, tired, messy, and confused. And, worst of all, they'd taken my cell when I'd stepped from the plane, so I was now stranded on some island in the middle of nowhere with no way of contacting anyone.

"All right, Harmony. You got yourself into this mess. Now it's time to see it through."

I knew Callum hadn't stranded me. Slate had told me Callum would only leave me stranded if I didn't follow the rules, and I'd been nothing but compliant. I looked across the beach to the stand of trees where the man had pointed. It wasn't close, and the sun was beating down on me.

"Bring clothes for warm weather were the instructions, and what do you do? You wear a leather jacket, jeans, and boots. Way to go."

Taking my jacket off and tucking it into the handle of my carry-on, I walked, dragging the bag behind me through the sand. After several minutes of teetering, I removed my boots and socks, letting the hot sand sink between my toes and promising to buy flip-flops the next time the warm season hit.

I trudged on, getting sweatier and stickier by the minute. There was a path in the trees where the boater had pointed, so I followed it, gingerly stepping with my bare feet, thankful that sand covered it. The walk took forever. By the time I broke through the tree line, sweat soaked my tank top and my hair, and I was out of breath. Clearly, my hours at the gym had failed to help with my endurance.

Stopping short of exiting the trees, I stared in awe, my jaw dropping. A luxurious pool sat before me, glinting in the bright sun and harkening me to its cooling water. Beyond the pool lay a patio that led into an open house. No windows, no doors.

A compound. I'd seen enough of Slate's compounds to recognize its purpose. It was Callum's compound in the middle of some island. Maybe even an island he owned. Shit, was he rich enough to own an island? This was ridiculous. It seemed like I was in some twisted movie where the wealthy playboy psycho killer traps the naïve, ambitious reporter in his lair and tortures her to death. It was a script I could have written and sold for big bucks to a streaming service. And I'd walked right into it.

"Fuck me."

Brushing a sweaty strand of hair from my cheek only to find it stuck there, I took a deep breath and admitted that my plan of looking hot when I arrived had gone down like a burning plane. Oh well, time to face the music and either my impending doom or embarrassment.

I walked the length of the pool, trying to hold back the saliva pooling in my mouth and tempting me to jump in. I was thirsty, hot, and tired, and I looked every one of those things as I took in my reflection in the pool.

"Hello?" I called as I entered the home, cool air brushing over my skin the moment my feet hit the tile.

No answer came, and I spotted a note alongside a pitcher of ice water that immediately had my parched lips craving it. I dropped my bag and ran to it, forgetting where I was for a minute. I didn't bother pouring it into the glass that stood next to it. In true unladylike fashion, I drank it right out of the pitcher, gulping it down like I'd had nothing to drink in years.

With my parched mouth satisfied, I looked at the note. The writing was elegant in an old-fashioned way, making me wonder even more about Callum.

> *Make yourself comfortable. The room to your left is*
> *yours. Help yourself to food and water, and please take a dip*
> *in the pool—the weather here is perfect for it. I'll be back in*
> *a few hours.*
> *—Callum*

I looked back at the pool, which sparkled temptingly at me. Swimming in my bra and undies would not leave an excellent first impression, no matter how sexy it might look. And since swimsuit weather had been far from my mind when I'd packed, my ancient one-piece was still in my drawer. The only time I ever swam was when I was at Slate's. He had a massive indoor pool that stayed heated all year long. The perv that he was, he always insisted I wear a bikini, so I left the ones he bought me there.

So, no Callum, no swimsuit, and no electronics. I glanced at my watch, thanking myself for refusing to get one connected to my phone, which was the only reason they'd let me keep it. My watch read six p.m., but it wasn't evening yet, so we must have crossed into at least one other province. I had no idea what time it was or where I was.

Sighing, I dragged my bag into the room on the left. If Slate hadn't insisted on spoiling me, I would have gasped at the room. The fabric on the windows and the bed were the finest materials, and the pillows that sat on the king-size bed looked like the softest feathers filled them. An elegant rug over the tile led to a massive bathroom with a walk-in shower and a tub that could fit four people. The decorations were minimal, but no less tastefully ornate.

The perk of being best friends with the most powerful man in the province meant he ensured I lived comfortably. While I insisted on getting my apartment, against his arguments of letting him buy me a house, Slate insisted on furnishing it. He didn't care that I had a decent job and excellent pay. He continued to buy for me, and I'd stopped fighting him years before. It was for this reason Callum's compound didn't surprise me as I took in the rest of the home, admiring the top-of-the-line furnishings, the top-shelf liquor in his cabinet, and the few high-end foods that stocked his shelves. Slate had me accustomed to seeing how the powerful and wealthy lived.

Trying the door on the far end of the one-story home and finding it locked, I returned to my room to rummage through my suitcase for anything suitable to wear. That's when I noticed the bag on the bed.

Curious, I reached into the bag, coming back with two small pieces of material held together by the thinnest strings I'd seen on a bathing suit. I thought Slate's taste in suits was revealing, but this made his choices look like onesies.

I held up the black two-piece and studied it, wondering if the small triangles would cover anything more than my nipples. The bottom was no better, and I thanked the gods that Slate's sister, Kanta, had insisted I tag along for her laser treatments when we were younger.

Staring at the suit, I contemplated my choices. I could stay inside, leaving on my sweat-stained tank top and hoping I cooled down by the time Callum returned. Or I could change into a less smelly and drier outfit, then dip my toes in the pool while I waited. Or I could wear this piece of eye candy, drown myself in the inviting water of the pool, then time my emergence from the water at just the right moment when Callum returned.

"Watch you struggle to keep this thing on as you trip up the stairs is more like it," I mumbled. I blew a strand of hair from my face and decided it was worth a risk. The guy clearly had done no research on me, thinking I was like any other tiny wanna-be lover who pined over him. He was in for a surprise if that was the case.

I stripped and wrestled with the strings of the suit, noticing how perfectly it fit. If this guy didn't know what I looked like, how had he chosen a suit that hugged my ass so pristinely and cupped my breasts in such a taunting way?

"Holy crap," I said, checking myself in the bathroom mirror.

Even the suits Slate bought me didn't make me look this good. This highlighted everything about me that I loved: my hips, my ass, and my breasts.

With that in mind, I strolled out of the house and plunged into the pool. I was confident that I'd have Callum Montrose wrapped around my fingers and spilling his secrets before he knew what hit him. A small part of me hoped I wouldn't be the one wrapped around his fingers, even if the thought of those fingers deep inside of me did light my body on fire.

CHAPTER 5
CALLUM

Harmony was here. I remained in the shadows, watching as she broke through the tree line. Her hair fell in long waves down her back, a few strands sticking to her forehead, where beads of sweat rolled. I followed their path down her neck and into the cleavage the black bra below her white tank top accentuated. I wanted to follow the trail of those sweat beads with my tongue and bury myself in that cleavage.

I shook my head, trying to clear the thought away as I observed her reaction to my compound. I had enough background on her to know she spent time with Slate Dimetre, so she had experience with compounds. Her history with the powerful man caused my hands to clench into angry fists, the heat of jealousy seeping through me. They'd been together for years and intimate for a duration of that time. His hands had touched her the way mine now wanted to touch her, and I didn't like the envy that slinked within my veins. That past shouldn't have bothered me. And I shouldn't have been watching the swish of her ass as she walked past where I'd shadowed myself, wishing I was pounding into it with my hands gripped on her waist. None of these thoughts should have been in my head, the images plaguing me like they were…but they were.

She stepped into my home, her bare feet making soft slaps on the tile. She'd removed her boots at some point during her trek, and I looked longingly at her feet with the cherry red toenails, imagining what the feel of her heels digging into my back would do to me.

Shit, I needed to stop before I came right there, spilling in my pants. As it stood, my dick was so hard that it was painful. There was no explanation for why this woman was having this impact on my mind and my body. None ever had. What was it about her that had me ready to give everything up, to turn my back on the life I'd always known just to have her clenching around me as she came undone?

She disappeared into the house, and I waited patiently, curious to see if she'd take my bait. I was torturing myself by leaving her the swimsuit. It was risky on many counts. I'd assumed she didn't have a suit. The Rikelin Province sat in the northern part of our world, bordering the Nilike Province, which was the coldest province. Mortals in Rikelin didn't know tropical weather. The province barely had a warm season. I'd also assumed this woman would drop everything after her long, heated walk through the jungle and take a dip in my pool to cool down. Then there was the assumption that she wouldn't find offense in the revealing pieces of clothing I'd bought her. I didn't care if I offended her; I was in charge here. And I was hoping her relationship with Slate, whom I'd found had a similar controlling personality, would cause her to disregard any offense.

Waiting was torture, and I was about to give up and just start this game when she walked out of the home. Fuck, my reaction was worse than I'd expected, my dick jerking powerfully against my pants. She had a figure made to be fucked. In fact, her build was like our female Shadows, with curves and thickness in the places that needed them. Harmony Decker was not a petite, fragile thing. She was a commanding presence that demanded all eyes be on her. The swimsuit covered just enough to leave me guessing but revealed enough for me to know I'd give it all up for a taste of her.

She dove into the pool, smoothing her dark hair down as she resurfaced. I needed to walk away, the sight too tempting. This was business, and I'd set myself up for failure, lured in by the breathtaking woman who was my mark. But I couldn't pull my eyes away as she walked from the pool, her fingers tucking below the edges of her bottoms where the material clung beautifully to her ass. I wanted those fingers to be mine so badly that it bordered on perverted. The sight was too much, and I tore my eyes from her, walking further into the dense trees as I chastised myself for my weakness.

I needed to step away, to reassess, to convince myself to call Gerrand and tell him to send someone else and be done with it. I'd never been so out of control, so desperate to have something as I was to have Harmony. The further I walked away, the calmer I became and the more rational I was until I readied myself to do what I didn't want to do—kill Harmony Decker.

AFTER TAKING the time to reset, I broke through the trees and stepped closer to Harmony, fortified. I could do this, no matter how it tortured me. But as her blue eyes lifted, meeting mine, I wavered, my heart pounding so hard it nearly jumped from my chest. She was laid out on a recliner, her long legs stretched before her, her breasts sitting pert and full under the drying swimsuit.

There was no denying the rise in my pants. Nor could I deny the way her eyes trailed down my chest, which I'd left bare. This was an island; the fewer clothes, the better, and I hadn't bothered to don a shirt. There was no hesitation as she perused my body, pausing briefly to rest her sight on the bulge she'd caused. A smirk formed on those beautiful full lips, and I imagined them sinking over my hard-on and bringing me relief before she brought her eyes back to mine.

"Callum Montrose, I presume," she said, her eyes twinkling. She had the soft drawl that was prominent in people from her province, and it only made me want her more. All thoughts of my mission disappeared the second she said my name, although they'd been holding on by a thread long before that.

"And you must be the relentless Harmony Decker. I see you found my gift."

Her cheeks grew a lovely shade of pink, but she kept her poker face. She had a confidence that bolstered her attractiveness, and it called to me, tempting me to test it.

"I'm inclined to say you've done your homework on me with the perfect fit. Do you give tiny particles of clothing to all your female guests, Mr. Montrose?"

Only to the ones I want to fuck.

That voice and the intensity of those eyes were enough to break me. "Only to the special ones."

She moved her left leg, propping her knee up, and I couldn't stop my eyes from following the movement, trailing up her leg to the dip between them. Dirty thoughts polluted my mind, and the discomfort in my pants grew. She was killing me, and I was the one who should have been killing her. This was going terribly wrong, and I had no one to blame but myself and my curiosity.

Her eyes flicked down, then back up at me, a coy grin on her face. "And you assume I'm special?"

She was playing with me, just as I was with her. A tit for tat and how I wanted to reach over and touch her tits. They fascinated me with how they sat so perfectly, almost defying gravity. I pulled a chair over and flipped it, straddling it and resting my arms over the back.

"I assume nothing. I knew you'd look fuckable in that suit and wanted to see you in it."

Her calm composure slipped, her mouth forming the sexiest *oh* before she pursed her lips. I wondered if I'd pushed it, but this was my game, and since she was willing to play, I wanted to see how far she'd go. It made no sense; I didn't need to be playing a game where I tempted her into my bed. That was the last thing I needed, but the one thing I wanted.

She rose from the seat, all legs and luscious skin, and said, "You were right, I do look quite fuckable. It's a shame we have business to discuss."

I couldn't stop my eyes from perusing every inch of her, especially when she turned, exposing a curvy back layered with intricate tattoos I wanted to trace with my tongue. She walked away, leaving me wondering if she'd won whatever battle of words I'd started and fighting a throbbing hard-on that was aching to be relieved by the pretty mouth that had formed it. The game was on, and I'd found my match, perhaps in every way.

CHAPTER 6
HARMONY

I leaned against the shut door, my heart thumping embarrassingly loud and my legs about to give out.

Callum Montrose was nothing like I'd imagined and everything I wanted. I'd known from his profile, and the few blurry pictures taken of him, that he was hot, but that word did nothing to describe what he really was. There wasn't a flaw I could find, only perfection. From that tattooed chest to the bulge that looked invitingly large, to those hazel eyes. I'd never wanted a man as badly as I wanted him.

Words fell from his mouth like silky liquor I wanted to lick up. I'd held my own, but when he'd taken my bait and told me he knew the swimsuit would make me look fuckable, it was over. It had taken every ounce of strength not to strip and let him see how fuckable I was. He had me so turned on that it surprised me he hadn't noticed the puddle that had formed in my bottoms.

"This is business, Harmony. Nothing more," I muttered.

It was the truth. I needed answers, and he had them. There was a high probability he was the killer, and I couldn't find myself in bed with a psychopath who murdered people in a string of random, unconnected killings. Not to mention the tattoo on his shoulder was the same as the markings on each victim, a nod to the Shadow. I'd gotten a good look at it, confirming that my suspicions had been right. But if the Shadow existed, and he was tied to them, I was in deeper than I could swim.

I hurried to my suitcase and changed, picking the cutest pair of lace panties and a matching bra to wear under my jeans and another tank top. This one was black, so it hid the mauve bra underneath, but I pulled it down enough to let a bit of the mauve peek out. Just because I was intent on sticking to business didn't mean I couldn't distract him.

When I emerged from the guest room, I found Callum in the kitchen. Much to my disappointment, he'd covered his chest and was wearing a short-sleeved shirt that enhanced his chiseled arms.

"So where are we?" I asked, taking a seat at the bar on the edge of the kitchen. He lifted his hazel eyes. They were now a blend of amber and emerald, stealing my breath.

"Nowhere and somewhere," he replied with a smirk that only made him more delicious.

I rolled my eyes. "That's a big help."

He plopped a glass in front of me and poured a good amount of whiskey into it.

"I'm not here to help."

Taking a sip of the liquor, I noted how smoothly it coursed down my throat. He'd done his homework. Whiskey was my favorite, and the high-end label on the bottle told me he'd spared no expense to provide it.

"Then why am I here?"

"You're here," he chugged his glass, then leisurely licked the remains from his lips, and I wondered how that tongue would feel on my clit right after he'd chased down the whiskey, "because you're nosy and I'm tired of your questions."

I almost dropped my glass at the terse response, but I knew Callum's type. Slate was the same—playful and teasing one minute, cold and calculating the next. I could handle myself with the best of them.

"That's my job."

"No, your job is to report the news and stay out of my business."

"What is your business, Mr. Montrose?"

He lifted a brow, his eyes growing darker. "So quick to return to formalities, Miss Decker? Should I have you prance around in that bikini again to bring back your relaxed side?"

My jaw tightened. He was egging me on, trying to see if I'd bite, to see if he could beat me, maybe even tame me. "Should I strip and interview you in my bra and panties instead?"

I spotted the tug at the corner of his lip and knew I'd beaten him.

"I do believe I'd enjoy that, but I can guarantee I wouldn't stay focused for long. Nor would you remain upright for long."

The inhale I took was louder than I expected, and I hoped he hadn't noticed it or the way my chest had heaved. Good gods, would I have invited that. I bit my lip hard, the sting bringing my focus back as I reminded myself that this persuasive, sexy man was likely a murderer plotting my death as we spoke. "I suppose I'll remain fully clothed then. Now why don't you tell me something useful aside from how you want to get in my pants."

A cheeky grin overtook his face, and it only made him look even sexier. But his phone rang, breaking the moment and smothering the look. He glanced at the number and then excused himself, walking out near the pool to talk in a hushed tone.

I tried listening, but all I caught were a few words that made no sense. Something about marks and deadlines. Picking up my glass, I perused the place again, settling myself on the soft leather sofa that looked toward the kitchen. After several minutes, he returned, apologizing that he had to leave and would be back in a few hours.

"I thought you booked this time for me?" I asked, hearing the disappointment in my voice.

He stopped as he was about to head out. "Oh, I'll have plenty of time for you, Harmony. Trust me. I'm yours for the next few days, and I'll give you everything you want."

He left before I could reply, leaving me with only the silence of the house and the rambling of my thoughts.

THE DAY DRAGGED ON, and I found myself curled on Callum's couch, reading a book I'd picked from the small bookshelf that lined the back wall of his home. It was a fantasy I hadn't heard of, and I quickly immersed myself in the world, only drawn back out when I heard him ask, "Have you been there all day?"

I jumped, dropping the book, and nearly falling from the couch, knowing he'd just seen the real side of me, the one that was clumsy and unkempt. One I kept hidden from the outside world.

He studied me as I pulled myself together and tried to think of a comeback. His eyes were serious, as if he saw something he hadn't expected in me. He came over and sat on the coffee table across from me, a smile growing.

"So, the sexy exterior is a cover for..." He picked up the book, glancing at the title quickly. "...a clumsy book nerd?"

I snatched it back and sat up. His eyes dropped to my cleavage, which was now precariously displaced with my movement. I fell back on the couch with a huff, blowing a loose strand of hair from my face.

"Let me guess, you left your nerdy glasses in your bag?"

"I don't think we know each other well enough for me to divulge that information." I didn't know why being near him constantly stymied my efforts to feel hot and put together. I'd had my moment at the pool and thankfully hadn't slipped on my ass when I'd walked over the tile floor. My trek here and now this situation had foiled any other attempts. "In fact, we don't know each other at all."

"I know your bra and pantie size," he said with a playful wink.

"Creepily, yes, you do. And I'd rather not know how you found that information out."

"I have my sources, just as you have yours."

"Well, I know Slate didn't tell you."

I could have sworn his eyes hardened, his jawline growing tense. If I didn't know better, I would have said it was jealousy, but that didn't make sense.

"No, he didn't," he said with what I could have read as a growl before he stood up and walked to the kitchen. Whatever it was, it left my legs twitching.

I pulled my shirt up and followed him, only then seeing the food containers on the counter.

"You brought dinner?" Right on cue, my stomach growled. I wanted to punch it, but I flipped my hair back in an effort to retain some form of dignity.

He peeked over his shoulder at me. "Just in time." I cringed, knowing he'd heard my rebellious stomach. "A woman who lives on the mainland makes the best fish and vegetables. Her husband catches the fish fresh, and she harvests the vegetables from her garden. I picked some up on my way back."

I scrunched my eyes, trying to figure out how that made sense. I'd spent two hours on that boat, which meant that he'd have a four-hour round trip, plus the boat had been an hour's drive down the shoreline from the town. He couldn't have been gone for more than a few hours. The sun was only beginning to descend.

"Don't try to figure it out. Just trust me," he said cryptically before turning from me and pulling plates from the cabinets.

It seemed such a mundane thing for a man like Callum to be doing that I let my math confusion go, content to watch the muscles of his back flex below his shirt with his movements.

"So, we're having a nice dinner date?" I asked as he placed the plates on the bar and gestured for me to open the containers.

He threw me a sly grin that had my thighs clenching. "Is this a date? If so, I expect sex for dessert." I caught the drop of my jaw before it was visible, but he still noticed my surprise. Chuckling, he said, "I'm just joking, although I wouldn't turn it down."

I snatched a fork from him. "You seem to think I would offer."

"From the blush on your cheeks and the way your legs are quivering, I know you would."

My inhale was one I couldn't stop, and I bit my lip in irritation.

"Contrary to popular belief, I prefer my women nerdy and spatially challenged. They're the kinkiest in bed."

He walked away, but my laugh had already escaped, and once it was loose, I couldn't stop the snort that accompanied it.

"See, that's hot." He threw me a wink and pulled a wine bottle from the fridge.

I flopped on the barstool, defeated by my inability to control myself around this man. "I'm glad you think so."

"I bet you make some sexy noises when you're on your knees."

"Just moans. My gag reflex is long gone."

His focus had been on opening the wine bottle, but his eyes flew up to mine at that comment, and the opener slipped, jerking his body with the force.

I raised a brow at him. "Looks like I'm not the only one hiding an awkward side of myself."

He appeared speechless, his mouth still slightly gaping, his sexy eyes widened. It gave him a boyish quality that did nothing but make me crave him more. He ran his hands through his hair and dropped his eyes. For a moment, he almost seemed like he was unsure of himself, and it was unexpected from the suave, confident man he'd been only seconds before. It made me think there was more to Callum Montrose than he allowed the public to believe, more than the rumors attributed to him.

He cleared his throat and went back to opening the bottle, his hazel eyes sneaking peeks at me.

As he poured me a glass of white wine, he continued to observe me quietly, and I wondered at his change in demeanor. The self-assured man who'd openly perused my body earlier while telling me he wanted to fuck me was still there, but it was underneath an additional layer—a more relaxed, maybe even vulnerable one.

I scooped some fish and veggies onto my plate, then did the same to his, never breaking my eye contact with him as he leaned forward on the counter across from me.

I propped my elbows on the counter and leaned over my food closer to him. So close, I could smell him. It was a mix of rustic cologne and island air. I was tempted to sniff along his arm, but I refrained, thinking it might completely ruin the moment.

"What are you thinking, Callum?" I asked, curious who this man really was.

His eyes glinted playfully. "Just wondering if having those tits wrapped around my dick would make me as happy as I think it would."

I pursed my lips.

"Shit, don't pout like that, Harmony, that's even more tempting." I sat back and folded my arms. "So is that."

"Do you always cover your true thoughts with sexual innuendos?"

"First, those aren't innuendos. Those are direct comments. Second, no."

"No?"

His confident grin faded, and he looked vulnerable for a minute. "Only around you," he mumbled.

He turned away quickly and rummaged in the drawer for something, but I didn't think there was anything he was looking for. He was trying to hide that vulnerability.

"Who are you, Callum?"

He froze, and I could see the tension in his neck.

"Someone you shouldn't know, someone you shouldn't have asked questions about."

"Why? Because the answers will frighten me? Because I've seen plenty, and it takes a lot to frighten me."

The muscles in his arms tensed, and he turned to me, the playfulness gone from his eyes, replaced with a gleam that made me reel back. The air stuck in my chest and not from the same reaction I'd had earlier. There was something deadly in his eyes, something that had me wishing I could take back my question and return to the sexually charged banter we'd had.

"Because it will lead to your death."

The air returned, rushing from my lungs in a whoosh that resounded in the room's silence.

"By your hands?" I asked with an uncomfortable pitch to my voice.

He didn't answer, instead storming off to the other side of the house and retreating to the room with the locked door. I stared at it, waiting for him to emerge and for some sign that the answer didn't point to him. With a shaking hand, I downed my glass of wine, pushing the plate away now that my appetite had disappeared completely.

AFTER GIVING up on a return appearance from Callum, I cleaned up the kitchen, pouring myself one more glass of wine to ease the trembling in my hands. Callum's words drilled through my mind like a jackhammer. My questions would lead to my death. It was a blunt statement and there had been no hesitation in his delivery of it. But he hadn't answered my question. If he would be the one to kill me. I wanted to believe the man who had bantered playfully with me wouldn't hurt me, but I didn't know Callum. I only knew what he did to me. The way my body reacted to him, the way my heart beat faster when he looked at me.

It hadn't all been a nightmare, I thought as I walked into my room, unsure of what to do now that Callum had disappeared. Most of it was nice. And I had to admit, I'd been enjoying Callum's company. There was something more to him than the good looks, the charm, and the body. He was sharp, witty, and intelligent, and every time he looked at me it left me soaked. Even being in his presence made my hands clammy. If I didn't know better, I'd say I was falling for him, but I hadn't been in his company for that long. Gods, I'd only just met him today; people didn't fall for each other that fast.

It had to be infatuation, lust even. And damn, was I lusting for him. It would be a miracle if I could sleep without fingering myself to thoughts of him, I had it so bad. I wouldn't because nothing I could do to myself could come close to what I imagined that man could do to me.

After pacing the room, I gave up on returning to the central area of the house. I didn't want to run into Callum; something about my question had upset him, leaving me with mixed emotions. I should have been terrified. He hadn't said my death would be by his hands, but he hadn't said it wouldn't. He had, however, confirmed that my questions had put me in danger. I simply didn't know from whom. If he were the murderer, he would have killed me already. Every part of me now prayed he wasn't, because I wanted to pursue whatever this was between us. I wasn't threatened by him, but he carried a tension that had been noticeable when he wasn't hitting on me.

"Gods, Harmony, you talked to him for barely an hour." Which was nothing. How could I possibly know Callum Montrose after a mere hour of talking…no, flirting with him? I couldn't.

The tension that had sat so tight in his muscles worried me. He knew something. Enough to suggest my life was in danger.

With a sigh, I headed to the bathroom for a much-needed shower, my mind churning. The shake in my hands as I turned the water on belied the nerves that were threatening to overtake me. No matter how shaken his words had left me, no matter the risk I'd taken to get this story, it was too late to back out now. I had no way off this island, no phone to call or to text for help. Callum had stranded me here and there was a high probability he planned to murder me. But no matter how I tried to convince myself, I couldn't grasp that the man who'd let his vulnerable side slip today could be a cold-blooded murderer or pose any threat to me. I wasn't naïve; I was sharp and usually an excellent judge of people. And the man who made my legs clench uncontrollably could not be a murderer.

He could, however, have ties to the Shadow.

Toweling my hair dry, I walked back into my room, ignoring the sensation that my legs would give out on me with each step. Maybe it wasn't Callum who posed a threat to me; perhaps it was the Shadow, and he was embroiled with them enough to know my digging had put me on their radar. My curiosity had made me a threat.

I plopped onto the bed, gnawing my lip. Then why bring me here? Goosebumps formed on my arms, and the hairs on my neck rose. Maybe Slate had been right to be concerned, and I'd walked right into the fox's den, following the pup while the true predator waited patiently for me to arrive. Swallowing back the fear that had pooled in my chest, I wondered if Callum was regretting luring me here, and that's why he'd stormed from the room. The Shadow were the true threat, and I'd walked right into the trap, taking the bait.

"Fuck."

I could do nothing now but hope to find some answers tomorrow. I didn't know how long I had, but I was hoping my questions wouldn't hasten whatever the consequences of my meddling were. The need for answers was like an itch that I couldn't scratch, no matter how hard I reached for it. I was close, too close to give up now.

Deciding there was nothing more to do and feeling the weight of my long day, I threw my tank top back on and a clean pair of lace underwear, thinking if I was going to die, I might as well die sexy. I crawled into bed and snuggled under the soft sheets, wondering randomly why the air felt so cool when the windows were open before I drifted off.

Dark wings and the scent of Callum mingled with death and fear in my dreams, and I jerked awake. Running my hands over my face, I looked at my watch. It was still dark, and I'd only slept for three hours. Knowing I would get no more rest, I stretched. My hair was still damp, but most of it had dried surprisingly fast for how thick it was.

I walked from the room, needing water to wake my mouth up, my hands playing absently through the few damp spots in my hair. The kitchen was dark, with no light even from the moon, but the dark had never bothered me. I made my way to the fridge, found a bottle of water, and quickly shut the door to fight off the blinding light.

"Shit," I muttered, wiping my eyes.

I stumbled into the bar before I found my way around it and muttered a few more expletives. I intended to make my way to the couch and chill in the dark while I bemoaned my current situation, but before I could, the light at the end of the room flicked on.

I jumped, a yelp escaping as my water bottle flew from my hands, landing on the floor with a muted flop. I stared at Callum, my heart revolting against my chest for a way to break through. He sat in the big leather chair in nothing but his boxers and I couldn't stop my eyes from taking their fill of him. Gods, he was yummy, and if I hadn't been coming down from an adrenaline high, I would have orgasmed just looking at him.

His hazel eyes were dark in the dim light, but his sly grin reassured me that his mood had lightened from earlier.

"Do you often roam around the dark muttering curses while in your lace panties?" he asked teasingly. "Not that I mind the look."

"Only when I think there might be a sexy man in his boxers waiting to scare the shit out of me."

His laugh was a hearty one, his abs emphasized with the movement. I knew it was wrong to wish I could feel them contract while my tongue licked them, but I thought about it anyway.

"Why are you up at this hour, Harmony?"

"I could ask you the same, Callum."

I was so drawn to him that I'd unconsciously walked a few steps closer before realizing it.

"I don't sleep much at night."

His hand moved, and I noticed the glint of silver near it. A knife. Not a kitchen knife or even a pocket knife. This was a well-worn dagger that sat in his hand so comfortably I didn't need to question if he knew how to use it.

My eyes flicked back to his, my legs trembling.

"I won't hurt you, Harmony," he said, putting the knife aside.

"Which explains the dagger?"

"The inability to sleep explains it. Old habit, I guess you could say." He brought the dagger up, running his finger over it.

"An old habit is biting your nails, not playing with knives. Callum, tell me what's going on."

He looked down at the dagger before picking it up and hurling it across the room. I followed its path as it flew within inches of me and landed perfectly in the center of his bedroom door.

"You're what's going on."

"Me?"

"You're a distraction, a beautiful distraction I can't ignore no matter how much I need to. I want you, Harmony, in a way I've never wanted anyone before, in a way that's dangerous to you and me."

I stared at him, unable to form the words to respond. This gorgeous man wanted me, and it was conflicting him. There may have been more to Callum Montrose after all. I walked to him, his eyes following the movement of my body. If his conflict was due to some impending threat to me, if I was going to die at the hands of the Shadow, I would go out happy. There was no way I was turning down the chance to experience this man. He was a temptation I'd happily take, no matter what it cost me. And I had a growing suspicion that it would cost me everything.

CHAPTER 7
CALLUM

I was a fool. Falling into a comfortable banter with the woman the Goddess had ordered me to kill, the mark I should have already killed. Falling for her with every witty comeback, every flick of her thick eyelashes, and curve of her smile.

Gerrand's phone call had given me a chance to walk away from her, to regroup. I'd returned to The Blight, listening as he broke it to me that the Goddess had not agreed to give me three days. She'd sliced it down to one. At mid-day tomorrow, my mark was to be dead or Trias would take my place as second, and I would suffer the humiliation of having him kill my mark and take my position.

There was nothing more to say, so I'd left to clear my head and refocus before returning to Harmony. But then I'd found her curled up with a book, the look too adorable and very real. This wasn't the confident, sexually charged woman I'd met earlier, but the softer side. A clumsy, sweet, vulnerable side that grabbed my heart and wound it around her completely. From the cute snort she'd made to her quick wit, I was drowning in her, too lost to come up for air. There was no saving her, but saving her was all I wanted to do now, aside from kissing her. Sure, I'd wanted her body, but now I wanted all of her.

I was lost, and when she'd asked me who I was, I'd been honest. She needed to run, but there was nowhere for her to run. She was safer with me than she was at home, safer with her soon-to-be killer…a killer who wanted to rescue her.

I hadn't meant to storm out. I'd wanted to eat a nice dinner with her, hear the hum of her voice, lose myself in the ocean blue of her eyes, and pretend to be normal for just that moment of relaxation she'd provided me. Never had I felt so free from the bounds that dictated my life, the same ones that demanded I snuff out the life that made me feel so alive. For the first time in centuries, I was awake.

I had listened as she cleaned up, hearing her pour another glass of wine before retreating into her room and closing the door. All the while, I'd sat on the corner of my bed, cursing myself for being a fool, remaining there until I heard her finally settle in. I tried to sleep, but sleep often eluded me. It had been that way my whole life, and I chalked it up to one of the side-effects of being a Shadow, like my accentuated hearing and sight.

But it was frustrating when I needed to sleep; I knew I needed my mind to rest, but it wouldn't. I'd finally risen and taken a seat in the dark, letting my dagger drift between my fingers as I contemplated my next move. Killing Harmony was something I didn't want to do. I'd known that from the moment I saw her, and now I was confident of that decision, but I had no way of protecting her once I defied the Goddess. I wondered why the Goddess hadn't struck me down yet. She had to know I was wavering, had to have sensed it, but I'd found that the gods only saw what they wanted to see in the mortal realm. Harmony may have been a necessity to kill, but the way she died was irrelevant. As long as someone confirmed the kill by tomorrow afternoon, the Goddess would be satisfied.

Lost in thought, I heard Harmony come from her room, fumbling around in the dark and muttering a bevy of curses. The woman had a mouth on her, and I loved it. Now she was walking over to me with a determined look. I'd bared my soul, stopping to the point where I'd almost admitted that it hurt to breathe when I'd left her presence. Or that my heart was aching so that it was breaking into pieces at the thought of killing her. That I'd fallen for her in a matter of hours, something that made me suspect we were more than either of us knew.

She lifted her tank top, revealing the rest of those lace panties and the trail of perfectly groomed ebony hair that led to the warmth I suspected awaited me. I followed the shirt's movement and the bounce of her breasts when she drew it over her head. The sight left me so mesmerized that I didn't stop her from leaning over and straddling me. Good gods, she was destroying me, and I was about to let her.

"You want to fuck me, Callum? All you had to do was ask."

Her bright blue eyes shimmered in the low light of the room. Every part of me wanted her, and as she ground herself down on me, I knew I wouldn't resist much longer.

"I don't just want to fuck you, Harmony."

"What do you want, Callum?"

I reached out, letting my fingers skim the swell between her breasts. "All of you."

She inhaled sharply, and I moved my fingers over her breasts. I'd already touched her, already broken my vow, and by morning Gerrand and the others would know. I would be a fugitive, and they would hunt us both. I touched the firm skin, loving the way her nipples responded to my touch, and reveled in the rush of breath that slipped from her.

"I want every sigh, every cry, every gasp, every orgasm to be mine." Winding my hand around her neck, I brought her closer while I continued to rub her nipple. "I want it all, Harmony."

"Then take it," she murmured, breaking me completely.

My mouth was against hers before I could think, that unexplainable draw to her guiding my moves. She slid her hands up my chest, grinding down on me so hard, I could tell how damp her panties were. There had never been a woman I wanted as desperately as I wanted Harmony Decker, never one worth giving up everything I was.

I kissed my way down her neck, licking her skin and tasting the sweet floral scent of her lotion. Sucking her nipple into my mouth, I teased it with my tongue, her feral moan my reward. Nothing was timid about her as she reached down and scooped my length from my boxers. The mere touch of her flesh against it had it jerking in her hands. I yanked her closer, scraping my teeth over her nipple before smashing my lips into her mouth. Our kisses were ravenous and needy, her tongue barely waiting for my mouth to open before she was provocatively exploring it. I pulled her against my chest, relishing how her tits squished against my muscles, and tipped her forward. My fingers pushed aside her panties and plunged into the drenched arousal that had me twitching in anticipation. She moaned, and I kissed her harder, loving how her one hand threaded through my hair and the other gripped my shoulder.

I slipped my finger to her clit, and she threw her head back, bucking against me. The move was too much, and I ripped her panties and lifted her further. With a confidence that drove me mad, she dropped her hand and grabbed my length, shoving it into her warmth. My groan rattled from my throat and I gripped her ass. She enveloped me before I could prepare myself, a cry escaping her which I stifled with my mouth. Every inch of me was on fire, my dick pulsing with a pleasure that erased every prior sexual encounter and imprinted this one on me forever.

Her breathing grew shakier with each rise of her body, and I could sense her cresting. I slowed my pace, watching her. Her blue eyes met mine, a haze of pleasure shadowing them as I moved my hand to her breast, rubbing her nipple until her mouth fell open with another cry. The tremble of her legs matched that of her lips, and I knew she was close. She clenched around me, and my need became too great to ignore. Pulling her to me, I kissed her, squeezing her hips and guiding her motion until she came, her muscles convulsing so intensely that I couldn't contain my climax. I lost all grip on reality and clung to her, pumping into her until I could do nothing more than hold her.

She dropped her head to my shoulder, and we remained as one, our bodies entwined and breathing in unison. There was no denying what she did to me now, no taking back what I'd done, no hiding it from the Goddess or the Shadow. I'd just taken the step to ensure both our dooms, and I'd gladly take it again.

Harmony's lips brushed my neck, and she lifted her head, those blue eyes heavy now with satisfaction, but I wasn't done with her. If I were to die the next day, I would take every ounce of pleasure from Harmony she could handle. As if knowing my intentions, her hips moved, a slow, sensual rise and fall that coaxed my body back to life within seconds. She leaned back on my knees, her breasts pushed forward, and I took one in my mouth, sucking the pert nipple that protruded from it. I had all sorts of ideas about how I wanted to pleasure her and me with those breasts...if we ever had the time.

I slipped my finger between her legs, finding her clit and playing with it until she was wriggling, her rhythm sporadic. She fell forward, and I brought her mouth to mine, our tongues dancing in a seductive play that had my heartbeat increasing.

"Take these off," I said against her mouth, my finger yanking at the edge of what remained of her panties.

She stopped and looked at me.

"Go on. I want your ass naked when I take it."

The inhale that comment evoked was one I committed to memory. It was as beautiful as the twinkle in her eyes that lit when I'd said it. Shit, she was killing me because I could tell she was my match in every way, just from that reaction.

She lifted herself slowly until my cock flopped against my stomach with a depressed thump. The ache of no longer being nestled inside of her was throbbing through it. But she didn't rise and stand as I'd expected. No, she dropped against me and slowly lowered her body, her breasts sliding down me and over my dick, which lurched to stay snuggled between them.

"Fuck, Harmony," I moaned, wrapping my hand in her hair, intent on keeping her there until her tongue hit my tip. The groan that came from me as she licked her way down my length was one I'd never emitted. She grasped my shaft, her mouth descending on me until I hit the back of her throat. She hadn't lied; her gag reflex was non-existent, and the sensation mixed with that thought almost had me coming in her mouth.

I rested my hand on her head, my fingers threading through her hair as I resisted the urge to still her head and use her mouth until I was exploding in it. No matter how good it felt, I wasn't ready to come yet. I intended to thoroughly fuck her a second time and maybe a third. Her tongue teased along me, then swirled around my tip before she rose, her hair drifting through my finger as I thought of how it would feel to pull those strands.

As she removed her shredded underwear, I perused every inch of that luscious body that now belonged to me, whether or not that had been her intention. She was mine, and if I found a way to keep us alive, no man would ever touch that body or that mouth again.

Her eyes burned with lust as they hungrily devoured me.

"Take mine off, too," I commanded. I wasn't a dom in the

bedroom, but I did like the occasional commands and giving them to her had me so hard it was difficult to stay seated.

"Mmm, happily," she replied, licking her lips.

"And no more of that until I've thoroughly fucked you."

"We'll see." She was on her knees before I could stop her, her fingers tugging at the band of my boxers and taking them from me. Those lips were around me again without warning, and I grunted at the impact.

"Damn, you don't listen well, do you?"

"Occasionally," she said, her words humming around me. "When I'm in the mood."

She took me all the way again, and I arched forward in reaction, unable to control how my body spasmed at her touch.

"Shit, Harmony. You need to stop that."

I pulled her hair, her teeth scraping erotically against my skin as I jerked her head back. Based on the devious glint in her eyes, I could tell she liked it rough, which was exactly how I liked it. Bringing her up, I stood and yanked her to my chest.

"I said you needed to stop," I growled.

"And I wanted to taste you more. Now pull my hair again."

I fisted her hair and jerked her head back, sliding my lips down her chin, then her neck, cherishing the moan she let loose as she gripped my arms.

"Fuck me, Callum. Take me again," she cooed, a sound that sent the blood rushing through me.

I released her hair and scooped her ass, picking her up in one quick move that had her giggling until her lips crashed into mine. I walked her toward her room, but it was too far, and she was too demanding, her kisses rough, her nails digging into me. Deciding the bed was too far, I slammed her against the wall outside the room and plunged into her. The scream she let loose pulsed through my ears, tugging at my desire. I took her there, pounding into her as her breasts heaved below me, her legs so tightly wound around me that her heels dug into my back like I'd imagined earlier that day.

The harder I thrust, the more turned on she grew until, with a cry that tore at my core, she came, clenching so tight around me I nearly fell over the edge with her. I continued to fuck her through it until I sensed her building again, her legs tightening, her kisses frantic. As she tumbled over the cliff of ecstasy again, I let myself fall with her, my orgasm rushing through me with such force that I almost blacked out, my grip on her slipping slightly.

Her nails dug into my shoulder, and I hoisted her further under her ass, thrusting into her a final time as the remains of my pleasure fled me.

"Gods, you're too much," she muttered, her breaths coming irregularly.

"I haven't even started," I whispered into her neck. "Are you telling me you can't keep up?"

She grabbed my head and forced me to look at her, digging her heels further into my back. "Did I say that?"

Smiling, I nipped her lower lip, dragging it back with my teeth before letting it go. "I must have misunderstood. That would have been a shame because I need you to keep up with me, Harmony. I have plans for you and this body that I haven't even begun to explore."

The shiver that traveled through her was reward enough, so I didn't let her reply. I kissed her fiercely before carrying her the rest of the way into her room, where I fulfilled every fantasy I'd had since the moment I'd seen her.

MORNING LIGHT FILTERED through the windows of the room, waking me to the reality that faced me. The night had been the most fulfilling of my life. I looked over at Harmony, who was still sound asleep, her dark hair covering her eyes, soft breaths coming and going in a peaceful rhythm. She'd been amazing, and I'd explored every inch of her, touching and tasting her as much as she had me. She matched me in ways I'd never expected, almost like she was my other half.

I rolled to my side, my fingers tracing the strange tattoos that layered her back. I'd noticed them when she'd worn the two-piece and again when I'd taken her from behind, my hand gripped so tight on her waist that her cry had urged my climax too soon. The series of markings started on her shoulders and made their way down her back, where they stopped in the low dip right before they met her ass. They covered her back down to her hips, the more prominent ones spreading out from her spine. I traced them, wondering how long she'd had them and the reason for them to cover such an expanse of skin.

I had my own tattoos, including ones that layered my shoulder blades, but nothing as extensive as hers.

I lingered over the larger ones, then followed them down to the curve of her hips and brushed the sheet aside, sliding my palms over the smooth skin of her ass. I shouldn't have touched her again, but our time was short, and last night hadn't satisfied me completely—I wanted more of her. She sighed as my hand moved lower, spreading her thighs to give me access. I could tell she was still sleeping from the smooth rhythm of her breathing, but she wouldn't be for long.

My hand slid between her legs, and I stroked my fingers along her clit before shoving one into her. The move had me hard, and the noise that slipped from her lips didn't help. I added a second finger, noticing how tight she was and aching to be inside her as the dampness surrounded them. She'd been tight last night, and I wanted to experience that again. Her ass rose the more she woke, and another moan filled the silence of the room. Straddling her, I continued my movement, growing harder each time she bore down on my fingers.

I kissed her back, licking along her spine as she tried to rise.

"Uh-uh," I said against her skin. "Not until you come for me, and even then, I might want that face pressed down into that mattress while I fuck you."

My words elicited a soft cry from her, and I slid my fingers out, bringing my hand around the front of her and dipping my wet fingers to her clit. I was aching to take her, but I wasn't ready. Slipping through her wetness, I teased her with my tip. She pushed against me, complaining about how she wanted me inside her.

"Patience, baby. I need you to come first."

She quivered, the shake of her thighs around my hand like a caress along my dick. Her arousal was soaking me, and she was fighting to rise, so I pinned her with my body, slipping my other hand around to touch her breast. Taking her nipple between my fingers, I twisted gently. She cried out, her climax pummeling her so powerfully that her entire body was trembling. I pulled her hips up and thrust into her, the residual spasms surrounding me as I went deep enough that I couldn't stop my grunt. She tried to rise, but I slammed her back down, a move that may have disturbed another woman, but Harmony only moaned, her body shaking.

She enjoyed it this way. I'd discovered she was even more of a vixen than I'd imagined. She splayed her arms out, grasped the sheets, and shoved her ass back to meet my thrusts, sending me so deep that it nearly broke me.

"You feel so good," I muttered as she tilted her ass higher. I yanked her back, jerking her body up so that her back met my chest, and gripped her neck with my hand. "Are you going to come for me again, Harmony?"

"Not until you come for me," she countered, enticing me more with how she played to my aggressiveness, matching it and inviting it at the same time.

"Together?" I gritted against her ear.

"Gods, yes."

I gave her two more hard thrusts before pulling out against her protests. I rose, knowing exactly how I wanted her this time, the same way I'd had her the first time, but she crawled over the bed to me, distracting me. My preference for lower beds would be my downfall because this one left her positioned perfectly on all fours. She sat on her knees and motioned me closer before swiping her tongue over those full lips.

"Shit, there's no way we're both coming if you do that."

She shot me an annoyed look and motioned me over until I was close enough, and she dropped to all fours again, jerking me forward into her waiting mouth. My eyes rolled back as her mouth devoured me so that my legs shook. I wouldn't last enough for her to come with me if I continued to let her pleasure me with her mouth. Still, it felt so good that before I knew it, I had my fingers twisted in her hair while I drove into her mouth. Just as I was reaching my limit, I shoved her away before she could protest.

"Fuck, Harmony. That's not fair," I said, ignoring the ache in my dick as I tried to settle it down. "Now stand up before I spank you for misbehaving."

Her eyes lit, and I wondered what limits this devious woman had. I had a suspicion they surpassed even mine. Slowly, she crawled off the bed, deliberately moving so that it was nothing but sheer temptation. She knew exactly how to use her body and sexuality, and the thought stirred envy in me that she'd developed that confidence with other men.

She tilted her head like she'd noticed the reaction, a coy smile forming before she kissed me, assuaging my jealousy. I pulled her against me, my hands gliding over her body, claiming it as mine. Moving from her, I sat on the edge of the bed and guided her to my lap.

"Ride me," I demanded, leaning forward and licking her stomach. She positioned herself over me, and I never lifted my mouth from her skin. I kissed her breast, sucking her nipple between my teeth and loving how she squirmed before she enveloped me. My groan forced me to release her nipple, and I threaded my fingers through her hair, bringing her lips to mine. With every lift and drop of her body, my need grew, flames of desire flickering higher. Our kisses slowed, and I noticed the shift, the difference, the emotion that clouded us as the moment took over, and I lost myself to her. Our bodies became one, and nothing else existed but Harmony. As our connection deepened, I sensed her growing closer, her rising climax different this time, coaxing mine nearer to the cliff where hers waited. The quiver of her legs grew more intense and extended through her body, her stomach trembling against mine.

At some point, her position had shifted from her knees, and her legs wrapped around my waist so that she was sitting on me. My pelvis thrust with each squeeze of her thighs, but I never stopped kissing her. My tongue leisurely stroked hers while our mouths remained connected until I sensed the change in her. Her climax hit her, and her muscles bore down upon my dick, giving it no choice but to explode. I smashed my mouth against hers, drawing her closer as my orgasm splashed through my body like a tidal wave that drowned me with her.

I could do no more than ride the tide with her, my body out of my control as if it no longer belonged to me. I held her tight, and she clung to me until our bodies calmed and I had filled her with every ounce of my essence.

Harmony dropped her forehead to mine, her blue eyes piercing and alive with something that looked too much like love. It was the same emotion pounding through me, waking every part of me that had been asleep for centuries. Her eyes searched mine, and there was no way she didn't see the same ghost of emotion there.

We said no words as I brought her down beside me and held her. I didn't want to let her go; I knew what lay ahead of us, the imminent curse of death that sat in our futures. So, I chose to hold her a bit longer, soaking her in and accepting the place she'd carved into my hardened heart.

CHAPTER 8
HARMONY

Reality didn't seem to have me in its grip because Callum had me in his. My head was resting against his powerful chest, and I couldn't help but think of how comfortable it was, how perfect. I felt safe, secure, and content like I hadn't ever felt before, even with Slate. I'd given Callum my all, and he'd taken me as I was, taken all I'd given him, returning it with his everything. And he'd brought me to ecstasy over and over. The night had been unbelievable, and I didn't want it to end. I wanted his touches to continue, his kisses to meet mine, his body to drown me again.

He kissed my head, murmuring, "Go shower, and I'll make us some coffee."

I lifted my head, meeting his eyes, the hazel holding a touch of blue in the amber today. "What if I want company?"

His laugh shook my body. "Then we'll never leave that shower." He kissed my head again before he glanced toward the windows, his expression shifting. I could see his jaw twitch, tension overcoming the relaxed look that had been there seconds before.

"Callum?"

"Shower, Harmony." He untangled himself from me, pushing me to my back.

I wrapped my arms around his neck, and his eyes sparkled, the tension fleeing. His lips brushed mine in a tenderness that set my heart ablaze. I didn't want to admit what this man did to me, the way mere hours with him had opened me to emotions I hadn't had since I'd been young and in love with Slate…and even then, the way my heart leaped at Callum's touch was more intense, like my heart was tied to him on a level I didn't know existed.

His kiss deepened, but then he lifted himself from me, and I watched him walk from the room. I couldn't drag my eyes from the muscles in his back or from the tight ass that moved with his muscular legs. He was nothing but strength and living force, so it was no wonder I felt so safe with him. Nothing could get through Callum, and from his actions this morning, he would let nothing get through to me.

I sat up, sighing as my eyes remained on the space where he'd been. I'd fallen for him, I had no doubt, and that conflicted me. Gnawing at my lip, I thought about how quickly things between us had progressed. I'd come for a story and found my soulmate. Soulmate? I didn't know why that thought had come to me so quickly and why it sounded so right.

Shaking my head, I made my way to the bathroom, pulling my hair up and brushing my teeth before I rinsed the traces of Callum from my body. As I dried myself, I realized I didn't want him washed from me; I liked his mark on me. I wanted him to claim me so that everyone knew I was his. In the same way, I wanted to mark him so that no other woman touched him again. Those touches, those groans, those climaxes were mine now and no one else's.

I stared at myself in the mirror, trying to figure out where this possessiveness had come from and why I felt entitled to claim a man I'd only known one day. Or why I was so easily handing him my independence, my identity, my everything without hesitation. It was a frightening thought, made even more terrifying by how natural it was.

Emerging from the bathroom, I dropped my towel, only then noticing Callum leaning against the wall, his arms crossed and a gleam in his eyes. His hair was damp, and I could see the beads of water on his bare chest that let me know he'd showered much quicker than I had. He wore a pair of tan pants that emphasized the bulge below. He was raw sex in a package that no one could resist. I couldn't help how my body reacted to his presence, how my mouth fell open, and my heart burst to life again.

He gave me a devious smile. "Lay on the bed, baby."

I shivered. The way he called me baby reached the depths of my soul and jerked it.

"I thought you were making coffee," I said, following his instructions and spreading out on the rumpled sheets.

He came to me, yanking me to the edge of the bed, and my heart raced in anticipation.

"It's cooling off, and I thought I'd have dessert first."

Gods, he was too good to be true. His hands moved along my inner thighs, which shook in expectation. His tongue was a weapon that rendered me helpless against the onslaught of pleasure. As it swiped along my clit, I knew it wouldn't be long before he had me weakened again.

He teased me, deliberately moving back to my thighs, kissing and massaging them, leaving the cool air to tingle against my damp skin. His fingers stroked between my sensitive area, scooping into the wetness that had gathered. He lifted himself, and my legs clenched to keep him in place.

Laughing, he brought his fingers to his mouth, his eyes never leaving mine as he licked them clean. He leaned over me, kissing me so passionately that it threatened to fracture every cell in me, further cementing his ownership over me. As he trailed his lips down my neck, his hands kneaded my breasts so that my nipples were painfully protruding. His tongue circled one while his fingers pinched the other, and I bucked, feeling his firmness against me.

"Callum, please," I begged, pushing him further into me.

He smiled against my skin as my stomach clenched. "Not this time, baby." And that word sent a gush of dampness from me. His hand drew down the curve of my body until his fingers sank into me. I groaned, clinging to his shoulders as he dropped his head to my stomach. "Fuck, you're drenched."

"Keep calling me baby, and it'll be a fucking tsunami."

He chuckled and peeked up at me. "Is that so? You like that?"

"Gods, no, but from you—"

I couldn't finish, his fingers twisting in me and hooking to hit a spot that shook my entire body. I cried out, my head falling back as all thoughts fled me.

"Good, because nobody else gets to call you that," he murmured as he dropped back down and dragged his tongue against my clit. "Now come for me, baby."

I lurched forward, his tongue replacing his fingers as he wrapped both hands around my thighs and brought me into his face. He stoked the fire he'd ignited in me until every part of me was ablaze, and I came undone. My climax rippled through me like the tremors of an earthquake, tearing at my foundation and burying me in its aftershocks. He didn't stop, his tongue taunting me until a second climax hit, ripping a scream from me that was feral. My body rocked against him as I rode out the waves, only for him to plunge his fingers back into me.

I heard his reaction, the growl that escaped him as I continued to come around his fingers. "Fill me, Callum. Please."

I hated the pleading but wanted to come with him inside of me, to have him deep in me, alleviating the throbbing that each thrust of his fingers was causing. I could barely breathe as he pulled them from me, his tongue sinking back to my clit, which was so sensitive now that I jumped. He nibbled on it while he laughed, then kissed his way up my stomach, pressing his length against me. Wiping his mouth with the back of his hand, he hovered over me, a humorous glint in his eyes.

"I like it when you beg, Harmony. You don't strike me as the begging type, but you'll beg for me, won't you?"

I wanted to snap back and shoot him a dirty look because he was right; I hated begging and anything that made me look weak. That's why I tried so hard to hide my insecurities, my proclivity for clumsiness, and the nerdy side of me. But I couldn't make my body cooperate; I was too exhausted.

He leaned closer to me, brushing his lips against mine. I could taste myself on his lips and swiped my tongue over them, eliciting the groan I'd expected.

"Beg for me, Harmony."

Shit, he was killing me, but I didn't sense any degradation behind his intentions. If anything, he was empowering me, hiding it below a word that carried no power. He had handed me the control; if I begged, he'd do what I wanted. I let my mouth fall open, watching his eyes as they lingered on my lips before returning to mine.

"Fuck me, Callum. I want to feel you inside of me. I want to come around you so hard that it breaks you, and you can't help but fill me." I could see the reaction etched on his face, the desire in his eyes. "Please, Callum, I need you."

He dropped his head to mine, murmuring "Fuck" before he reached down and freed himself, penetrating me so hard and fast that the only reason my scream didn't reverberate through the room was that his mouth captured it first. He pushed my legs back, going deeper, and I could barely breathe as pleasure careened through me, grabbing hold of me so fast that I came again. I'd never climaxed so quickly, but I was starting to see that my body's reaction to Callum was anything but normal.

His groan rumbled through his chest, vibrating against my skin. I held onto him, forcing his lips to mine and kissing him with the hunger currently tearing through me. He'd moved me further up the bed and was thrusting into me so hard that the bed was emphasizing each thrust with a bang against the wall. His kisses became more desperate. I could sense his body tensing, calling to mine as another wave of ecstasy poured through me until I came so intensely that it left me obliterated. He growled, his climax hitting as mine was rampaging through me, leaving me weakened and numb.

He was holding me so tight I thought he might crush me, but I had no energy left to fight it. I was too far gone, and the last thrusts he gave me only intensified the aftereffects of my orgasm. His chest was heaving, but so was mine, and I wondered if my heart had exploded; it certainly seemed like it. He raised his head, dropping his forehead to mine. I saw the vulnerability there, that same emotion I was fighting—love. Love that shone in his eyes but that neither of us could admit because people didn't fall in love in one day. Sex didn't equate to love, but what we'd done was more than sex—it was spiritual, no matter how much I didn't want to admit it.

I brought my fingers to his cheek, caressing his firm jaw, the tension returning as his eyes shifted, hardening to cover what he'd let me see. I opened my mouth, the words wanting to slip out, but he shook his head, his thumb coming to close my lips before he brushed it along my cheek.

"Don't," he murmured. "Not yet. You don't know me, Harmony. You don't know who I am or what you've walked into, and I can't afford to let my guard down. Otherwise, I don't think I can protect you. I need to be hard, cold, unfeeling right now."

I studied him, searching his eyes for the softness that had been there moments ago. "But you're not that."

"Because you bury that part of me, bringing out someone I didn't know still existed." He dropped his head to mine again. "But that man can't exist right now. Otherwise, I'll lose you."

He lifted himself, pulling his pants up and walking away again. "Get dressed and come get coffee before it's too cold."

I stared at his back, wondering what had just happened and why a shiver of fear settled in my soul, which had been content with love only moments before.

CALLUM STOOD at the island sipping his coffee, his eyes scanning the windows and doors, giving the impression that he was waiting for something. The open world no longer blended with the home's interior; thick glass panes now stood between us and the outside. I glanced over at him, picking up my mug and wondering where the glass had come from and why he looked so tense. I was more relaxed than ever, like I'd done an hour of hot yoga followed by a deep tissue massage. Yoga was something I'd only tried once with Slate's sister, Kanta, and it hadn't left my body nearly as limbered as Callum had. Callum should have been more like me after what we'd done, but he wasn't. The man who stood before me was the closed-off man I'd first met.

I sipped my coffee, noticing the cinnamon flavor to it. "How did you know I like cinnamon in my coffee?" I asked, thinking it was a strange thing to know.

His eyes turned to me, hard and closed off. "I did my research."

I arched my brow. "You researched me?"

"I had to know who was poking around and who I was inviting into my den."

Den. It seemed an odd word for what had formerly been a home. And it reminded me of the reason I was here. The murders, the Shadow, and Callum's connection. In my rush to satisfy my sexual hunger, those things had slipped from my consciousness. With Callum's tension, they had returned. "I thought I was the one researching," I said. "Speaking of which, you owe me answers."

He set his coffee cup down and walked around the island. I didn't know what to expect, so I stayed seated on my stool, following his movements from the corner of my eye. He stepped behind me, his hands going under my shirt, his touch calming me immediately, sweeping those thoughts away once again. He pushed my shirt up, his face brushing my exposed neck. I'd forgotten to take my hair down, and his warm breath against my skin made me happy I had.

"Why did you tattoo your back in such unique designs?" he asked, kissing my neck.

He drew back, his fingers tracing my tattoos.

"I didn't," I answered honestly. His fingers froze before they lifted from my skin. The loss of his touch was agonizing. He moved beside me, turning my chin toward him with his hand.

"What do you mean?"

"You clearly didn't do enough research on me," I played, but his expression remained serious. Huffing, I continued, "My parents did."

He scrunched his brows, trying to understand what no one understood, not even me.

"The tattoos were already there when they left me on the doorstep of the orphanage. Fresh and still bleeding from what I've been told."

His face reflected the shock that everybody had when I was open enough to reveal my past.

"How old were you?"

"About six months."

His mouth slammed shut, his jaw flexing. "Your parents tattooed a baby? With something this expansive?" His teeth were so tight that it came out as a growl.

"Parents of the year, right? It is what it is, Callum. It's been thirty-some years; it doesn't faze me anymore."

"Why didn't you have them removed?"

"They're a part of me, a part of my identity. The only piece of my parents I have. I guess I never wanted to remove that, no matter what an asshole move it was that they abused their child. At least they knew enough to give me up before the abuse turned deadly." I shrugged, having long ago come to terms with a past I couldn't remember, one I was glad I hadn't been old enough to remember.

His lips thinned, the creases around his eyes deepening. "They look as though someone just did them recently. The ink never faded or stretched?"

I shrugged, having stopped questioning those facts long ago. "Never. They grew with me." It had always seemed an odd thing to me, but there was no explanation for it, so I'd chalked it up to some ill-fated reminder of my horrible parents.

Callum was about to respond when his head jerked up. His eyes darted back and forth, the tension in his body palpable. He walked to the other side of the counter and picked up two daggers, the one the same as he'd been holding the prior night. My breath caught, and fear climbed my spine.

"Harmony, I need you to go back to your room. Hide and do not come out, no matter what you hear."

"Callum—"

He turned to me, eyes deadly. "Go, now, and don't question. If we make it out of this, I'll give you all the answers you need."

"But—"

"Go, now!" His command gripped my soul and shredded it. I scrambled from the stool and ran to the room, glancing back to see him move to the other side of the counter, both daggers gripped tight in his hand. A shadow fell over the doorway, traveling to the windows and blanketing the room in darkness. A chill tiptoed up my spine, and I slammed the door just as the sound of shattering glass filled the room. I backed from the door, fear digging its talons into every inch of my body.

"Trias," I heard Callum growl, the sound not having the same effect as it had when he'd been ravishing me.

"Oh, how the mighty Callum has fallen." It was a male voice, one that caused that chill to dig its claws further into my gut.

The door muffled their voices, but I could still hear them as I moved closer to it.

"You touched your mark," the voice said mockingly. "That's one I never expected from the perfect Callum. No one touches their mark, yet you thought you were better than the rest of us."

"Fuck you, Trias."

"I think you've done enough fucking. You were supposed to kill her, not fuck her."

There was a snarl and a scuffle, but I'd backed away at that point, no longer listening. The words resounded in my head. He was supposed to kill me. I'd been right; he was the murderer and had lured me here to kill me. His words returned to me—*because it will lead to your death.* He'd struggled with doing it…or maybe he hadn't, and it had all been a sham. I tripped, landing on the bed, my hand stifling the cry that was scraping its way free.

I needed to get out of there. The door shook, and the tip of a blade shredded through it.

"She's my mark now, Callum! You couldn't do your job, so now it's mine."

I scrambled to the window, adrenaline coursing through me. There was no lock or access to lift it, so I grabbed the lamp as another thud hit the wall beside the bedroom door. It sounded like a war was happening outside it. Throwing the lamp through the window, I climbed through, paying no attention to the glass slicing my hands and jeans as I fell to the ground. Rolling to my feet, I ran, praying I could find some place to hide from the chaos that my world had just become, even if I couldn't run from the storm of emotions that were now crashing through my heart.

CHAPTER 9
CALLUM

Trias was armed and ready, his arrogant words increasing my hatred toward him. I didn't know how the day had changed course so quickly, although I should have expected it. Making love to Harmony had been a highlight. Making love was the only way to describe what we'd done when I'd woken her up, the way we'd shattered together, and every piece of my soul had become hers. I'd walked away, intending to be done, needing to focus on the war I expected to come to us. Yet I'd returned to her, needing her one last time, because if we were to die today, I wanted her body to be my last memory.

I hadn't meant to be so harsh to her when I'd sent her from the kitchen, but I'd sensed Trias, sensed my link to the Shadow with his presence. And I wanted her nowhere near his reach. I realized I would fight to the death to protect Harmony, to protect what we had, even if it meant we had to go on the run for the rest of our lives. I was already a target, a traitor to my kind who had broken the most sacred rule—no touching a mark.

Trias made another snide remark about Harmony, and I

charged him, my knives drawn and slicing into his forearm. He retaliated, striking back as I dodged his moves and countered them. We were both trained warriors, but I was older and more mature. My countless centuries enhanced my quick reflexes and ability to anticipate his young moves. His hundred and fifty years had nothing on my time as a Shadow.

The intensity of the fight grew with each flash of steel and at one point our bodies slammed into the bedroom door where Harmony had hidden. The last thing I wanted was for us to break through it and hand her right to him. She needed to stay where she was until I could cut his tie to the mortal realm long enough to buy us time. It was difficult to kill my kind; our wounds healed almost as if we were immortal, but if wounded enough, our bodies would transport us back to the realm for healing. There was only one way to kill a Shadow, and only a handful had ever suffered that extreme punishment. No matter how he grated on my nerves, I wouldn't do that to Trias unless it came to Harmony's life. Then I wouldn't hesitate to send his soul back to the gods.

As he threw me into the wall, knocking a random painting down, I heard a crash from Harmony's room. Trias stopped, his head spinning toward the pool. My heart screeched to a stop as I saw Harmony run past the shattered window where Trias had entered. I could smell her fear and blood permeating the air.

"Fuck," I said as Trias gave me a smug look and ran.

Running after him, I hurled my dagger at him, slicing his arm, but doing no damage. He jumped at Harmony, taking her down, but I slammed into his back, my knees digging into his spine and snapping it. Ripping his neck back, I yelled for Harmony to run, but Trias grabbed her ankle as she scrambled up, sending her falling to the cement with a hard thud.

"Asshole, I didn't want to do this, but you're giving me no choice." I twisted my dagger into his shoulder blade as he struggled below me, howling in pain. I dug my other dagger down his spine, severing it. He threw me as he writhed in agony, and I landed beside Harmony, who was pushing herself from the ground.

"You'll pay for that, Callum," he growled, but I drew another blade from my pants and tossed it into his chest, sending his back arching and giving me the perfect target. Kicking him with all my weight, I sent him flying into the pool. His wings burst open as his body evaporated just before he hit the water, and his soul dragged him back to the realm to reform.

I turned, searching for Harmony, and not finding her.

"Harmony!"

I spotted blood drops heading away from me and I tracked her, catching her scent, the tangy smell of blood mixed with fear.

"Harmony, stop!" I yelled, spotting her as she tripped over a tree root.

She was a fast runner, but that adorable klutziness slowed her down. "Dammit, Harmony, stop running!"

I grabbed her, but she kicked at me, her knee too close to not retract back, and my grip slipped enough for her to break free. I didn't understand why she was running from me. Trias was gone, and it would take a few minutes before he reformed and returned to finish his task. Minutes I was losing chasing his mark.

I leaped, tackling her to the ground. She fought, scratching and hitting me until I pinned her completely. "Harmony, stop struggling. We're running out of time."

"Get off of me."

She was strong, a fighter, which I hadn't expected, although, given her personality, I should have.

"That's not what you said last night, and definitely not this morning."

The glare she gave me was meant to upset me, but it did little to sway my need to get her somewhere safe. "Stop struggling.

He'll be back, and I need to get you out of here before he returns."

"Why bother? You're just going to kill me anyway. That's what you were supposed to do instead of fucking me."

Ah, so she'd heard Trias. "I'm not going to kill you."

"You were supposed to. Was that all I was to you? A mark? A hit?"

I flinched at her words as they sliced through the heart she'd released from its bounds. "No, you weren't just a mark."

She stared at me, disbelief still in her eyes.

I didn't have time for this, but she would run if I didn't explain. "You started as a mark, but I couldn't do it." The hurt in her eyes gutted me. "Harmony, I'm serious."

"You lured me here to kill me."

"No, I lured you here because I wanted to get close to you. I was curious. If I'd meant to kill you, I would have done it before you came here."

She relaxed, the strain in her arms fading. "Why?"

I sensed the change in the air. Our time was up, and Trias was back.

"Nice move, Callum. Now send my mark out so I can kill her as you should have."

Harmony's lips trembled, and I brought my finger to them.

"I can smell her, asshole. You have no idea how satisfying this is. First, I get to take your mark, and then I get to bring you back for your sentencing. The Goddess is angry at your betrayal, Callum."

My mind was going in a million directions as I tried to figure out the best way to keep Harmony out of his grasp.

"Stay," I whispered, hoping she'd obey.

I rose, keeping myself low to the ground. I'd lost both my daggers, which pissed me off because they were my favorites.

That left me with two options: fighting him with my hands or running with her.

"I could smell her on you, and I still do. Did you fuck her this morning? One last goodbye pounding before I kill her?"

The growl rumbled through my chest before I could stop it.

"Found you."

My heart stopped as he stepped through the trees. I grabbed Harmony, knowing I had one chance to escape.

"Hold on," I said, pulling her against me. Before she could respond, I swept us away, noticing the touch of Trias' magic on me as I stole us away to safety.

HARMONY BACKED FROM MY ARMS, stumbling and looking around frantically. I bent over, the blade of Trias' dagger embedded in my back. It had missed its mark, but the metal was still burning, the pain thrumming through me.

The shock was settling into Harmony. I could hear the rapid pace of her breathing as she searched for a way to escape me.

"Harmony," I said, stretching my fingers to my back, the blade just beyond my reach.

"No, Callum. Let me out of here. I want to go home."

"There's no going home. Now calm your ass and pull this fucking blade from my back."

She stopped, her eyes hardening until they moved to my back. They went wide, and her hand rose to her mouth. "That was an actual knife...a dagger. Why do you and your friends have daggers?"

"Trias is far from my friend. He was my underling until today."

She didn't move, chewing on her lip.

"Dammit, Harmony. Take the fucking blade out."

Tilting her head back, she glared at me. "You've got a lot of nerve commanding me."

"You're lucky that's all I'm doing right now."

I sensed a shift in the air but not the heaviness that usually accompanied a Shadow. "Now, Harmony," I hissed, and she jumped slightly.

A golden light spread through the windows. "Fuck, do it now, or I won't be able to protect you."

She stared at the golden light for a split second, then ran to me, pressing her palm against my back and tugging on the dagger.

"Use your foot for leverage, then drop the dagger in my hand."

"What?"

"Just do it!"

The windows shook, and I cursed my choice of location. This was one of my many safe houses I sometimes used to get away. Only a few of my fellow Shadow knew of it. The Torch, however, should not have known it, and it wasn't a Shadow who burst through the door. Harmony's foot pressed into my back, the dagger freeing. It dropped, and I caught it just as my wound healed and Krinle entered the compound, his ivory wings spreading wide behind him.

Shit, one more thing to explain, I thought as Harmony's scream filled the room.

Krinle rolled his neck, his muscles bulging. I hated the Torch, and Krinle was at the top of my list.

"Well, well. Callum. Rumor has it you failed to kill a mark."

"What does that have to do with the Torch?" I asked, confused as to why he was involved. This wasn't a demon kill; this was an order from the Goddess, and the Torch should not have been concerned.

"That's not your business, but I'm happy to take your mark from you, as she's my mark as well."

"Your mark?" I was confused, and he took advantage of it, soaring into me and sending me into the wall. His presence irked the magic in me, and it flared as I punched him.

Harmony was now on the floor, curled up in the corner.

"You were always a weak punch. I was looking forward to watching you fail when you took over for Gerrand. Shame I won't get to watch them kill you for your betrayal."

I threw him from me. "Shame I don't have time to send your soul back to be reformed, fuckhead."

"You're such an uncouth being," he spat, taking a defensive stance. "Of course, I wouldn't expect anything else from a—"

I tore through the room, grounding the blade into his neck, blood spurting from the wound. While he fought to grip it, his hands slipping over the bloody handle, I stole his daggers and gauged them into his eyes.

"Gods, I've always wanted to do that," I said over his screams. "You Torch think you're fighters, but you're weak excuses who constantly fail against our strength."

I kicked him in the ribs and ran to Harmony, encasing her in my wings and fleeing to another safe house, one fortified with the strongest of my spells, so I was sure no one could trace us to it. I kept Harmony in my arms once we landed, her body shivering against mine. My heart hammered so hard in my chest she had to have heard it.

Finally, I pushed her back slightly, taking her face in my hands. Her eyes were wide with fear.

"You're safe with me, Harmony. I promise you."

I didn't know how to reassure her. She'd heard Trias, she doubted me, and now she knew the truth of who I was. That was a lot for a mortal to comprehend. Brushing her hair back, I noticed the bruise on her forehead from where she'd fallen, only then seeing the rest of the wounds on her.

"Shit, you're hurt." I took her hands in mine, seeing the cuts from the glass where she'd fled through the window, the tears in her jeans red with her blood.

"You're…you're…" she stuttered.

I led her over to the table, sitting her in a chair. This safe house was tiny and sparse on furnishings, but it would have to do. "I'm not going to kill you. I told you that," I said as I grabbed a towel and dampened it before bringing it over to her. I studied her wounds, finding no shards of glass and only surface wounds. No arteries had been severed, or I would have lost her before getting her to safety. I cleaned her up, hating her silence, but knowing she needed it to digest what she'd seen and heard.

When I was done, I took her hands in mine. They were still trembling as I gently rubbed the spots where I'd stopped the bleeding. "I didn't know how to tell you the truth, and even if I had, I didn't have time. I was lost to you the minute I saw you. The second I gave in to my need for you and touched you, you were no longer my mark. I don't think you ever were."

"Mark…" She said the word so softly it was barely audible. "Like a hit. There's a hit out on me, and you were the hired killer."

"Not quite."

Her eyes looked up from her hands. "You killed those other people, didn't you? Everything I suspected was true…and you." She drew her hands back, standing suddenly, the chair screeching in the silence. I remained stooped before her, afraid any movement would set her off.

Shakily, she walked around me, her fingers touching my back and tracing the tattoos over my shoulder blades. "Show me," she said.

I stood slowly, stretching my back and freeing my wings,

sensing them appear and uncurl behind me. Her gasp was loud, but I didn't hear her move. After a brief silence, her fingers touched one, gently brushing my ebony feathers.

"Shadow," she said, dragging her fingers over them as she walked around me. I didn't deny the title, for it was who I was, as much a part of me as the black wings that defined me.

Her blue eyes searched mine. "You're real."

I drew my wings back in and noted how she didn't react, as if seeing the movement had been a natural occurrence for her. "Yes."

"Did you kill those people?"

I thought of all the kills I'd made over my lifetime, only leaving my calling card over the past decade for fun. How curious that she'd been the only one to tie me to them. "Yes."

Disappointment spread in her eyes, but she didn't move from me.

"Why?"

The truth of what we did, of what we hunted, was more traumatizing than what we were, but I had to tell her at this point. There was no going back.

"They were demons."

"Demons?" she asked, her lips quivering.

"Yes, demons."

"And am I a demon? Is that why you were supposed to kill me?"

I smiled, taking her hands in mine. "No, the Goddess wants you dead. You are a direct kill from her...." I let the thought go as another took over.

She was on to her next question before I could verbalize my thought. "But why me? What have I done to warrant a death sentence from the gods?" She said the word gods in a hushed tone.

"You asked too many questions and pieced it together." I

creased my brows as I continued, "But that doesn't make sense. You're not the first to look into the Shadow, to say we exist, or to question a murder. In fact, the mortals knew of us centuries ago, but that knowledge faded over time until we became only the things of myth."

"Centuries?" She teetered on her feet.

I steadied her, ignoring her sudden shock about the time. "Why does the Goddess want you dead? And why are the Torch hunting you?" It made no sense. The Torch didn't care what kills the Goddess assigned us. They only concerned themselves with the demons, always intent on capturing them before us.

"That was a Torch. Oh gods, that was a Torch, and you're a Shadow. And a goddess wants me dead." She grasped my arms. "Which goddess?"

But I could see from her eyes that she knew which goddess. "Harperia."

Her knees gave out, and I caught her, folding her into my arms. She resisted at first before she leaned into me, her arms wrapping around my waist. She was weak, I could tell from the shaking of her body, the weariness in her limbs. Finding out the gods were real and not just constructs to help mortals face their brief lives, that the hunters of the gods existed and walked among them, was a lot for any mortal to take in. And Harmony was taking it better than I'd expected, although I suspected she was still in shock given the circumstances.

I scooped her up. There was a double bed in the room, and I gently placed her on it. Her body had gone limp, and she'd passed out while I'd carried her. I brushed her hair from her face, taking her cheeks in my hands. She was so pale, too pale. A few scrapes and bruises wouldn't cause that. Quickly I checked the rest of her, my eye catching the blood that had stained my forearm. I rolled her, seeing more blood and a blade wound in her lower back, close to the spine but just missing it.

Ripping her shirt, I studied the wound before running to the bathroom and rummaging through my supplies. I did my best to clean the wound before stitching it up, glad she'd passed out, so she didn't have to endure the botched stitch job I was giving her. Mortal wounds weren't something I dealt with, and the only reason I had these supplies was in the rare case a wound wouldn't heal. It was uncommon, but occasionally the blasted Torch would spell their weapons to make a wound slow to heal. The assholes were a thorn in my side, always getting in the way and stealing our kills. No one understood the reason, other than the Galere gods detested the gods of Blight, the Errant gods, and because they did, Torch and the Shadow detested each other. Since we couldn't kill each other, we tried our best to aggravate each other.

Once I'd dressed the wound, I sat back, rubbing my neck. The tension I'd carried since Trias had crashed into our day was tight in my shoulders and neck, so I tried to stretch them. My eyes wandered to the markings on Harmony's back. I couldn't understand why anyone would ink an infant, let alone in such a brutal fashion. There was no rhyme or reason to the strange markings, which were haphazardly placed, so they barely formed a pattern. Nor was there any explanation as to why they looked as if they were new instead of faded and stretched like any other tattoo would be after so many years. Almost as if there was an enchantment on them.

Tilting my head, I looked closer, tracing my finger over one. Something bothered me more than just how her parents had placed them on an innocent child, marking her for life. There was a familiarity to them.

"Marking," I muttered, going against instinct and tracing another path over the marks, my mind filling in the image it created.

Reeling back, I stood quickly, the air in my lungs burning as it refused to flee. "That's not possible. Fuck, it can't be."

I ran to the bookshelves on the other side of the shelter, thanking my instinct that I'd chosen this safe house to keep the books I'd stolen from the realm years ago. They held the lure of our kind, the origin of our existence, and the language of the old ones—the first Shadow and Torch created by the gods. I prayed I was wrong, hoping the gods didn't hear my prayer and find us. Needing to be incorrect because if I was right, there was more to Harmony Decker than I would ever have imagined, and there was a good reason the Goddess wanted her dead. She threatened everything that Shadow was, everything Torch was, everything the gods had established as order in our world.

CHAPTER 10
HARMONY

My dreams were fitful. Webs of feathers, blood, and pain entrapped me until I could no longer breathe. A single white feather drifted past me, an ebony feather freeing from its hold on me and dancing with it in the space before me. They weaved around each other, the color bleeding from them until only two streams of ivory and ebony remained. They turned on me, drowning me, pushing me from the web in the force of their flow and suffocating me with the weight of it. My vision faded, two lines of white and black imprinted in the gray that remained until the breath flowed into my lungs and I woke.

I blinked, my eyes adjusting to the dim lighting of the room. Pain flared in my back, and I stifled the cry that wanted to escape. I didn't know where I was as my memories slowly returned. The attack, finding out I had been Callum's mark, that he was a Shadow, a killer for the gods, a myth I'd unearthed and, in doing so, had pissed the gods off. And not just any god, Harperia, goddess of discontent. The most powerful of the gods of The Blight.

As if my life couldn't get any more complicated.

I pushed my hair from my face and gingerly sat up, finding that Callum had moved me to a bed. I must have passed out because I didn't remember getting there on my own. I looked around the small space that held a tiny bathroom and a kitchen that could have fit in the bathroom from the tropical home I'd fled. Rising, I ignored the stab of pain it caused me, my knees yelling at me for the abuse they'd taken. Callum sat at a small round table, his head in his hands as he stared at the pages of a book. Books surrounded him, pages wrinkled and left open as if he'd been searching for something.

Shadow. Callum was a Shadow. I didn't think it was possible that they existed, even when I'd touted the possibility. But I'd seen it, his black wings wide behind him, beautiful and powerful —the wings of a killer. I studied him, my heart flittering at the sight of him. Did it really matter what he was? That he was some immortal weapon of the gods? It should have. It should have freaked me out more than it did, but it was Callum. A man I'd known for only a day, yet I felt like I'd known my entire life.

I walked over to him just as he looked up from the book. His eyes carried something I'd yet to see in him: fear. I didn't know what it took for a Shadow to have fear, but it had to be something serious. Legend said the Shadow were warriors made by the gods to fight their fights, to kill for them, and to hunt for them. Made from every bit of darkness The Blight held just as the Torch held the light of The Sect.

"Callum, I—"

"Tell me what you know of your parents, Harmony." His voice held no softness, only authority. The fear was still there but masked behind a hardness, the kind Slate took on when he didn't want his emotions to get the best of him. It surprised me how similar the two men were.

Swallowing, I answered, "I told you all I know of them. They left me on the steps of the orphanage. No note but a small line that said my name was Harmony. I went from foster home to foster home, never quite fitting in, never finding a family who wanted a daughter who carried the scars of her infancy so visibly. Slate was the only family I knew. He took me into his fold when we were children, and his family became my family as much as the state would allow them to."

"He didn't act very brotherly," he groused.

I gaped at him. "Are you jealous?" I could see it in the grip of his hands.

"He touched you—"

My laugh cut him off. "Are you kidding me? We dated years ago, and he hasn't touched me since. He's my friend, my closest friend, and one night of fucking me doesn't give you the right to think you own me or have any claim to me."

His eyes creased, becoming dangerous, something that should have frightened me, but a warmth simmered through me. He stood and moved closer, towering over me as my breath caught. He took a handful of my hair and pulled my head back, another move that only soaked me further. I didn't understand the power this man had over me.

"You are mine, Harmony. I have claimed you, and no other man will touch you again. I will kill everyone who tries and die protecting you so that no one does."

My lips parted, his words echoing through me like a call I couldn't deny, tugging at my heart and my clit, and I couldn't tell which one he had affected more.

"Do you still have a problem with that?" he asked, his lips hovering over mine.

"No."

"Good. Now, who owns you?"

All self-respect fled, all confidence, all the time I'd spent to make myself a formidable presence, a woman who held power, all gone with the mere tug of my hair. Callum waited for my response, his hand tightening in my hair, my arousal flooding me further.

"You," I breathed.

His lips curved into an impish smile. One I wanted to run my tongue over.

"Now that we've settled that, take your shirt off."

My knees quivered, and he raised a brow. "We'll get to that later." His expression changed, slipping back to the stern seriousness it had held earlier. "First, we figure out why both legions of the gods are after you."

His fingers released my hair and slowly moved over my neck to caress my cheek. As his thumb brushed my lips, I parted them, my body ignoring the scream from my mind that echoed in reaction to his words. Torch and Shadow hunted me, but that meant nothing compared to the draw I had to Callum. It overrode my need for survival, putting only my desire to have him take me again in the forefront. He pushed his thumb further into my mouth, and I slid my tongue along it, seeing the flicker of lust in his eyes as his façade fractured. He dropped his hand, wrapping it around my neck and dragging me closer, his lips smashing against mine, and I melted into him. No matter who he was or what his past held, I wanted Callum Montrose. I needed him like a fish needs water; there was no denying what he did to me or how my heart and body responded to him.

"Take your shirt off, Harmony, before I fuck you right on this table," he commanded against my lips.

"Saying things like that might tempt me to leave it on just so you do," I teased back, my hands slipping under his shirt and scraping up his chest.

He squeezed my waist, his fingers digging into my wound, and I cried out in pain.

"You're still wounded too badly. Now stop teasing me and let me see your back."

I stepped from him, glaring at him, but my reaction only caused him to chuckle.

"I don't think I was the tease. You were the instigator on that one," I grumbled as I lifted my shirt over my head.

His inhale was my reward, placating my irritation. Not that this was the best time to have sex—my world crashing down around me, the gods hunting me through Shadow and Torch. It would have been a pleasant distraction, though, and having Callum buried deep inside of me would have been worth it. That need for his touch screamed through me, making everything else a minor distraction. It was as intense as a need for food or water, like a primal need I couldn't ignore.

"So pulling your hair and gripping your neck are kinks I should remember?" he asked.

"Only if you do it hard enough."

He grimaced and yanked me against him, the move sending searing pain through the injury in my back, the one I'd forgotten about in the adrenaline-filled flight to safety. I barely remembered pulling the knife from my back before running again.

Callum dropped his hands from me. "I'm sorry; I didn't mean to hurt you. That's what I'm trying to avoid."

"Then stick to pulling my hair or choking me," I purred, grabbing him through his pants and stroking him.

"Fuck, Harmony, you need to stop, or I will hurt you." He grabbed my hand and pinned my arm behind my back, spinning me around before I could protest.

He bent me over the table, sending the books falling to the floor. I could sense from the tight grip on my wrist that he was holding back, trying not to hurt my injury more.

"Let me figure this out," he said, letting my arm go and dragging his hands down my sides before gently squeezing my hips, "and then I promise, I will fuck you all night long until we're forced to run again."

He dropped his head to my back and squeezed harder. He was fighting the same desire that was eradicating every rational thought in my mind. It made no sense. I'd almost died, and the situation was dire. Sex should have been the furthest thing from both our minds. But his firmness was pressing to get to me, and I wanted it so badly that I pushed back against him. He groaned, a sound that rumbled through him. I didn't want to wait for him to figure out whatever this was. I wanted him to remind me why I was falling for him and why my body responded to him uncontrollably.

His fingers moved to my stomach, and he undid the button, then the zipper of my jeans. My heart somersaulted as I heard his breathing come in short, strained breaths, each a caress against my clit as if his fingers had already reached me. They were closing in fast, and before I knew it, they were inside of me.

"Shit, you're soaked," he muttered against my neck, destroying any sense of reality I had left.

I no longer cared what was happening outside this space. Nothing mattered but Callum's touch. "Take me, Callum. Show me why I'm yours and no one else's."

His rumble was feral this time, and it reverberated through the touch of his skin against mine. He unhooked my bra with his other hand, his erection pushing harder against me as his fingers scooped between me and the table. His touch to my breast caused rivets of pleasure to course through me. His lips brushed my back, and I purred, needing him in me like I needed food to survive.

I tried to move to free him, but he pinched my breast before he shoved my body down onto the table.

"You teased me; now you'll come for me, Harmony." His breath was warm against my back, and the shiver that ran through me was a heated one. I no longer cared if the gods wanted me dead. That was a lost thought to the stimulation that was coursing through my body.

He ran his hand over my curves and pushed my jeans down, freeing his hand from my clit long enough to pull them down and rip them off. He did the same to my panties, his hands running back up my legs as he returned to my naked body. I tried to lift myself, but he held my neck down, threading his fingers into my hair and ripping my head back as he lowered over me, his chest against my back. The wound that had pained me earlier was a distant memory, because all that existed was the pleasure of his fingers dipping back into me.

"Where do you think you're going, baby?" he asked against my neck. "You're going to stay here until I'm finished with you."

"And then I get to finish you," I said, vaguely wondering where my grasp on reality had fled to.

"Fuck, there won't be anything left to finish because I'm going to tear you up until my cum is leaking from you." His dirty talk sent me closer to the edge, and a cry escaped me, my body trembling. "That's it. Come for me, baby."

He pulled my hair again and thrust his fingers further into me, his thumb playing with my clit so that there was nothing but the sensation of a thousand currents in my lower body. As he released my hair, he removed his hand, sliding it up my body, my arousal leaving a trail until he reached my breast. He kneaded the flesh as his other hand joined, pinching my nipples until they were so hard they ached. I could barely breathe, my body was on fire, and I was so close to succumbing to the heat that I didn't think my legs would hold me much longer.

"Fuck," he grunted, biting my shoulder. "This is not what we should be doing right now. But you feel too good to resist."

It was the same argument I'd been having internally, the one I'd lost the moment his fingers entered me.

He removed his hand from my breast, the other continuing its tormenting ways until I was gasping, my body trembling as I reached the brink of oblivion. I vaguely heard his zipper drawing down, but not until he plunged into me did I realize he'd freed himself. The impact forced a cry from me, my body falling into the fire after just a few thrusts. My nails dug into the table as my orgasm tore through me, leaving me a weakened shell. He didn't give me time to recover. His hand reached into my hair and forced my head in place as he reamed me so hard I was climbing again within minutes. I screamed out as I climaxed a second time, his thrusts slowing as I bore down on him, my body a cascading quiver that wouldn't stop.

Callum gripped my hair and yanked me back against him, my legs shaking so badly I worried I'd fall. As if he knew, he drew out and flipped me, picking me up and placing me on the table before he plunged back into me. The kiss he gave me as he wrapped his hand around my neck and yanked me closer was enough to burn me to the core with the passion it held. I twisted my legs around him, pushing him deeper, loving the grunt that escaped between our lips.

His mouth devoured mine as his body lit mine with a fire that burned through every cell. I wanted nothing more than to leap into the inferno with him and never return. Nothing I'd ever experienced came close to how it felt to have his body against mine, his dick buried so far inside me I didn't know where I ended or he began. The way his hands touched me, squeezing my breasts like he never wanted to let them go, had me soaring to another climax, and as my hold on it broke, he tensed, his hands dropping to grip my hips so tight I cried against his lips. His growl filled my ears as I came, clenching my legs around him while his climax hit. He squeezed me tighter, pumping into me with long, deep strokes that lit my body with pleasure until he fell against me. The sparks of my orgasm continued to assail me even as he held me tight, his breathing ragged and uneven.

"Gods, Harmony. You break down my resolve, undoing me with just your touch until I can do nothing but want you." He moved his cheek against mine, the stubble that had grown lightly over the last day scratching my skin until his lips met mine. The kiss he gave me reached down to my very soul, claiming it, calling it to answer, then weaving its way to my heart, ensnaring it so that Callum and no one else marked it. "I can't love you, Harmony," he murmured against my lips.

My heart fluttered in the cage in which he'd captured it. "But you do," I replied, running my tongue along his lips. He moved back, his eyes searching mine. They were a breathtaking amber, the sage peeking through behind it. "Just like I do."

His eyes widened, and he touched my cheek, brushing his knuckles against it.

"I can't resist you, Harmony."

"Then stop trying to. Claim me, own me, love me. As long as I can do the same to you."

He lifted his brow. "You want to own me?"

"Damn right, I do. There's no chance another woman is ever touching you again." I squeezed my legs, noting how he remained embedded in me, his erection not fading. I moved my hips, watching his lip curl into that adorable smirk I loved. "I'll fucking kill anyone who tries because you're mine, Callum Montrose."

His hand had moved around the back of my neck, and he encircled it, his eyes twinkling with a devious look. "I'm going to take you again, Harmony, and I don't care if the gods themselves are knocking on that door to get to us. They can wait. I want you to come again for me. This time, you're going to scream even louder, and I'm going to pound you even harder."

I inhaled so sharply that my ribs hurt. "How about you make love to me first?" I asked once I regained my control. With it, the ache in my back returned, and I tried not to let him see my discomfort. Still, my desire for him screeched within me, dimming the pain and pushing aside all thoughts of the danger that lurked.

"I can do that," he said, his eyes mischievous, "but the other sounds more tempting."

I threw my head back and laughed, his hand wrapping around my neck as I did and drawing my mouth to his. He kissed me again, the emotion held within that kiss enough to ease the sting of my wound. His hands moved under my ass cheeks, and he picked me up. I clasped my hands around his neck, wondering how he was carrying me so easily if I was light as a feather. His kisses brought my attention back, and as my back hit the bed, a flash of pain careening with the pleasure of his thrusts, I opened my heart completely to Callum. I could sense how it connected to his in our moves, in our kisses, in our matching breaths, and our touches almost like fate had meant us to be together, to be one. Fated. The word should have frightened me with its power, but it didn't because it felt right, as right as being in his arms. As right as being his did. And as we finally came undone, our cries in unison as the ecstasy of our release coursed through us, he whispered, "I love you, Harmony" into my ear.

And I whispered, "I love you, Callum." The words took root in my soul, sealing it to his forever.

CHAPTER 11
CALLUM

Harmony lay snuggled in my arms, and nothing had ever seemed so right. I didn't know how the impending doom that hung over us had taken a backseat to fucking her, but it had. I hadn't been able to defy my desire for her; I needed her like I'd never needed anything. And somehow, the fucking had turned to something more, something more profound and emotional. I'd made love to her, losing myself to her, sensing how my soul bound itself to hers, my heart imprinting itself to hers until I didn't think I'd ever be able to live without Harmony in my arms.

Love. It was a concept that had escaped me for too long. What I'd thought had been love in prior fleeting romances was nothing compared to what I felt for Harmony—a woman I'd known for two days. It made no rational sense, but I wasn't about to argue. I wanted her, and now no one else would have her. She was mine, and she'd accepted it, claiming me as much as I'd claimed her. Fated was a word that held power in my world. The Shadow revered the word as much as the Torch did, and we did not take fate and destiny lightly. But fated was what this seemed like. Fated love that implied the gods had destined her to be mine. Like she'd been waiting for me to find her.

I kissed her head, and she peeked up at me, a pile of hair falling over her face. I pushed it back, letting the strands run through my fingers. It seemed like something I'd done a thousand times, just like holding her seemed like something I'd been doing my entire life.

"All right," I said, kissing her nose. "I need to see that back of yours."

She scrunched her face. "What's so important about my back?"

Something that could change the path of Shadow and Torch forever. I'd had my suspicions, but the books confirmed them. The markings on her back weren't random. They were deliberate symbols that dated back to the original Shadow, and I needed to figure out what they meant and what they were hiding. And I'd squandered time, acting as if our hunters weren't scouring the provinces for her. Like my destiny hadn't taken a turn that sealed my death along with hers. But if I was right, and she was my fated, there was no stopping my hunger for her. Touching her was as necessary as breathing.

"Stand up," I said, ignoring her question and sitting up, fighting the instinct to touch her again. I squared my jaw, focusing my mind on the situation and not on her naked body.

Her eyes twinkled. "Aren't you tired out yet?" she asked, rising from the bed as I positioned myself on the edge.

"It takes a lot to tire me out, baby." I pulled her to me, letting her breast fill my waiting mouth and relishing the wiggle of her body as I tormented her. She was so easy to torment, too. Of course, so was I. "Fuck," I said, flicking my tongue over her nipple. "That was a bad idea."

And just like that, my resolve dissipated. There was no off switch with her. I could take her over and over for days and never tire of her. She was an addiction I couldn't get enough of, one I craved like a drug. I spun her around, smacking her ass and loving the squeal that slipped from her. My girl liked it in all the right ways—sometimes rough, sometimes submissive, sometimes aggressive, and sometimes soft. She was a match for me, like no other woman.

Finding that ass too hard not to touch, I squeezed it, letting my finger drift up her crack and wondering how tight she'd be when I took her there. And I planned to, especially after she moaned as I put some pressure on it. Gods, she was too good to be true.

"I promise I'll deepen that moan and sink into that sexy ass of yours." My dick twitched at the thought, and her legs clenched. "None of that," I said, scooting closer to the edge of the bed and pulling her between my legs.

Part of me wanted to take her again, to pull her onto me and let her ride me until I was exploding again. But I'd wasted time and still needed answers. That fact irritated the Shadow in me and it was demanding I put my physical desires aside and figure out what was going on. Both Shadow and Torch were hunting us, and I needed to find a way to keep her safe.

"Lean forward," I said, convincing myself to focus.

"Are you going to fuck me again?"

"Of course I am. But not yet." She grumbled, and I grabbed her waist, squeezing tightly. "Don't worry, I'll bury myself deep inside of you soon. Trust me, I intend to use you until you break, Harmony."

"Then your stamina better be excellent."

I pushed at her back, straightening it. "Are you saying it isn't?"

She laughed again, and I pinched her waist, only then noticing that we'd ripped her stitches, the bandage soaked with blood. Shit, I needed to get a grip.

"Your stamina is fine, Callum. In fact, I'm inclined to say you're the first man to keep up with mine."

I squeezed her waist harder. "And how many men have you had, Harmony?" The question came out as a growl.

She looked around at me, throwing me a dirty look. "I'm guessing my thirty-three years have nothing on your long life, Callum. Should I ask how many women you've tested that stamina on? Or how many have matched it?"

"No," I grumbled, knowing she was right.

"Then don't get jealous about my past. And for the record, there hasn't been a man who has ever kept up with me...until you."

"Not even Slate?" I didn't know why I was being so snippy. Her past didn't matter, and neither did mine.

She rose before I could keep her in place and stood before me, crossing her arms over her chest.

"You know, if you're trying to be intimidating, that look does not help. You're buck naked, and your breasts are entirely too tempting."

"Don't change the subject. You need to stop with your jealousy. I told you about me and Slate." She dropped her arms and climbed onto my lap, straddling me so that I was instantly hard. "And he was close, but I suspect you could outlast him any day."

From the way my dick was aching to be inside of her, I didn't doubt it.

"Besides, I'm sure you've screwed quite of few women, including Shadows. If the female Shadows are anything like you, then I'm the one who should be jealous."

And they were relentless. It took a lot to wear any of us out, male or female.

"Damn, I'm right, aren't I?" She slapped my chest, and I grabbed her wrists.

"Now who's jealous?" I asked, as her lips formed a delectable pout.

She remained quiet, and I couldn't help but reassure her. "You by far outlast any of them, and none of them ever came as much as you do so beautifully for me." It was true. She'd surprised me when she'd demanded more of me, her sex drive rivaling any Shadow I'd been with and certainly any mortal female.

Her mouth lifted to a smile until her lips thinned. "You're just saying that."

"No, I'm not. We all have unnatural stamina, but you are my match in ways none of them were, Harmony. Just as I imagine, I'm your match in ways that Slate never was."

The smile lit her face, and she leaned in, kissing me. Weaving my fingers in her hair, I pushed her lips further into mine, sliding my tongue in to play with hers. I could have kissed her all day. It was a delicious taste and an action that sent trails of tingles bounding through my body, cementing the connection we'd forged and reaffirming the fact that there was no question I would die for her.

My hands slid up her body, hitting the blood from her wound, and I stopped, pushing her away and seeing the trail of blood seeping from it. I lifted her from me before she could protest, cursing myself for putting my need for her over that blasted wound on her back and the danger that hovered over us.

"Callum, I—"

"No more, Harmony," I said as I pulled my pants back on.

She frowned, but my eyes dropped to the blood pooling on the wounds in her hands.

"Fuck, let's clean you up, then I look at your back. No more tempting me."

Her worried frown curved into a questioning look. "Me tempting you? I believe that was you pulling me into your lap."

I threw her a look. "And whose pelvis was grinding into me? I didn't hear you complaining, sweetheart."

I walked to the bathroom, throwing the shower on and smiling at the grumbles coming from her.

"Get your ass in here, Harmony."

"Are you showering with me?" she asked with a naughty grin.

"Damn, you're devious."

"If you only knew."

Smacking her ass, I forced her into the shower, peeling the soaked bandage from her back and carefully helping her wash the blood off her skin. It took all my effort not to take her there, knowing the wound on her back had reopened and was weakening her with every minute I delayed restitching it.

"It's bad, isn't it?" she asked, her tone finally serious, sobering me up and calming the throbbing in my pants that had me desperate to step into the shower with her and take her against the tile.

"I've seen worse, and it won't be bad if you stop seducing me," I teased, handing her a towel.

She snorted, a sound I found as adorable as the first time I'd heard her do it. "Again, I'm not taking full blame on that."

I stood back, crossing my arms and watching as she dried off. It didn't help my uncomfortable hard-on, but I couldn't deny myself the entertainment. She peeked up at me, her eyes playful until she read the serious expression I'd assumed.

"Do you want to tell me what you expect to find on my back, other than this stupid wound?"

She tucked the towel around her, and I motioned for her to return to the main room.

"Not until I see if my theory is correct."

I grabbed my first aid supplies and a bottle of whiskey.

"What's this for?" she asked as I returned and handed her the bottle.

"Drink it. You're going to need something to take the edge off."

"I have you and that tongue of yours." The shimmer in her eyes had me swelling uncomfortably. I wasn't sure how I would get us anywhere if we didn't stop the incessant playing.

"Just drink it and drop your towel." I pulled a chair from the table and brought it to where she was standing, turning her so I could access her back. Chastising myself for letting my desire distract me enough to re-injure her, I went to work yanking the ripped stitches free and restitching the wound. All the while, I ran through my suspicions, growing impatient to figure out what the markings on her back were. If I'd stayed focused earlier, and not given into that damned incessant need for Harmony, I would already know. But I hadn't, and as much as I hated myself for it, I wasn't certain I could deny her again if she turned around and straddled me.

Harmony didn't make a sound as I stitched her up. I knew it hurt. I could see it in the shake of her arms and her grip on the whiskey bottle as she drew a few more swigs from it. But she didn't scream or even curse me. Harmony was definitely a woman made for me. Strong women were a turn-on, a challenge but not one to break, one to encourage because I loved their strength and the fight in them. And I loved Harmony's strength, the way she'd fought me when I'd been trying to catch her as she'd run, and now the way she bore a pain that would have made most men whimper.

When I finished, I left the wound exposed. There was a tattoo close to the stitches, and I was intent on figuring out if my theory was correct. To do so, I needed all her tattoos accessible. I kissed the dip in her back, squeezing her ass, which was thankfully still covered by the towel. If she'd left that piece of her exposed the entire time, I wouldn't have been able to concentrate.

"Do you trust me, Harmony?" I asked, rubbing her back.

"Yes," she answered quickly.

"Could have fooled me when you were running from me on the island."

"That was before. Now I trust you."

It irked me that she hadn't trusted me before, but I needed to remember she didn't know me then. She still didn't really know me. She knew the truth, however, and the way I felt. I would die before I ever hurt her.

I stood, moving the chair away with my foot. "I don't think your tattoos are random, and I don't think your parents were abusing you. I suspect they were protecting you."

She tried turning to me, but I grabbed her and kept her facing forward. "Don't turn," I said against her ear. A tremble ran through her as the hand I was grasping her hip with slid up her stomach and to her breast. There was a part of me that wanted to put this off longer, to play with her again. She relaxed, leaning into me, her towel dropping.

Damn, that had been a bad idea. I squeezed her breast, loving how her flesh flowed over my hand, firm and reactive. A moan fell from her lips as I licked her neck and rubbed her nipple between my fingers. The swelling in my pants was hard to ignore. I'd just had her, though, and time was against us.

"Later, baby," I said, breathing on her neck to cool the dampness my tongue had left. Her legs quivered at the word *baby* like they did each time, further increasing the discomfort in my pants. "I promise I will fuck you for days when this is over, and you're safe."

"Days?" she repeated, her pulse quickening.

"At the least."

The sigh from her was titillating, and I nipped at her neck, fighting my need to let go of my theory and just take her again. I suspected she could keep up with me for those days and still demand more. And the marks on her back might hold the reason for that insatiability. I needed to know, and that need overrode the persuasion of my dick.

Reluctantly, I let her breast go and gently pushed her from me. She let out another sigh that gripped my cock and squeezed it.

"Cut that out, or I'll fuck that mouth of yours instead."

"That's not a threat, Callum. That's a tease."

I gritted my teeth. That mouth was a deadly distraction, one I wanted around me again. I'd yet to experience more than a few teases, wanting to be buried in that pussy of hers instead. But I had plans for that mouth just like I did for her.

I jerked her head back by the hair, saying, "I'm serious, Harmony."

Her moan was my response, and I realized I'd made a mistake. Gods, everything I did to assert my dominance and show her I was the aggressor turned into a mistake because my girl was dirty, and that drove me over the edge.

"Fuck," I muttered. This was turning fast, and I needed to gain control again, to stop this before we ended up losing more time.

I shoved her away, and she glared back at me, darkness overcoming her blue eyes and revealing her irritation.

"No," I said. "We will wait until I figure this out. Now, turn around and let me do this."

She eyed me, seeing if I'd bend.

"Harmony, both Shadow and Torch are hunting us right now, and it won't be long before they find us. The Goddess wants you dead, and now there's a death sentence on my head. And you want to have sex again?"

Saying the words brought the reality down around me, and

the pain beneath my pants simmered. I'd let my desires take over my common sense, and now I might lose her. She undid me in ways no one ever had, making me lose grounding in reality. Centuries of training disappeared within seconds of being in her presence. I was a warrior; this was what I did. I hunted, I stayed in the shadows, I killed, and I survived. Within two days, Harmony had erased all of that from me, her body all I desired now.

Her expression changed, her brow creasing. She swallowed, and I could see reality descending on her, revealing the fear her teasing had been covering. "You're right, but—"

"Harmony," I warned, crossing my arms.

"Callum," she returned, crossing her arms to mimic me, the move pushing her breasts up. "When you figure this out and we're safe, I want you to use my body and my mouth until all of this is just a fading memory."

Damn, she'd summoned my unruly dick again. "I don't want to just use your mouth, baby. I want to mark you so every man knows you're mine, and no man will dare touch you again."

"Mark me? That's a little possessive, isn't it?"

I stood, knowing I needed to put a stop to this, but the Shadow in me was battling with the fated mate who wanted her to know she was mine. Running my hand up her neck, I squeezed and yanked her to me.

"I am possessive of you, Harmony. I will mark you every way I can to ensure there's no question you're mine. If I want to mark you with my touch, I will. If I want to mark you with my tongue, I will. And if I want to mark you with my cum, I guarantee I will. You're mine. You've been mine since the moment I claimed this body."

"It's a good thing I like my men possessive, Callum, otherwise, I'd be worried about how toxic that sounded. But you're assuming I'll let a drop of your cum spill to mark me."

"Fuck yeah, all over those beautiful tits of yours."

She gave me a devious smile. "I'll have to think about that. It's been a long time since I let a man's cum spill."

She was playing with fire, and she knew it, so I turned the table on her, narrowing my eyes. "How many men have come in that mouth, Harmony?"

The thought sent a red-hot rage searing through me. I didn't have any explanation for why I was so jealous about the idea of even a man in her past touching her, but it burned me up. She gave me a coy smile and turned her back to me.

"I've lost count," she said, and that heat flared, switching my mood to an aggression I didn't understand.

I yanked her back against me. "That mouth is mine, as is your body, your ass, and that soaked pussy. I don't want to hear about any other man touching any part of you, or I will hunt each one down and bring them excruciating pain before I kill them."

My mood was no longer playful, her words triggering the Shadow in me, along with a possessive aggression that had me seeing red. I was deadly in any situation, but at this moment, I was lethal. She could have read me wrong, and the hand around her neck could have slipped and crushed her bones easily before I even realized it, but she was smart, my equal in every way.

"Will killing my former lovers bring you pleasure?"

"Great pleasure," I said in her ear before nipping it.

"But it won't erase their touches from my memory."

I froze, my hand precariously tighter around her neck as I fought the instinct to hurt her. "And what will? Because I want every trace of them removed from your mind and your body."

"There's only one thing that will do that, Callum."

"Tell me, Harmony. Otherwise, they all die."

"You."

The word drifted over me, dampening my mood and calming the ire that was cascading through me.

"But I need you to promise that grip around my neck and that aggressive talk will be part of it because you have me so wet right now that I'm about to come."

I drew a sharp breath, her words reaching deep to my core and claiming me like I never thought possible. Loosening my hold on her neck, I caressed my fingers along it. I didn't know if it was possible to love her more than I did now.

She reached her hand around and squeezed my dick so tight my fingers clasped her neck again.

"Harmony," I warned.

"Oh no, Callum. If you get to threaten, then so do I. I may like it when you get all aggressive and dominating like that, but make no mistake, I'm just as controlling. I want no thoughts, memories, or touches of any other women in your mind ever again. I may be yours, but you are just as much mine, and I will hunt them down and rip them to shreds if you even think about one."

And yet it was possible to love her more because her hold on my heart dug further with those words so there was no piece she didn't own.

"Gods, I love you, Harmony."

"More than any other?"

"Fuck, yeah. And I can promise you, there will never be another, not even the thought of another, because you take up every space in my mind, body, and soul."

"And because you fear the repercussions."

My laugh was uncontrollable. "And that. You are a force I didn't see coming, Harmony Decker."

"Oh, you've seen me coming plenty of times now, and you'll see me plenty more. Now get this done so I can watch you cover my body in your cum before I shove your head between my legs and make that tongue lick up this soaked mess you've made me."

I groaned and released her neck. My hard-on was raging

again, and I cursed myself for letting my envy get the better of me. She was still completely naked, and as I adjusted my bulge, I tried to ignore how sexy her ass was. The image of covering her in my essence was in my head now, and it was one that only had competition with the other picture she'd placed there, my tongue disappearing into her warmth and lapping it up.

Swiping my hand down my face, I tried to clear the image from my head.

"Any day now, Callum. It's running down my leg."

"Dammit, Harmony, you're killing me. How am I supposed to keep you protected and figure all this out with you saying shit like that? You're a distraction."

"Good. Maybe it'll work, and you can satisfy this burning between my legs." She clenched her legs and wiggled her ass.

"What in The Blight? You're naughtier than any Shadow I've—"

She turned her head toward me, shooting me a look that carried daggers. "Don't make me hurt that cock of yours, Callum. It'd be a shame to damage it before it can bring me more pleasure."

I narrowed my eyes at her. "I don't take well to threats, Harmony."

"Well, it's a good thing I do, or you wouldn't have me as turned on as I am right now. Besides, that wasn't a threat; that was a promise."

My lip curved as I fought the smile that was growing. "Fine, you win this one. You're naughty, plain and simple. You threaten my dick again, and I'll remind you what it's like to gag."

Her eyes lit, and I shook my head. She was naughty. Even as deviant as Shadow females were, she outshone them all. But I couldn't tell her that, just like she couldn't tell me anything about the men she'd been with. We were both possessive, and I suspected once I figured out the markings on her back, I'd have confirmation for the reason her possessiveness matched mine.

I touched her back, ignoring the sigh from her and concentrating on the markings, clearing my head of the word foreplay, the sexual innuendos, and the teasing that clouded it.

"I need you to trust me, Harmony. No matter how bizarre I sound or what you feel, I need your trust."

"What do you think they mean?" she asked, her tone serious.

"Something that could shape the course of our world."

She tried to turn, but I held her steady. "Callum, what does that mean?"

"Shhh. Trust me."

Starting with the top left marking, I slowly deciphered each symbol, speaking the ancient language of the Shadow aloud. A language from the earliest of our ancestors, one no longer used but taught to every Shadow as a child. A revered language that held power. And one the markings on her back contained.

The further I progressed, the more Harmony fidgeted. "It tickles like my leg has fallen asleep," she complained.

"Stop moving and stay quiet," I hissed, not wanting to break the magic pooling around the markings.

There was no way my suspicion could be correct. If it were, it would answer questions whispered on the wind for decades. Never spoken aloud for fear of the Goddess' reaction. Never spoken because it was a part of our history we wanted to forget. One that reminded us that we had no control, that the gods owned us and held the power to snuff us out in one blow.

I continued reading the markings aloud, a dusting of gold appearing the further I got, and Harmony's agitation grew until she was trying to reach over and scratch at her back.

"Harmony, stop!"

"It hurts, Callum. Really bad." And if it was painful enough for her to complain, it was severe. She'd barely flinched when

I'd sewn up a gaping wound in her back; this had to be agonizing.

"Just a little more to go. The pain is going to worsen. I'm sorry, but please trust me and stop reaching back."

The gold started to fade, and I knew I needed to continue, or I'd lose the spell. I tuned out her complaints and continued translating the words in my head as I spoke the ancient language.

> *The curse of the forbidden will bind you.*
> *The love of the forbidden will protect you.*
> *The pain of the forbidden will raise you.*
> *The death of the forbidden will drive you.*
> *The taste of forbidden love will seal your fate.*
> *And release the bindings to free the fruit of the*
> *   forbidden.*
> *Only then will the fate of Shadow and Torch*
> *   reveal itself and bring the gods to their knees.*

The gold glowed so brightly on the last word that I stumbled back, watching as it weaved into an ebony hue that rose like ash from her back. A wind funneled around us as the spell broke. Harmony screamed in pain, but I could only stare as the magic of the Torch spread from the markings of the Shadow. She doubled over as what the spell had hidden burst forth, her scream shredding my soul, my eyes too transfixed for me to move.

Wings of ebony and ivory unfurled, filling the room with their beauty and the weight of their existence. Black wings edged with ivory feathers. Harmony wasn't being executed for her curiosity. She was being executed because she was everything the gods feared. The result of a forbidden love that had shaken the gods and their hunters in ways that still reverberated to this day.

CHAPTER 12
HARMONY

The pain was excruciating, burrowing between my shoulder blades and pulsing through my body. Callum had said to trust him, and I did, but with every strange word he spoke, the itch that nagged at my skin became more painful until I couldn't take it anymore. My skin blazed like it had ripped open as screams poured from my mouth.

Callum had grown silent, but I wasn't sure it hadn't been because my screams covered the sound of his voice. As the burning stopped, a destabilizing weight overcame me, and I tipped forward. Callum's hand wrapped around my waist to keep me on my feet, but that didn't help the fear that encapsulated me as I realized something was on my back. I shrieked and jerked from his grip, stumbling as he tried to calm me.

"Harmony! Stop moving, you're okay."

"Okay? There's something on me, Callum!" I spun, hearing things falling to the ground and catching sight of feathers from my periphery. I reached my hands to my back, trying to free myself from whatever had its grip on me.

"Dammit, Harmony, stay still!" He grabbed me and stopped

my motion, teetering as my weight nearly toppled me and dragged him with me. His eyes were wide with wonder, a boyish excitement on his face. "You need to keep calm for just a moment while I show you what's on your back."

My heart pounded and a strange flutter tingled from my back, a wind kicking up with the movement of wings.

"Oh gods, the Torch are back, aren't they?" I cried, reaching to his chest and digging my nails into it, wishing he'd put a damn shirt on so I could tear at something besides his skin.

"No, they're not. Look at me, Harmony." His voice was soothing, so I brought my eyes back to his. "No one is here. That's you making the noise."

"Me?" I didn't understand, but then that flutter happened again, and I became unbalanced, falling into him.

"Yes," he replied, stabilizing me. "Harmony, those markings were a spell hiding the truth of who you are."

Panic gripped me again for some irrational reason, and I found myself suddenly exhausted. "Who am I, Callum?"

I wasn't sure I wanted to know with the weight on my back trying to pull me down to my knees.

"The daughter of Landon and Trinity. Shadow and Torch, hunted by the gods and slaughtered for loving each other."

My gasp was so loud it would have cracked windows if there had been any. A chill climbed along my spine, my body quaking with the impact of his words. My legs gave way, and I collapsed, but something stopped my fall. It was then that I saw the curl of wings coming from behind me, outlined in a bright white with black feathers through the rest. I grasped Callum's shoulders tighter, my mouth opening and closing as I tried to find the words.

My world came down around me, shattering everything I'd thought I'd known about myself and my past. Everything I'd ever attributed to the parents who had scarred me and abandoned me on the steps of a building, never looking back. Leaving me with nothing but their marks and a name.

The room spun, my body shaking with a chill I couldn't ease until the weight of the last few minutes and that of Callum's words became too much, and darkness seeped into my eyes. The last thing I heard as it took me away was Callum saying my name. Then there was nothing.

I DREAMED of ebony and ivory feathers floating before me and gently falling to the ground, leading me on a path that had no end. The further I walked, the more muddled my mind became until I could no longer see the feathers or determine which direction to go. Lost, I swirled around frantically until I sensed something familiar, a calm, strengthening presence that reminded me of Callum. Following it, I woke, blinking to adjust to my surroundings. The softness of the bed was below me, and across the room, Callum paced. He had his face screwed up in thought, his eyes narrowed, looking to the ground as he mumbled to himself.

"You know, I hear talking to yourself is the first sign your sanity is slipping," I teased, sitting up and noticing the weight was gone from my shoulder blades. The thought brought back the sight of the wings, and I wobbled, slipping sideways to flop back on the pillow. Callum was across the room before I could curse myself for my clumsiness.

His fingers brushed my cheek, his eyes searching mine with a fear that didn't sit well on him.

"Were those my wings?" I asked, hearing the shake in my voice and not bothering to lift myself from the pillow. "Because if they are, my clumsy game just got upped to a level I don't think anyone should bear."

Smiling at me, he kissed my nose, saying, "You'll get used to them."

"They were real?" There wasn't a need for me to ask him. I'd seen them, but it seemed too surreal to be true.

"Yes, and they were glorious." He was awestruck, his eyes bright with excitement, and I didn't know how to take it.

"Gloriously precarious is more like it. People like me shouldn't carry that much weight on our backs. We already deal with balance issues."

As he helped me sit up, I reached around to my back for the damned feathery things, but found nothing.

"They're tucked away now. They retreated when you passed out."

I gave him a confused look.

"They don't act like normal appendages," he said.

"So they act more like your dick? Coming out to play when they get worked up?"

"Funny," he replied with a laugh, trying to give me a stern face that wasn't sticking. "You know, if you weren't working my dick up all the time, we'd get a lot more accomplished."

"But then it wouldn't want to come out and play," I said with a pout on my lip. One he leaned toward and nibbled away.

"Concentrate, Harmony."

"Does fucking feel different when your wings are out?" I didn't know why the thought made my thighs tighten, but his wings had been sexy. A pressure built on my back, and the damned things burst out, pulling me down with their unexpected weight. "Shit, guess that answers the question about them getting worked up."

Callum climbed on top of me, pinning my body and wings down. I'd forgotten I was still completely naked, and my body responded instantly. "No fucking with the wings until you've gotten used to them," he said, pushing his hardness against me and caressing my breast.

"But they're already out. It'd be a shame to put them to waste."

"How do you get anything done in life? Are you this distracted when you're at work?" A shadow came over his face. "Am I going to need to kill every man you work with?"

He was possessive and jealous, and that should have scared me, but he was a Shadow. He was my Shadow, and I loved that possessiveness.

"Am I going to need to work now that we know I have these things? You don't work."

"I run businesses and collect the cash while others do the work for me. I don't have to work."

I tipped my head and looked at him. "Why bother? Don't you have some magical Shadow hangout where you guys all live?"

"Guys and girls," he said, his hand still massaging my breast as if it was a comfort thing. I didn't complain. My thighs were soaking by the minute, and I was close to humping the bulge in his pants. I did, however, mind the addition of the word girls, and he must have seen my frown. "We live together in that place you refer to as a hangout."

"Having orgies all day?"

He pinched my nipple, and I bucked against him, my pelvis tipping his hardness further into my wetness. "No, we don't have orgies all day. Stop your jealousy, woman."

"Only if you stop with yours."

"Fuck, all right. Let's move on. I don't like living in that realm. The mortal realm is more exciting." He leaned closer to my ear, whispering, "And the women are fun to fuck."

I snarled, which was a completely new sound for me and one

I liked. He was taunting me, and from his chuckle, he was enjoying it.

"The men here are fun to fuck, too. I've had quite a few who left an impression." If he wanted to play, I could play with the best of them.

He dropped his lips to mine, kissing me with a force that left me breathless before he bit me.

"Ouch!" I complained, my lip throbbing as I spied the blood on his. "You prick. You bit me."

Licking his lips, he stared at my wound, a devious smile playing on his face. "I'll be damned."

"Don't even pretend you did that by accident."

"I didn't. I did it purposely. Now stop being a pain in my ass and sit up."

"You started it with your comments about fucking women," I complained as he lifted himself from me. He was so hard it was a wonder his zipper hadn't broken. I wanted to jerk him back to me so I could play with him, but I sat up, wiping my lip and noting the bleeding had stopped.

"It's not there anymore," he said nonchalantly, looking my new appendages over. Each time he touched them, it sent a shockwave of pleasure through me that differed completely from other touches. "Your blood carries our healing gifts. The spell must have released them."

He took my hands in his and flipped them over. The cuts and scrapes were gone. I flexed my hands in and out, staring at them in awe. Healing. The word seemed so foreign, a concept for books or movies, not for my reality.

"Stand up and let me look at your back," he commanded, standing.

He'd taken on this methodical, serious mood, and I couldn't help but reach up to his face, running my fingers over the tightness that sat in his jaw. The playful lover he'd been moments ago was gone.

"I'm a Shadow, Harmony. Softness is weakness. Now turn around."

Dropping my hand, I did as he ordered, thinking how different he was now. Yet that wasn't entirely true. This was the man I'd met with his guarded comments and innuendos, tough and untouchable. Yet the part of him he revealed for me had been there then, just as I knew it was there now.

His hands touched the place where he'd stitched me. The pain had been almost unbearable at the time, but nothing like the agony of my wings breaking through.

Wings…I had wings. The surreal thought hit me, and my chest tightened, my balance wavering as my anxiety rose.

Callum grabbed my waist. "Stop thinking about them. They'll become a part of you, as natural as your fingers or toes."

"My fingers and toes don't disappear, then appear to fill an entire room."

"They weren't filling the room before you started freaking out."

"I don't freak out," I snapped. But I knew he was right. They hadn't risen before I'd thought about them. "How do I make them go away?"

His finger drifted up my back, light and seductive. "Your magic healed your wound. The stitches are gone."

"That didn't answer my question," I said as his lips dragged along my neck. "And that definitely isn't answering it."

"I can't help myself. You're completely naked and absolutely stunning."

My wings fluttered, and I gaped at them. "What the fuck was that?"

"That was your arousal," he replied, nipping at my neck.

"The wetter you get, the more they react. And when you come… good gods, when *you* come, they'll be incredible."

"And I'm guessing you know that from other lovers you've had with wings?" I huffed.

He bit my neck, and this time the ache it caused sent a heat through my belly that I couldn't deny. "Only Shadow, baby, and I can promise you, you come better than any Shadow I've had. I can't wait to see you break with your wings around me."

My exhale was louder than I'd intended.

"You need some clothes on, Harmony. We have a lot to discuss, and that body of yours is making me so hard it's distracting me."

He drew away, his fingers drifting through the feathers of my wings so seductively that my legs almost gave out. The sensation that tumbled through me was like a tongue to my clit.

"I can take care of that if you want me to," I teased him. I tried to turn around, but my wings tangled in everything. It was hard to be sexy when my clumsiness was twofold. "Damn, tell me how to put these things away, Callum."

He was laughing, which only caused me to pout more. My wings seemed to sense it, and they flicked back, knocking into him. The laughing stopped.

"Control those things, Harmony, or I may need to punish you."

Punishment? Why had that word soaked me so badly? I'd never been into that kink. Slate had tried spanking me once, and I'd kicked him in the balls. Hair pulling I enjoyed, but not that… at least not before. Something about Callum called to a part of me I didn't know. One who loved the way he called me baby, the way his hands held my neck so tight I could barely breathe, that dark side of him that brought out a dark side in me.

"Don't tempt me, Callum."

I heard a low rumble that sounded like it had come from deep in his chest, further drenching me. It surprised me I wasn't dripping on the floor by now.

"Concentrate on them and command them to retract," he said, slightly hoarser than usual.

"Concentrate, he says," I mumbled.

Closing my eyes, I tried to think of them as I would my arms or legs, sending the thought out that I wanted them to disappear. The weight shifted on my back as the air whooshed and I became steadier. Turning around, I tried to contain my excitement, but I was still bouncing on the balls of my feet.

"I did it!" I looked from side to side, noting no wings in my periphery.

Callum had a smug smile on his face. In his hands were a T-shirt and my panties. "Not quite, sweetheart." He gestured behind me, and I reached my arm around my side, touching the soft feathers that remained. "Fuck." I'd only managed to bring them in, but the blasted things were still there.

"You know, I can't decide if I want you in the shirt with your panties or without your panties," he mused, as if I weren't struggling like a newborn bird.

Scowling, I ignored him, which was hard to do when he brought the panties to his nose and sniffed before tucking them into his pocket. "I think we'll forego them. Watching you prance around in my shirt, knowing that ass is bare, will make my dick happy."

"I have a few more things that will make your dick happy if you make these stupid things disappear."

"Uh-uh, don't insult the wings. They're part of you. Respect them."

I muttered a few obscenities as I tried to make the things go away, but they refused to listen.

Callum came closer. "I can't take you like this much more, or I'm going to ravage you. Now relax and stop trying so hard." He brought me against him and kissed me. It wasn't the hungry, aggressive kiss he usually gave me. This was sensual and emotional. A calm settled in me, and as I wrapped my arms around his neck, I perceived the shift in my back as my wings retracted completely.

His hands slid down my back and to my ass, pressing them into me so hard my pelvis tipped. The moment his lips left mine, I knew he was denying himself again. He dropped his forehead to mine, breathlessly saying, "I want you, Harmony, but there's a lot you need to know, and I cannot protect you if I'm entangled with your body."

"I didn't start that this time, Callum. That was all you."

The color in his eyes danced in the room's light, the hazel leaning more to a golden sage that made my heart flutter. Giving me one more gentle kiss, he handed me the shirt and walked away, the panties still tucked in his pocket.

I pulled the shirt on, seeing that he'd taken a seat at the table, his eyes following my movements. Thinking it best to keep a distance between us since my body was craving him again in a completely irrational way, I remained where I was. "All right, tell me why I have these humongous wings and why you think I'm the downfall of the gods."

"To understand, you need to go back to the beginning. When the world was first created, the gods got along. There was no strife among them, no separation, no Errant gods or Galere gods. They were one family. Somewhere along the way, there was a fallout between Harperia and Farinthion. We don't know what happened; the gods don't share their secrets. Whatever it was, it was serious enough to fracture them. They formed The Blight and The Sect as separate realms and began vying for souls. As time passed, the Goddess created the Shadow, and Farinthion, the enemy god, created the Torch. Everything she did, he countered, and everything he did, she countered."

I scratched my head, wondering at how petty the gods were.

"So, where do my parents come in?"

"Well, that's where it gets interesting. Shadow and Torch were enemies from the beginning. We hate each other. They're a pain in the ass who steal our demons and—"

"Demons?"

"Yes, the Goddess thought it would be fun to create demons and let them run amuck among the mortals, another way to irritate Farinthion. But they went rogue, and now we hunt them. We're hunters for the gods, remember?"

"Yes, but you have to remember this was all legend before yesterday," I told him.

Giving me a smirk, he said, "You didn't think so, as you so determinedly chased me down for answers."

I had. And now look where I was, knee-deep in a mythical world I didn't understand and barely believed in. "You said those people you killed, the ones you marked with the wings, were demons, right?"

"Yes, they find a host, a weak soul, and invade. Once they do, they devour the soul of the host. The mortal is no longer there. All that's left is a shell for the demon to use and wreak more havoc with."

I gaped at him, the thought terrifying. Demons devouring souls and walking around the streets looking like anyone else. "And you hunt them and kill them."

"We hunt them, kill the host body, and sometimes the demon. Or we take the demons back to our realm and pass judgement on them there. Our leader likes to use them as target practice, but I prefer just to kill them."

I had no words, and I imagined I looked like a confused child, my eyes large as I listened to the stories of the gods and their hunters as if it was an everyday thing.

"Anyway, the point is Shadow and Torch are enemies,

forbidden from communicating with each other in any way except during a demon hunt if one gets in our way."

"That's how you knew the name of the one who found us?"

"Krinle? No, he's the leader of …"

He trailed off, and I wondered what had caught his attention. It was hard to remain silent while he worked it out.

"Damn, why didn't I see that?"

"See what?"

His brows creased, his face lined with tension again. "Krinle is the leader of the Torch. Leaders don't hunt. They rarely leave the realm. When they accept the position, they leave hunting behind. I should have known it was something serious for him to be here."

"But your leader didn't come after me, so why would that have told you something?" I was having a tough time following.

"In two months, Gerrand, the leader of the Shadow, is stepping down. I'm his second, the one who will step into his role, the one he's groomed since I was a child. I'm the leader of the Shadow, by all accounts."

I sucked in a harsh breath that stung my chest.

"That's why the Goddess chose me to kill you. I thought it was a last gift before my promotion locked me away in the realm."

"You thought of killing me as a gift?" The thought had me scooting further back, adding more distance between us.

He gave me an annoyed look. "We've been through this, Harmony. I didn't know you were anything more than a kill. But I would have killed you the first day I saw you if I'd wanted you dead. You intrigued me. That's the reason I asked for more time. Something drew me to you. I just didn't know why until now."

Relaxing some, I moved back to my original position. "Why is it so important that I die?"

"Because of what you stand for. Remember how I said the gods are enemies, as are Shadow and Torch?"

I nodded.

"I don't know the entire story. Only the gods' Guard does—"

"The gods' Guard?"

"Yes, they're like the Shadow, only stronger. They're close to the gods, particularly the Goddess, guarding The Blight from Farinthion and the gods in The Sect. If you think we're frightening, you should meet a Guard."

"I think I'll pass." I couldn't imagine anything more frightening, and all this talk of gods was making my head hurt.

"Good, now stop interrupting."

I stuck my tongue out playfully at him.

"Put that away. I'm not ready for it yet." He grabbed himself, gesturing to his bulge. "But I will be soon."

"I'd suggest you get your hand off that thing before I take over. Now, finish the story."

His eyes glinted playfully. "Don't give me commands, Harmony."

I lifted a brow at him, but he disregarded it and continued talking. "I only know pieces of the story. The gods brought the Guard in to deal with the situation, leaving the Shadow out, since it was one of our own who had caused the issue."

My heart thumped, knowing that by one of their own, he had meant my parents. I sat closer to the edge of the bed in anticipation.

"Trinity was the leader of the Torch. She was fierce and loyal and fought her way to the top. That much I know because, as a third, I had to deal with her on formal occasions."

"Wait, third? I thought you were second to the leader."

His smile warmed my heart. "You are sharp, like your father. I am now, but your father was second. Landon was in line to lead the Shadow. He was the strongest Shadow I knew, lethal and terrifying. I was content knowing I'd be his second and still get to hunt. I can't say I ever wanted to lead…although I don't think that's something I need to worry about now."

He ran his hand through his hair, a forlorn look on his face, and it hit me then how much damage my presence had done to his life. I'd taken everything from him, and what did he get in return? A life on the run, the constant threat of death, having to protect me?

His eyes met mine, understanding in them, and I wondered if he'd read my thoughts. "I'd give it all up in a heartbeat if I had to do it again, Harmony. As I imagine Landon would have."

I gave him a nod, still not feeling good about the fact that I'd destroyed his life. "What happened to them?"

"They fell in love. Shadow and Torch leaders will meet occasionally. That's how the top Shadows know who the top Torch are. Only during those times are we civil to each other. It's boring shit, like territory arguments. Sometimes we'll do prisoner exchanges if they need a demon for a specific reason, and it's still alive. Boring business talk that I hate. Any other time, we are enemies, and the laws of war apply."

"So they knew each other?"

"Yes, but only on a strained civil level. There was nothing that seemed out of the ordinary when we would meet."

I chewed my bottom lip, wondering how two enemies suddenly became lovers. "But something changed that."

"Yes," he confirmed. "A few Shadows captured Trinity. It still amazes me that they captured her, but they wounded her and then jumped her when she was healing. No one really knows why she was hunting since she was a leader. But she was, and we took her hostage. Gerrand thought of it as a bargaining chip. Landon didn't like the idea and was vocal about it, but the gods agreed with Gerrand. They clipped Trinity's wings—"

"You cut her wings off?" I asked, horrified at the thought, my stomach knotting in revulsion.

"No, it's an expression," he said, with the shake of his head. "It's a spell that kept her bound to our realm. Gerrand assigned Landon to guard her, taking him off hunting duty until we negotiated with the Torch."

"But he fell in love with her." It sounded so romantic if taken out of its context.

"I think so, although it may have happened before then and they'd kept it hidden."

I leaned in further, anticipation building in me, my nerves on edge because I knew something terrible had happened to them. Otherwise, they would still be alive. "He helped her escape, didn't he?" I asked, my voice sounding distant.

Callum nodded, running his hand through his hair. "He freed her and ran away with her."

I scratched at my hand, my mind churning with the information. "But if they got away—"

The shake of his head stopped my words. "Torch and Shadow are enemies, Harmony. There is no happy ending here. What they did went against everything the gods have imbued in our ranks for centuries. It was a scandal that rocked both realms. The gods were outraged, furious that a Shadow and Torch would break their vows of antagonism and fall in love."

The tightness in my chest built, my level of frustration rising. "But they weren't hurting anyone. I don't understand why what they did was so wrong." And I didn't. Love was love and if my parents loved each other as deeply as what I felt for Callum in just this brief time, then there was no way they could have resisted it.

"It hurts the factions, Harmony. I know you don't understand, but these are the gods you're talking about. There are rules we must follow, both Shadow and Torch. Our entire existence rests on the animosity between the gods and that hatred funnels down to us."

With a sigh, I knew I had to accept that answer, whether I liked it or not. This world was new to me, as were the rules enforced within it. "So, what happened to them?" I asked, needing to know even if part of me wanted to run from it.

Callum's eyes grew sad for just a moment before they hardened, and I wondered at the toll the war between the gods had taken on their warriors. "The Guard were called in on both sides, hunting for them. They were on the run for a few years when the Guard captured Trinity. She was weak, distraught, a shell of the warrior I had known. We handed her over to the Torch, and they executed her." My heart lurched, tears pushing against my eyes. "Landon turned himself in when she died. I'd never seen a man so destroyed. He didn't even fight as the Guard brought him in. The Goddess delivered the killing blow, executing him for treason to our kind and his gods."

Silence fell upon his last word, and I embraced it. I didn't know what to say. All the thoughts I'd had of my parents had never come close to what I'd just heard. Tears made their way down my cheeks, and I brought my fingers up to wipe them away. Callum gestured for me to come to him, and I did, not questioning the subtle command. I curled into his lap, and he wiped the rest of my tears away, kissing the salty trails they'd left.

He was the only solid piece of my life left, and I didn't want him to be any further away than he was. I wanted to stay in his arms, safe and secure for the rest of my life, and leave the outside world with its gods and hunters far behind. Reality was too much for me to grasp, and I wanted no part of it except Callum.

CHAPTER 13
CALLUM

Harmony's body was curled up in my arms, and I could sense the vulnerability in her. I didn't like it there; it wasn't her. She was my strong girl, full of life and witty comebacks. But as much as I'd taunted her earlier, the situation was serious. Watching her wings unfurl had knocked the breath from me. I'd been stunned at their unexpectedness, even though I'd suspected the spell held a secret that tied back to Landon and Trinity. Seeing them compounded my fear of losing her, fear of the past rewriting itself through the two of us. She wasn't just a Torch; she was a combination of both factions —half Torch, half Shadow, the epitome of everything the gods had executed Landon and Trinity for.

Reliving Landon's death had brought the pain of that time back. Landon had been as much of a mentor to me as Gerrand had been. The scandal had rocked the Shadow. It had rocked the realm. There was no one unaffected by it. The Goddess had brooded for months, the other gods avoiding us as they contemplated the misstep of one Shadow and what it said about the possibility of any of us making a similar mistake. There had been days when we weren't sure the gods would let any of us live. Even the Guard had been nervous, rumors circulating that there was dissidence among them as well. The leader of the Guard, Belkair, was Landon's brother after all.

The situation had been tense for too long, and the wounds had only begun to heal after decades of loyalty tests doled out by the gods.

Now it turned out there was a reason Trinity had been weak enough to be captured. She and Landon had thought there was no other choice, and so she'd let the Guard find her. Landon doing the same once her gods had executed her. Why else would they have given Harmony up? Taking the chance that a spell would hide her identity, that having mortals raise her would keep her hidden from the eyes of the gods? Giving themselves up and facing the persecution that awaited them took the gods' eyes from the mortal world long enough for Harmony's existence to go unnoticed. Until the Goddess finally discovered her thirty-three years later.

I hooked my thumb under Harmony's chin, lifting her face to mine. My heart hurt for her; my soul longed to shelter her from what I knew was outside the doors of the safe house. The same life Landon and Trinity had faced to be with each other. I didn't want our ending to be the same. I didn't want to watch as the Shadow captured Harmony, knowing her fate, and handing myself over as her death tore my soul in half.

"I won't let them hurt you," I promised, unsure how to keep that promise.

She dug her fingers into my chest. "I don't want to know any more. Take my mind from reality, Callum."

Her hand wrapped around my neck, and she brought my face to hers, kissing me desperately.

"This won't solve anything, Harmony."

"No, but it will numb the pain and remove the fear."

I shook my head, my body reacting to her touch, my stomach sucking in as her hand slid down my chest to unhook my pants.

"Harmony," I warned, grabbing her wrist.

"Please, Callum. I need you. I don't want to hear any more about Shadow or Torch or executions. Everything I knew is gone, and everything I thought..." Her voice cracked with emotion, the tears welling in her eyes, and I didn't know how to ease the pain. "All of it is a mess of death and war between beings I didn't genuinely believe in until today. The only real thing is you."

I wanted to give in, to make love to her, to use her body and her mouth and take the pain away the only way either of us knew how, but I knew it wouldn't be anything but a temporary salve.

Her kisses traced their way down my neck, her hand stroking me through my pants, and I wrestled with my need to do the right thing and the need to seek the same escape she was seeking. As she unzipped my pants, her hand guiding me out, I lost the battle to do the right thing, to be the good guy I desperately wanted to be. I wasn't the good guy and if she needed this to make her whole again, I would give it to her with no hesitation.

I threaded my fingers through her hair and brought her lips to mine, giving over to her request. I draped my other hand up her body, caressing her breast as her hands spread up my chest. The revelations of her existence faded to a distant memory as her hand stroked me confidently. Lifting her shirt, I pushed her back, raising it over her head and searching her eyes for any chance that this wasn't what she wanted. But I found none and so I brought her against me, loving the breathless way she returned my kiss.

I lifted her and set her down on my length. I didn't stop kissing her as she encompassed me, riding me with moves that broke every level of resistance I had until I was nothing but putty in her hands. My usual aggressive dominance disappeared, caving to the man who loved the woman now using his body. That matching dominance reminded me she was my equal in every way.

As she shattered, her body shaking uncontrollably against me, I picked her up, taking over and reclaiming my dominance. We worked the balance perfectly, stepping in whenever one of us was beginning to submit. And she was submitting now, her body clinging to mine as I dropped her on the table and pushed her down. Her legs remained clenched around me, the remnants of her orgasm continuing to tear through her.

I drove into her, teasing her clit and grabbing at her breasts until she was trembling again. "Turn around," I commanded, pulling out and stroking myself as she sat up. "Shit, no, stay there," I said, dropping to my knees and yanking her legs forward, sinking my tongue into her and hearing her drop back to the table with a loud grunt.

She tasted like exquisite champagne, and I rode her with my tongue, my thumb circling her clit, feeling it harden the closer her climax drew. With a cry, she came, falling apart against my mouth as I continued devouring her. I didn't let up, needing to weaken her again until she was screaming, her legs squeezing around my head, her muscles shaking. She crashed, coming so hard she dug her nails into my shoulders, ripping the skin.

My wings broke free, flaring wide behind me. Giving her one last lick, I forced her up, seeing her eyes widen, lust filling them, which only made me harder.

"On your stomach," I said, shoving her over. I rubbed her back, knowing the spot that would drive her mad, her wings breaking free and spreading behind her. They were glorious, and my own flickered in anticipation. The moan that fell from her lips when I dragged my fingers over her feathers drove me to the edge. I shoved her to the table and penetrated her, grunting as she enveloped me, her soaked pussy causing waves of desire to pulse through me.

I curled my fingers into her hair, pulling her back against me, then brought my wings around her, encasing both of us in our wings as I took her so hard sweat drenched us. With one hand around her neck, the other on her clit, I continued to fuck her until she was trembling, the waves of her oncoming release about to overtake her. I knew now what her signs were, and I held her tight as she came undone. Her muscles clamped down around me so tight I succumbed to the orgasm that had built in me waiting to erupt, my body convulsing as release tore through me.

On the fourth thrust, my legs gave out, and I collapsed, dropping us both to the table as my wings retreated with hers. I wrapped my arm around her waist and held her, the two of us lying on the table, breathing rapidly and loudly. When I recovered some, I lifted myself from her, licking the beaded line of sweat on her back. I slipped from her and helped her turn over, bringing her against me and kissing her. This kiss was gentle and emotion-laced, and I held her tight against my chest before picking her up and walking us to the bed.

Lying next to her, I curled her into my chest. There was nothing like it, and I never wanted to let her go again. We fell asleep that way, the day too long to grapple with anymore, both of us wanting to keep reality at bay for a little longer.

IT WAS PAST DAWN. We'd slept through the night, losing too much time. Harmony remained snuggled into my chest, like she didn't want to be far from me, even in sleep. I slipped from her hold and pulled the blanket over her, watching her lips turn to a grimace at the absence of my body before they relaxed.

Quietly, I dressed, taking a moment to look at her again before I left. With the Shadow and Torch after us, I knew it was only a matter of time before they found us. I needed to get a plan in place, but I couldn't keep Harmony safe by myself, not against the warriors of the gods. Softly kissing her head, I left her behind, hoping she didn't wake before I returned. My spells were secure around the compound and as long as she remained inside, she would be safe.

As Shadow, we could wrap ourselves in our magic and transport to any destination. It helped with our job and kept the world oblivious to our presence. If we kept the magic bound to our bodies, it left no trace for others to follow. The only reason Harmony and I were still alive was because of that ability. I landed in another of my safe houses, my wings closing behind me in a flurry of magic.

I stashed extra phones in various safe houses. The one where Harmony was still sleeping had one, but I didn't want to take a chance and inadvertently lead someone to her by using it. This safe house was larger and on the edge of another province, so there was no chance of anyone finding her if they traced me here.

Shadow had standard-issue phones we all carried that connected us to The Blight. It kept our communication discreet and blended with the mortals. I'd been at this long enough to imbue my magic to my own phones for emergencies. They were untraceable even to other Shadow, allowing me to keep my safe houses undetected and giving me the autonomy to live among the mortals when I needed to escape the boredom of The Blight, which was often. It had pissed Gerand off until he realized I was better left to do my own thing when I wasn't on duty.

Digging around in the small office, I found one. Rather than use it immediately, I sat on the couch, staring at the phone and wondering if this risk was too considerable.

I thought about Harmony and my emotions for her. Fated love was rare among my kind, but when it happened, it brought about a powerful tie and, eventually, a stronger breed of Shadow. My parents had been fated, and I was stronger than even Gerrand. Landon had been his second only because I was so much younger.

Although fated love only happened between our kind every few centuries, I suspected Landon and Trinity were an exception. Her death had devastated him too deeply. Losing a partner was paralyzing but survivable. Losing a fated mate was soul-shattering. There was no recovering, and the other mate couldn't survive. When one died, the other died, either by their own hand or with the withering of their heart within months, if not sooner. That's why it was so rare. Landon had handed himself over when he'd lost Trinity. There had been no fight in him, no anger at her death, nothing but pure devastation. He'd wanted to die.

That was the way I felt about Harmony. Love that deep didn't bloom in a few days and certainly didn't root itself in a soul that fast. But fate had meant us to be mates. There was no denying it now. No matter how my kind revered that term, it hadn't saved her parents, and it wouldn't save us.

With a sigh, I dialed the number. I had two calls to make, and both would be hard. One could prove deadly if the receiver betrayed me.

"Who the fuck is this?"

"Shut the fuck up, Slate, and listen." Slate was an arrogant shit, but he was smart, and he had resources—ones I would need now that I was on the run.

"Callum? Where's Harmony? You promised she'd text me this morning, and she hasn't texted. If you even dared to fucking hurt her or even touch her—"

"Shut your fucking mouth, Slate. I haven't hurt her, but I can't say I haven't touched her." His snarl gave me pleasure. I'd forgotten I'd told the prick I'd have her home by now. Not that I'd had any intention of following through. I knew I would have killed her or owned her by the time her visit was up. Since Slate was a few hours ahead of us, I had no doubt he was ready to kill someone because he hadn't heard from her. If it was one thing I'd discovered about Slate, it was how protective he was of Harmony. "I need to call in a favor."

"A favor? Not until I know she's safe."

"She's not safe. That's the issue."

"What the fuck, Callum? You promised—"

He was grating on my last nerve, and I was about to disconnect, but I needed him, for Harmony's sake. "I know what I promised. I haven't hurt her, but there are others after her. Others neither you nor I can fight." I was strong, but I couldn't defeat an entire army of Shadow and Torch alone.

"What's going on?"

He'd calmed, his business persona coming out to cover his emotions. I learned when I settled in the city that Slate was someone to keep in my pocket. I had enough money and my hand in enough assets through the city to threaten his greedy empire, but I didn't need to own the town. I simply wanted to skirt unseen, remaining in the shadows while I built a reputation and a small empire within his. There was no need for any of it, but it satisfied a drive in me, keeping life interesting. And after centuries of trudging through this world, doing the bidding of the gods, the mortal identity of Callum Montrose was a much-needed reprieve. Slate could have been an obstacle, but I'd worked my way into his trust, making a few business deals with him that benefited him and kept him as an ally.

It had worked well and put Harmony in my hands at just the right time. Another thing I could have chalked up to coincidence but given how fate seemed to hold the deck in our lives at the moment, I didn't think it was.

"I need you to fortify your compound. Place your guards on alert and do not let anyone in. Make sure they know Harmony is the exception. If she comes to you, you protect her like she's your most precious asset. Do you understand me?"

"Of course. I always protect her."

"Not like you always do, Slate. Make no mistake, this is not an everyday situation. This is war, and anyone around her will be collateral. She's the mark, and until she's dead, they will kill anyone who stands in their way."

"What the fuck did you get her involved in, Montrose?" The anger in his voice was almost palpable through the phone. Good, he needed to be angry. He was at his most dangerous when he was angry. Nobody fucked with Slate, just like nobody fucked with me.

"I didn't get her involved in anything…well, except my dick." I smiled as he started going off on the other end. Baiting him had been deliberate and worth it.

"I'm going to kill you, Montrose!"

"No, you're not because Harmony will kill you if you even try. Trust me, she enjoyed every minute of it. Now settle down. You have a safe house, right?"

He remained silent.

"I asked you a fucking question."

"Yes, I have a safe house. I have a few." Of course he did. He was methodical like I was.

"I need you to ready it, and I need to know where it is. Pick the one furthest away, the one you'd use if your rivals were picking your family off one by one."

"I'm not telling you where it is."

Shit, of course, he wouldn't. I wouldn't have either. So, if Harmony and I got separated and Slate hid her, I wouldn't be able to find her. Again, that fated love thought came back to me. If it was true, and fate connected our souls, then I could sense her. That was likely the reason Landon had known they'd taken Trinity. And how he'd known Farinthion had executed her.

"Callum?"

"Give me a minute." I closed my eyes and thought about Harmony, letting my heart fill with emotion for her. Relaxing, I calmed myself so nothing existed in my mind but my love for her. I let my soul stretch, reaching for its other half, searching for the piece of it that would fortify it. There was nothing at first, but then a warmth filled me, a sensation that washed over me, and I could sense her soul respond. In that response, I could tell where she was.

"Shit," I muttered. "It worked."

"What worked? Where's Harmony? I want to talk to her."

"No, she's safe. Trust me."

"Trust you? You're telling me I need to protect her, that she's some kind of target someone wants dead. Why the fuck would that make me trust you?"

"Because you have no other choice. Now hunker down and pull all your men in for security duty. If Harmony comes to you, you keep her safe, or so help me, I'll rip that dick off and shove it up your ass so far you'll never reach it. Keep her safe, and I'll forgive the fact that you used to touch her, and I'll leave it attached."

Not giving him time to reply, I disconnected. I considered crushing the phone and getting rid of it, but Slate had the number. He was the only one who could trace it, and if things went wrong, I could give it to Harmony.

Pocketing it, I pulled another out and made the call I'd been delaying. With each ring, I could feel the sweat beading on my brow. Tension wound my muscles so tight I could barely sit still.

"This better be important."

"Gerrand, it's me."

The silence on the other end was stifling, and with each passing minute, sweat trickled down my neck.

"Like I said, Fledgling, this better be important."

The fact that he'd used the nickname he'd had for me when I was young and he was busting my ass to mold me into a leader told me two things: he wasn't alone, and I'd made the right call. Gerrand was my closest friend and ally. He may have been my commander, but I trusted him with my life. I trusted him enough to risk bringing him in to help me.

"I need your help."

"So I've heard. You've called me at an inconvenient time."

"Can you get someplace private? This is my neck on the line, Gerrand."

There was no response. I should have hung up and dumped the phone, but my instinct told me to stay on the line. Instinct made me a Shadow to be feared. One the others, even Trias, didn't question.

When the silence became almost unbearable, Gerrand exploded. "What the fuck have you gotten yourself into? You couldn't keep your hands off your mark long enough to kill her? Is that why you made that sorry ass excuse to give you more time? To fuck her and get a mark on your head?"

"Gerrand, listen to me. It's not what you think."

"Not what I think? You didn't fuck your mark? Shit, Callum. You've always tested me and the gods, but this is too much. I can't save you on this one."

"You have to. She's not just any mark—"

"No," he hissed. "She's the Goddess' mark! That means no questions, no delays, no touching!"

I held the phone from my ear, cringing at the anger in his voice.

"She's Landon and Trinity's daughter. That's why the Goddess wants her dead."

There was a long pause before Gerrand responded. "What?" The anger was gone. Landon's death had torn Gerrand. They'd been best friends, growing up together and training together to become the top two Shadow reigning for centuries. I was close to Gerrand, but he and Landon had been like brothers. That's why I knew he was the one to call.

"She's their daughter. They hid her wings beneath a series of markings and a spell, Shadow and Torch magic."

"Fuck. Callum, you know what this means."

"Yes, which makes it even more important that I protect her. The Torch are hunting her, too."

"Those dumb-asses know who she is?"

"I think so. They sent Krinle."

"Then they know. He'd only leave the realm if the gods ordered him. If Farinthion had ordered him."

"Exactly my thought." My heart rate calmed the more we talked.

"Why call me? I can't save you, either of you."

"I know. Gerrand…she's my fated."

Silence again. The word carried a weight that was substantial.

"That's why you touched her." It wasn't a question. He was stating the truth, what we all knew about the fated. A fated couldn't ignore the call to his soulmate once he found her.

"Yes. I have to protect her, and I will die doing so."

"Fuck, Callum. I knew I should have taken the assignment when the Goddess gave it to me."

"Wait, she wanted you to kill Harmony?"

"Yes, but I convinced her to send you. I know how much you like hunting, and being trapped in this job means losing that thrill. I figured it would give you one last meaningful hunt and reinforce your merit in the eyes of the gods. I didn't know I was sending you to fuck it all up."

"Well, that wasn't my intention." Both leaders had been called to kill Harmony, called directly by the gods when leaders didn't do the hunting. They'd wanted no chance of escape, no chance there would be a slip-up, so they'd sent their top Shadow and Torch to do the deed, ensuring Harmony's death. But one change had saved Harmony. I was beginning to think fate was involved in more ways than I'd initially figured. "The Goddess let you decline her command?"

He ignored my question. "What do you need from me, Callum? The gods have my hands tied on this."

"I need you to meet her, to see what I see."

"Are you mad? Your head is on the line. You're not dragging mine onto the chopping block as well."

"Gerrand. She's special. Landon and Trinity recognized it. I'm sure of it. That's why Trinity let herself get captured. They wanted to keep her hidden."

"Because she threatens to undo everything the gods have built."

"Maybe. But why is her death so necessary? We don't even know what she's capable of."

"She's capable of bringing down both Shadow and Torch with her mere existence."

"I think it's more than that, but I need you to witness her, to stand with me when they bring me to the Goddess for execution."

"Callum, you're asking me to be an accomplice in treason against the gods."

"I'm asking you, as a friend, to meet and look at her. That's all. Then you'll return to the fold and tell the Goddess you know where I am."

I suspected his reaction before his curses left his mouth.

"There's no fucking way I'm turning you in. That's insanity." I could hear the desperate plea in his voice.

"I wouldn't ask it if I didn't mean it. Doing so will take any suspicion from you and bide me time to get her to safety. You don't have to be the one to capture me. Trust me, you don't want that fight. I'll kick your ass."

He snickered. "You wish."

I gave him time to think, my plan developing as I waited.

"Fine, tell me where and when. But I can't save you when they bring you in, Callum."

"I know. I don't expect you to."

And I didn't. I was hoping another would and that he would be Harmony's saving grace.

CHAPTER 14
HARMONY

Callum was gone. I'd found a note on his pillow, the familiar handwriting telling me he'd be back soon and not to worry. As if not worrying was an option. After taking a long shower, I slipped into another of Callum's shirts and decided against underwear. All my clothes were still at the island house, and evidence of my body's reaction to Callum stained the only pair I had.

I found a coffee maker and made myself some much-needed caffeine. I wasn't sure what time it was since Callum had taken my phone and I'd left my watch behind. Not that it mattered. I wasn't even sure if we were in the same time zone anymore.

I suspected it had been three days since I'd begun this journey, naively stepping into a car that would inevitably lead me into the arms of a man who completed me like no other had. It seemed surreal. To be so endlessly in love with Callum after three days. But that's what it was. Love that reached down to the tips of my toes and leaped to my head. The kind that embedded in my core and soared through every cell of my body. It was unlike anything I'd ever experienced, and even waking up without him beside me was gutting. It was like a part of me was missing.

A strange sensation came over me as I sat staring into my coffee cup, thinking about how drastically my life had turned upside down in so little time. I didn't know how to describe it, but it was akin to what Slate's mother would describe as someone walking over her grave. The expression had always been odd to me, but that's exactly what it was like—someone reaching out and touching my spirit. The touch was familiar, protective, and loving. Callum. Somehow, wherever he was, he'd sensed me. Our love connected us now in ways that went beyond normal love and closer to spiritual. The sensation drifted away but left a residue of his touch on my soul.

Smiling to myself, I picked up my mug and walked around the small apartment space. I didn't think it was an actual apartment, but it gave the impression of one. I bent and picked up the books that had fallen from the table when Callum had taken me. The memory sent a stream of warmth between my legs. I missed his touch even though I'd had it only hours before. I thought briefly about bringing myself satisfaction, but I knew it would be nothing like him and only leave me disappointed. If I was coming today, it was going to be by Callum's hands. My breasts tingled thinking about it, but I ignored their call and sifted through a book.

What I would have given a few days ago to have access to the information that it contained. Before reality had knocked my identity on its ass and reconfigured it into something I didn't understand. I scoured the book, reading through a more detailed version of what Callum had told me. This was a history of the Shadow. Confirmation that they existed. Not that I needed any more confirmation. My wings were proof enough.

Wings. It was such an unsettling concept to think there were magical wings hidden somewhere in my back that could break free at any moment. Callum had coaxed them free last night, his own bursting forth while he'd taken me. The level of sensual intensity they'd added was indescribable, and even the thought had my legs twitching.

"You grip that table any harder, and I'm going to be suspicious that you've been playing with yourself while I've been gone."

I twisted to see Callum across the room. I wanted to run to him, but that wasn't my style. His black hair was messy, strands falling across his forehead. Tension sat on his shoulders, his hazel eyes not as vibrant as they usually were. But when they met mine, they flared to life. Whatever stress he was carrying lifted from him, and his lips turned to a sexy smirk.

"Were you touching yourself while I was gone?"

"I thought about it, but I'd much rather have the real thing."

The corner of his mouth lifted higher as he walked over to me. "You keep that ass in the air while you're bent over that table and I'll give you the real thing." He pulled me against him. "I'm starting to like this look, you in my shirt with…" his hand slipped between my legs "…no panties on."

"I don't have more than that one pair."

"That's a shame. You'll have to go without them from now on." He furrowed his brow, his expression concerned suddenly. "And that's going to be a massive distraction. Damn, there's no way I'll be able to concentrate knowing you've got nothing covering that pussy."

I shrugged, ready to say something witty back, when his fingers slipped into me. All thoughts fled, my mind and body overtaken with pleasure as his fingers fucked me. His eyes stayed on mine, watching my expression. I couldn't cover my reaction, and his grin rose. He dropped his head to my breasts, sucking a nipple into his mouth through the fabric of the shirt. With his other hand, he gripped my ass, tipping my pelvis so his fingers could go deeper, and I moaned so loud it echoed through the room.

He chuckled, dragging his teeth against my nipple as he released it. I wanted to shove his head back, but it wouldn't have mattered. He had his own agenda, one he'd likely thought about the entire time he'd been gone.

"Where did you go?" I asked between breaths.

He pulled his fingers out so fast that I dug into his shoulders to keep from falling. "Don't talk, Harmony. I'm going to fuck that luscious ass of yours now, like I've wanted to, and you're going to keep your mouth shut for anything but my tongue, my cock, or your cries. Understand?" He brought his fingers to his mouth, licking each one in a slow, deliberate way that had my clit pulsing. I wanted to say something snide, but I also wanted to comply because I knew the pleasure his words promised.

Knowing I wanted exactly what he wanted, I lifted my shirt over my head, watching his eyes twinkle with excitement. He brought his hands to my breasts, touching them the way only Callum could, my nipples his to command. But then again, he commanded every part of my body.

I tucked my fingers under his waistband and brought his shirt up, hating the brief moment when his hands lifted from my skin before I pressed my chest against his and kissed him.

His mouth was hungry for me, calling to the fire that was simmering deep in my belly. I unhooked his pants, needing my hands around his hardness and to have the warmth of it pulsing against my skin. A deep rumble went through his chest when I began stroking him and it sent desire clawing through me.

"Did you think about me when you were gone?" I cooed, stroking faster. I wanted to take back the role of aggressor and thought he was letting me until he shoved me to my knees and yanked my head back.

"I thought I told you no opening that mouth unless my tongue or cock was filling it."

The wave of arousal that splashed through me had my legs trembling and when he grabbed his length and stroked it in front of my mouth, I actually salivated.

"Show me how sorry you are, baby."

Pre-cum was dripping from his tip, so I reached my tongue out and licked it clean, moaning at the taste of him. Without warning, he shoved into my waiting mouth so hard I gagged. He pulled out, studying me with those sharp eyes.

"I thought you didn't gag, sweetheart."

"I guess you just bring it out in me."

His grin was adorable and sexy at once. "Don't do that too much or I'll explode before I can have some real fun."

"Is my mouth not enough fun?"

"You're talking again, Harmony. Open those pretty lips and make it up to me."

Gods, I should have hated how he stripped my dignity like that, but he did it in such a way that I wanted to obey him. I opened my mouth, knowing he wanted to be the aggressor but needing to take back some power. Instead of waiting for him to take the lead, I engulfed him, encircling his base with my hand and reasserting my dominance. The grip in my hair softened and he brought his other hand to my head, holding on as I sucked and licked until his legs were shaking. He took control back, and forced my head forward, driving my motion and showing me he was in charge again.

We had a dance we played each time we had sex, a power game that bounced between us, neither of us having complete dominance. It drove me mad and left me dripping.

He tugged my hair, my mouth freeing from his length with a pop, saliva dripping down my mouth and onto my breasts. I knew I looked like a scene from a smutty movie, but I didn't care. I could see from the lust in his eyes that it did nothing but turn him on.

"Damn, you are hot, baby," he said with a growl that stoked the fire in me.

Licking my lips, I went to speak, but he stopped me with a look, one that warned me he'd fill my mouth again if I did. Not that I would have complained.

Grasping my neck, he pulled me to my feet. He stepped from his pants and picked me up in one quick move that had my heart quickening. His mouth was on mine, kissing me with a fever until my lips parted from his upon the impact of my back hitting the wall. He dropped me and flipped me around so fast I barely caught myself from falling. Jerking my waist back, he ran his hands up my body before caressing my breasts. Every part of me was blazing with heat and I pushed back against him, sending him sliding through my wetness and hitting my clit so that he had me cresting within seconds. I bucked against him, straining for more as he played with my nipples, his lips pressing against my neck.

"That's it, baby. Come for me before I sink into that beautiful ass and make you come again."

Those breathy words whispered in his deep baritone sent me over the edge, and my climax rushed through me with such intensity that I could barely hold the wall. He reached down as the waves continued to barrage me and buried his length into me, grunting as I bared down on him with my convulsing muscles. His hands were holding my hips tight, but the heat of them only increased my spasms. He continued to ravage me, bringing my climax back to a peak before he slipped from me. I complained, missing having him inside of me, but as he dragged my wetness over my ass I shivered, the complaints turning to a moan. He penetrated me, stars lighting my eyes as a fiery pain lacerated me, then transformed to a pleasure that I hadn't had in years. I closed off the cry that I'd been emitting, bringing my teeth down to bite my lip and thrusting back to meet him.

"Gods, you feel amazing. You like me any way you can get me, don't you, baby?" he said, his voice hoarse. He reached around and shoved his fingers into me, his other hand gripping my waist and holding me still as he continued to own the part of me that only Slate had taken before. Now it was Callum's to claim, as was every part of me. "Fuck," he grumbled as my climax hit me so hard my entire body clamped down on him. He shattered, his hand leaving my warmth to hold my waist, slamming me back into him as his body met mine, his cum filling me more with each penetrating thrust he gave me.

My legs gave out, and he grabbed my waist, holding me up as he slipped from me. He pulled me against his chest and I noted the sweat that had gathered there, his heart beating rapidly below.

"If I die today, at least I'll die with the memory of your ass clenched around my cock and milking every ounce of cum I have to give you."

"Gods, you sound like a cheap erotica."

His laugh shook against me, and he kissed my neck, licking a bead of sweat from it. "Not cheap, but definitely erotic." He gave me a smack on my worn-out ass before he lifted me and tossed me on the bed. "Clean up and get some clothes on. We're meeting someone in about," he looked at his watch, "fifteen minutes."

"Fifteen minutes?" I yelled at his back as he walked through the bathroom and turned on the shower.

"Fifteen. I knew I had enough time to get my fill of you before we left."

"Dammit," I grumbled as he disappeared into the shower. He'd known we were leaving, yet he'd still taken me. I dropped my head to the pillow, thinking of how he'd fucked me. His cum was leaking out of my ass, causing a quake in my lower belly at the thought. I peeked toward the shower. He'd owned me that time, taking the lead as he used my mouth and my ass. It was time to take the power back. If we had fifteen minutes, I was going to use them to my advantage.

Scooting from the bed and ignoring the mess I left, I snagged a rubber band and pulled my hair back, then made my way to the shower. I took a moment to appreciate Callum before I stepped in. He was all muscle, rock solid everywhere, including the hard-on he was still sporting and taking his time cleaning in long strokes.

"Thinking about me?" I asked, stepping in.

He turned his eyes to me, perusing my body. "Thinking about that tight ass of yours."

I pushed his hand away and pinned him against the shower wall. "I think it's my turn to take the lead," I said over his lips.

"Is it now?" he replied playfully. "And what did you have in mind?"

"You're going to fuck me against this tile wall until I have *my* fill of *you*. You don't get to come until I'm completely satisfied, which starts with you on your knees and your head between my legs."

"Damn, I love you," he said with a grin.

"I know. You're wasting time. I believe we're down to twelve minutes and your tongue isn't against my clit yet."

His eyes sparkled, the amber overtaking the brownish blue as he dropped to his knees and obeyed every command I'd given him, multiple times.

WE WERE LATE, but so was whoever we were meeting. Callum had taken us to another of his safe houses, this one larger but with even less furniture. It reminded me of a warehouse.

He was pacing, the tension returning to his shoulders and his jaw. If I had any strength left in my muscles, I would have been tense, but he'd wiped whatever was left away with his tongue in the shower. That man and his tongue were going to be the death of me. My ass and clit were so depleted, I didn't think I'd be able to have sex again for months. Although one look at Callum and his taut muscles had butterflies stirring in my lower belly. I had a suspicion all he needed to do was to speak, and I'd be wet again.

"You look like a starving lioness ready to devour her prey," he said, interrupting my dirty thoughts. "Aren't you satisfied after our shower?"

"Aren't you?" I asked, raising a brow and throwing him a sexy smile.

"Satisfied but still hungry."

I swore my nipples ripped through the shirt I'd taken from Callum's small closet. It was a white button-down dress shirt, my mauve bra below just visible enough to tease. Callum had insisted I leave enough buttons undone for my cleavage to distract from the bra color. His eyes landed on that cleavage, and the heat in them had me growing uncomfortably damp in my jeans. With no underwear to catch my arousal, that was a disaster waiting to happen. I really needed to get some clothes.

He adjusted himself and rolled his neck. "You're too tempting, baby, and I can't afford to be tempted right now."

"Then don't call me baby if you're not planning to do something about the wet spot that's growing in these jeans."

His groan was wicked, and he ran his hands through his hair. "Noted, Harmony."

I could listen to him call me 'baby' all day, but it wouldn't help him focus on anything other than me, and from the stress in his body, I could tell he needed to focus. He turned away, looking at his watch and pacing.

"Who are we meeting, Callum?"

He hadn't told me anything other than we were meeting someone. My leg shook, my body rigid with the irritation at being left in the dark. Callum's spine went straighter, his muscles flexing as he backed closer to me. I noticed the air move before I saw the Shadow across from him. His ebony wings were the size of Callum's, his muscles just as large as his presence. This man, however, terrified me in a way that Callum didn't.

I scooted further away to the end of the couch where I sat, the man's eyes turning to me. They were a muted brown, emotionless and hard.

"Gerrand." Callum's voice shattered the silence with its force. He was authoritative and deadly serious.

"Callum. So this is the mark you couldn't kill?" He turned his eyes back to me and I saw nothing there but the intent to murder.

"I told you why I couldn't kill her."

The man pulled his wings in, and they disappeared. I thought it strange how they could wear shirts, yet the wings didn't destroy the fabric. The realization should have been the last thing on my mind as Gerrand walked closer to me.

Callum stepped into his path and Gerrand pushed his chest out. Callum didn't flinch, although I was flinching for him.

"You brought me here to see her. I'm risking everything to be here, Callum. Let me see her."

"Don't fucking touch her, Gerrand."

"Having a change of heart? You were the one who told me I needed to witness. This was your call, Callum. Now stand down or I'll leave and bring the Shadow down on you before you have time to hide her."

My heart slammed against my chest as fear pounded through

me. I stood, unable to take this display of testosterone between the two men.

"I have a name, and it's not 'mark' or 'her.'"

"I know exactly what your name is, Harmony Decker. What I need to understand is why you're still alive, and why my second ignored his orders to risk his life for you."

He crossed his arms, his brown eyes not leaving Callum's. "I suggest you show me what you need to show me before I change my mind."

My wings. That's what Callum wanted him to see, proof of why I was being hunted. I didn't know what difference seeing them would make, but if that had been Callum's plan, I needed to show him. I pushed Callum aside. Fear needed to take a backseat. I would die at this man's hand or another Shadow's or even a Torch's, so there was no reason to be afraid. If it was now, then so be it. The death sentence stood, no matter who let the axe fall.

As I unbuttoned my shirt, Callum grabbed my wrists.

"This is what you wanted to show him, right?" I asked him.

He didn't release my arms, and I could see the possessiveness behind his eyes. This wasn't about fear of what Gerrand would do to me. He would protect me if the man tried to hurt me. This was purely possessive. He didn't want anyone to see me exposed or to touch me.

I wrapped my fingers around his hand. "It's fine, Callum. He's not going to touch me and I'm sure he's seen breasts before."

"Not yours," he snarled.

Gerrand stepped back, his look of strength melting as one of shock overtook it. "Shit, you weren't joking."

Callum's head snapped around. "Did you think I'd joke about something this serious?"

"No, but fated, Callum? It's so rare I thought you had to be wrong."

"Fated?" As the word left my mouth, it answered all my questions. Fated love. That explained my reaction to him, how I couldn't stop touching him, how I was insatiable for him, how I'd fallen in love with Callum within moments of seeing him.

"Fated," he said. "You and I are fated. Just like I suspect your parents were."

"And yours, Callum," Gerrand said. "It's rare and to have two children of fated lovers also fated is unheard of. Fuck, Callum, what have you gotten yourself into?"

"Besides me?" I asked, unable to resist a little comic relief.

Callum shot me a look and Gerrand laughed. He pushed Callum aside, ignoring the terrifying growl that surfaced from him. "Let me look at her."

"Stop calling me *her*."

He frowned and grabbed my chin. Callum tensed, his body ready to attack. Gerrand tipped my face and looked into my eyes. "Trinity's eyes. She had the most amazing blue eyes. You couldn't help being mesmerized by them even if they were on a filthy Torch."

My offended expression must have slipped through, and he snickered. "Calm yourself. We don't like Torch, no matter what they look like. The only one who ever fell for one is your father. And damn if you don't look like him now that I see you. Fucking same cheekbones and hair color." He pushed my shirt down, and Callum lost it, attacking him and landing several punches before Gerrand threw him off. They crouched down in fighting positions, and the hairs on my neck stood as their wings expanded. This was the Shadow, brutal, deadly, and terrifying. And half that blood ran through my veins.

"I want to see her wings," Gerrand gritted through his clenched jaw.

"Then you should have asked. I warned you not to fucking touch her."

"I don't want your mate, asshole. I'm the only one standing between her life and death, so back your overprotective ass down."

There were a few seconds when I didn't think Callum would, but his wings curled in and disappeared, Gerrand's doing the same. They stood, glaring at each other, and I knew I needed to step in. Things were too volatile.

I took my shirt off and turned around, unhooking my bra.

Gerrand inhaled sharply upon seeing my back. "Good gods."

"Yeah, I always thought my parents were just abusive assholes, but it turns out they tortured me with a purpose." I noticed the venom that slipped from my mouth, the remnants of years of pent-up hatred for the monsters who'd left their imprint on my body. I swallowed it back, remembering that they'd done it to protect me, to hide me from the gods who would have killed me in my crib.

"She's had them since she was a baby."

"And no one noticed. All this time, right under our noses, under the eyes of the gods." His fingers traced the pattern of my tattoos, and I heard the low growl that rumbled through Callum. "And you never tried to have them removed? To hide them?"

"No. They're a part of me. When I was young, I wore them as a sign of rebellion. Flaunting them as a 'fuck you' to the parents I thought had abused and abandoned me. In high school, I embraced them, accepted them as a part of me. That's what they are now." Slate had helped me see that, telling me how beautiful they were. Now wasn't the time to admit that, not with Callum on guard the way he was. That admission could throw him completely over the edge. "I did my best not to hide them. After the first few stares and snide remarks, I had everyone wanting ink like mine." I glanced over my shoulder at them. "It only takes heads turning to the strangely tattooed girl with the nice tits and curvy ass for the jealous girlfriends to want the same thing. Lucky for them, Slate had already claimed me and would have beaten the shit out of their boyfriends if they'd even tried touching me."

Callum narrowed his eyes, a grimace forming that made him even more darkly beautiful. I saw the flash in those amber eyes that told me there would be consequences for that comment, so I gave him a sexy grin to let him know I looked forward to it.

Gerrand looked between us. "Fucking fate. I hope that guy Slate is far from the picture or Callum here will ensure he doesn't live long enough to consider touching you again…that is, if you two survive this."

"I don't think so," I said. "I'm as protective of Slate as he is of me."

"Callum's not the sharing type. Few Shadow are, and fated definitely aren't. Hope you said your goodbyes."

"Just look at my fucking back and keep your comments to yourself," I said.

Gerrand ground his teeth and gave me a look that would have had most people running in fear, but I knew his type. I flashed him a sweet smile and turned around to face him, crossing my arms over my chest. His eyes dropped for an instant before Callum stepped in front of me.

"I like her, Callum. She's a spitfire like Landon. That jackass would never stop with the smart-ass comebacks. Show me your wings. If you really are Landon and Trinity's, a daughter of fated, you should have some impressive wings."

I tapped Callum on the back, turning his attention from Gerrand to me. The only way they'd ever emerged was through his enticement, and I was fine with showing this guy my tits, but I wasn't about to give him the whole show.

He didn't have to ask. He understood just with my look. "You need to learn how to command them, Harmony."

"You don't know how to use your wings?"

"How long did it take you to learn to use yours? Because I've only had mine for two days," I shot back.

"She's right, Gerrand. We've had ours since birth. We learned to command them the same way we learned to walk."

"Well, you better teach her fast because there are two armies hunting for her right now and they won't give her time to take lessons."

Callum handed me my shirt. "Put that back on."

"But—"

"The magic protects the material." So that's how it worked. This wing thing was going to take a lot of time to adjust to. And time was something I didn't have.

I hooked my bra and put the shirt on as he walked behind me. His fingers slid up the back of my shirt and with each button I reached, I grew warmer. Gerrand stepped back, leaning against the wall and taking a stance that left me uncomfortable. It gave the impression he was a voyeur watching an intimate moment.

Callum's fingers massaged my shoulder blades, the heat spreading through my body until he hit a specific spot between them and my wings burst forth. Gerrand lost his balance, his foot slipping at the shock of seeing them. His eyes were wide with disbelief. Callum took the moment to run his fingers through my wings and a strange *mewl* sound slipped from me. He leaned in and whispered in my ear, "Save that sound for later. That's the sound that makes my cock jump."

I shivered as he walked away, throwing him an annoyed look for getting me so worked up when we had an audience.

"Beautiful, aren't they?" he said to Gerrand.

Having both of them staring at me left me self-conscious, but I brushed it off and stood taller. I hated that feeling.

"She's a mix of both factions," Gerrand muttered. "No wonder the Goddess wants her dead. She undermines the divide between Shadow and Torch and the gods."

"Now do you see why she needs to live?"

"No, I don't."

My wings slumped, and I watched Callum's expression harden.

"I see every reason she needs to die like the Goddess commanded."

Callum stepped in front of him, shielding me again while I struggled to make my wings disappear. The situation had my nerves on alert, leaving me shaky, and the wings wouldn't heed my command.

"If it comes down to her or you, I will fight for her," Callum said in a low, threatening snarl.

"I know you will," Gerrand replied, his voice soft. "I won't hurt her, Callum. Watching them bring Landon in killed me. He was a pain in my ass, but he was my best friend and it left me empty when they executed him. He died to protect her. I won't let his death be in vain."

I breathed a sigh of relief, my body relaxing, the wings folding in as I'd instructed them to.

"I can't fight with you, however. None of us can. To stand against the gods is suicide and will do nothing to help her."

The anger rolled off Callum in waves. He slammed Gerrand into the wall so hard the plaster shattered.

"Watch yourself, Callum," Gerrand warned, taking a defensive stance.

"How can you stand by and do nothing just like you did with Landon? Just like all of us did?"

"You don't think I would have given my life to save him?" Gerrand's voice shook the room.

"No, I don't!"

Gerrand shoved him and pinned him to the floor as I stepped back, holding my scream in. He punched Callum so hard I heard cartilage in his nose break. Blood poured from his nose but stopped within seconds as it healed. "Fuck you, Callum. I would have given everything! But he wanted to die."

He rose, turning his back on Callum and running his hands through his hair. I saw the frustration behind his anger, the emotion that he shielded.

"You tried, didn't you?" I asked, my voice soft in the simmering anger that still filled the space. Callum had pulled himself from the ground and was wiping the blood from his face.

Gerrand turned to me, his eyes unguarded for a brief second. "Yes. I went to him as he was awaiting judgement, promised him I'd find a way to free him even if it meant my life. He was like a brother to me, as close as his own brother, maybe closer."

My father had a brother. That was news, but I didn't want to interrupt the moment, so I refrained from asking the questions the statement had created.

"He refused. Trinity was dead, and he couldn't survive without her. Fated, he'd told me. I'd only seen fated in one other couple. Your parents, Callum. But I knew enough of that bond to understand that with her death, his life would cease with the burden of fated love. Her death had already destroyed him; the man I knew died the day they killed her."

"This is your chance to help him, Gerrand." There was a desperation in Callum's voice that hurt my soul.

Gerrand looked at me, his eyes perceptive as he studied me. "When I was trying to convince him to fight back, he said something to me, something I didn't understand then. I thought it was just the effect of Trinity's death messing with his mind. They say if one half of a fated love remains, losing that bond slowly brings them to madness. So I assumed it was taking hold quickly in him." He moved, ignoring Callum's broody stance, and stood before me. "I see a lot of Landon in you."

"What did he say?" Callum asked with an edge to his voice.

"'She's safe. They won't hurt her now. You can't save me,

but you can save her. Make sure they don't hide the truth of what can be.'" The weight of his words hung in the air. My father's last words to the man in front of me had been about me. "I thought he was talking about Trinity in his madness, thinking she was still alive. But he wasn't. All this time, it was about you."

"Trinity didn't slip up, Gerrand. She meant for them to capture her. It was strategic. They knew what they were doing, and their sacrifice kept Harmony safe for thirty-three years. Trinity and Landon needed to face execution so no one would notice Harmony. Their sacrifice turned the gods' eyes away long enough for her to slip through the cracks."

There was a shift in Gerrand's features, the softness replaced with the clenched jaw and lethal eyes, serious and deadly once again.

"Three days, Callum." He turned his back to me and walked back to Callum. "Three days was our deal before, and I give you that again. Make sure she's trained by then. She needs to know how to fight and how to use her wings. If they wound her, she'll heal, but once they realize what she is, they'll go for the kill, and she won't have anywhere for her soul to replenish and heal."

"Fuck." Callum glanced at me, a shadow of fear in his eyes.

"Exactly. She's not Shadow, she's not Torch, so neither realm will pull her home to regenerate. We don't even know if she'll have that ability. And if she can't get to a realm, she'll die. Make sure she's as deadly as you are. Train her like I trained you."

"I will. Thank you, Gerrand," Callum said, his voice holding a seriousness that hung heavy on the air.

Gerrand's eyes creased as he studied Callum. "Are you sure this is the way? You can run like they did."

"She deserves better."

"She doesn't deserve death."

I saw the shiver that ran through Callum, the one that mimicked my own.

"Three days." Gerrand's wings unfurled, encasing him before he disappeared. I had to force my mouth closed because the sight was so surreal.

"What did he mean by three days, Callum?" I asked, trying to remember how to breathe after the intense interaction.

"It means we have a lot of work to do." He walked to me and grabbed my arm. "But first we get you some clothes. Stay close to me and do not move until I tell you to."

He didn't give me time to reply, sweeping me up in his wings and taking me away as though another life-changing conversation hadn't just taken place. I needed time to comprehend everything that had just happened, but there was no time. Whatever was going to occur, we had three days to deal with it. Three days had seemed like a long time when I stepped into the car to meet the mysterious Callum Montrose, but now, three days seemed like nothing when what waited at the end of that time was my death.

CHAPTER 15
CALLUM

The clock was ticking, and I needed to move fast. Harmony was in no shape to face an army of Shadow, let alone Torch. The odds of this going the way I wanted were low, but I would take every chance I had to keep her safe. First, I needed to get her some clothes. She couldn't train in my clothes, and I couldn't concentrate with her in my dress shirt. Shit, she looked so hot I'd almost lost control while Gerrand was there.

Gerrand was a wild card, but his loyalty to Landon ran deep and I'd always known he carried the weight of Landon's death heavier than the rest of us. Seeing Harmony was something he needed, and he'd keep his word. Maybe he'd even do more. If word spread in whispers in the halls of the Shadows, if somehow it spread to the Torch, there might be a way. There was no guarantee; the gods gave us life, they could easily take it.

At the very least, I was hoping Gerrand would talk to Belkair, Landon's brother. If Belkair found out he had a niece, it might make a difference.

Belkair was the most lethal of our kind. He'd risen through

the ranks of the gods' Guard to become their leader. It was the most prestigious position in our realm. He'd led the Guard for centuries, cold, hard, and ruthless. He'd even stood by as the gods had killed his brother for treason. The Goddess had taken Landon's life for the transgression, forcing Belkair to watch. He'd accepted her command with no hesitation, no reservations, no anger or aggression toward the Goddess for taking his brother's life. As the commanding Guard, we weren't sure the Goddess hadn't ordered him to give the fatal blow to prove his loyalty. He'd remained emotionless, hard, and calculating since then, as if his brother had never existed.

I moved us to Harmony's apartment, taking the chance that both Shadow and Torch would know I wouldn't be stupid enough to bring her there, which I was.

"Stay here," I commanded before proceeding to search her apartment, trying to ignore my temptation to stop and take in the life she'd had before that fateful day when I'd seen her on the street.

Returning to her, I instructed her to pack a bag quickly. I didn't want to be there long. With both factions hunting for her, they would sense us and descend on us if I didn't get her out of there. She hurried off, and I took a few minutes to look around. It was a small apartment but well furnished, too nice for a reporter's salary. Slate. I didn't know what to make of that relationship. I wanted him nowhere near her ever again, but I knew they were friends. From what she'd said, he'd been instrumental in shaping her into the woman she was today. I needed to open myself to letting her tell me about him, but it hurt to think of her with another man. The damned fated bond was too strong now.

I picked up a picture of her with him. They were young, in their late teens. Harmony's smile lit her blue eyes. Slate's face was bent toward her neck like he was kissing her as he peeked at the camera.

"If you break my picture frame, I'll make sure I bite next time you have your cock buried in my throat."

Grimacing, I glanced over at her. She'd walked back into the room and was pulling a tight black low-cut T-shirt on, her tits spilling over the top. Maybe my shirt had been less distracting. "If you bite, I bite," I countered.

I lowered the picture, flipping it upside down and ignoring the glare she threw at me. Pulling her to me, I dipped my mouth to her ear. "And I promise, my bite will hurt more."

She trembled, and I had to resist pushing her against the doorframe and taking her. We'd squandered enough time, and I needed to get her to safety. "Grab your bag."

"Not this?" she asked, cupping my newly formed bulge in her hands. The damned thing never seemed to go down around her.

"Not now." Smacking her ass, I let her go.

"You know, spanking is one thing I've never liked."

I raised my brow. "Yet choking and hair pulling you like?" Her eyes sparkled, and I shook my head. "I'll ensure you grow to like it."

"It's growing on me already," she said, picking up her bag.

"Good, because I want to mark that ass with more than my cum. I think a nice handprint would look good on that pale skin of yours."

"Would it now?"

"Definitely."

I yanked her toward me and encased her in my wings, taking us to another safe house.

"How many of these places do you have?" she asked, trying to keep her balance when we arrived.

"One in every province. My parents taught me early to watch my back." I checked the doors and windows, ensuring my magic shielded the place so it was undetectable.

"Is that snow?" she asked, running to a window. I'd forgotten her province was cold most of the time but never had precipitation other than rain. Sleet was the closest it came. The atmosphere over that section of the world was a strange one.

"Sure is." I couldn't help but smile at her excitement. Her eyes were wide with wonder as she watched the flakes fall.

"Can we go out in it?" She sounded like a child begging for a piece of candy.

Chuckling, I replied, "Maybe later. It might make for good terrain to train you harder in. But for now, we work on those wings." Her full lips pouted perfectly, and I tried to stave off the desire they stirred in me. "Later."

"Fine." She looked back out the window, steaming it up with her breath. "Where are we? If it's cold enough to snow, we must be pretty far north."

"We're in Snepore, the province just northwest of yours. In fact, we're only a few miles over the border."

She gave me a look of doubt. "It never snows in Rikelin. How can we be that close?"

"Because your province was the site of a fierce battle between the Errant and Galere gods."

She squinted her eyes, and I could see her trying to comprehend the statement. "What does that have to do with the weather?"

"The gods' magic infected the weather system over Rikelin during their battle. To this day, the seasons do not change more than the slight taste of warmth you get in the early part of each year. That's only because Marinasta, the goddess of seasons, took pity on the people of your province and snuck her magic into the realm about a hundred years after the battle. Otherwise, you're stuck in the dead of winter where it's too cold for snow."

Her head had tilted, and she studied me, almost like she was seeing me in a new light.

"How old are you, Callum?"

I lifted a brow. "Do you really want to know that?"

"Yes."

"I lost track a long time ago, but I'd say somewhere between seven or eight."

"Seven or eight what? Decades?"

"Don't diminish my standing among the Shadows, sweetheart. Centuries."

Her mouth dropped open and my dirty mind couldn't help thinking of how good it would feel driving into it. Moving to her, I brought my fingers to her lips and dipped them into her mouth. Her tongue brushed them. "Leave that mouth open any longer, and you'll force me to use it." She closed her mouth, sucking my fingers in a stimulating way that made me uncomfortably hard. "Don't tease, baby."

"Don't call me baby. Remember? Unless you're deep inside of me, that nickname is off limits."

"Oh, I don't think so. I like how wet it makes you. It's only off limits when I want it to be. Now, since you've already damaged my reputation with the Shadow and insulted me by removing a few centuries of experience from my life, I get to decide your punishment."

"Experience?" she asked, her mouth turning into a gorgeous frown. "And what kind of experience would that be, and with whom?"

Damn, that fated possessiveness was alive in both of us, and I'd slipped with my choice of words. "Experienced enough to know how to make you come with a few flicks of my tongue." I draped my tongue up her neck, but she didn't react. I pulled back to look at her, seeing the fire in her eyes. "And to know you taste better than anything I've ever sunk my tongue into."

"Not helping."

I nipped her lip, saying, "You're the best fuck I've ever had, baby. The only one I want, and the only one who matches me. Nothing comes close to fated lovers. Anyone before you was just practice. And don't get me started on how you can take my entire length without gagging, because that tells me just how many times you had Slate's cock down that pretty throat. The thought of it makes me want to kill him more than I already do."

"Point taken, although his wasn't the only one," she said with a wicked smile.

I slipped my hand up her shirt, pulling down her bra and cupping her breast, fighting the rage that comment sent storming through my body. Instinctively, I pinched her nipple, seeing the flash of pain and the danger that lit her eyes. "I don't want to hear about other men, or I will burn the entire province down so that no one who has touched you lives to hold that memory."

She leaned into my hand, her lips parting. "Then I get to rip the wings from every Shadow you've fucked until The Blight is nothing but blood and feathers."

The current that flooded through me with her words had me throbbing. Heat surrounded us as the fiery mixture of jealousy, rage, and desire seeped from us. The sensation was ecstasy that stroked me like her hands and pushed me closer to her. I palmed her breast, her nipple puckering below my skin and pressing to be toyed with. She grasped my neck and pulled my lips to hers, taking the lead of the aggressor, and I followed, but only enough that she thought she was in control. I was about to take that lead back; I wasn't ready for her to have it.

Threading my fingers in her hair, I pulled her head back, dragging my teeth along her neck as she pressed her breast further into my hand. I pulled her bra down and sucked her nipple into my mouth, playing with it through the material of her shirt.

Three days. The words resounded through my head, reminding me that a deadline hovered over us, that I didn't have time for play if I wanted her to survive. The hunters were coming, and she needed to be ready. But she'd slid her hand down my pants and was stroking me so firmly that I didn't think my body would listen if I dared tell it to stop. There was no resisting her, no resisting the fated link between us and the desire that neither of us could deny. I scraped my teeth along her nipple, releasing it from my hold and kissing her again.

"If you don't stop that, I'm gonna come in your hand, sweetheart."

"But I might like that."

"Oh, I know you would, and I'd enjoy watching you clean up the mess with your tongue." I pushed her hand away. "But if I come, it needs to be deep inside of you." I dropped my head to hers, hating what I was about to say because my dick was already aching from the thought. "And it's going to be after we train."

The way her face fell could have broken me if her life wasn't on the line. Kissing her forehead, I dragged my lips down her face, taking time to pull her earlobe into my mouth and gently bite it. "I promise you, Harmony, I'll have this sweet little body of yours covered in sweat by the time we're done and I'll lick every bead from every inch of you until you're screaming for me to stop."

Her eyes sparkled. "And why would I ever do that?"

I groaned and tore myself from her, adjusting myself and putting some distance between us. There was a wet spot on her shirt, her nipple still protruding under it where I'd sucked on it. She slowly lifted her shirt, her exposed tit sitting there, waiting to be taken again. I rolled my neck, trying to maintain control while she fixed her bra and lowered her shirt again. Her cheeks were flushed, and it only added to her beauty.

"You will fuck me tonight," she said in a commanding tone that had me smiling. "Until I'm thoroughly satisfied."

"You are wicked, sweetheart. And I bet you're soaked." I could only imagine, and the thought was a dangerous one.

The vixen dipped her hand down her pants, and I watched, breath hitching, as she slid her fingers through herself and brought them back out. She walked to me, a dangerous move that I wasn't certain I could ignore, and placed her fingers to my mouth. They were drenched, and I licked each one, savoring the taste of her as a surge of need flushed through me, making that ache in my pants worsen.

"Very," she said in a naughty voice. Without removing her fingers, she brought her lips to mine, her tongue sweeping over her fingers before meeting mine. As her fingers dropped, I took her waist and moved her flush against me.

"You're playing with fire,"

"I know. I like the burn."

"Shit, Harmony." My warrior blood called to me to stop this madness, the Shadow in me shutting the other parts of me down. The danger was too real, too near to ignore. I pushed her hands down, holding them to her waist. "Enough. We need to stop. I promise I'll fuck you until you're begging me to stop, but right now, I need to train you. I can't risk losing you. I won't, no matter what I need to give up to keep you safe."

She stopped fighting and studied me, her blue eyes growing brighter. Releasing her hands, I pushed a strand of her hair back before gently tracing the curve of her face with my fingers.

"I love you too much to lose you, Harmony."

I could see the emotion in her eyes, the awareness that what I was asking was necessary. "I know. What do you need me to do?"

Dropping my head to hers, I remained there, thinking through all the years of training I'd had from the time I could walk and through the centuries. There wasn't enough time for me to teach her everything about our ways. Even if I could, she was half Torch, and I didn't know their ways. I only knew the Shadow side of her blood.

"Callum?"

Her voice broke through my racing thoughts, and I looked back into her eyes. Understanding greeted me, dressed in a haze of dusty blue. I brought my hands to her face, brushing my thumb over the corner of her eye as she clasped her hands over my forearms.

"I trust you," she said. "I trust you with my life, and there's only one other man I've ever trusted that much."

"Slate," I said, gritting my teeth.

Laughing, she replied, "Yes. But although I loved him desperately at one time in my life, that love doesn't come close to what I feel for you, Callum."

"Do you still love him?" I didn't want to hear the answer. I'd been in love, nothing earth-shattering or desperate like I thought she'd had with Slate. Never anything that lasted long. In fact, I hadn't opened myself to it in centuries, preferring the unattached interactions with women that left me satisfied enough to survive.

"Yes," she answered confidently, my heart twinging with the confirmation. As I drew my hands away, she stopped me. "But only as a friend, or even a brother. We learned a long time ago that we couldn't be anything more. I knew there was someone out there and that he wasn't that someone. You are."

Her words fortified my heart, knocking away any doubt, the honesty in her eyes securing the foundation of my love for her. Kissing her, I brought her against me. This kiss wasn't one of lust or want. It was pure love, an expression of the emotion I held for her and she for me. It was a sensation that I'd only ever experienced with Harmony, spiritual where our souls touched with the same force our tongues and lips touched until it connected us completely. As if our spirits fed on each other, entwined and longing for the other.

Slowly, our lips parted until the moment was gone, and reality returned. "Teach me, Callum."

I gave her a nod, knowing there was no more delaying it. They were coming for her, and I was her only defense. I knew I would plow down as many Shadow as I could until they overcame me. It didn't matter if they were friends or not, I would tear them down until there was no fight left in me. But I didn't want her completely defenseless. She needed to know how to fly, to run, to flee to safety for my plan to work. It was the last precaution and the reason I'd made the call to Slate. If I couldn't protect her, I knew he would. It gave her a chance at a little more time, and that's all I needed.

"CAN'T WE REST YET?" Harmony complained.

I shot her a look. "We rest when you learn how to punch."

She looked sexy, even as exhausted and worn as she was. We'd been at it for hours, only taking a slight break to eat something. I hadn't realized we'd gone so long without food. It wasn't a necessity to eat as often as mortals ate, but considering Harmony had been mortal only days before, her body needed the fuel.

She blew a loose hair back from her eyes. She'd pulled her hair back in a high ponytail, but strands had broken free. Her tight shirt was sticking to her. And since she'd been a tease and removed her bra because it was too soaked with sweat, the shirt was clinging to her breasts, emphasizing their ample size. I'd been having a difficult time not staring at how they bounced when she moved, or how her nipples popped out at various times, like now. No female Shadow had come close to distracting me the way she was, during training or any other time.

The jeans she wore were riding up her ass so far I knew she'd never put underwear on, and that thought was enough to keep me hard for hours.

"I know how to punch," she argued.

"You call that a punch? I know toddler Shadows who hit harder than that. Now bring it again and try to knock me down this time."

She was stronger than I'd expected. Slate had taught her to fight, insisting she train with his men, something I'd have to thank him for if we made it through this. I supposed it was a precaution considering she traveled in his circle, and he had enemies outside the province. She took an attack pose, and I gestured with my finger for her to move, imagining that I had that finger embedded below the camel toe she was sporting. Her tits jiggled as she moved toward me, a determined look on her face, and my sight wandered to them. They were hypnotic, and she took advantage of my distraction and struck at me. Her fist made contact, but only in my palm as I caught her hand and flipped her to the ground, pinning her.

"Dammit," she grumbled as I hovered over her.

"You might want to try lifting your shirt and flashing me next time," I said, inching my fingers up her waist. I'd been waiting for hours, and the sweat that beaded on her cleavage needed to be licked.

"Is that the secret? So if a group of Shadow are coming at me, I just need to lift my shirt?"

I narrowed my eyes at her. "I take that back. Nobody sees these tits but me." I shoved my hand up and encased the soft skin of her breast, kneading it with satisfaction, my thumb brushing over her nipple until it was rock hard.

"I take it we're done?"

"No," I said, pinching it. "You rest when you get a punch in."

I pulled my hand back against my protesting body's desire to have it stay there and offered it to her. The tick of her jaw was worth making my body wait. Those baby blue eyes had a darkness to them that assured me I'd have her riled up by the time I gave in.

Helping her stand, I eyed her, seeing the fire that remained in them, the determination that she was going to get that punch in sooner than later because she wanted it just as badly as I did. It was a wonder we'd gone this long without touching each other, but the Shadow in me had overruled the fated mate in me. Its hold was slipping quickly, though.

Rolling my neck, I turned from her, catching her movement in my periphery too late. Her punch hit me square in the jaw with enough force to make me smile. I forced my reaction back, swiveling to her and grabbing her wrists. Her breath caught as I forced them behind her and stepped into her space.

"Now we're done," she said, with a devious glint to her eyes.

In one quick move, I had her pinned on the floor again, my knees caging her legs, her wrists now in my left hand secured above her head.

Pushing her shirt up and over her arms, I wrapped it around her wrists. "Oh, we're done training, but we're far from done." I sat back, removing my shirt. "It's a good thing you got that weak attempt at a punch in, because I have so many things I want to do to you, sweetheart." Her chest heaved, and I spread my hands around her waist, letting them drift up her body until I reached her breasts.

"And what do you want to do to me, Callum?" There was a rasp to her voice that was like claws on my desire.

"Everything. I want to fuck these tits until my cum covers them. I want your cunt over my face while you ride my tongue until it breaks you. And I want my cock buried so far in your pussy that you're screaming with each thrust." I dropped over her, loving how short her breathing had become, her body arching toward me with each word. Dragging my lips over hers, I snagged her bottom lip between my teeth, biting gently and hearing her hiss as her breasts pushed further into my hands. "And don't forget how I want to use this mouth of yours. How I want to fuck it so deep that you remember how to gag." My tongue swiped over her lips.

She inhaled so sharply that it sent my body into a frenzy.

"What are you waiting for?" she asked, her eyes lit with hunger.

There was nothing that bothered my girl, and I loved it. I could talk dirty to her, and it soaked her. I could use her delectable body any way I wanted, and she'd scream for more.

I pulled her breast into my mouth, thinking of how I wanted them surrounding me as I used the sweat gathered between them to hasten my thrusts. I flicked my tongue over her nipple, sucking the swollen skin around it until she bucked below me. With a laugh I released it and worked her pants off, taking my time to kiss each newly exposed part of skin until she was naked, her shirt still binding her wrists.

I stood and removed my pants, seeing her eyes light when my dick bounced free, ready for her to feed it. Lowering myself over her body again, I spread her legs with my thigh before sinking into her. I couldn't help the groan it evoked. She felt so good, so wet and ready to be taken, that I wondered if I'd be able to go through with any of my fantasies before I lost control. Kissing her, I knew it didn't matter. If I came, I'd take her again. There was plenty in me to ensure we were both thoroughly pleased before the night was over.

She arched her back, her skin warm and lush against mine. Ignoring my body's complaints, I pulled free of her warmth and brought myself forward until her tits surrounded me. Sitting back slightly, I pushed her flesh around me, and just like I'd imagined, I fucked the dip between her breasts tucked within their warmth.

I played with her nipples, my eyes never leaving hers and watching how it turned her on. She dipped her chin, sending her tongue out to lick my swollen head each time I moved forward.

Releasing her hands from where I'd left them tied in her shirt, I pushed further into her cleavage, saying, "Play with your tits while I fuck them."

"Gods, you're dirty," she muttered, bringing her hands up to engulf the flesh and squishing it around me.

"Just like you want me, sweetheart," I replied, leaning over and increasing my speed.

It was almost as good as being deep inside of her, and a growl rumbled through my chest. Her moan cut through the sound of my thrusts, and I felt my release mounting. The feel of her flesh and the flicks of her tongue were too tantalizing. I steadied myself and she swiped her tongue around me in such an erotic way that I knew I needed to change position, or I'd come too soon.

With reluctance, I pulled free from her and stood, taking my swollen length in my hand and stroking it. "Get on your knees, baby."

"Are you going to come, Callum?" she asked, bringing herself to her knees like the good girl she was. She swept her tongue tauntingly over her lips and the move demolished me. The hours of watching her body, of imagining what she would do to me, proved too much. My release shot free, splattering her chest.

"Fuck, that's hot," I said, watching my cum drip down her breasts as I squeezed out the last of my essence. "I think this is my new favorite vision of you, sweetheart, marked with my cum, so every man knows you're mine."

Her brow lifted perfectly. "You want to clean this mess up?"

She was ready to take the lead again, but I wasn't ready for her to take it. I dipped my finger into my cum, smearing it around her nipple. She gave me a mischievous smile, and I brought my finger to her mouth, mesmerized by the way she licked it clean.

"I think I'll watch you clean it up," I said. "And don't miss a drop, or my hand will leave a print on your ass."

Her breath hitched before she dragged her finger over her stomach repeatedly until she had devoured every drop of me. She was something, and I planned to continue testing the limits she didn't seem to have. When she was clean, I grabbed her shirt and stood over her, wiping her skin with it as she looked up at me with those gorgeous blue eyes.

Tossing the shirt, I picked her up, throwing her over my shoulder and smacking her ass.

"Ouch! You said I only got the smack if I didn't clean up," she complained.

"I changed my mind." I threw her on the bed and made my way to the head of the bed, sitting up and saying, "Now get that ass over here before I smack it again."

She chewed her lip and I could see her working out how she was going to take the control from me, but she wouldn't win. This was my game for now.

"Move it, Harmony."

She crawled up to me and I saw the determination there. She was a stubborn one. Dropping over me, she took me in her mouth. I hadn't expected the move, and I threaded my hand in her hair before I could stop myself. Closing my eyes, I embraced the sensation of her tongue draping along my shaft before she deep throated me again. All thoughts fled, all the plans of what I wanted to do to her disappeared as her mouth took control of my body.

But then I remembered this was my game, and she'd hijacked it. I gave in to the dominating Shadow side of me and pulled her hair, hearing the growl she gave that reverberated around my dick. I took my other hand and shoved her head down, guiding her moves as I lifted my pelvis to meet her lips, pushing her so deep she released me, a gag escaping.

I couldn't stop the laugh that accompanied my feeling of accomplishment. The sound had sent my need cresting too close to the edge for comfort. I jerked her from me, seeing the scowl that was etched on her face. My hand still wrenched in her hair I moved her lips against mine, grinning as I kissed her. "Not the position I was planning to tear that gag from you in, but that will work. That's the second gag I've freed from you. That gag is mine and mine alone and I can promise you, it won't be your last, sweetheart. All your gags are mine and I claim them just like I claimed you."

"Again with that toxicity, Callum. If I were a different woman, I wouldn't find that such a turn on." She bit my lip, and I lowered my hand to her neck, caressing it with my thumb before I squeezed. Her eyes were blazing, and it drove me mad.

"But you aren't a different woman. You're mine and I'm not ready to relinquish control, baby. This is my game, and you'll play by my rules."

She went to respond, but I grabbed her ass and shoved her forward so she had to grab the wall to stabilize herself. I heard her grumble until I lifted her and sat her over my face, my tongue plunging into her. She cried out, her body relaxing as I licked up the sweetness that lay between her legs. I continued to devour her, holding her firm against me so she could barely move. I thrust my finger into her, keeping her steady with my other hand, my tongue flicking and sucking her clit so that soon she was grinding down on my face. Replacing my finger with my tongue, I dipped it into her as far as I could reach while grasping her ass, the flesh of it squishing around my fingers.

She trembled, and I moved my tongue back to her clit until she was bucking against my mouth. With a few more licks, she came, her cries music to my ears as I held her through it, lapping up the taste of her until she went weak in my arms. I gave her one long lick and lowered her, pushing her over and yanking her hips into the air. I'd left her too exhausted to rise, and that was fine with me. This was the angle I wanted her in. I rubbed my mouth against her ass, kissing the red mark I'd left. The way her ass was sitting there tempted me to take it again, but I wanted to be buried in that soaked mess I'd just made. Sliding into her, I grunted at the tremors that were still going through her body.

"I love tasting your pussy, sweetheart. It's like the nectar of the gods, and I could eat it all day."

Harmony shivered, and I pressed her head into the mattress. I ravaged her, squeezing her hips as I lost myself to the rapture of her. She pushed against me and I could sense her building again, so I leaned over and gripped her neck.

"Gods, Callum," she moaned as I tightened my grip, all the while continuing to drive into her.

"Show me how you like it and come around my cock like a good girl," I growled.

The mattress muffled her cry as her orgasm raced through her body. Her legs trembled, and she clenched around me, her body quaking so intensely that it destroyed me, my release barreling down on me like an unrelenting storm. I yanked her hips back as I filled her, the euphoria of my climax drowning me until it depleted me.

Collapsing beside her, I pulled her onto my chest, trying to calm the deep inhales and exhales that were pouring from me. Her arm draped over me, and I pushed her hair back, noticing how it was heavy with perspiration. I kept her there, as my body relaxed, unable to fathom how I'd existed without Harmony in my life. How my body had survived without her to satisfy it.

She kissed my chest, slowly making her way up along my neck and cheek until she reached my lips. Her kiss was sensual.

With it, the remains of my aggressiveness slipped away. I wanted her to take control, wanted to leave the roughness behind, and take the tenderness she was offering. We remained like that, our mouths finding pleasure while our bodies rested. As her touches woke me again, I knew I was ready for the softness she was offering. We made love until exhaustion finally won over. As I drifted off, holding her in my arms and listening to the rhythm of her breathing, I let the day go, knowing only two remained. Two days to get my fill of her, two days to teach her, two days to protect her or die trying.

CHAPTER 16
HARMONY

I've done this a million times."

"And you'll do it a million more until I say you can stop."

I huffed at Callum, but he didn't flinch. We'd been working all day, and I was exhausted. He'd given me time to gulp down a quick breakfast while he traveled to our previous safe house, returning with the stack of old books he'd been studying. I had given him a funny look, saying I could occupy him if he was that bored, but he shot me a smug grin and dumped the books on the table. Grasping the back of my neck, he'd yanked me from the chair and fucked me hard against the wall until I'd come so intensely that he'd broken with me.

"You ever suggest I'm bored with this body, sweetheart, and I'll rip the pages of those books out and slap that sexy ass of yours with them while I'm filling it," he'd said, dropping me and pulling his pants up before he picked up his coffee and began running me through training exercises.

I wished I had control of my magic so I could wipe the smirk from his face, although that smirk had a way of keeping me soaked. He'd been working me so hard since that moment I wasn't sure I could even appreciate that smirk at this point. I was bruised and infuriated at how I couldn't get a hit in no matter how I tried. It didn't matter how fit I was, how many years I'd trained with Slate's bodyguards, I couldn't beat Callum.

Now he was having me open my wings and spread them, over and over. I'd lost track of the hours, but the sun had descended, and my stomach was long past the growling stage.

"I know how to spread my wings now."

"No, you don't."

I glared at him and forced my wings out, crossing my arms in a told-you-so-manner.

"Close them," he snarled.

I concentrated, and they disappeared to wherever they went when I didn't need them.

"Now open them again."

"Shit, Callum, this is a waste of time!"

"Open them." His command was enough to send a flicker of fear running rampant through me.

He'd been growing more tense as the day went by, the veins in his neck protruding more, his eyes darkening to a deep amber.

I concentrated, but before my wings obeyed, he had me pinned against the wall, a knife to my throat. I squealed in fear, a reaction I cursed myself for as soon as it was free.

"You don't have control, you force the responses, you're thinking too hard, and that moment of thought is your weakness."

"I don't know how to do it any other way, Callum."

He lowered his knife, dragging it down my cleavage. "You can't think about it, Harmony. It should be instinctual."

"That's easy to say. You've had yours since you were born."

He picked his eyes up from my chest. "The hunters coming for you won't give a shit. These wings are your only means of escape, the secret weapon they won't expect. You need to control them."

I saw it then, the truth behind his words. He wasn't planning to survive. He wanted me to run while he sacrificed himself to save me.

"Callum." His name broke on my voice and his eyes softened. "I can't live without you," I said in a hushed tone of desperation.

"There's an army coming for us, Harmony. Trained warriors. I can take most of them, but I can't take them all, not at once. They will take me down and while they do, you are to flee. The moment the Shadow descend on us, the Torch will know and there will be two armies after you."

"But—"

He brought his knife to my lips, the metal cold against my flesh. The acceptance behind his eyes broke my heart. The thought of not having him with me broke my soul.

"Now, open your wings." He walked away like the conversation hadn't happened, like he hadn't just admitted he was sacrificing himself for me but killing me in the process. "Instinct, Harmony. Your wings should be like any other part of your body, naturally part of your movement."

Sighing, I did as he asked, knowing there was no arguing. He'd hidden the soft lover he'd been moments before behind the hunter again, and there would be no breaking him free. He continued to run me through wing training until, with a frustrated grunt, he tossed his dagger at the wall beside me and returned to fighter training.

By the time my yawns had become too loud, I was sore and irritable. He wasn't faring any better, his mood darkening with each hour that passed. I watched him search the cabinets for food. He plunked a can of tuna down and I turned my nose up.

"No fancy meals here, sweetheart. You take what you get,

and you need the protein." The nickname was back, and it gave me hope that the man who'd brought me to ecstasy earlier in the day would return.

"Why don't you need to eat, then?"

"Because my magic fuels me."

I couldn't help my reaction. Hopping on the counter, I leaned closer to him. "Magic?" I sounded like a child at story time. It made sense that he had magic—the wings, the moving from one place to another, the mere fact that he was a hunter of the gods— but I hadn't really thought about it before now.

"Yes. Tomorrow morning, we'll work on summoning yours and on flying."

"Holy shit. Really? I have magic?"

"All Shadow and Torch have magic," he said with a snort, like I'd asked a foolish question.

I pursed my lips at him, irritated that I hadn't considered I'd have it as well. My parents were Shadow and Torch. But the thought seemed so surreal to me, and it still hadn't settled in me that I was like Callum. Even with the wings. Putting my hands on my hips, I said, "Show me."

He frowned. "I'm not some puppet for you to command."

"You could have fooled me," I teased, walking my fingers down his chest. He snatched my hand away, holding it tight.

"It's not magic like you think. It's part of us, activating while we hunt or while we kill. If the kill ends up fighting back, we sometimes resort to using it."

I knew my eyes had grown large. He shook his head and spread my legs with his body, inserting himself between them.

"Eat your dinner so I can eat you out, then thoroughly fuck you, baby. We've got an early morning."

I entwined my legs around his back, ignoring the dampness that pressed against my pants. "The food can wait. I want you first." I tried to sound sexy, but the bruises on my legs were a dull ache that throbbed. It seemed odd that I was frisky again, especially with how sore I was, but from everything Callum had told me, it was the fated in us that drove the need for contact, for sex, for the touch of our mate. And that need burned through me, erasing all other cravings in my body until I met it.

He lifted my shirt, pulling it over my head. I tipped my head back, waiting for him to devour my breasts, but he kissed my arm, leaving kisses on each spot where a bruise was forming. He worked his way up my arm, lingering momentarily on my cleavage before dipping to my ribcage. His lips caused me to flinch at the painful contact.

"Hmm, that should have healed by now," he mumbled. "Your parents' magic healed you last time and your body hasn't learned to heal on its own."

He pressed his lips into my aching ribcage, and I hissed through the pain. "It should be natural," he said, licking over the spot. "Stop thinking you're mortal, sweetheart."

His lips dragged across my stomach as he dug his finger into a particularly large bruise on my arm.

"Ouch!" I swatted his hand away, but he grabbed my arms, pinning them behind me.

"Stop acting like a mortal. You're no longer one of them. You are an immortal. There is only one way to kill you."

I swallowed. "And what is that?"

"If you're wounded enough in the mortal world and your body is bound here so you can't get back to your realm to fully heal. As long as you can make it back to the realm, your body regenerates, perfectly healed."

Immortal. The word sounded so intangible it couldn't have been true. But there was no sign from Callum that his words had held anything but truth. Shaking off the strange sensation that my reality was morphing too far and too fast from what could be possible, I said, "Is that what happened to the guy on the island?"

I remembered hearing his body hit the water, but he hadn't resumed his chase as I'd run away.

"Exactly. Our bodies will disintegrate if we're too gravely wounded to heal here. They reform in our realm, healed."

I tried not to gape, but it was difficult. The concept was so foreign that I could barely grasp it. Swallowing back my shock, I asked, "Has anyone ever died here?"

His hand rubbed my arm, the sensation grounding me. "Only a handful in my lifetime. Usually, when a nasty fight occurs between a Shadow and Torch. We have rules of engagement, but there have been times when some have overlooked them. The only other way to die is by the hands of the gods."

Fear pummeled me as a thought occurred to me, Callum's plan returning to my thoughts. "So if they take you down tomorrow…if you can't fight them…" My words were barely a murmur, as if saying them would make it happen.

He shook his head. "The Goddess will want to execute me. They'll take me back to The Blight to face that execution."

His words came out with no emotion, but they had my heart pounding against the fear that was scraping over my soul.

He took my face in his hands. "There's no other way."

"I can fight—"

His eyes grew dangerous. "No. You will not stay and fight. You will run. Do you understand me?"

"But I can't leave you."

"You will leave me and save yourself. You need to promise me that, Harmony. I can't fight them, knowing you won't run."

I couldn't speak, the thought strangling me, drowning me under a sea of helplessness.

"Promise me. You will flee and not look back. Run to Slate. He'll protect you until I can figure a way out of this. Promise me."

His eyes held a plea I couldn't ignore, so I nodded.

"Tell me what you'll do. I want to hear you say it. While I'm fighting them, what will you do?"

"Escape." I swallowed the sandpaper that sat in my throat. "Leave you behind and find my way to Slate's."

"And don't look back. The only way I can survive this is if I know you survived. If I know you made it out."

I nodded, leaning my head into his. "Why not go to Slate's now?" I asked, hope suddenly filling me. "If you think he can help, why not go now?"

"No, he's the emergency. Only if I can't handle the situation should you run to him."

"But—"

"You'll be safe there. They don't know the extent of his power or his network. It's you they researched." Researched was such a dry word. Like I'd been a job, a task to check off their list. And I supposed I had been. I tried not to think about how minimal that made me, a small mortal whom the gods' hunters could strip from the world without a second thought. Callum continued, not noticing my inner thoughts, and I was glad. He had enough to worry about. "I only knew about Slate because your city is my territory. It's rare that another Shadow would work it."

"Territory? You have territories?" Gods, this was getting more convoluted by the minute.

Callum noticed my confusion, which I knew he could see in the creasing of my brows. He took my hands in his, tracing his fingers over mine absently as he explained, "We each have our own. They won't know where you are unless they ask the gods, and the gods ignore the mortal world unless it influences them."

"Which I do," I said, a distinct quiver to my voice.

"Yes, but they'll leave it to the Guard since the Shadow came back without you."

That fact sent a chill down my spine and Callum let my

hands go, rubbing my back as if to chase it away. "But you said the Guard are more terrifying than the Shadow. How can that be better?"

I couldn't read his expression. He kept it shaded before he responded, "You just need to trust me. Run to Slate's. I'll ensure you know the direction. We're close to your province, and he's expecting you. We'll cover it in the morning with your training."

I ran my fingers along his arm, feeling the muscle below, the strength that was the man I loved. "We have one more day, right?"

"Yes. At some point tomorrow, the Guard will track us down. Harperia will remove Gerrand and the Shadow from the hunt and turn her attention just enough to locate you."

I couldn't halt the quiver in my lip, his eyes softening as he gently brushed his thumb over it. "I have a plan, Harmony. Trust me."

The pressure in my chest was heavy, strangling the air in my lungs, and I grabbed his shirt, pulling him closer to me and letting my need for him take away the terror that was assailing me. "Fine. Tomorrow we train, until then we fuck?" I asked, trying to turn the mood. I tightened my legs around him, pushing the firmness that was growing in his pants against me, but he pulled my legs apart, freeing himself from my hold.

Frowning, I scrunched my eyes, trying to figure out what he was doing. My stomach fluttered as he unhooked my jeans and scooted me out of them. "No."

"No?" I could hear the disappointment in my voice. "Tomorrow we don't train?" I asked, hoping that was what he meant.

He chuckled, squeezing his hands up my legs. Each time his hand hit a sore muscle, I cringed, his observant eyes catching each reaction. "Good try." He squeezed harder, and I cried out in pain. "Oh, sweetheart, I love it when you scream, but that's not the scream I like. No, we're not fucking yet. You need to heal before I touch you like I want to."

"But Callum—"

He squeezed again, and I gritted my teeth. "You are no longer a mortal. Own who you are, just as you did as a mortal."

"And who am I, Callum? Aside from a hunted mistake the gods want dead."

A growl resounded through the room, his eyes narrowing. "You are not a mistake. You are the daughter of a fated pair—Trinity, leader of the Torch and Landon, second of the Shadow. There is no other like you. And you are mine. Now own your heritage and your place at my side."

I sucked in a breath, his words opening my eyes to the reality that I hadn't completely opened them to. Shadow and Torch were legends. Renowned and feared, turned to whispers in the dark and hushed words that carried the power the two factions held. As revered as the gods. A leader of either fraction would hold power above the others, royalty in their own right, and I was the daughter of Torch royalty. My father would have been leader if they hadn't killed him. And my lover was now next in line for that title.

"Who were your parents, Callum?"

His eyes creased. "My mother was a hunter, my father was leader of the Shadow before Gerrand took command."

My hands shook at the revelation. "Why isn't he still leader?"

"A Torch killed him when I was young. Remember those exceptions when a Shadow can't make it back to their realm?" He looked down, taking my hands in his. Brushing his fingers along mine, he continued, "There's a forced peace now, but there were times in our history when our factions were viciously antagonistic. The Goddess sent him on a special assignment.

Farinthion found out her intention to kill the mark and sent the leader of the Torch after my father."

"My mother?"

He shook his head. "No, this was before your mother led. She was his second. He stepped down a few hundred years later and yielded his lead to her."

I didn't understand why it mattered so much to me. It wasn't like I knew her. But it did, and relief settled on my shoulders. "He killed your father?"

"Yes. He trapped my father's wings, binding them in cement. They wouldn't dissipate when he needed to return to The Blight." I could see the tension in his jaw as he spoke. His eyes remained focused on my hands. "They were too heavy with the cement and so he bled out. Ritak, Torch's leader, stabbed him so many times that he was unrecognizable. My mother was inconsolable. As happens with fated mates, she withered away within months, her wings shriveling with her heart until it gave out and she was gone." The sadness in his voice was almost palpable, but as he met my eyes, I could see the fight in him, the warrior overpowering it and pushing it aside.

"Oh Callum, I'm so sorry." I didn't know what else to say, so I scooted to the edge of the counter and pulled his head to me, letting it drop to mine. His hands slid to my waist, holding it tight.

"It was a very long time ago, Harmony," he replied with no emotion.

"But still…she loved him so much her love for you couldn't save her?" I didn't understand. A mother's love was supposed to trump all, so why had she given up?

"Fated lovers can't live without each other. It's the curse of the blessing. They are two halves of a shared soul."

"Is that…is that what will happen to us?" Two halves of a

shared soul, he'd said. It felt that way, like something had severed my soul and half was now housed within him.

"Yes. That's why I can't lose you. Why you must learn to let instinct guide your wings and why you must learn to heal yourself."

His statement angered me, and I shoved his hands away. "You assume I can lose you? That leaving you behind to face your execution is something I can handle?"

"I told you to trust me."

"Trust you? You just said fated can't live without each other, yet you're planning to give yourself up so that I can fly to safety?"

His jaw clenched. "I have a plan and if everything falls in place the way I want it to, then I will be by your side again."

"And if it doesn't?" I didn't want to hear his answer because I knew what it would be. I knew from what he'd told me, and the horror of it was overwhelming.

"You'll know the minute they kill me."

I let out a wretched cry, bringing my hand over my mouth to halt it. His words had affirmed my suspicion and hearing them ignited an urge to flee. To run from this and force him to run with me. To change his mind about facing the Guard, about leaving me.

"Harmony, stop," he said, taking my hand. "I need you to be strong."

"Strong? You need me to be strong?" I pushed him away, sliding off the counter, the situation taking hold of me and drowning me. Everything he'd thrown at me the last few days compounded so that I could barely breathe. "How can I be strong? My entire life is now nothing but a string of mistruths, death, and violence that will forever haunt me. I'm being hunted by the Shadow, the ghosts of darkness that we learn to fear as children, the boogeymen under our beds, the stealers of souls.

And the gods want me dead. You want me to be strong, yet my parents died fighting what you're asking me to fight. If they couldn't stop it, how can I?" I rubbed my arms against the chill that had set in my bones. "I can't do this, Callum. I can't lose you. I can't be what you want me to be."

He grabbed my arms and pulled me to him. "I don't want you to be anything but what you were before all of this began. A strong, confident, self-assured woman who didn't take any bullshit, who braved meeting a man she suspected was one of those monsters." I tried breaking free from his hold, but he held me in a firm grip. "The woman who walked through a jungle in bare feet with her head held high. Who donned a skimpy bikini that same man left her knowing he could easily rip it from her body and strangle her with it." He smoothed his hands along my arms and tilted my face up, his expression stern but his eyes soft and matching his tone. "You are not some fragile damsel in distress, Harmony. You're a fighter and if anyone can get through this, you can. And right now, I need you to get through it because if there's any doubt you can't..." He took my face in both his hands, his voice holding a vulnerability that he never showed. "I won't make it. I'll let them kill me because I'll already be dead."

Searching his eyes, I tried to relax, to find my center and let his words embolden me. He was right. I was a fighter. I survived foster home after foster home. My best friend was the deadliest man in the province. My lover was a Shadow. "You were watching me?" I said, realizing what his words meant.

He gave me a crooked smile, the sexy Shadow in him returning. "Sure did and damn, you were hot. The way your tank top had slipped down, so your tits and bra were hanging out of it. It took all my strength not to break through the foliage and take you right then."

"You're a bit of a perv, aren't you?" I said, chuckling. The change of mood and subject calmed me immediately, and I didn't want it to stop.

"Damn right I am when it comes to you."

"Shame we didn't bring that bikini. I may have liked it wrapped around my neck."

His grin widened. "That's my girl. Better now?"

"No, but I will be as long as you don't give up on me."

"I won't if you don't."

"Deal. Can you fuck me now? Because I could really use some release."

He yanked me against him, his kiss almost knocking me off my feet. If his hold on me hadn't been so tight, I would have lost my balance.

"Heal yourself first, then I'll give you all the release you need. If this is my last night with you, I'm going to use every part of you until you can barely walk in the morning, let alone talk. You'll need that healing power if you're going to keep up with me."

I shivered inadvertently, and he chuckled, kissing my neck and nibbling on my earlobe. "Heal. I'm losing patience and my cock wants to be buried so far in you that you won't be able to keep from coming all over it. I want those pussy muscles clenching so tight around me that you milk every drop of cum from me."

My sharp inhale accompanied the flood of arousal that drenched me. Callum gave me a wicked grin, like he knew exactly the reaction his words had caused. "You're so wet now," he murmured in my ear. "I can't wait to lick that up."

"Gods, you need to stop or I'm going to come right now." I was already rubbing against him, loving how hard he was.

"No, you won't." He dipped his hand down into my panties, shoving his fingers into the drenched evidence of his effect on me. They teased my clit until I was moving against them, longing for them to bring me release. "Do you want to come, baby?"

His voice was like a brush along my clit, and I lurched forward, the move forcing his fingers further. He let out a groan and dropped his head.

"Please, Callum," I begged, hating that I was begging him but needing the release he was promising with every dip of his fingers. I was so close that I was trembling.

The movement stopped, and I pushed forward, needing more as he pulled his fingers free. I cried out, but he stepped away, licking his fingers one by one.

"You taste so fucking good. I can't wait to sink my tongue into that."

"Then do it now," I said, my body on fire with the pain of the letdown he was causing me.

"Not...until...you... heal." He licked a finger between each word, dragging out the motion. My legs twisted in response. "None of that, sweetheart. When you come, it's going to be me that rips it from you."

"I don't know how to heal," I said, throwing my hands up in frustration.

"Yes, you do. You're a child of Shadow and Torch. It's as instinctual as flying. It was there when you were a baby, and it never went away. It's only been asleep all this time. Be a good girl and wake it so I can relieve that twitching between your legs. And if you don't hurry it up, I'm going to fuck that pretty mouth of yours instead and make you wait for your release until you've swallowed every drop of me."

It wasn't a threat that held much danger. I could easily come that way, but I didn't have the energy to argue. His words had me dripping even more, and I needed release so badly I was about to hump the couch. It wouldn't have been my finest moment, nor would it have felt as good as he would, but I wasn't picky at this point. Not with my body burning like it currently was.

He crossed his arms and stared me down, that broodiness only further affecting me.

"Harmony." There was that scolding tone. I was being a bad girl.

"Don't scold me, Callum. It only makes me wetter."

His lip tugged, but he didn't break the façade.

"Damn, you're an asshole," I grumbled.

"I know. I'm a Shadow. I'm not a nice guy and I never claimed to be. I'm as bad as they get."

"That's what you want everyone to see, but I know the truth." He flinched slightly, the façade cracking. "You're a good guy hiding behind a tough exterior."

He shifted so he was looking down at me and I wanted to back up, knowing he could kill me within seconds. But he was mine. The warrior hunter and the gentle man below who would give his life so that I could live. He was trying to intimidate me, to have me take the words back, but I wouldn't. I brought my hand up to trace the tension in his jaw, and his eyes softened. "I love the man below the Shadow, but I need the Shadow that hides the man. I own both sides of you, Callum. They're mine."

He gave me a lopsided grin and pulled me against him, nuzzling my nose. "You are something, Harmony Decker."

I leaned into his chest, liking his strength and the way my name fell from his lips. "I know," I said, peeking up at him. "Say my name again." I wanted to hear the way his deep baritone reverberated through his chest when he did.

He jerked me closer to him so that it was almost hard to breathe. "Why?"

"Because I like the way you say it," I replied, the corner of his lip lifting in response.

"I thought you liked the way I called you 'baby'."

Every nerve in my body flared to life in confirmation. "Damn, do I ever. But I like how my full name rolls off your tongue."

He dropped his head, his tongue draping along my neck. "I have other ways to bring you pleasure with my tongue. Better ways than just saying your name, baby."

The shiver that ran through me was more like a convulsion, and his chuckle rumbled in his chest. "You know that's not really your name, right?"

I tipped my head back, meeting his eyes. "What do you mean?"

"Decker. It's not your last name."

My head tilted as I thought about it. My parents had left me with only a partial identity, my first name. The orphanage must have picked Decker for me. Once again, my self-awareness faltered, another part of my existence toppled like a house of cards. "What was my father's last name?" I asked, finally finding my voice and noticing how his shirt had bunched in my hand.

He shook his head. "That's not how it works with us. Our females don't take another name. There's no marriage ceremony when there's a decision to mate for life."

"So, your last name is… Is it even your last name?"

"A combination of my father's and my mother's. And yes, it's Montrose. Children take a version of their parent's name that represents both sides of their heritage. Yours would be Bentire, from Landon Shatire and Trinity Benratin." He narrowed his eyes as I grappled with this piece of information.

"Harmony Bentire doesn't have the same ring, does it?" I asked, thinking of how odd it sounded.

"No," he muttered absently.

I studied him, seeing the distracted look in his eyes. "Callum?"

"You said there was a note when they left you? One that insisted your name remain Harmony?"

I nodded. "It was the only thing the note said."

"Harmony," he mumbled, moving away from me to pace back and forth. "Torch and Shadow in harmony within you." His hazel eyes turned to me. "I think there's more to you, Harmony. More that hasn't wakened. That name was deliberate, representing what you are to two factions that have been enemies since the moment the gods created them."

"What more could I be?"

"Aside from a disruption of the norm? Of everything my kind has known? We have a fragile peace with the Torch that can fracture at any time. My father's death was evidence of that. The gods have driven the wedge between us, compounding our differences and the divisiveness that exists. You are a slap in the face to everything they have shaped us to be."

The titillation that had been fluttering through my body dissipated, replaced with a nervous anxiousness that was compounding.

He stopped his pacing, running his hands down his face. "That's why it's so important to kill you. Your parents knew that, hiding evidence of you within that spell but leaving a fuck you to the gods in your name." He looked at me, his eyes large, the amber within the hazel bright. My heart was pounding so hard I wasn't sure I could remain standing. The fear that had been a constant companion since this journey had begun was now embedding its claws into my gut. "It's imperative that you live, Harmony," he continued, his voice taking on a level of seriousness that caused my heart to stutter. "Not just because I need you, but because the Shadow and Torch need you...maybe even the gods need you." His brows knitted just before his eyes grew wider. "They just don't realize it. Shit, Harmony, you could change the course of the world with everything you represent."

I stumbled back, my fear shredding me and shaking me to my core. Those words carried a burden I didn't want to shoulder, one I didn't think I could deliver on. Callum read my reaction, his eyes hardening, the hunter in him returning.

He grabbed me by the shoulders. "What did I say about your self-doubt, Harmony? Own who you are now, just as you did before. You're no different."

"No? Aside from the wings and the fucking fate of the world on my shoulders?" I spat, freeing myself from his grasp. "I'd say that's a big difference from where I was a few days ago."

He yanked me back to him. "You're still the same person who taunted me in that black bikini." He gave me a sly grin, his fingers loosening to skirt my arm. "The same one who walked to work the day before sloshing your coffee around while you talked with your hands."

I gaped at him, his words stunning me and simmering my ire. "You…you were watching me," I said, thinking back to that morning and the sensation that seemed to tingle through me. "I sensed you. I remember thinking I needed to see something that morning, like there was something important in the distance that I couldn't set my sight on. It was you?" My heart beat unexpectedly hard, a strange fluttering like wings stirring in my belly.

"You looked my way," he mumbled, his voice full of wonder. "I remember the moment your blue eyes turned my way, and you stole my heart. I didn't know it then, but I do now. I fell in love with you at that moment. I used excuses to keep you alive longer so I could see you, so I could meet you. I tried to deny it, to rationalize it, but I couldn't fight it. Gods, Harmony, that spell your parents placed on you should have covered any supernatural part of you, including any call to a fated, yet…" His hands rubbed along my arms as he dropped his head to mine, running his face through my hair.

"Yet, it didn't. There was no stopping it, was there?" I said, my voice unsteady.

His laugh was warm against my head. "No. Two children of fated love have never been fated, but we are, and it's stronger than any fated love before." His voice had dropped to a hush by the last word.

I clung to him, not wanting to let go. Not wanting time to move forward, not wanting anything to exist but this moment with him, with our love, with us. He folded me into him, holding me like the same desperate thoughts were going through his mind. I breathed him in, knowing there was no place else I belonged but in his arms. If it meant I was everything he said I was, then so be it.

I lifted my head, looking deep into his eyes. "If I am half Torch—"

"If?" I saw the shift in his eyes as the vulnerability tucked itself away.

He was waiting for me to own my identity, the powerful pieces that had formed me and that now defined me.

"I am half Torch, half Shadow," I said, correcting myself. "I am not mortal. I am an immortal child of...of the gods." I gave him a naughty smile. "I am the fated half of the sexiest Shadow, next to lead, owned by him, claimed by him. And I..." Something inside of me was waking, slowly releasing, like it was leaking from behind a barrier. I could sense that it wouldn't break open at once but would be a slow trickle as I grew to accept my place in this messed-up history. "And I am something to be feared."

He arched a brow, his lips turning. There was a tingling through my body, and his lips formed that sly grin that made me drenched. He picked up my arm, smoothing his hand over it as I watched my bruises heal with wide eyes.

"Like I said, own the fact that you are no longer mortal, my little Shadow."

"I like that nickname," I said, embracing the way it had sunk into my soul like a call I couldn't resist. "But I prefer baby."

A rumble came from his chest.

"Does this mean you'll give me release now?" I leaned further into him. "I want you to fuck me and take me from this chaos for one more night before the armies of the gods come to ruin my day."

His eyes lit, his fingers tracing higher on my arm. "Only my girl would describe impending doom as ruining her day."

"If your dick isn't filling me by the end of the day tomorrow, it will ruin my day."

He smirked. "Only if my cock isn't snug between your legs? Not if we're both dead?"

"Eh, if we're both dead, then I won't know it's not there, right? And who said it was between my legs?"

The sparkle in his eyes lit my body on fire. "Gods, I love you, sweetheart." His hand rose, his fingers skirting the swell of my breasts where they pushed above my bra, before they surrounded my throat, tugging me forward so my lips crashed into his. "I'm going to fuck every part of you I can plunge into tonight and again before dawn. I want that mouth, I want that ass, and I definitely want that pussy clenching around me as I fill you."

My breath hitched, my body arching into him. Death may have been looming over us, but we had each other to ease the pain. "I want you, Callum. I want you to be the last touch on my skin, the last taste in my mouth, and I want your name to be the last that falls from my lips as I come undone for you."

He lifted me, walking us to the counter, his hands working my panties from me until he gave up and ripped them. I unhooked my bra, which he quickly threw aside, dropping his mouth to my breasts and sucking them like they were sustenance for him. As I worked to free his length, he slipped his fingers deep inside of me. My body lurched, heat coursed through me with his touch, and I forgot what I was doing as I rocked into his motion.

"That's it, sweetheart, come for me. I want to hear you call my name as your cum coats my fingers."

He smashed his mouth into mine, his tongue playing with mine until my climax tore through me. I threw my head back, bucking against his hand and screaming his name while he chuckled. He dragged his fingers from me, the spasms still rocking me, and plunged into me with a ferocity that sent another scream from my lips. The combination of his hand wrapped around my neck and the force of his thrusts coaxed another climax from me. It plowed through me so fast I squeezed my legs around him tighter. My toes curled and my heels dug into him. The growl he emitted enhanced the torrent in my body, but he didn't stop the pounding he was giving me.

As I descended from my back-to-back orgasms, Callum slid his hands to my ass and walked us out of the room into the bedroom. He dropped me on the bed. I didn't have time to protest because he fell to his knees and licked me so deep my groan rattled through my chest.

"Gods, that's delicious. I'm going to need more of that to tide me over, baby." He nibbled my clit, and I squirmed, but his hands gripped my hips and pulled me further to his face. I'd never had anyone's tongue torment me the way his did. He slid his hands up and squeezed my breasts, his tongue flicking against my clit. "Time to come for me again, sweetheart," he breathed against me.

I groaned, arching my back as his tongue slid deeper than it should have been able to. My soul soared from my body, then careened back in as my orgasm hit me, breaking me into so many pieces I couldn't think as he thrust into me. He didn't let up, making good on his promise to use every part of me. I relished every second, knowing this could be our last night together, the last night to experience his touches, to have him wreck me like only he could.

Each time he filled me, I begged for more. Every time he took me over the edge and fell over it with me, I pleaded for more. I didn't want it to end because I knew when it did there would be nothing to do but wake in the morning and face the consequences of our love. The consequences of my existence, of my parents' love, and the constructs that made all of that wrong. And I didn't want those consequences because I knew what awaited us—the inevitable that sat on the cusp of our ecstasy like a lioness watching its prey frolic before the kill. Well, if the lioness was watching, I'd give her a show to remember. Because like Callum, I wanted to taste, to touch, to be used, and to use until there was no part of me that didn't bear his mark. No part of him that didn't bear mine. I would claim his soul and he mine so that nothing they did to us would matter. So that nothing would tear us apart because our souls would find each other and fuck their way into the afterlife. And as I broke one last time, Callum's groans matching mine, our bodies soaked with sweat and lust, I sent one final *fuck you* to the gods who wanted to destroy us.

CHAPTER 17
CALLUM

Dawn was approaching, and I hadn't slept. Harmony and I had made love into the early morning hours until sleep finally took its hold on her. Making love was how we'd ended, but we'd done nothing but dirty fucking early on. There was no dampening the need I had for her. It was continuous, and she met that need with her own level of fierceness, one that took me over the cliffs and sent me to oblivion.

I slid my hands down her back, squeezing her ass, the ass I'd taken the prior night. Her tightness had bared down on me so that I'd had no choice but to come. I'd used her in every way, marking every inch of her, finally making love to her, setting aside the unfiltered lust, and letting my emotions free as she did the same. The passion was on a level that surpassed anything we'd done to this point and was layered with the fear and desperation of our predicament.

Harmony sighed, and my cock jerked to life. Touching her had been a mistake. Our time was limited, and I didn't know when Gerrand would report to the Goddess. I did, however, know she wouldn't send the Shadow this time. She would send her Guard. The thought was enough to stop my hand, and I gently rolled Harmony from me.

"No," she moaned, grabbing my chest and pulling me on top of her.

"Oh sweetheart, that was a dangerous move," I said, cursing myself for getting harder. There was no stopping my hand from caressing her breast and bringing her nipple to my mouth. I could suck on them all day. They were my favorite thing about her body. Her ass was my second favorite thing.

"Have you always been a breast man?" she asked, her fingers playing in my hair.

"Always, and yours are the best." I licked my way down her stomach, biting her hip. "Although your hips and this ass are amazing, too," I said, inching my fingers underneath her and giving her ass a squeeze.

"You like your girls curvy then?"

"Of course I do. All Shadow men do. Our women aren't tiny like those scrawny, weight-obsessed mortals." She picked my head up and peeked down at me, giving me a curious look. "The gods created all Shadow women like you—round asses, curvy hips, and big tits…although you take the prize for the best ones."

"All of them?"

"Definitely. You're fighters, built to fight."

"How do big tits help them fight?"

"Rumor has it the Goddess' brother, Trinibus, insisted on the larger breasts." I shrugged. "Don't ask me why, but I'm not complaining."

She rolled her eyes, and I laughed.

"Typical man insisting the tits be big," she groused.

"Again, I'm not complaining. The gods designed the rest of your body to suit your warrior needs."

"I thought we were hunters. I'm confused. You use the word interchangeably."

She was running her fingers through my hair, and I closed my eyes, resting my cheek on her stomach. I could have laid there all day. "We're both," I replied lazily, the words slow and drawn as my entire body relaxed into her touch. "The gods created us to be warriors, but they use us as hunters. They had their Guard, using them as guardians, warriors within the realm. They didn't need us to guard the realm as well, so they used us on the ground instead. The Guard never leave the realm except in extreme circumstances. Their job is to protect The Blight and maintain the separation between the realm of the gods and the mortal world. Shadows maintain stability in the mortal world by hunting the demons and fighting the Torch. The gods call us hunters, but we still refer to ourselves as both."

"Huh, so we're both. And I have the gods to thank for the taunting I received in junior high when my body developed into this," she said, her tone snarky.

I picked my head up and looked at her. "You are perfection, Harmony. There's no other way I'd want you. You're built to be a Shadow and to be desired by a Shadow."

"You?" she asked in a coy tone.

"And only me." I licked my way up her stomach, the sensation of her skin against mine revitalizing me. Pulling her nipple into my mouth, I let my teeth graze it. "Every part of you is mine, Harmony."

She shivered, and I released her nipple. Replacing my teeth with my hand, I brushed my mouth along her neck until I reached her lips. Dawn was rising and with it the threat to the woman I loved, but I ignored it for one last taste of her. I pushed her legs apart and buried myself in her, enamored by how wet she was.

"Should I make love to you or fuck you, sweetheart?" I said against her lips.

"So many choices. Should I come in your mouth or on your dick?"

My laugh was one that rocked us both. "If that's the option, then maybe I should come in your mouth instead."

She pushed me over and, not expecting it, I rolled, dragging her with me. Pressing against my pecs, she brought herself up, tipping her head back as her body moved in stimulating gyrations. Gripping her hips, I slid my hands up her body, her head falling more as she arched her back and pushed her breasts further into my hold.

"I think we should do them all. And I want your cum splattering my throat and my tits. I love how turned on that gets you."

"Fuck, does it ever. Even the thought makes me hard. But we don't have all day, baby. So why don't I just fuck you rough and dirty like we both enjoy, and I'll make love to you when we make it out of this mess?"

She dropped on me, crushing her mouth to mine, and she didn't need to tell me her answer. Twisting my hand into her hair, I took back the power, needing to dominate this time. I yanked her head back, waiting for her attempt to reclaim control, but she read me, relinquishing it to me and saying, "Ravage me one last time before those bastards arrive and ruin my day."

"I thought you said not coming on my cock would ruin your day," I replied, curving my tongue around her lips.

"No, not coming on your cock tonight will ruin it. I mentioned nothing about this morning."

My laugh filled the room as I flipped her to her stomach and took her hard like she wanted. By the time we were through, she was back on top of me, riding out the currents of her climax, while I bucked below her, my hands clinging to her hips as the waves of my release drowned me one last time.

"WAIT, WE'RE GOING OUTSIDE?" Harmony asked me as I dug a jacket from the closet. "It's cold out there."

"Tough shit. Now grab your coat and let's go."

"I didn't bring a coat."

I stared at her, only then remembering I hadn't told her what to bring as we'd hastened to her apartment and packed a bag. I looked down at the jacket in my hand. It was entirely too large for her and would have impeded her ability to move. Rummaging through the closet, I found a black hoodie and threw it at her.

She picked it up, glancing back at me. "Hoodies don't seem like your thing."

"Just put it on," I groused.

"Is this someone else's?"

I shot her a look and snatched it from her. Holding it up to me to show that it was my size, I replied, "Does it look like someone else's?"

"You did say Shadow women are bigger."

"Don't make me smack your ass, Harmony. Put the fucking sweatshirt on and let's go. It's likely not warm enough, but once we start moving, you'll warm up."

She tugged it over her head, and I couldn't help but think how adorable she looked in it. It was entirely too big for her—the arms draped past her hands and the material hung loose over her. Thankfully, she was tall, but I still had a few inches on her and so it hung well past her waist. The sight stirred my heartstrings.

She pulled her hair out from under it, tying it up in a pony-tail, which made her look even more like she was playing dress up in her father's closet. I shook my head, trying not to think about how dressing up in her father's clothes triggered some strange desire to hear her purr the word *daddy* to me. The last thing I needed was another kink for either of us. We were dangerous enough with what already turned us on.

But I couldn't deny how young she was compared to me or any of my former colleagues who were hunting her. Too young to know what any of us knew, to understand how to control her powers, her wings, her strength. Running my hand over my face, I turned away, heading toward the front of the compound.

"Callum," she called, worry in her voice.

"You shouldn't be dealing with any of this, Harmony. Left alone your entire life, raised apart from us." It wouldn't have changed our love if she'd lived her life in The Blight instead of the mortal world. I still would have fallen for her, likely when she was younger. We were fated mates and there was no ignoring that draw.

Her hand rested on my back, rubbing at the tension I'd been carrying since we'd dressed.

"It's okay, Callum. It was better this way."

I turned to her. "Was it? To not know who you are? Not know your parents or your heritage?"

"Yes. My life as a mortal made me who I am today. I know myself. I understand pain and grief, hate and agony. I know the joy and freedom of being young and alive. And the realization that life is short, that chances need to be taken, love needs to be risked, and that every day needs to be lived as if it's the last. Can you say the same?"

I couldn't. None of us could because we were immortal, taught to fight and kill from the moment we could walk. Nothing existed but that purpose, which was why I preferred to live away from the realm and among the mortals. They made me feel alive in ways I didn't when I was in The Blight. "No," I murmured, brushing a wisp of hair from her cheek.

"Meeting the way we did would never have happened if my life were different."

"We would have still fallen in love, Harmony. We're fated, it's unavoidable."

"But circumstances made it deeper, richer, more than something that just is."

I smiled. She was right. The situation had plunged us into our love and made the fated piece settle faster than it did for other couples. They didn't have the threat of death or separation hanging over their heads, so they could take their time exploring the depths of their love. Harmony and I didn't have that luxury and so we dove in headfirst, never looking back, and embracing it for what it was without hesitation.

"Now, stop your pouting before I bite your puckering lip," she teased.

Narrowing my eyes, I pulled her to me and kissed her, sucking her bottom lip between my teeth. "Don't threaten me with something that only makes me hard, sweetheart."

Her giggle was infectious, and I nuzzled her cheek before releasing her. "Let's go. Once we walk through that door, there's a chance we won't have time for Gerrand to warn us."

"What do you mean?"

"My protection is only over the compounds themselves. I spell them with a shading of sorts so no one can sense me. I don't have that control over anything but a physical space."

"So we step outside, and what?" Her eyes were enormous, and I noticed the tremor in the hand that rested on my chest.

"There's a chance they might sense me."

She backed away, but I tugged her to my chest. "We need to go outside to practice your magic and your flying. If you can't fly, you can't escape."

"But—"

"No buts, now let's go."

Her hands cinched my shirt, her eyes darting nervously. "Callum, I don't want to lose you."

Bringing my finger to her lips, I said, "Have faith and trust me. What do you do when they attack, and I have them distracted?"

"I run…or I fly away."

"And go where?"

"Southeast toward the province until I reach Slate's."

"You follow the direction of the sun and stay hidden. Take to alleyways, to shaded spots. Travel at night if you end up on foot. Do not trust anyone because you don't know how to spot another Shadow or even a Torch." She nodded, swallowing loudly. "Save the swallowing noises for when we're safe and your lips are encasing my cock again."

I didn't give her time to respond. Handing her the phone that held Slate's number, I walked to the door and opened it, my eyes surveying the snowy landscape before I walked out. "Keep that on you. Unlock those legs, Harmony, and get your sexy ass out here."

My nerves were on edge, every sense alert. I'd stored a set of daggers in my belt and my hands were itching to take them out. Each step further from the compound added more tension to my body. I heard Harmony come up behind me, taking small steps as if she were as alert as I was. Bringing her out there was a risk I shouldn't have taken, but we were almost out of time anyway, and she had yet to take flight. If she didn't know how to fly, her wings would be useless.

"Your wings run on instinct," I said, reaching my hand back to ensure she was close to me but not turning around.

"You've said that, but I don't know what it means."

"It means you use them as you would any other limb. You

don't think about it, you just do it. You don't tell your mind to walk, you just walk. It's instinctual. The same with your wings. They should expand when needed and retract when they're not. They should take flight when necessary, without thought."

"You make it sound so easy."

"Because it is." I took her hand and pulled her in front of me. "Remember how you healed last night?"

"No."

"Exactly. Because it happened instinctually. Your magic is driven the same way. When the Shadow or even the Torch in you is active, your magic will be as well."

"We've been practicing for two days, and I still can't do what you're saying."

She chewed her bottom lip, and although she was trying not to show it, I could see the nerves in the drop of her shoulders and sense her hesitation.

"Harmony," I said, taking her by the shoulders. "You tapped into it last night—"

"Because you were seductively coaxing it out of me."

Chuckling, I replied, "Then imagine me rubbing your clit every time you need to access that part of you."

She hit me, but I grabbed her wrist and flipped her to the ground, where she landed with an *oof* in the snow. Her glare was worth risking her wrath.

"What was that for?" she complained.

"I thought I taught you to never let your guard down."

The handful of snow hit me before I could stop it. I wiped it from my face, giving her my most lethal stare, but my phone buzzed in my pocket before I could retaliate. Only one person had this number.

I pulled the phone from my pocket and read the message, though I knew instinctively what it said.

They know. Run.

I looked at Harmony, who had pulled herself from the snow and was looking at me quizzically. My heart raced as fear barraged me. We were out of time, and she was defenseless, with no control of her wings, no access to her magic, and barely any connection to her healing power.

"They're coming." As I said the words, I perceived the shift in the surrounding air. It was too late. They were already here.

CHAPTER 18
HARMONY

Callum's words reverberated through my ears like a fire alarm that wouldn't stop. They were here. The reality smacked into me, waking me to the idea that this was really happening. It hadn't seemed real before, more like a dream with the alarm going off in the periphery, just out of reach. But now, I couldn't ignore it. I'd never seen fear in Callum like I saw in him then and it tore through my soul, shredding it because I knew what it meant. I watched as he hardened himself, becoming the hunter, the Shadow I loved, the one who was about to sacrifice himself for me.

He turned, his muscles flexing as he drew two daggers from his belt.

"Run, Harmony."

"Callum, I—"

"Now."

The wind stirred from every direction, and he backed up, wrapping his arm around my waist. My chance to run was gone, and I couldn't help but think it was my fault for questioning him.

Three men appeared, unfurling their dark wings. I'd thought

the Shadow I'd seen at the island was intimidating, or even Callum when something aggravated him, but these men were terrifying. But they weren't men. They were Guard. I could see the difference in their stance, their postures, the way their eyes scanned Callum as if he were nothing more than an annoyance standing in the way of their prize.

"Callum," one said, his voice a heavy baritone that held authority.

"Belkair," Callum returned with a snarl that caused the hairs on my neck to rise.

"You stand charged of treason to the gods, of turning your back on your sacred duties, and breaking your oath of obedience."

"So, I've heard."

"Then you understand why we're here?"

Callum rolled his neck, his muscles flexing. I had my hand pressed to his back still and could feel the tension in it. "You're here to get your asses kicked."

Belkair's expression turned sour. "I don't think you understand the gravity of the situation."

"Oh, I understand clearly. The gods don't send their prized general for just any kill. I'm surprised you three even know how to leave the realm, they've had you locked away for so long."

"Don't make this harder than it should be, Callum," another one said, his voice low and gravelly, further intensifying the chill that wouldn't leave my body.

I didn't know what to do other than to cling to Callum's shirt. Sure, I was a fighter, but these were immortal warriors who saw me as nothing more than an assignment from their gods. A kill to satisfy the Goddess.

"I wouldn't want to make it easy, Brigan. I'm not surrendering and if you lay a finger on my mate, I will tear your wings from your bodies and feed them to you." My heart would have swelled with the protective fierceness of his words if death didn't stand in the form of three Guard in front of us.

Belkair's brow lifted as he peeked around at me. "Mate? You've lowered yourself to fucking a mortal and now you're calling her your mate?"

Callum's growl thundered through him.

"You've been here too long, Callum. I've heard you had your fill of mortal flesh over the centuries, but claiming one as a mate?" Brigan said.

It was my growl that escaped this time, and Callum snickered. "I wouldn't piss her off. She bites and if you enjoy it, I'll make your death more painful."

I wanted to add a witty comeback, but the situation was too dire, and I couldn't seem to find the confidence I always had. It had fled the moment the reality of our situation took physical form.

"Enough talk," Belkair said, moving closer. "The mark is to die, and you are to—"

He stopped talking, his head turning to our right as the Torch who had come after me a few days earlier appeared. As if this wasn't bad enough, the gods thought one more immortal hunter was necessary. I would have found humor in the idea that the gods feared me enough to send so many bulky killers after one mortal, but I couldn't because I knew they weren't all for me. That Callum was the threat, and I was what they saw as easy prey.

"Krinle?" Belkair said. "What the fuck are you doing here? This is Guard business."

"He may be, but she is Torch business."

The fear those words imbued caused palpitations in my chest. Callum pushed me back a few steps as they started arguing, but Belkair snapped his attention back to us. I took another step back and something crunched below my shoe. Risking a peek down, I saw my phone wedged in the snow. It had slipped from my pocket when Callum had tossed me to the ground.

My fear escalated, and I fought to keep my reaction under control, to not scream in frustration because that's what I wanted to do. To scream at the impossible odds that faced us, at the frustration of being so helpless when I'd never been that kind of woman, at the horror of knowing the gods wanted me dead and there didn't seem a rational way to escape that fate. And now, my chance at escape was gone, along with my one lifeline.

I tried to calm the ferocious beating of my heart and tore my eyes from the phone and back to Belkair.

"Krinle, the mark is ours. If you interfere, I will attack," he said, without looking at Krinle. His eyes were on me and held nothing but malice and a need to kill.

Krinle cracked his knuckles, and I forced myself to look away from Belkair's glare. "I welcome it, Guard."

He launched himself at Belkair, but the other two Guard engaged him. Belkair hadn't even turned in his direction like he was nothing but a nuisance the other Guard needed to clean up. Callum stepped forward, and Belkair attacked. I stumbled back, unsure of what to do. Their moves were so fast and powerful they were almost magical. The two who had taken on Krinle separated, the one staying to fight him while the one Callum had called Brigan made his way to me.

Callum struck Belkair, sending him flying through the snow, and soared toward Brigan, tackling him.

"No one touches her," he snarled as he dug his knife into Brigan's chest.

Two more Guard appeared, their reaction instantaneous. They pounced on Callum. Belkair returned, glancing at them and then at me, a nasty gleam in his eye that sent terror gripping my insides so badly I almost puked. Callum roared, throwing the others from his back and freeing himself, but Belkair turned sharply, driving his blade into Callum's chest.

I screamed and started running to him, but Callum caught my eye as he yanked the knife free, giving me the warning that I was not to interfere. Brigan plunged another knife plunged through his back and Callum arched in pain. Belkair had a second knife in his hand and drove it into Callum's chest as the third Guard incapacitated his wings and Brigan sliced through one. The sound of it ripping was one I would never forget. The agony on Callum's face was like a thousand daggers plunging into my heart. My screams cut the air as he fell to his knees.

"Run, Harmony," he wheezed. "Run."

Belkair turned toward me like a predator. Even with all his wounds and two Guard holding him down, Callum grabbed him, struggling to keep him from reaching me.

The Torch broke free from the other Guard, turning his attention to me. With one last look at Callum, I ran.

"Instinct Harmony!" he screamed before he went silent, the only sound a deafening grunt I forced myself to ignore. I understood the underlying meaning. He didn't want me to run. He wanted me to fly because flying was my only escape, the trump card none of them would expect.

Instinct. The word played through my mind as I heard the wings of the Torch spread, and another set flapping further away. I filled my mind with thoughts of Callum. Letting my fear slip away, I sent the thought of freedom through my mind. My wings burst open, and I let them take over, hearing the startled reactions as my feet left the ground.

Don't think, don't think, don't think. Over and over I repeated the mantra, trying to ignore the way the ground was getting smaller, the air colder. Trying not to think about the fact that I was flying or Callum was on the ground fighting for his life, maybe even dying.

Something grabbed my ankle, disrupting my concentration. My wings froze, and I began to fall, but then I thought of Callum. If I gave up now, it had all been for nothing—all his training, the promises we'd made to each other in our touches, the faith he had in me. I looked down. The Torch had my ankle, and he was yelling something to me that I couldn't make out. Belkair was closing in behind him, his eyes narrowed with determination to get to me.

"No!" I yelled, kicking with all my might. Something broke in me, the last pieces of whatever internal lock had been keeping the two magical sides of me apart. My wings flapped as my foot made contact and a scattering of black and gold sparkles exploded as I kicked the Torch and sent him spiraling into Belkair.

I turned and flew, letting my wings guide me. I soared and dove, flipped and climbed, the jubilant freedom of flight skipping through my senses the further I was from harm. I'd never been so free, so light, yet powerful. Magic tingled on my skin and for the first time since I'd discovered my past, I connected with it, understanding on an instinctual level who I truly was.

I crossed the border into my province, passing the few miles with ease, but Slate's compound was outside the city and the city was in the center of the province, miles from the border. Never having flown before, my wings tired quickly, exhaustion setting in along with the reality that they'd captured Callum. My flight faltered.

No, Harmony. He's still fighting, so you must continue fighting, I scolded myself. I'd promised him I would go to Slate's, and that promise was likely keeping him alive. At least for now. I didn't have the luxury of taking a break or walking. There wasn't time. I couldn't call Slate to come get me. That option was far behind me, buried in the snow. Callum had a plan, and that meant I needed to be at Slate's as quickly as possible, so I had no choice but to fly.

Fighting against my fatigue, I pushed on, the miles slowly piling behind me until the cold and the exhaustion became too much and I descended again. I fought to stay airborne, but my wings dragged me down, sending me tumbling to the ground. Something broke, and I clenched my teeth against the pain as I lay on the grass staring up at the sky. My wings had retracted. There was no more flying. Pushing myself from the ground, I winced as I tried to stand on my leg. My ankle had broken, but I could tell it was healing. The magic tickled my skin.

Within minutes, I'd healed, but I knew it had taken too long. I should have healed faster. I'd pushed my body, which wasn't used to its new identity. Callum had told me he suspected my body still thought of itself as mortal and I would need food and water to replenish until it grew accustomed to the magic. I hadn't eaten, and we'd skipped dinner the night before, too caught up in each other to even think about it. I was starving now, and my mouth was like a parched desert.

Looking around, I tried to get my bearings. I could see the city to my left. I was about a mile outside of it. While Slate kept a penthouse in the city, his main compound was just outside the city limits. A sign that he ruled more than the city, that the whole province was under his influence whether or not the governor liked it. I'd never understood why he hadn't simply taken over officially at this point. He'd always argued that the governor was a puppet and there was more power in the undercurrent than in the tide.

I walked, making my way to the trees beyond the open field where I'd fallen. Callum had told me to stick to the shadows, and that's what I'd do. Callum. The thought of him twisted my gut into rivulets of pain that threatened to send me to my knees. Seeing him covered in blood, his wing torn so that it was

216

drooping to the ground, had been agonizing. The fire had still been there, the fierceness in his eyes. He was strong, maybe stronger than they knew. At least I prayed he was. I didn't want to think of what they were doing to him, of what he faced if he couldn't make his plan work. He hadn't told me what his intention was, but it gave him hope and so I would cling to that hope. The alternative was devastating.

The further I walked, the more I realized I'd flown too far south. I stopped and headed back toward the city. Confusion set in. I never traveled this far unless I was in a car, and I had seen no roads. I was in the countryside, lost, cold, hungry, and weak. My teeth were chattering. The sweatshirt Callum had given me was too thin to stave off the cold in this region. But it hadn't bothered me while I'd been flying. It was cold in the air, but something had kept my body temperature regulated. Magic.

I needed to get airborne again. Callum had said the magic triggered when our Shadow was active. But I wasn't just Shadow. I was also Torch, and he had admitted he didn't know if they worked differently. Maybe I worked differently. I was something none of them had seen before; it stood to reason that my abilities were unique to what either faction knew.

Stopping, I closed my eyes and calmed myself. I reached inward to touch that strange magical sensation I'd had the day before when I'd healed and then when I'd kicked the Torch. I thought about how Callum said I always tried too hard, and I relaxed. Shortly before this had all begun, I'd taken a few yoga classes with Slate's sister, Kanta. I had hated it, having to sit quietly and look inwardly. I knew it was good for me, understood that I was gaining flexibility and core strength, but I just couldn't handle those moments of quiet. But maybe it wasn't the quiet, maybe it was the inward piece that flustered me. And maybe that was because inwardly a lock had bound me, keeping the true me caged behind a spell, asleep. In that moment of quiet reflection,

I'd come close to that lock and somehow I'd sensed it, intuitively knowing I shouldn't be that close to it.

My eyes flew open. I'd remained hidden from the gods for thirty-three years, yet the Goddess had discovered me now.

"Fucking spiritual calm," I muttered. I'd been the one to reveal myself and I hadn't even realized it. I'd touched the bounds of that spell, the core connection I had to my true self, and it had startled me so much I hadn't gone back. I'd told myself I was too antsy to sit there and contemplate my spiritual self in silence. When in reality, I had awakened that spiritual connection and set a beacon off for the Goddess to find me.

I wanted to curse myself for my ignorance, but I hadn't known and if the Goddess hadn't discovered me, I may have never met Callum.

Sitting, I crossed my legs and closed my eyes. I slowed my breathing and let all thoughts clear from my head. Reaching inward, descending further with each calming breath, I let only one thought slip into my empty mind. *You are not mortal. You are immortal, half Torch, half Shadow.*

I held onto the thought as I dove further until warmth filled my body, a golden shimmer flickering behind my eyelids, wrapped in streams of black. Me. The true me, the magic that made me complete now, the same way Callum did. Opening my eyes, I called on the magic, my wings expanding behind me as the gold and black spread into the air.

"No," I murmured to my wings. "Rest."

They closed, and I felt them settle in me, but the magic stayed. Callum had said my power was both Shadow and Torch, that both sides lived in me, only active when my wings were free. But that wasn't true for me. The blending of the two factions made me different. I saw that now as I let my fingers drift through the magic, awed at how it tingled over my skin. I thought of how I needed to find Slate's and the answer appeared in my mind, the direction, the knowledge of where to go and how long it would take. I was about an hour out, but at least I knew how to get there now.

Rising, I watched as the magic gathered back into my skin. I didn't have complete control of it yet. I was still exhausted and hungry, so I hadn't woken all aspects of it, but at least I knew how to reach it. Callum would scold me, saying no Shadow would give me time to sit and find my center, but this was all I had right now. Until I completely understood my power or even who I was, I would take my time with it.

Time wasn't a luxury I had, however, and as I started back on my trek, I wondered if it even mattered that I was finding my power. If they killed Callum, no power in the world would hold me together.

CHAPTER 19
CALLUM

Watching Harmony run from me was the hardest thing I'd ever done. Each step she took was a wrench in my soul. Each step Krinle took closer to her sent fear through me, like I'd never known. But when she'd taken flight, it had knocked the breath from me. She'd been magnificent, her beautiful wings spreading to their full glory as her body lifted. Belkair and Krinle both faltered, halting in their tracks to stare in wonder.

"She's one of us?" Brigan asked, his dagger still plunged deep into my spine, his foot pressing against it to keep it in place.

"No, she's more than any of us," I said, gritting my teeth against the pain.

I needed to return to The Blight and heal. My body was trying to pull me back, but I was fighting it, too afraid to go without knowing Harmony was safe. Brigan had pinned my wings after Belkair had severed the one almost completely. The pain had been excruciating, but the only thing on my mind was Harmony.

"Shut up, traitor," Ritork snarled, striking his other dagger into my chest as Brigan put more pressure on his. He and Brigan were two of four Guard now securing me. I was bleeding too badly to heal, and the four knew exactly how to keep me stationary.

My stomach lurched as Krinle grew close to Harmony. Brigan said something, but I paid him no heed, my eyes glued to her as both Krinle and Belkair chased her down. I watched until I could no longer see her, then held my breath, waiting for Belkair's return. I knew Krinle wouldn't return. If he killed her, he'd head back to The Sect; if he lost her, he'd still return to his realm. We weren't on social terms with the Torch and avoiding each other was the best thing, especially if the mark was dead.

Ritork continued to berate me, seeming to forget the sight of Harmony taking flight. And I continued to ignore him, my eyes scanning the sky for a falling body. Her falling body. But it was Belkair I spied instead, landing with a whoosh a few feet from us and stalking over to me.

"Is she dead?" I asked, not wanting to know the answer but needing to, even though in my heart I understood she was still alive. Otherwise, the discomfort of my wounds would be nothing to the agony of my soul.

He pulled his dagger out and placed it under my chin, pinning his knee to my chest so that he had me secured between him and Brigan. The pain flared through the wing that was too wounded to heal and the dagger in my back.

"You don't deserve the answer. You've betrayed us with your foolishness."

"Is she dead?" I asked again.

He lowered his face to mine, his teeth gritted, but his eyes inquisitive as they searched mine, hunting for something.

"Take him back and keep him contained until I can return to bind his wings. I need to report to the Goddess."

My chest tightened in fear. I'd miscalculated. He was reporting to the Goddess, confirming to her what she already knew, that Harmony wasn't a mortal. She was something else. He hadn't, however, told me if she was still alive, so I didn't know if his report would please the Goddess or anger her. My only consolation was that I hadn't perceived Harmony's death, and I knew her death would have left me in more pain than any of my injuries.

They jerked me up and took me home, parading me along the path that led to the prison. The other Shadow gathered, and I kept my head held high thinking of the similarities to the Guard walking Landon to his death. I met Gerrand's eyes, perceiving the flash of sadness before he hardened them. My eyes remained locked on his until we passed him. My fellow hunters remained quiet, the silence only stressing the inevitable fate that stood before me. If I couldn't get Belkair alone, I stood no chance. But he barked an order for his men to take me to the cells, then veered toward the palace where the Goddess was waiting for his report. Brigan and Ritork dragged me into a cell. My wounds had healed the moment I'd returned to The Blight, but they had continued to restrain me by my wings. They plunged their daggers into my wings and forced me to the ground, ensuring I couldn't escape. There were too many Guard at this point to fight even if a possibility for escape existed. They'd captured me, just like I'd wanted them to, but my hope for a solution was fading with each minute Belkair was gone.

TIME DRAGS when an army of Guard is holding your wings hostage while they stand on your arms and legs, making it impossible to move enough to even scratch your ass.

"Release him," Belkair's voice came from behind me, breaking the stoic silence of the Guard who held me. They let me go, yanking their daggers from my wings and my back, my body instantly repairing the damage. It wouldn't matter. Guard magic would clip my wings in moments and contain me to this cell to await the verdict of the Goddess.

Belkair's magic weaved over my wings and through my chest as my ability to control what had been a natural part of my body for centuries was bound. It took all my strength not to scream at the burning that wound through my wings, severing my connection to them. When he was done, he left, the others following, none saying a word to me. I had failed. They would execute me and kill Harmony. I had to believe she was alive, that our fated tie would tell me if she was dead. But it wouldn't matter. If the Goddess killed me, Harmony would be dead within days.

Left alone with my thoughts for far too long, I rehashed everything that had happened, from the moment I'd seen Harmony to the moment I'd lost her. There wasn't a moment I would have changed except the one when I called Gerrand. I could have kept her hidden, remaining in my compounds, keeping her safe. But it would have been selfish, guaranteeing me the pleasure of her body and her love while locking her away. It was no way to live. And she needed to live.

My incessant thoughts quieted when Belkair appeared in my cell, shadowed in the corner.

"Who is she?" he asked in a hushed voice.

Hope slunk from the depths of my soul. "Landon's daughter."

I waited for the denial or the questions, not knowing Belkair well enough to read him.

"It can't be."

And so it was the denial I'd have to grapple with.

"It's true. He and Trinity hid her, binding her wings with a spell before they left her." I paused, waiting for some reaction, but Belkair gave me none. He was as stoic and loyal as they came, but the fact that he had returned gave me hope. Hope that trickled into the devastated recesses of my heart. "Trinity let them capture her, and Landon turned himself in to take attention from Harmony while the spell worked its way into her system. She's lived hidden in the mortal world since."

He shoved me against the cell, his teeth clenched so tight I could hear them grinding. "How do you know this?"

"Because she's my fated."

He flinched at my words, then pressed me harder into the bars. "The last person to say those words to me died at the Goddess' hands."

"I know, but it's true. You've known me a long time, Belkair. I wouldn't risk my life for a mortal if there wasn't a good reason."

He studied me for what seemed an eternity, but I didn't flinch, knowing to even blink would be weakness.

"She's Landon's?"

"Yes. You saw her wings. You know the truth. She's half Shadow, half Torch."

Letting me go, he backed away, running his hand through his hair. "Why lead us to you? Why not stay hidden?" I could sense his anger rolling off him in waves. "Why wouldn't you stay hidden?" he hissed.

"Because it wasn't fair to her. And it wouldn't have worked forever. Look at Landon and Trinity. I didn't want to face the same fate as they did…I can't lose her, Belkair." I knew I sounded vulnerable. The slip would have cost me if he weren't already swaying to my words.

"But now you will."

"Not if you help me."

His head jerked up, his eyes narrowing. "You want me to risk everything to help you? Risk the wrath of the Goddess?"

"For your niece. She's Landon's daughter. We owe it to him not to let her die."

"Do we?" he growled. "He betrayed our kind, betrayed our gods."

"He fell in love, fated love. There's no stopping it, trust me."

He looked torn, his face scrunching as he wrestled with what to do.

This was my only chance and if he wavered, if he turned from the truth, Harmony was dead. "Belkair," I said, pleading with him and not caring that it went against the Shadow in me to do so. "We have the chance to make it right, to right the past and save her."

He shook his head. "No one can stand against the gods."

"Maybe we can't, but she may."

"Do you really believe that?" And in that instance, I saw the glimmer of hope behind his steely eyes, heard it beneath the gruffness of his voice.

But I wasn't certain if Harmony could stand against the gods. I didn't even know where the thought had come from. But Landon and Trinity had believed she could. Her name was evidence of that.

"How long have the gods been fighting? How long have we been fighting the Torch?" I asked him.

"Forever."

"But there was a time they didn't, before the Shadow, before the Torch. Harmony is a blend of both factions, a magnificent blend," I said, my nerves bounding in me as I desperately tried to win him over. "The two factions came together to form something amazing in her. If we can convince the others to rally with her—"

"They'll all die."

I didn't know what to say. His words were like a weight dragging me down. The likelihood of death for anyone who stood beside us was high.

"But if only a few of us stand with her, fight for her," he mused, "then only a few sacrifice themselves if we can't reason with the gods."

I looked back up at him, hope filling me again with his words. The binding fell from my wings, freeing from my chest.

"The gods are distracted, and the Guard are busy searching for her. Tell me you have a plan, Callum."

I did. It wasn't the most solid plan, but it was a plan.

CHAPTER 20
HARMONY

By the time I reached the gates of the compound, I'd hit my limit. My magical connection was long severed, my body no longer healing itself, too exhausted to do anything but put one foot in front of the other. Even that ability faded as I fell into Brach's arms. The henchman yelled for help, but my eyes had fluttered closed by then, too heavy to remain open.

Nightmares invaded my dreams. Black feathers that blew across a marble floor, cells with iron bars and no light, cold and dank. Pain that seared through every muscle in my body and a heaviness on my back giving the sensation of chains weighing down my wings.

I woke suddenly, searching for Callum, knowing instinctually that my dreams had been of him, our bond somehow strong enough for me to sense him. To know how he suffered. Drawing my knees into my chest, I shivered. They had him locked away, awaiting his execution. Whatever plan he'd devised, it hadn't worked, and now his fate was sealed. As was mine.

I looked around the dark room, my eyes adjusting. There was

a familiarity to it. I reached over and turned on the bedside table lamp, the guest room Slate reserved for me coming to life in the dim light. I pushed aside the covers and stumbled out of bed. Someone had stripped off my clothes and left me in a tank top and boy shorts.

Callum's sweatshirt lay across the room on a chair along with my jeans and I ran to it, picking it up and sniffing in the scent of him that still lay within the material. It gave me a sense of calm, even if it was short-lived. Throwing it over the tank top, I wandered out of the room and down the hall, meandering until I reached the main room where Slate, his mother, his sister, and a few of his men had gathered.

"Harm!" He leaped up from his chair, picking me up in his bear hug and holding me tight. "Holy shit, I thought you were dying on me."

"Don't suffocate her, asshole, or she will die on you," Kanta muttered, rising from the couch where she and their mother were sitting.

He released me and looked me over, inspecting every inch of me.

"Armando Dante Dimetre, step back and give the poor thing air," His mother said, coming up to us. When Slate's mother used his full name, even he didn't argue. "Ma, I'm just checking to make sure she's okay."

She smacked him on the back of his head and pushed him aside, wrapping an arm around me and bringing me further into the room.

"Kanta, get the food I set aside for her and some water. She needs to eat."

Slate rubbed his head as Kanta ran off to do as ordered. He may have ruled the city, but his mother ruled him. Slate studied me as his mother sat me down, his eyes guarded against the emotions he was fighting. I'd known him long enough to read him now.

"What's going on, Harm?"

"Let her rest—"

"No, Ma. Callum was insistent that I protect her and put the compound on emergency alert. I want to know what's going on and what he did to her."

She gave him a look that told me if it wasn't for me, she'd have him by the ear as she gave him a piece of her mind.

"He didn't do anything to me. It's…it's complicated." Just hearing Callum's name hurt. I missed his presence and his touch.

"Then uncomplicate it and tell me why I'm suddenly hiding you and who I'm hiding you from. You know how I am, Harm. I take great pains to ensure you stay safe. You're gone from my protection a handful of days and suddenly you're in danger. What the fuck did Callum do?"

"Nothing." I rubbed my arms, looking out the windows that led to the expansive deck beyond. Night had fallen, and I wondered how long I'd been asleep.

Kanta bustled back in, holding a tray of homemade soup and water. I could smell the scent of their mother's old country recipe wafting from it as she set it on my lap.

"Eat," his mother said, taking a seat in the chair across from me.

I didn't argue, scarfing it down along with the homemade bread Kanta had drowned in butter.

"Damn, Harm. I've never seen you eat so fast. That was a bit of a turn on," Slate said when I brought the bowl down from my lips and wiped my face with the back of my hand. I hadn't let a single drop of it go to waste.

"Always the perve, little brother," Kanta teased. "What's going on Harmony?"

Her green eyes were creased with worry, just like her brother's were.

Sitting back, I let Zeke, one of Slate's men, take the tray from me. How did I explain what was happening? There was no way I wouldn't sound like I needed to be locked up.

"Harm." I knew the tone. Slate wanted answers. He wasn't a patient man and the longer he waited, the more agitated he would become. And he'd waited since whenever Callum had contacted him.

Looking down at my hands, I finally said, "Callum didn't hurt me. He loves me." I brought my eyes up to Slate's. "And I love him. And they have him." My voice cracked. The weight of emotion I'd carried from the moment I'd discovered who Callum was, to who I was, to the sight of him bloodied and screaming for me to run came crashing into me. A floodgate broke that I couldn't repair.

Slate sat beside me and took me in his arms, holding me as I fought to regain control. I couldn't be weak now because Callum couldn't be. I had to be strong for him. Wiping my tears away, I pushed from Slate's arms.

"I'm fine. I'm sorry, it's been a long few days."

Slate tipped my chin, searching my eyes.

"I'll be okay," I lied, knowing if this ended badly, I wouldn't be okay. That he'd be holding me while my life drifted away, my heart shattered and empty, my soul screaming for its other half until it withered away to nothing.

"Tell us what happened, sweetie," Kanta said. She'd always been like a big sister to me. She'd been the one who had dragged me to the yoga class, saying I needed to be more centered. "Give her some room, Slate."

He gave me a kiss on my forehead before rising and taking his position across from me, arms over his chest, emotions hidden again. Why did I always fall for the men who sheltered their soft sides under hardness and power?

"I'm not sure how to explain it or if you'll even believe me."

"Try us," his mother said, sitting back in the chair.

What was there to lose? Taking a deep breath, I began at the beginning, telling them everything but leaving out the intimate moments. When I was through, I looked up from my hands. Their eyes were wide. Slate's mother was pale. I'd never seen her look so frightened.

Even Slate seemed shaken. His jaw was tight, his lips pursed as he stared at me.

No one said anything, the silence stretching an uncomfortably long time.

"I told you, you wouldn't believe me," I muttered.

"It's not that we don't believe you," Slate started. "It's that… fuck, Harm, Shadows? The fucking Shadow are hunting you, and Callum is one?"

"That's the scariest part? Not the fact that the gods are hunting her? That the Goddess wants Harmony dead?"

"Fuck you, Kanta. There's a lot to unpack in that story. I picked one part."

Kanta rose, and the two started arguing. They were both pig-headed, more like oil and water than brother and sister.

"Quiet, you two," their mother said. "Slate, what did Callum tell you to do when he called you?"

"He called you?" I asked, trying to figure out when he had.

"Yes. He told me you were in trouble and if you came to me, I was to take you in. Like I wouldn't do that anyway. Said I needed to be ready, to have everything locked down. He made it sound like a war was coming. Shit, a war is coming, isn't it?"

"Yes, and it's one you can't fight," I said. "It's not just the Shadow. The Goddess has the Guard hunting me. They're like Shadow on steroids and then the Torch are hunting me. They all want me dead and if Callum couldn't fight them, neither can we."

Slate wiped his face and started pacing. He reminded me of Callum, and my heart wrenched.

"Boss, we have a situation," Zeke said suddenly.

Slate's head snapped up, the fighter in him ready.

"There's movement on the outer gates, but the men can't get a look at what it is."

Zeke brought his finger to his earpiece, his expression turning deadly. "We need to move now. Three men are down—"

He didn't have time to finish. The glass in the windows burst forth, Belkair landing crouched before he stood, his wings stretching. Bullets were flying, but they didn't faze him. A Torch landed next to him, her white wings extended, blonde hair shimmering in the moonlight.

Slate grabbed me and started running, but the wall crumbled. Another Torch landed in front of us, his wings blocking the way. Slate shoved me behind him and began firing his gun. Bullet after bullet sank into the Torch's flesh, but the wounds healed within seconds.

"Mortals and your weak weapons. I prefer steel. It rips the skin deeper and faster," the Torch said.

He pulled a dagger similar to Callum's out and raised it at Slate.

"No!" I yelled as I stepped in front of him. The dagger plunged into me with a burn that tore a ragged scream from my throat and shattered the remaining glass.

"Dammit, Helios!"

I didn't know whose voice it was as I stumbled back into Slate.

"All of you, stop and drop your weapons. Helios, put your fucking dagger away!" Belkair yelled. I didn't understand why he would say something like that, but my wound was too deep to worry about anything else.

"You don't command me, Belkair. You're lucky I'm here."

"You're here because we needed to see," the female said as Slate lowered me to the floor.

The pain in my chest was so intense, I was having trouble concentrating on their voices.

"She's not healing. I thought she was Trinity's child?" Her voice held a desperate pain to it that made me turn my head in her direction.

"She is, according to Callum."

"Callum?" I mumbled, struggling to breathe.

"Somebody help her, dammit." Slate sounded broken as his hands pressed to my wound.

The female Torch came over to me. She threw a nasty look at the other Torch who shrugged before she kneeled next to me.

"Don't touch her," Slate snarled, hovering over me.

"It's okay, Slate. I think…" Something in her eyes gave me reassurance that she wouldn't kill me. If she wanted to, I would have already been dead. There would have been no reason for Belkair to stop the other Torch from finishing the job unless it had to be by his hand. But he hadn't moved from his spot.

"She's right," she said. "I won't hurt her, not if she really is Trinity's daughter. Show us who you are, little fledgling." Her voice was soft and left me drifting with the melody of it.

"Damn, Torch, that's not helping. Move aside." Belkair pushed her away, and she growled at him. "Fuck off, Triana," he grumbled, eyeing her. His presence ruined my calm, jarring me back to the pain that was flaring through my chest. She grasped her dagger and Belkair took a step closer to her.

"Stand down, Belkair," Helios said. "This isn't about you or even us. This is about Harmony."

Belkair gave him a side glance before turning his attention

back to me and saying, "Heal the damned wound. Callum's life lies in the balance. I risked everything to come here, as did they. If you can't prove you're my brother's daughter, then I'll drag his ass back to the Goddess and toss his battered body at her feet."

Brother…Belkair was my father's brother. That meant he was my uncle. The thought was overwhelming and would have had me desperate to question him, but for the one statement that eased the pain in my chest and made everything else seem irrelevant. "Callum's alive?"

"Of course he is. He said you're fated, you would have sensed it if he died…unless he lied about that, too. Fucking Shadow will suffer if he did."

"No, no, don't hurt him anymore." I heard the desperation in my voice, not liking how weak I sounded.

"Then heal yourself and show us who you are," Belkair groused.

"Stop bullying her. Heal her yourself, asshole," Slate said.

I squeezed his hand, hoping he wouldn't say anything more. These were vicious hunters, not some thugs on the street. Belkair's head snapped up, and I recognized the lethal glare coming from his eyes. My heartbeat quickened, causing my pain to intensify. Slate was dead if I didn't do something.

"It's okay, Slate. I'll try to heal," I said. "I'm still slow at it. Just leave Slate be, and don't hurt anyone else."

Belkair looked back down at me, his eyes hard and unemotional.

"Stop staring at her. You're making her nervous," Triana said, pulling him back. He swiveled to her, a dagger to her neck. Helios attacked him, throwing him off her, the two fighting viciously. Everyone in the room backed away, Kanta holding her mother close to her as they stood in a corner.

"Whatever you need to do, Harmony, you'd better do it before they kill everyone here," Slate whispered to me.

The two Torch and Belkair were fighting now, the walls cracking as their bodies hit against them. I tuned it all out, finding my core again, reaching in deep to the glow within me and perceiving how the magic tingled on my skin.

"Shit," Slate muttered as my wound healed.

The three hadn't noticed, even as Slate helped me up. His eyes were so large he looked like the young boy I'd met on the playground that day. I gave him a quick kiss on the cheek, saying, "I think this is my situation to handle now."

Turning, I put my hands on my hips, letting my wings spread the length of the room and hearing Slate and his family gasp.

"If you three could stop being shitheads for a minute, I have your proof."

They glanced at me, all three freezing, their expressions changing as they moved apart from each other.

"It's true," Triana breathed, her hand coming to her chest.

"So I've been told," I said, looking around at the mess they'd made. I supposed it was the least of my problems, seeing as I still had an army of supernatural beings hunting me and the gods asking for my head.

Triana came over to me, her hand reaching up tentatively to touch my face. Her fingers lingered in the corner of my eye and that's when I noticed her eyes were the same shade of blue as mine. She smiled, a soft, lovely smile.

"Trinity was my twin. When I lost her, my world fell apart. Helios, come see your niece."

My eyes flickered to Helios, who eyed me with curiosity. His blue eyes were the match to Triana's, his mussy blonde hair only slightly darker. He remained where he was, but Belkair didn't, pushing Triana aside and getting right in my face. He was a formidable presence, towering over me like Callum did. His eyes were dark and hard to read.

"I watched the day the Goddess executed my brother, making me stand by her side as her power burned through him, turning him to ash. His last words to me remain ingrained in my mind. They've driven me mad with every passing year as I tried to understand them. 'She will bring them to their knees.' That's what he told me after saying he wanted to die. He couldn't live without Trinity. They were fated, and he'd felt the moment they'd taken her life." Triana let out the small sound of a stifled cry, but it didn't faze him. "I never understood why Trinity let herself get caught. She was too smart to have fallen into a trap. But she did it for you, didn't she? They both gave up their lives for you."

"I think so," I said in a voice that sounded meek compared to his commanding tone.

I folded my wings in and turned, lifting my shirt and ignoring Slate's protective attempt to stop me.

"It's okay, Slate. They need to see my back to understand."

He nodded, his eyes guarded. I'd laid a lot on him today and now he stood in the presence of legends. The stories we would tell each other when we were growing up, whispering the word Shadow in fear that one would come and gobble us up.

"They hid you," Helios said.

Fingers touched my back, tracing the patterns.

"It's ancient Shadow from the time of the first," Belkair said, a certain awe layering his authoritative tone.

"That's what Callum figured out," I said. "The markings are Shadow. The magic that bound them was Torch. I think the markings bound my wings, the Torch my magic."

I heard the rustle of wings and turned back to see the three without them, no longer in a defensive stance. All looked like three normal people, aside from the menacing expression that never seemed to leave Belkair's face.

He ran a hand through his black hair and looked at the other two.

"What are you doing here, and where's Callum?" I asked, suddenly tired of being inspected.

"Callum is bound and caged at his compound."

"Bound?"

"Yes. Like the markings on your back, a rogue Shadow can have his wings clipped with a binding that weighs them down and locks them in place," he replied.

"Like chains surrounding them," I mumbled, thinking of my dream.

"Exactly. We have the same ability in The Sect, but only the Guard and Sentinel can lay the binding," Triana said.

"I couldn't risk him escaping. He's lucky I believed him or I'd have left his ass locked in a cell awaiting execution."

"Why did you believe him?" I asked Belkair.

"If I hadn't seen you fly away, I wouldn't have. But your wings confirmed his story."

"So you helped him escape?" I asked, unable to believe this man had risked everything for me.

He sighed, his eyes growing softer, although they were still dark. "Landon was my younger brother. He was mine to protect, and I couldn't do it." He dropped his eyes for a moment before meeting mine again and I saw the pain there, pain he hid behind the broody persona. "It was devastating watching him die, but I knew I'd already lost him when he surrendered. Trinity's death had killed the brother I loved. The Goddess merely took what remained of him." The softness left his eyes at the mention of the Goddess. "I miss him every day. There's a part of Landon in you. I see it in your features, in your hair, your wings. I couldn't protect him, couldn't stop fate and the Goddess from taking him from me. You can be damned sure I'll die protecting his daughter."

By his last word, his eyes were cold again, whatever emotion I'd seen now hidden behind the Guard in him. I'd seen the shift too often in Callum to not recognize it. I wanted to hug him but he was too intimidating of a presence and I wasn't sure if his kind hugged.

"After the Guard took Callum, and Krinle reported to the gods that you had gotten away, he came to me," Triana said, giving no notice to the warrior next to her who had just confessed the pain of seeing his brother murdered. "He told me how Callum had fought to save you, about your wings and the suspicion they garnered in him." She paused before adding, "He and I are close—"

"If you call fucking close," Helios muttered.

She jabbed him in the ribcage.

"You're fucking your commander?" Belkair asked, his brow raised.

"Don't your commanders ever fuck? No, you don't, do you? That's why you walk around like you have a stick up your ass," she retorted. I liked her even more now, but Belkair snarled at her.

"Watch your mouth, you dirty Torch, or I'll send you back to your realm for healing."

"Wow, you guys don't like each other, do you?" Slate said.

"They're sworn enemies, just like in the stories, Slate," I explained.

"So what does that make you, Harm?"

What did that make me? Something new, something different, something dangerous. "An anomaly the gods don't want around."

"No, it makes you an example of what happens when we get

along, and that pisses the gods off," Helios said. "When Triana told me about this, I was skeptical. But she's my little sister, as was Trinity, and so I acquiesced. Triana's a bitch when she's unhappy, and she's a pain in my ass if she doesn't get what she wants."

"Probably why Krinle agreed to fuck her," Belkair muttered.

"Don't make me put this dagger in your dick, Guard," Triana snapped.

"I thought our family had friction. You guys make us look like a picnic," Kanta said from across the room.

"We're not family," Belkair complained.

"But you are now," she said. "Harmony connects the three of you, making you family."

They all looked at her. None of them appeared happy about what she'd said.

"Huh, Harmony, that's the perfect name for you," Kanta mused, her green eyes calculating.

"It was the name my parents gave me. The one instruction they left with me when they left me as a baby."

"Harmony," Helios repeated.

Triana's eyes shimmered with understanding. "A peace between Shadow and Torch."

"Created with their love and embodied in me," I said, experiencing an unusual connection to my parents.

Slate's hand came to my shoulder. I reached up and squeezed it. Belkair raised his brow.

"It's not what you think," I said quickly, knowing his thoughts just from that one look.

"I'd suggest if we make it through this, you remember not to touch her again," he warned with a smirk. "Callum isn't someone you want on your bad side, and I guarantee that hand would not remain attached if he were here right now."

"I can handle Callum," Slate said with too much confidence.

Belkair's lips twitched, and I suspected he was holding in a laugh. "I highly doubt that," he said.

"Speaking of Callum, can I see him?" I asked, excitement tingling in me at the thought. I needed to see him, to confirm that he was safe and unharmed. To have his arms around me again.

"In due time. Right now, we need you hidden and locked down where the gods can't find you."

"And with us around, you've got three beacons sending them your signal when they realize Callum's gone," Helios said.

"Shit, Callum said we were to move you to my safe house." Slate looked around nervously.

Belkair shook his head. "That won't help."

"Callum's compound?" I asked.

"No, we breached the last one," he said.

"Then why can't you put a spell on Slate's like Callum does on his?" I really didn't understand this magic thing, but that seemed the simplest solution.

"The sneaky shit. That's how he's been hiding from us? I'm surprised Gerrand lets him get away with that," Helios muttered.

"Shadow have always been better than you Torch," Belkair said. "Though few have ever been as sharp as Callum. I'd venture to say Gerrand doesn't know about all his compounds or how he stays hidden when he's in the mortal world."

I smiled, thinking about him. "No, I'd say he doesn't."

Belkair gave me a slight grin before hiding it below his rough exterior. "You two go back to The Sect."

Helios balked at the order. "I'm not a fucking Torch, asshole. And we're staying. She's our family, too."

"Fucking Sentinel. I don't need you or the Torch underfoot while I'm trying to protect her."

I wasn't sure what a Sentinel was, but I thought maybe it was the equivalent of the Guard. Helios held himself differently from

Triana, more like Belkair did. "We'll be protecting her, too," he snarled.

"You're lucky I didn't send you both back to your realm when I spotted you," Belkair groused.

Triana put her hands on her hips and moved in front of Belkair. "I'd have liked to have seen you try. You Guard are all the same, and your Shadow are the worst."

"Enough, you three," Slate's mother said, bustling forward. "You're wasting time with your bickering. Slate, tell your men to ready the cars—"

"Cars? We don't need cars," Helios argued.

"Yes, you do. If the gods can sense you, having those wings out will only make it easier. Slate, get the cars. We head for the safe house like we planned. That's what Callum told you to do, right?"

"Right."

"Then we stick to the plan and don't let these three muck it up." They grumbled but Slate's mother was a spitfire and even at her tiny five-foot frame, she was a force to be reckoned with. "You three will fortify the building, then you," she pointed to Belkair, "will get Callum and bring him to her."

The three of them looked taken aback, even Belkair.

"Get moving, all of you!"

Slate motioned to one of his men and before I knew it, he had me tucked in the back of a dark sedan, barreling down the road and wedged between Belkair and Helios. If my life had seemed surreal before, it had taken an entirely new turn. My mind couldn't grasp what had just happened and how I now sat between these two massive burly uncles, my aunt gabbing away in the front seat on Slate's lap. Slate's baffled expression had amused me when she'd insisted she sit there because she didn't want to be left out.

As I stared out at the road before us, I tried to ignore the looming threat, and the reality of what these three new additions to my life meant for me. Instead, I concentrated on the pattering of my heart as it beat in anticipation of seeing Callum again.

CHAPTER 21
CALLUM

I hadn't expected Belkair to bind me again when I'd led him to my compound to discuss the plan. I'd wanted to go with him to get Harmony, but he insisted I stay. That's when I knew he still had doubts. He wanted to see her up close, to study her before he turned his back on the gods and became a traitor like me. Binding me and leaving me behind was his assurance that he could make some excuse for leaving the realm.

I knew how he thought. He was like me—sharp, calculating, cold. If things went sour, he'd kill Harmony and take me back, claiming I was bait to lure her out. It was exactly what I would have done. He'd left me tied to a chair in an uncomfortable position, and I planned to show him how unhappy I was about it when he finally freed me.

The wait was unbearable. As each minute ticked by, the worry grew. There was a digital clock on the wall across from me, making the wait even more miserable because it wasn't moving fast enough. After a few hours I'd about given up hope, cursing myself for believing Belkair would sacrifice for her, when the air stirred. He walked to me as he appeared, his wings curling into him.

"She's safe. She's locked down in Slate's safe house. Triana and Helios are guarding her."

"What?" I erupted as he freed me. I grabbed his dagger and brought it to his throat, slamming him against the wall.

"Krinle told them about her, and they were curious. They know who she is, Callum, and trust me, if Triana has anything to say about it, nothing will touch her. She's about as possessive of her as you are."

I pushed the dagger into his skin. "No one is as possessive of her as I am. If she's hurt, I will rip your feathers out one by one and stuff them down your throat as I slice your heart out."

"You Shadow are always so dramatic," he groused, shrugging me away.

"Fuck you."

"I'll pass, asshole."

"Take me to her now or I'll show you how dramatic I can be."

His eyes bore into me as he grabbed me. His magic took us from my compound and dropped me in a hallway lit with a trail of lights along the floor. I turned to him, shrugging his grip from my shoulder. I hated it when I couldn't travel with my magic. Having someone else's magic on my skin irritated my senses.

There was something else agitating me, and I frowned. "Torch magic? You fortified his safe house with Torch magic?"

"I used what we could. Between the three of us, it's hidden."

"Where are we, and what is it with those lights?" I said, looking around at the lights that ran along the floor of the hallway.

"Seems the Slate fellow has some eclectic decorating preferences. He told her to get some rest, but I doubt she's sleeping. She's in that room." He gestured to a door a few feet from us.

"He has his men stationed at both ends of the hall and throughout the house. Helios is on the perimeter with more of Slate's men scouting the area."

"So, she's locked down."

"As well as we could. She's safe, Callum."

"She's not safe. But she will be."

He snatched my arm. "You couldn't protect her when we came for her."

"No?" I said, with a lift of my brow. "She's still alive, isn't she?"

I jerked free and walked toward the door, where I could sense her presence.

"I'll give you a few hours, Callum. Then you're on duty."

Stopping, I glanced back at him. "I'm not one of yours to command, Belkair."

"You weren't, but now you are. Consider yourself my second."

Gritting my teeth, I replied, "I'm no one's second, but I'll be there as long as you remember this is my show now."

"You're not the only one with something to lose," he said.

"No, but I'm the one with the most to lose."

I entered the room silently, spying Harmony in front of the window, her eyes scanning the sky. I took a moment to look at her, my heart complete again just from being in her presence. Her legs were bare, my sweatshirt hanging loosely on her and just covering her upper thighs. She had her arms wrapped around her waist, as if letting go would send her tumbling to the ground. Seeing her like that hurt because she didn't look like the strong woman I loved, and I knew the worry and fear had gotten to her. Quietly, I closed the door and walked toward her.

"Are you standing in front of an open window with your legs out for everyone to see?"

She spun, her expression one I'd hold in my memory

forever. It was a blend of relief and excitement, her eyes large in disbelief, her smile lighting every aspect of her beautiful face.

"Callum," she said breathlessly as I moved to her, taking her in my arms and kissing her before she could say another word.

Nothing in my life had ever been as comforting as that kiss. It was like returning home. My body woke, the stress lifting from me, my mind calming. I backed her against the window, taking her face in my hands and scanning her, a part of me not believing she was back in my arms. She was doing the same, touching my face, then my body in every place where my injuries had been, her fingers shaking.

"I was so scared," she murmured, her fingers grazing below my shirt and causing my stomach to clench in anticipation of her touches.

"I'm fine. I'm here and I'm not going anywhere again."

Her eyes searched mine, looking for any sign of doubt.

"You promise? Because I don't think I can take it again. I need you here with me. Otherwise, I don't think I'll survive next time."

She looked so wounded, and I hated that I'd done that to her.

"I promise you, Harmony, I won't leave your side again. I will die before I do."

I brushed my knuckles over her cheek, lingering on her lips, my eyes lost in the endless blue of hers. The tightness in my chest was uncomfortable because it bucked against the tough Shadow in me. But Harmony brought out the softer side of me, the part I'd never allowed to surface, having no one who meant enough to me to give it that freedom before her.

She leaned against me, and I held her in my arms, feeling the soft beats of her heart and the calm, steady rise and fall of her breaths. Those small things were precious to me, and I nestled my face in her hair, breathing in her scent. I didn't want to let her go, and, by the way she was clinging to me, I could tell she felt the same way.

"I promise, sweetheart," I murmured, knowing it was the truth. No matter what happened, I didn't think I could bring myself to ever leave her side again. Being away from her had been worse than having my wings bound.

I tipped her face up to look at her again, soaking in the sight of her once more. As her fingers traced my jaw, I said, "You did it, sweetheart. You spread your wings and flew, and I don't think I've ever seen a sight that rivaled your naked body until that moment."

A light blush filled her cheeks. "I did! It was exhilarating, Callum. I flew so high and they did just what you said they would."

I remembered the thrill of my first flight. Even after all these centuries, there was nothing like it.

"You can show me again when we get out of this mess."

"And you'll fly with me?" There was an innocence in her voice that made me smile.

"Shadows of my rank don't mingle with newbies, sweetheart," I teased, nipping at her bottom lip when it pouted.

She raised a brow and tipped her head back, eying me. "Considering my pedigree, don't I pull rank on you?"

My laughter felt good, and I loved that my feisty, confident mate was playing again.

"There's no way you're pulling rank on me, baby. You're just a kid with wings compared to me." The truth of that statement should have bothered me, but it didn't because she was my fated, regardless of how much older I was. I ran my hands down her body. "But I'd be happy to let you prove yourself worthy of that rank."

She looked like she was about to snap back. I could see the jealousy in her eyes, the possessive mate wondering how many

Shadow I'd made that offer to. Shaking my head, I skirted my fingers up her sweatshirt, intent on shutting that thought down with a pinch, but my fingers hit something that immediately changed my mood. I looked down, pushing her back as I noticed the dried blood. I lifted the torn bloody spot in the center of her chest, my heart in my throat.

"Who hurt you?" I snarled, meeting her eyes.

"I'm fine. I healed. Helios stabbed me."

My blood boiled, a low feral growl rumbling through my chest. The need to punish him for daring to touch her, let alone hurt her, overtook every thought. "I'll kill him."

"It healed, and he didn't mean to. He was trying to kill Slate. It was chaotic when they arrived—bullets, wings, knives."

Her words didn't relieve the need I had to rip the Sentinel to shreds. It would be a fierce fight. Sentinel were the equivalent of Guard in The Sect. But it was a fight I'd win because no one touched my mate.

"Callum." I registered her words, but the white-hot searing heat that had overcome me didn't let me do anything but think of horrible ways to end him.

But Harmony knew me too well, her hand finding its way down my pants, stroking me until my attention shifted.

"Don't kill him, but you're welcome to take that aggression out on me," she purred.

Desire roared through me, taking the anger and possessiveness and transforming it into an insatiable need for her. I pushed her against the window, her sharp inhale stirring my need for her. Thoughts of her wound fled as she applied more pressure to my hard-on.

"I need you inside of me, Callum, as close as I can have you. I need you to remind me I'm yours."

"Did you forget?" I asked, kissing her neck and gliding my hands up the shirt to caress her bare breasts below the material.

"Never."

Her word sent my cock jumping in her hand. Lifting the sweatshirt from her, I threw it aside. I pushed my shirt off as she unzipped my pants, freeing my length, her lips parting as mine smashed into hers. She worked my pants down and I kicked them the rest of the way before I pinned her hands above her head.

"Were you really standing in front of this window with nothing on but a sweatshirt and panties? Showing the legs I own to everyone out there?"

"It's dark in here. They can't see in."

"No? Helios is out there, and I guarantee he can see in. Another reason I'll need to kill him when I see him."

"Eww, he's my uncle."

"One who only just met you and I can promise you, even he's taking in the sight of your naked back against this window and that perfectly curved ass below these tiny lace panties. We have exceptional sight, sweetheart."

"That's gross."

"Should I mention the four men Slate has positioned outside your window?" I asked, licking her neck.

"I know they can't see in."

"You'd be surprised what a man can do when a half-naked woman is present."

She pressed her pelvis against me. "Should we give them a show?"

"Fuck, baby. I don't want to share this body with anyone."

"It's not sharing if they're only watching. Stake your claim on me, Callum. Mark my body so they all know I'm yours."

The idea of anyone seeing her body made me see red, but there was a part of me that found the idea of them watching as I owned her tantalizing. Making it known that no one would touch my girl, that no one made her come like I did.

Her hands slid up my chest, and she pulled my bottom lip between her teeth.

"Fuck it. I want you too badly to worry about curtains." I flipped her and ripped her panties off before yanking her hips back and plunging into her. Her cry was amazing, and I yanked her head back, my hand twisted into her hair, eliciting another cry. Slamming her up against the glass so any of them could see her entire body, I drew her back to my chest, bringing my hand up her stomach and over her breasts until I had it firmly wrapped around her neck. Her moan was like chains on my dick. Knowing she would wreck me completely if I continued, I slipped from her and dipped my fingers between her legs.

"Come for me, baby. Show the world how you fall apart for me."

Her groan was my reward, her body trembling in my hands. I tightened my grip around her neck, and she bucked. I was so hard by now I was throbbing to be buried back inside of her, but I needed her closer, right on the edge of her climax, so I could feel her come around me. Dropping my hand to her breasts, I pulled at her nipple, getting it so hard my mouth salivated to have it between my teeth. I bit down on her shoulder, trying to calm my need as I continued to bring her closer to her edge. Her body was quivering, her breathing coming in shortened heaves, and I knew she was ready to break.

Just as she was on the brink of surrendering to her body's need, I jerked her hips, my hand pressing her back down as I plunged into her. She came undone, her hands curling into fists as her climax hit her with a force that had her clenching around me. I grunted from the intensity of it, her muscles spasming so tight that it almost sent me tumbling with her. I fought it, needing more of her before I gave in.

"Callum," she cried.

"That's it, baby. Scream my name so they all know who you belong to."

I pounded into her harder, squeezing her hips and thrusting her back into me with each dip of my pelvis. As much as I loved fucking her this way, I wanted her skin on mine. Freeing from her, and chuckling at her mewling protest, I turned her and shoved her against the window. I picked her up by the ass, my fingers digging into her soft skin before I buried myself in her.

"Gods, you're so wet, baby." She dug her heels into my back in response.

I wanted her to come again, to have her fall apart in my arms before I finally gave in. She arched her back, her breast filling my mouth as I continued to thrust into her. Her climax was rising. I noticed it in the quiver of her legs and the way her stomach muscles were tightening. I sucked and pulled at her nipple, walking my fingers to her ass and sliding one inside. Her reaction made me jerk inside of her.

"Damn, sweetheart, I think I'll take that ass again tonight before I'm done with you."

Her moan reverberated through her chest. Rolling my tongue around her nipple, I tipped her pelvis, thrusting deeper until she screamed my name. Her climax overcame her, and her muscles clasped around me so tight it destroyed me. My orgasm washed over me in waves that drowned me repeatedly, and I pushed my essence into her until there was nothing left. Her body went limp in my arms, her breaths coming in rapid pants. I remained there until the muscles in my legs stopped quivering. Walking her to the bed, I lowered her, bringing myself over her and kissing her.

I didn't give a fuck who was watching anymore. If they'd made it through that show without wanking off, they were stronger than me. I'd kill them all in the morning for finding pleasure in my girl's body. For now, I was going to make love to my fated before I fucked her again. It had been a long day, and I needed her to replenish me, to refuel me in ways only she could.

"I love you, sweetheart," I muttered in her ear.

"You just love the way I come for you," she teased.

"Oh, I love that, too. Now spread those luscious legs for me because I want to hear you scream my name a few more times, so everyone knows there's only one name that will ever fall from your lips again."

"Gods, I love you, Callum."

"Spread, baby, and come for me again."

I took her again, making love to her like it was my first time touching her. Memorizing every curve, every sigh until my body couldn't hold on any longer and ecstasy took me in its hold. It was a place I never wanted to leave, because this was my place, in Harmony's arms with her body against me, her heart entwined with mine, our souls as one. As she took the lead from me, claiming every inch of me again and forcing her name from my lips, I knew I had finally found my reason for living. After centuries of looking, I'd found it in Harmony.

CHAPTER 22
HARMONY

Callum left after ravaging me. He'd been insatiable, but then, so had I. We hadn't been apart long, but it had seemed like forever. His every touch had brought me to an ecstasy that only continued to grow each time he took me. And oh, how he'd taken me. Being pressed against the window, vulnerable and exposed, had been exhilarating. And although it had been an unguarded moment, being with Callum erased that feeling. I was never weak with him around. He strengthened me with just his presence. The way he let me take control when I needed to, empowering me to rule him just as he did me, was intoxicating. He knew me, even after this brief time, better than any lover I'd ever had.

I pulled my knees up to my chin, thinking about him. He was patrolling the inside of the house; I was certain he wouldn't have gone outside, especially not after what he'd told me about being detected beyond a spelled compound. Helios and Triana had taken turns scouring the outer grounds before I'd gone to bed. The gods and their warriors weren't hunting them like they were Callum, and likely Belkair.

I couldn't get over how drastically my life had changed. Within days, I'd fallen in love with my fated mate, discovered a hidden past, a new identity, and now a family. Slate had been the only family I'd ever known, he and Kanta and their mother. Now, I had two uncles and an aunt, and parents I wasn't ashamed to claim anymore. I belonged to someone. I belonged to Callum.

Shivering at the thought of him, my legs clenched, and I knew I needed to get out of the room or thoughts of him would lead to me satisfying my need for him. A need that should have abated but never seemed to. It was a constant burning for his touch.

Rising, I rinsed myself off and threw some clothes on. I had brought none, so Kanta had given me some of hers. She had a smaller build than me, and her leggings left nothing to the imagination when I pulled them on. They gave camel toe a whole new meaning. The T-shirt she'd given me was a size too small and hugged my curves, my breasts popping over the low neckline. My stomach was showing since the waistband of the leggings sat low on my long waist. I glanced in the mirror, wondering if Callum would block me from everyone's sight for how sexy I looked.

"Definitely not my usual style, but damn, I make it work."

Throwing my hair up in a clip she'd given me, I made my way from the room, determined to have her give me a sweater when I finally found her. Zeke eyed me as I made my way down the hall, a devious grin on his face.

"I'm guessing you had ground duty earlier," I asked as I passed him, the reality of what we'd done starting to settle in.

"Quite the show, Harmony. It's a wonder Slate gave you up. I knew you were sexy, but damn. I had to change my pants when I got in."

"Don't let Callum hear you say that. You'll be lucky if he lets you live if he finds out you watched."

Maybe the window action wasn't the turn on I thought it was. Callum was going to flip. I was sure he had considered nothing but making a statement when he'd slammed me against that window.

"I think your boy wanted us to watch, Harmony. He was staking his claim and daring any of us to even think about touching you. Not that I wasn't thinking about it with my hand on my dick."

I cringed. That's exactly what Callum had been doing. And now he'd be a possessive, angry mate I'd have to keep from killing everyone.

"That's great, Zeke," I replied with a roll of my eyes. "Glad you enjoyed the show."

"It's a memory I won't forget. But let's keep all that to ourselves. Your man intimidates even me."

I threw him a wink and put my finger to my lips. Zeke was one of Slate's longest standing henchmen and I knew he'd lay down his life for me just as he would for Slate. I didn't care that he'd watched. The guy worked 24/7; he needed a treat now and then. It was Callum I worried about.

Shaking my head, I continued down the hall. The living room was empty, so I made my way to the kitchen, knowing Slate wouldn't be sleeping. He'd be too on edge and sleep was something he barely did anyway.

"Well, well. If it isn't the little performer," Kanta teased.

I stuck my tongue out at her.

"Did you use that on him?" she asked, laughing. "I heard it was him using you. Something about the window and amazing tits. Nothing about your mouth except the scream you made when you came."

Slate was staring at the knife in his hand, carving it into the island. He was strangely quiet, which unnerved me.

"Aren't you going to chime in, Slate?" I asked.

He slowly lifted his head, his eyes dark. "About how that prick had my girl spread-eagle in the window for my men to see as she got her brains fucked out?"

He was in a mood.

"First of all, I'm not your girl. I think we've had that conversation many a time."

"We have," he said, rising from the stool. "And I think I've made it clear you'll always be my girl."

"She's no longer your fucking girl and if you call her that again, I'll pull your internal organs out one by one while you watch me." Callum's baritone cut the quiet of the room, adding a weight to the air that spoke of angst and possessiveness.

Slate didn't back down as Callum eyed me, his gaze taking in every exposed curve. He licked his lips and pulled me to him, kissing me with a hunger that clawed at my soul. I teetered when he let me go. He moved behind me and wrapped his arm around my waist before kissing my neck.

Slate's face held a mix of envy and animosity, his hands gripping his knife so hard I worried the handle would shatter.

"Woah, this just got tense," Kanta muttered, moving from where she'd been leaning on the counter. She started rummaging through the cabinets.

"You put her on display like that again, and I'll fill you with so many holes you won't have time to pull a knife on me," Slate snarled, moving closer to us.

Callum brought his other arm around my neck so that he had me wedged protectively in his hold.

"Who said I'd need a knife to kill you?"

"Damn, would you two stop?" I protested, knowing this could only lead to something disastrous. I tried shrugging from Callum's hold, but he only tightened it.

"This guy comes in, demands to see you, steals you off to some secret location and suddenly your life is in danger?" Slate grumbled, gesturing to Callum with his knife. "How long have you known me, Harm? Have I ever put you in danger?"

"No," I said, rolling my eyes. "But it wasn't Callum's doing."

"The fuck it wasn't. If he'd stayed away, you'd still be safe."

"If I'd stayed away, she'd be dead by now," Callum argued. "The only reason she's still alive is because she's mine." I could feel the muscles in his arms bulging and the way his abs had hardened behind me.

"Harm, this guy is dangerous."

"You're dangerous, Slate, and that never stopped me," I argued.

Callum's arm tensed. Any mention of Slate bothered him, and now the man who had once owned me stood across from him. But Slate had never owned me the way Callum did.

"I'm not yours anymore, Slate."

"She was never yours," Callum growled, the sound soaking me every time he made it. "She belonged to me long before your young ass was even born."

I threw Callum a 'you're not helping' look over my shoulder and heard Kanta snicker.

"This is great," she muttered, opening a bag of cheddar popcorn.

"Are you really eating popcorn?" I asked, giving her an irritated stare.

"Damn right I am. There's enough testosterone in here to turn me straight. I swear if that man's arms bulge one more time, I'm gonna grab one of Slate's men and make him ease this ache I have." She glanced at the ceiling, a devious look on her face, "Or maybe I'll just see if that sexy Torch is around. I'd like to sink my tongue into her. I bet she tastes delicious."

Slate turned to her and Callum tensed even more.

"I'd go down on you, Harm," she continued, oblivious to the

increased tension in the air, "but he doesn't look like the sharing type, and you never were into letting me taste what Slate got to savor all those years ago."

The bulge that pressed against me had me as wet as Kanta's words. She knew how to tease, and apparently it had worked on Callum.

"See, he'd be into it," she said, scooping some popcorn and throwing it in her mouth.

"No, he wouldn't," Callum grumbled. "I don't share."

"Mm-hmm, not what that tension in your neck says." She wiped her hands together, the cheese remnants falling onto the floor from where she had positioned herself on the counter.

"Or that hard-on," I muttered, elbowing him.

He squeezed my waist tighter and dropped his mouth to my ear. "I was imagining my tongue sunk into that wet pussy, baby. No other tongue gets to taste my nectar."

"Good gods, I'm done," Kanta said, throwing her hands in the air. "I think I saw Zeke down here. I'll have a go at him since there aren't any free pussies around here to play with."

"Harm's never been into that, Kanta," Slate said as she hopped from the counter. There was a distinct sneer to his words, and I knew Callum had pushed him. "She prefers a cock in her mouth, don't you, Harm?"

Callum's chest rumbled against my back as Kanta left the room. This macho toxicity was too much, but Callum was in no mood for me to bring that up.

"You like how she doesn't make a sound when she's blowing you, Montrose?"

Callum remained silent, but I noted the strain in his muscles as he held back from hurting Slate. Shit, between the two of them, this was getting ugly. Two possessive men who both held distinct parts of my heart.

"Took her some practice," Slate moved closer, daring to

reach his hand out to touch my cheek, "but she can take it all now without a single gag. Makes the ride last longer and hitting the back of that pretty throat for that long makes for an amazing fuck."

Callum's arm snapped from around me and grabbed him by the neck. I didn't know how he'd moved so quickly, but he had Slate pinned against the island before I could even react.

"She gags beautifully when I'm ramming down her throat. Guess she needed the right man fucking her mouth. She comes amazingly while I'm spilling down her throat, too. Bet she didn't do that for you either."

He let go of Slate's neck and walked back to me. I expected Slate to do something rash, but he let out a belly laugh instead. Callum stopped, his brow creasing.

"Damn, Callum. I guess she is all yours. She is amazing when she's coming, though. Fuck, I miss that."

"You two need to stop talking about me like I'm not here," I complained. I didn't mind the claim of ownership I'd let Callum have over me, but I wasn't keen on being dragged into his macho attempt to one up Slate. And Slate's behavior had my jaw ticking because he knew better than to pull that toxic shit. "Besides, don't you have Mandy or Missy or whatever her name is for that?" I said, waiting for Callum's tension to leave his shoulders. I grabbed his shirt and pulled him to me, exerting my claim of ownership over him. Sliding my leg along his, I kissed him, forgetting my irritation at him when his hand caught my leg. He cupped my breast and caressed my ass, making me wish we hadn't left the room.

"No, the bitch is miserable in the sack, and I told you, she gags way too much to last long enough to enjoy it. Can't even take me all the way. And don't get me started on the fucking," he said, leaning on the island.

"Why do you keep her around if she's not worth the fuck?"

Callum asked, finally relaxing. He repositioned himself behind me again, his hand still cupping my breast below the shirt. He was staking his claim again, and this time, Slate didn't bat an eye. The asshole had been testing him, seeing if he could play his game, and he had. Men, I didn't understand them, no matter how much I loved them.

"She's got a nice ass. It's tight, and she lets me take it when I want it. I'll put up with her until I find something more interesting. That chick with the wings is pretty hot."

"Triana?" Callum sounded sick when he said her name. "She's a Torch."

"Hey, I'm half Torch," I said, swatting his arm.

"Yeah, but that Shadow half is enough for me to tolerate the other half."

I tried to slip from his hold, but he pinched my nipple. I had to bite back the groan, and Slate only shook his head and grinned.

"Damn, who am I to argue with that? She's yours, Montrose."

"I never doubted she was."

Slate hopped on the island and stabbed a few pieces of popcorn that had fallen from Kanta's bag with his knife. "So, guess this means you no longer need those businesses your invested in?"

"Who said that?" Callum asked.

"Eh, just seems you're preoccupied now. If you need to divest a few of your interests, I'd be happy to take them off your hands."

"So, you go from some macho possessive play on me to business talk?" I asked, confused as to what direction this conversation was going.

"You're mine to protect, Harm," he answered, causing Callum's hand to tighten around my breast. I jumped slightly.

"Always have been, and like I said, you'll always be my girl, whether or not Montrose agrees. So, if this is the guy you're gonna go down with and on, he's gotta pass through me first."

"I don't have to pass through anyone," Callum gritted, the air thickening with tension again.

"Back down. I approve, but I don't like the exhibitionism. Harmony's body isn't one to share, no matter how exquisite it is."

"I made my point and there won't be another who ever dares touch her."

"Because you've made it known she's yours. I like how you work, Montrose. Just don't do it with my girl again or I'll plug you full of so many holes you'll be bleeding for weeks."

"Enough, you two," I said as Callum's teeth ground in my ear. "Slate, I remember a few times when you made it clear I was yours when we were younger. You were never shy about fucking me wherever you wanted."

He lifted a brow, his lips turning to a sly grin at the same time as Callum's hand dropped to my waist, squeezing my hip painfully. There was so much tension in his body, I thought he might burst. There was no questioning how possessive he was.

"No, I wasn't, was I? My favorite was the time you dropped to your knees behind the bar. That was before I bought it and if my boss hadn't enjoyed the show so much, he would have fired me on the spot."

Callum squeezed tighter.

"Ouch," I complained.

"If you say another word, Slate, I'll cut your tongue out and shove it up your ass so far you'll be coming on it."

"Someone's a little possessive." He hopped down just as Belkair stormed into the room.

"There you are," Belkair snarled, attacking Callum and ripping him from me.

He slammed Callum so hard into the wall that the plaster cracked. Callum fought back as I jumped out of the way, Slate pulling me to the corner of the kitchen. Callum punched Belkair, and the two began a fight that was a flurry of wings and moves I could barely follow. I screamed as Belkair grabbed Callum by the neck and punched him into the floor, the tile breaking.

"Fucking Shadow," Belkair said through gritted teeth. "You fucking do something like that again with her, and I'll tear your wings from you."

Callum gave him a devious smile and sprung to his feet, flipping Belkair onto the island, which toppled from the force.

"That's gonna be expensive to replace," Slate complained.

I thought it had been bad when Slate and Callum had been going at it, but now there were three overprotective men in the room and the testosterone was overwhelming.

"You're getting slow, old man. Too much time kissing ass to the gods and not hunting," Callum snarled.

Belkair kicked him away, but Callum landed on his feet, his wings spread behind him. I took the moment to look closer at him. He was beautiful, a beautiful killing machine. And he was mine. The thought caused a flutter in my belly.

They circled each other, Belkair pulling a weapon and Callum pulling his.

"Are we really going to do this, Guard?"

"I've wanted to do this for a long time, Shadow."

"Am I missing something?" Slate whispered to me.

"There's animosity between the Guard and Shadow." Callum had made enough snide remarks about the Guard while we'd been training to lead me to believe the gods viewed the Guard as stronger than the Shadow. The Shadow resented it since they did all the dirty work and the Guard never left the realm.

"You think?" Slate said, sarcasm underscoring his words.

"Remind me to have you explain the difference between a Guard and a Shadow when they aren't tearing up my home."

Belkair leaped, and the two began a vicious fight that toppled the remaining furniture and almost brought down a wall. It was frustrating to watch because I wanted them to stop. Slate was on edge, cursing each time they broke something. By now, the table was in pieces and the chairs looked like kindling.

Callum had Belkair by the wings, his knives drawn when Helios stormed in. He grabbed Callum by the neck and bashed him face first into the floor. Belkair looked stunned as Callum lifted himself and turned to Helios, his lips in a snarl, his eyes dark, the hazel almost completely brown.

"Fucking Sentinel, I'll send you back to your realm in pieces," he growled.

"Fuck off, Shadow. You really think I wanted a show while I was out there stuck on sentry duty?"

"You saw it, too?" Belkair asked Helios as Callum wiped blood from his face. "Gods be dammed, Callum, I'm going to send you back to The Blight and let the Goddess have you."

Callum glared at him, his muscles so strained they were bulging.

Helios ignored the deadly hunter in front of him, replying to Belkair, "Gods, yes. Fucking sexiest thing I've seen in centuries."

"Eww, we're related," I complained, finally waking up to the reality that more than a few men had witnessed Callum's display of possessiveness. Our sexual escapade was now the talk of the house.

Helios glanced at me. "I've been your uncle for a matter of hours. I don't know you, but damn, do I know how you come now."

"I'm her fucking uncle, too, and I can guarantee I wouldn't have watched that, asshole," Belkair muttered.

Helios flashed him a naughty smile that turned my stomach.

"But…but you're the good guys, you can't watch that…" I was at a loss for words and beyond grossed out.

"I didn't just watch that," he said, that smile even more deviant. "I haven't jerked off that intensely in a few years."

Callum's punch hit him fast, sending him to the floor.

He rubbed his jaw. "If you didn't want anyone to react, you shouldn't have let us watch so clearly. And who says we're the good guys? Is that what the mortals think?"

"Yes, it's what they think, and I was making a point," Callum said.

Helios laughed. "You made a point all right."

"Making a point?" Belkair asked. His jaw was clenched way too tight. "You ever make a point like that again, Callum, and I'll haul your ass to the Goddess myself. Keep my niece's body off display."

I gave a sigh of relief. "Finally, someone who makes sense."

"Because we're the good guys, not these jackasses." He pointed to Helios, who shrugged.

"Wait, I'm really confused," Slate interjected.

Belkair stared at him. "What's there to be confused about? Shadow and Guard keep this world safe. All these shitheads do is make a sport of getting in our way."

"We keep it safe, too," Helios grumbled.

"So both factions watch over the world and keep the demons from the streets. But you also kill on behalf of the gods, sometimes innocent people like me, just because a god has a vendetta against them?" I asked. "Sounds like you're both a mix of good and bad, neither one nor the other…except you Helios, perv."

He grumbled, but I ignored him.

"You're not so innocent, Harmony," Callum said.

My glare did nothing to deter his penetrating gaze. "Yes, I am. I haven't hurt anyone. I was living my life—"

"Digging your nose where it shouldn't have been," Callum said.

My jaw ticked, and I was about to retort when Belkair did it for me.

"Which she wouldn't have done if you played by the rules," he said. "Don't interfere with the lives of mortals. Stay in The Blight when not hunting. Don't touch your mark."

The veins in Callum's neck thickened.

"Don't start fighting again!" I yelled, my irritation piqued from all the commotion.

Rolling his neck, Belkair said, "It wasn't the curiosity that got her in trouble. You know that as much as I do, Callum. It was her heritage."

The tension dissipated with his words.

"You're an anomaly that should not exist," he continued, glancing at me. "Our factions have been at war for longer than even we've been alive. You are living proof that the war isn't necessary, that the two sides can be—"

"Harmonious," Callum finished for him. "It's already begun. You have a Shadow and Guard working with a Torch and Sentinel."

"Sentinel?" Slate asked.

Helios raised his hand. "The Sect's equivalent of the Guard. We don't get out of the realm much."

"Which explains your perv move, Uncle," I muttered.

"Nah, I guarantee if Belkair had been there, he would have done the same."

Belkair grimaced at him. "No, I wouldn't have. That's not normal."

"Neither is Callum fucking his fated against a window, knowing I'm out there."

"It was a test, and you failed," Callum stated. "Don't think I'm ever leaving her alone with you. And don't even try to touch her or you'll be reforming in your realm before you can even open your mouth to scream in agony."

Callum moved in front of me, but I pushed him aside.

"I can handle myself," I argued.

"She can," Slate added.

Callum gave him a side glance. "I know."

Belkair rubbed his hand over his face. "You are a balance between what has never had balance, Shadow and Torch, Blight and Sect. Binding two unstable powers and two realms within you. The gods need you dead so we don't see the possibility. So we don't question. That's why they hunted your parents so fiercely. They despised them for what they did, crossing barriers like that. A Shadow and a Torch cannot mate. They certainly can't be fated, they can't fall in love because the gods trained us to hate each other. We're the epitome of the hatred Harperia and Farinthion have for one another."

I let his words take root in my mind as Helios spoke.

"They imbued that hatred in us, ingrained in us from birth," he said. "Trinity and Landon had something that broke the boundaries and the rules, challenging everything the gods had instilled in us. And you, you are a fuck you in the face of the gods. A show that the two sides can make something amazing together if permitted to."

"And the Goddess and Farinthion cannot have that," Callum said.

I bit my lip, thinking through all they'd said, all Callum had taught me during our brief training time. I thought about the fated love, wondering at how my parents could have been fated if the gods wanted the two sides to hate each other. Or how Callum and I could be if Torch ran through my blood.

"Someone's interfering," I mumbled, meeting Callum's eyes. "One of the gods isn't happy. One of them is manipulating things."

They stared at me, no one responding.

"What?" I asked, not sure why they were looking at me like I had two heads.

Callum chuckled. "Things don't work that way, Harmony."

I frowned, not liking the way he'd written off my suggestion as if I were a child. "How do you know?"

"Because the gods in The Blight despise the gods in The Sect. It's always been that way." Helios crossed his arms to emphasize his disdain at my suggestion.

"But what if one was unhappy?" I didn't think what I was saying was that impossible.

"They're gods. They're cranky most of the time," Belkair grumbled.

"This is hurting my head," Slate complained, taking a bottle of rum from the cabinet. He turned quickly to set it on the island, forgetting Callum and Belkair had decimated it, and the bottle crashed to the ground. "Fuck, that was a fresh bottle."

The other three were shooting him daggers, but he didn't seem to notice, turning back to the cabinet and pulling out a bottle of gin this time. He opened it and poured it straight into his mouth. Wiping the back of his mouth with his hand, he glanced at us. "What? This shit is serious. Now you're talking about the gods as if you walk…fuck, you do, don't you?"

"These two ass-kissers do. I do my best to avoid the gods," Callum grouched.

"That's because you're a Shadow. They don't give a shit about you errand boys," Belkair retorted.

I grabbed Callum's arm before he could attack. "Don't, please. No more fighting."

He creased his brow, his lips turning down, and I had a suspicion there would be repercussions later for stopping him, especially when the corner of his lip twitched. The sight caused my legs to involuntarily squeeze.

"Damn, just one look and she's wet. She's got it bad for you," Slate muttered.

"Good, and stop looking at her legs."

"Hard not to notice in those tight leggings. Besides, I know every inch of that body—" The bottle in Slate's hand exploded as Callum's dagger soared through it, hitting the cabinet behind him.

"Are you shitting me?"

"Stop fucking talking about her body or the next one goes in you."

Slate's jaw twitched, and I knew he wanted to fight, but the odds weren't on his side. Thankfully, he refrained, dropping the bottle with its remains. He walked over to us, slapped my ass, and stormed away before Callum could hurt him. The ire in Callum's eyes flickered in the green of the amber and I knew if Slate had stayed there would have been no stopping the bloodshed. If Callum didn't retaliate, I would have. As much as Slate and I teased and bantered, the slap crossed the line. He'd only done it to irritate Callum and remind him I once belonged to him.

"You gonna put up with him touching your mate like that?" Helios asked.

"Shut up, Helios," Callum barked. "You fucking wanked yourself off to her. I'd be careful with your words. I'm still ready to slice you to pieces."

"I'd like to see you try."

"Is it always like this?" I asked.

"Yes," they answered in unison.

"You need to put more clothes on," Callum complained.

"And you need to get back to rounds," Belkair commanded.

"I told you, I'm not your second."

"And I told you, you are now. You dragged me into this mess, you get to pull sentry duty like the rest of us."

Callum grabbed my elbow and yanked me from the room, grumbling about Guards and their stick up the ass attitudes.

"Where are you taking me?" I asked, not liking the grip he had on me.

"To get you something decent to wear."

He was pulling me along, his pace hastened so that we were through the main living space and down the hall before I could jerk my elbow free. "It didn't bother you when you took me against the window for the world to see."

He had me pressed against the wall before I could finish my words, and I was glad we were out of sight. "I thought you enjoyed that, sweetheart." And suddenly, that seductive side of him that made me gush had returned.

"I did until I realized what the consequences were."

His hand slid up my shirt and scooped my breast under my bra. "I don't want another man ever seeing an inch of your skin again," he said, rubbing my nipple between his fingers, his firmness flush against me.

"No? I think you like how they want what you have. That you got to show them I'm yours."

He groaned in my ear as he licked my neck. I didn't like how worked up I was getting. My reactions to him were uncontrollable.

"Maybe I did."

"So why aren't you fucking me back in the kitchen where everyone can see you?"

"Who said I was going to fuck you, baby?"

He slid his other hand down my pants and tipped my ass forward before sinking his fingers into the dampness that was rampant between my legs. I pressed into them, spreading my legs so they could explore further.

"Are you ready to come for me again?"

His eyes held a wicked glint to them that had my stomach cartwheeling. "Always for you, Callum."

A kiss so needy it stole my breath was his response, and I clutched his shirt as my body answered his call. I bucked against his hand, his thumb stroking my clit so that I threw my head back, biting my lip to suppress the moan that was mounting with his every move.

He freed his fingers, and I dropped my head to his chest, my cry muffled in his shirt as my climax teetered on the edge of an endless fall.

"Callum," I cried, clawing at him. He grabbed my hands and linked them, holding them by the wrists above my head as he brought his soaked fingers to his mouth, his tongue gliding over them.

"I want to hear you beg, Harmony." He'd called me by my name, a sign the hunter in him was present. My heart thudded in my chest. "Tell me what you want," he murmured, pulling my shirt and bra up and caressing my breast before bringing his mouth to it.

His tongue flicked against my nipple, sending currents through me that teased at the orgasm that was burning for release.

"Please, Callum." I hated the pleading in my voice, the power he was holding over me, and the idea that I wouldn't get that power back this time. I knew he was going to torment me and leave me here as punishment for stopping him earlier when he was ready to fight Belkair again. I'd stepped in, asserting my dominance when his Shadow side was in control and that was never the side of him that liked me that way.

"That's not how you beg, sweetheart." The nickname was back, and I trembled in anticipation, not caring that he'd stripped me of any leverage. All I wanted was for him to touch me and bring me to ecstasy.

He continued to hold my hands hostage, working my pants down over my hips and plunging his fingers into me. I cried out, the sound filling the silence of the hall and likely warning anyone daring enough to walk down it that Callum was at it again. Each thrust of his fingers had the fire in me burning higher until he removed them again and pushed his firmness against me.

"Beg for me. Tell me what you want," he said against my lips before his tongue licked along my lower lip and penetrated my mouth. I groaned, humping against his bulge, craving its fullness in me.

"Fuck me, Callum. Make me come and fill me, please."

He chuckled. "That's what I want to hear but say it louder. I want everyone to hear you beg for me."

His grip tightened around my wrists, his free hand playing with the breast that lay exposed.

"Please, Callum."

"Please what, Harmony."

Fuck, my name was back and with it, the darkness in his eyes that said this was going to continue to hurt if I didn't beg the way he wanted. He squeezed my breast tighter, twisting my nipple until I was squirming from the exquisite pain.

"Gods, Callum, please fuck me."

"I'm not going to fuck you, Harmony."

His fingers interrupted my cry of angst as they thrust back into me, hooking in just the right way that my release crashed down over me in never-ending waves. I rode his fingers as I rode out the gut-wrenching pleasure, not wanting it to stop.

When nothing but tremors remained, he leaned into me, releasing my hands and removing his fingers.

"You're a damned gorgeous sight when you're coming for me, baby."

He brought his fingers to my mouth this time, and I didn't

stop to question, knowing he wanted this show of my submission. The hunter in him was still on edge and not satisfied that he'd thoroughly admonished me for the interactions in the kitchen. I took them in my mouth and licked each one clean. I'd never enjoyed my taste, but I knew it drove men mad and that's exactly what it did to Callum. I saw the hard exterior crumble, noticing the jerk in his pants.

"Fuck, sweetheart, you're gonna ruin my plan."

"And what was that?" I asked, trying to catch my breath.

"To wreck you."

"It worked."

"I know, but now you're breaking me. I want that pussy so bad now, I can taste it." I brought his finger to his mouth and let him lick the residual off. "And it tastes like an aphrodisiac. You've got me so hard I might rip these pants."

"That's not my fault, but I can help with that." I stroked him through his pants, wanting him to fill me so I could come around him. But he grabbed my hand.

"No. What I want to do to you won't be quick. Be a good girl and go back to the room, take these clothes off and wait for me. I'll fuck you the rest of the night when I'm done with my rounds. I don't give a shit what the others say. And burn this outfit. It shows off entirely too much of that ass and those tits, and no one gets to see them again but me."

He drew me against him, kissing me so that my knees went weak. Releasing me, he slapped my ass, saying, "Go" before he walked away, adjusting himself.

His slap was a welcome one, and I slumped against the wall, watching him leave until he was completely out of view. He'd left me drained yet still craving more. I didn't think there would ever be a time when I wouldn't crave him. With a sigh, I made my way back to the room, glad Slate had a penchant for enormous houses, so I had time to walk off the heat Callum had left between my legs.

CHAPTER 23
CALLUM

I was having a hard time focusing on anything but the way Harmony had crumbled for me in the hallway. I'd done it to torture her, a consequence for her behavior in the kitchen when she'd stopped me from strangling Belkair. Not that I didn't appreciate how assertive and strong she was, but stepping between me and Belkair had irked the Shadow in me and it had enjoyed doling out the repercussions as her body had fallen apart for me.

My intention had been to leave her there without the satisfaction of release. Adding the threat that if she touched herself before I returned to finish her off, I'd withhold any orgasms from her for the rest of the night. But she'd been too sexy. Her begging had broken me, and I couldn't keep myself from taking her over the edge. She'd been glorious, like she was every time she came for me.

Rolling my neck, I adjusted myself again, trying to clear the thoughts away. I was serious about the outfit. Shit, I thought she looked hot normally, but in those skin-tight pants and that shirt that left her stomach bare, it was all I could do not to take her in that kitchen. But I'd never take her like that again. I didn't know what I'd been thinking, fucking her in front of the window. That animalistic need to flaunt my ownership of her had taken over my senses too deeply to think about the consequences.

I passed by one of Slate's men who dared to give me a smirk. Grabbing him by the collar, I snarled, "Wipe that smile off your face. And if I catch you even thinking about her, I'll rip your eyeballs from your skull and feed them to you."

He wasn't a small man. In fact, I had to hand it to Slate; all his men were large and intimidating. Perfect henchmen. The guy glared at me but knew better than to fight back. I was a Shadow, and he was a mere mortal. I could kill him before he even drew his weapon. After giving him one more shove, I continued my rounds. Every room I passed, I inspected. Every window I found, I looked through. And all the while, I wondered how I'd found myself locked away in yet another prison.

Wiping my hand down my face, I stared out at the grounds, my eyes detecting the movements of Slate's men but not spotting Helios or Triana. Wherever they were, they had shadowed themselves to remain out of sight. We couldn't continue this way forever. Locked away in a safe house—a sprawling mansion that was nothing close to any inconspicuous safe house I'd had in mind—patrolling for the inevitable.

"They'll find her," Belkair said from behind me.

"I know," I replied, without moving. "If the Guard and Shadow fail, the Goddess will find her, and no amount of spells will hide her from the gods."

"Don't forget the Torch hunt her as well," he said.

"Pfft, I don't take much stock in those imbeciles. It's our people I fear."

"The Torch hunt her for Farinthion."

I couldn't hide my surprise, turning to him quickly.

"Triana told me," he stated. "Remember, she's Krinle's second, so she would know. Helios confirmed it."

"If Farinthion wants Harmony, then he knows who she is."

"Correct."

"Did Triana know?" I imagined Farinthion had kept her in the dark, just as Harperia had done with us.

"No, none of them knew, just as none of us knew. Rumors were starting when we captured you. Whispers among the Shadow that fell silent before they could reach the gods but not silent enough to escape the Guard."

I smiled. Gerrand had played the part I'd expected him to. The more doubt we sewed, the more chance I had to keep Harmony alive.

"It won't help, Callum. We are but weapons of the gods, ones they can annihilate if we push back or question."

"Then why didn't they snuff us out when we voiced our discontent about Landon?" It was a question to which we'd never had an answer. The threat had been there, but they'd let us meander in our discontent until it eventually faded.

"Because it was never more than that. Harmony is not discontent, she is a revolution."

I let his words fall to the silence that surrounded us. They held power and truth I didn't want to admit, for it sealed her fate. Our fate. If she died, I died. There was no living without her, no existence where she wasn't with me.

"Whose revolution?" I muttered, angry we were in this situation that held no outcome where she remained in my arms. A situation that held no answers because those answers weren't ours to give. Harmony's words from earlier came back to me. "Neither Torch nor Shadow have the power to incite revolution, yet within her stands the possibility. What if she's right? What if one god has an agenda the others don't suspect?"

His brow furrowed as he thought about it. "Then perhaps

we're not doomed. If a god is behind this, manipulating fated lines, driving Landon and Trinity together to create Harmony, putting her in your path, this is bigger than us."

I frowned, not liking the idea that our love had been unnatural. "The Shadow in her formed that fated connection," I argued.

"Are you certain? I've seen fated couples—your parents, for one—and none come close to the intensity I see between you two. It was the same I saw in Landon before he ran off with Trinity."

"It's not," I snapped, clenching my fists. "A god's interference didn't bring us together."

His laugh aggravated my darkening mood. "What do you think fated mates are, Callum? Manipulations of love by the gods. No fated couple is ever by chance. Each one serves a purpose. Whether it be to strengthen the Shadow line or bring about a stronger Guard. Fated is a gift from the gods and you should take it as such, no matter which god drives it. Take it and revel in it while you can, because the only way it will survive is if the focus turns from Harmony to whatever god is stirring the discontent."

THE EVENING DRAGGED ON, and with each passing hour, I longed to be back with Harmony. With dawn still a few hours away, I gave up my pointless pacing and headed back to the room, only to find it empty. I'd spent the bulk of my time lost in thought as I walked the lower levels of the entirely too-large home. Three levels spread across an estate was not my idea of a safe house, and I planned to give Slate a piece of my mind when I saw him next. First, I needed to find Harmony and have her relieve the hard-on that had formed as my mind had played out all the ways I was going to take her again, beginning with her mouth.

Grumbling in irritation, I made my way up to the third floor, where Belkair had told me Triana was surveilling. I checked the rest of the second floor before heading that way, my ire growing with each step. I'd told Harmony to wait for me, instructed her to be naked and waiting, yet she'd disobeyed. I should have anticipated her not heeding my request. Harmony had a mind of her own, and it was something that made the balance between us so exhilarating.

As I neared the top of the steps to the third floor, I heard Triana. I stood to the side, listening as she spoke. I could see her sitting in an oversized recliner, a drink in her hand. Slate's sister sat in the chair across from her, her green eyes lazily watching her. I didn't know Triana enough to know whether she'd take the skinny brunette up on her advances, but from the way she was eyeing the girl, it wouldn't surprise me. I took her in as she spoke, thinking how strikingly similar she was to Trinity. They were fraternal twins, Triana's hair a darker shade of blonde, her features not as soft and closer to their brother's. I'd only interacted with Trinity a few times, but she was hard to forget. In fact, it surprised me how I hadn't noticed the similarities in Harmony, but then it hadn't occurred to me to look. I glanced across from Triana, my eyes landing on Harmony, who lay stretched on a long black leather couch, her feet on Slate's lap. She'd changed into a long sweater. The result was not much of an improvement, but at least it covered her skin and her ass.

"How did they meet?" she asked as a flare of jealousy raged through me. It was all I could do to stay hidden and not rip Slate from the couch. His hand rubbed her ankles too familiarly and if Triana's answer hadn't caught my attention, I would have burst in and torn it from his arm.

"She was in the field for a hit on a mark. Landon had the same mark."

"She was in the mortal world?" I asked, stepping through the doorway.

Triana shrugged. Slate's hands moved abruptly as my eyes went to them. "One of the gods sent her."

"For a mark?" I said, narrowing my eyes at Slate before turning my attention to Triana. "She was the leader of the Torch. Leaders don't leave the realm unless it's serious."

Triana shot me an annoyed look. "Maybe it was serious—"

"Then the Goddess would have sent Gerrand instead of Landon." I crossed my arms, staring her down as my mind went back to Harmony's words from earlier. "Which god sent her?"

"That was a long time ago, Callum."

"*Which god*, Triana?"

Her expression soured, but I could see her thinking. While she did, I walked over and snatched Harmony's legs from Slate. "I thought I warned you."

"You did, and I ignored the warning," he shot back. He was an insolent brat who was too cocky for his own good.

"Callum, it was harmless. Friends, remember?" Harmony said, but I could see the flicker of excited fear in her eyes. She knew I'd punish her for it, and she'd enjoy every bit of it.

"I don't touch my friends like that," I grumbled.

"You don't have any friends to touch like that," Belkair said, walking in. "What the fuck is going on in here?"

"I have friends," I snapped.

"Only the kind you fuck—"

Harmony's growl interrupted him, and I turned back to her. Her expression was dangerous, her eyes a dusty shade of blue that held the Shadow in her.

"Damn, you two are too much with this possessive thing," Slate's sister complained.

"It's the fated," Triana said.

"Keep your skin from Slate's hands or I'll describe every Shadow and mortal I fucked before you," I said to Harmony, giving her calf a tight squeeze. The deadly shade in her eyes sent a thrill through me that left my pants uncomfortably tight. I had the urge to throw her over my shoulder and haul her ass to a private room where I could test that jealous side.

"Marinasta," Triana said, and I dropped Harmony's legs, turning quickly to her. "Marinasta ordered her to go."

I glanced at Belkair, whose brows were drawn.

"Marinasta sent Trinity to the mortal world to hunt the same mark as Landon?" I asked, my chest tightening.

"Well, yes." Triana pursed her lips, and I could see her thinking about it. "I thought it was strange. It's usually Farinthion who assigns a special mark. The goddess of seasons doesn't involve herself in mortal affairs. But then she sent her on two more assignments."

"Two more?" It was Belkair who spoke up this time.

"Yes, each one coinciding with a mark Landon hunted. And each one ended up just being a demon, nothing special. I think Trinity might have been curious about it, but she was so preoccupied with what she was feeling for Landon that she wasn't up to her usual par."

"Of course she wasn't. She was fighting fate," Belkair said.

"And a goddess who was toying with that fate," I mumbled.

"Callum, what are you saying?" Harmony asked. I looked down at her, seeing it then. Exactly what she had suggested, the pieces falling into place clearly yet still fuzzy on the borders.

"Why would Marinasta need Trinity and Landon together? Why spark fated love in them if they were just going to die?" Triana asked, putting it together herself.

"Because they were only the first step," I answered. Harmony's blue eyes grew wider.

"Revolution," Belkair said.

Helios shifted his position, crossing his arms as he said, "Harmony was the end-game."

I looked into Harmony's eyes, which had brightened, confusion creasing around them. "Belkair, why was I given Harmony as a mark?" Gerrand had given me his story, but I suspected there was more to it.

"I'm not privy to that sort of information."

I glanced over at him, knowing his answer was bullshit. "You are commander of the Guard to the gods. You are in the presence of the gods constantly and privy to specifics on marks assigned directly from the gods. You must remember something."

"The Goddess doesn't share…" He trailed off, the light lines on his forehead deepening. "Seranik was there. The Goddess gave the orders to Gerrand, but Gerrand suggested you should go since you were taking command soon. Seranik agreed, convincing her it made sense. Fuck, Seranik is never there when the Goddess gives the directive of the gods, and he definitely never argues with her orders."

"Seranik?" Seranik was a god whose name sent a chill down even my spine. He was the most vicious of the Errant gods, dealing in death and torture. Diseases that delivered mortals an excruciating death. "Why would he care about a mark? He's the most aloof of the gods," I said, my mind pulling at that fuzzy part of the puzzle to make the pieces fit.

"Is it freaking anyone else out that they're talking about the gods like they're personal friends?" Slate's sister asked.

"Definitely, but I don't think this is the best time to interrupt," Slate replied.

Both Belkair and I glared at Kanta, causing her to shrivel back in her chair.

"Don't let those brooding assholes scare you," Triana said. "Shadow are full of themselves and don't even get me started on the Guard." She gave Belkair a side glance, her blue eyes sparkling with mischief.

I gritted my teeth and noticed the veins bulging in Belkair's arms.

Helios let out a bellowing laugh. "I believe you've got the enemy worked up, sis. I'd watch it or one might strain a muscle."

Belkair had Helios flipped to the ground, his foot to his neck before the Sentinel could say another word. He snarled. "You Sentinel are pitiful excuses for our kind, and you belong in Sect with the weaker of the gods."

"This is the reason they want me dead," Harmony said. I swiveled my attention to her. She'd risen from the couch, a perplexed expression on her face. "They like the fact that you want to kill each other all the time, that the hate they hold festers in their minions."

"Minions?" I sneered. "That's a harsh word, sweetheart. I'd watch your tongue, or I'll put it to good use later as I show you what a minion is."

The blush that filled her cheeks was rewarding, the look she shot me titillating.

"You know what I mean."

"I have to agree, I don't like that term," Helios complained, throwing Belkair's foot from him and rising. "It's quite degrading."

"But that's how they use you. Doing their bidding, killing their demons, cleaning up their messes, killing mortals they don't like, doling out their rules. They like the fact that you fight nonstop, that the animosity they hold toward each other is alive in you."

"Not all of them," I said, the pieces of the puzzle fitting together. The blurred edges now clear as the part Seranik and Marinasta played became clear. I glanced at Belkair, seeing the understanding reflected in his eyes.

He shook his head as he asked me, "Are you thinking what I'm thinking? That Seranik and Marinasta are not the enemies they're supposed to be?"

"Exactly," I replied as the power of that statement gripped me.

Triana's gasp reverberated through the room. "You think they're…" Her voice was barely a whisper, as if the gods might hear her accusation.

"Fucking?" I said, not caring how loud I was. They were already hunting me. "I have a pretty strong suspicion."

"Which would give them reason to want the realms united," Helios conjectured. "If they've been having an affair behind the backs of the other gods, they would benefit from seeing Farinthion and Harperia at peace. You think this goes all the way back to Trinity and Landon?"

"I think it goes back further than that, but that's the tipping point. Harmony is their ultimate play."

"She's the spark they need to disrupt the order the Goddess and Farinthion have in place," Belkair stated, his expression hard to read.

Slate handed Harmony the bottle of vodka he'd been holding. "You need this more than I do after that revelation." She took it from him, but I swiped it away.

"The last thing I need is for you to be drunk."

"She's quite a ride when she's drunk," Slate commented.

I held back from punching him, my fists wrapping around the bottleneck. "She's quite a ride when she's not, which tells me you didn't fuck her nearly as hard as I do."

There was an audible inhale from the others, but Slate only laughed. "You're growing on me, Montrose. Now that you've figured out what the fuck is going on, how do we stop the other gods and the rest of your lot from killing our girl?"

"She's not our girl," I sneered, stepping closer to him. "She's my girl."

Harmony stepped in my line of sight, her hand coming to my chest. "So how do you keep your girl alive?" she asked with a twitch of her lip.

I wanted to kiss that lip and take it between my teeth, but Slate was right. We needed a game plan, and I had nothing, no way to stop the inevitable. Leaning in, I pushed her hair back and whispered, "Keep those lips twitching. I'll put them to good use later."

She teetered, and I caught her, staring at her parted mouth and wishing the others would leave so I could fill it.

"If you two are done," Triana said, "Slate makes a good point. We can't stay holed up in this place forever."

"If the Shadow and Guard don't find us, the Goddess will," Belkair added.

Helios flexed his muscles, his expression no longer playful. "Don't forget the Torch. They'll have noticed our disappearance by now. Even the Sentinel will be hunting. Farinthion will step in if they don't do their jobs."

It was the truth, and once the gods stepped in, we stood no chance. I brushed my thumb along Harmony's cheekbone, wishing things were different. That we weren't preparing for war against an unbeatable force and instead enjoying the perks of our fated love.

"Why are we fated?" I asked absently, my mind stirring.

Harmony looked taken aback, her eyes growing sad.

"I didn't mean it like that," I said, trying to ease her concern. "I mean, what purpose does it serve?" Giving her a kiss on the head, relieved that her hurt shifted, her features softening, I turned back to the others. "It made sense that Landon and Trinity were fated. The outcome being Harmony, the physical exemplification that peace can exist between our kinds and the realms. But why me? Why us?"

"You unlocked the secret," she said in a hushed tone. "You broke the spell and freed my wings."

"Seranik specifically assigned Harmony as your mark," Belkair said. "And I have a suspicion he had some influence on Gerrand suggesting it, leading him to put the idea in Harperia's head so it wouldn't look so obvious. He needed the two of you to meet."

"No. He needed Callum to save Harmony," Helios argued. "Any other Shadow would have just killed her. You're fated for multiple reasons, all tying back to the need for Harmony to survive. You saved her over and over. I'm assuming Krinle wasn't the first to attack?"

"No, he wasn't," I said absently as my mind turned. "When I touched her, she became Trias' mark. He was the first."

"So you saved her from Trias, then from Krinle, and finally from the Guard. You're fated because Seranik and Marinasta needed you," Helios stated, his words falling like a heavy weight.

"That's it?" Harmony asked, her voice bitter. "I needed a bodyguard? Our love is this way because they thought I wouldn't live without him?"

"You can't live without him," Triana said. "He's the other half of your being. It's the curse of the fated. They may have tied you in the literal sense of needing protection, but now you protect each other. Without one, the other dies. I think you're both signif-icant in this and Callum is more important than we think. Look at Trinity and Landon. We know their being fated brought about Harmony…that sounds so funny to say, but it's true in so many aspects of the word. So many layered meanings to one name—"

"Triana, focus, please," Helios scolded her. I was glad he

had. I was about ready to strangle her if she didn't get to the point.

"Fine. They did more than that. They laid the seed of doubt, the embers of rebellion. I don't know what it was like in Blight, but in Sect, the sight of Trinity being marched in by the Sentinels and then hearing of her execution horrified us. Not just me and Helios, because she was family, not just her friends, but all the Torch and Sentinel. We knew the gods saw her act as treasonous, but we didn't really understand why it was so bad to fall in love with a Shadow, even if it made the rest of us sick." She shuddered and made a sour face.

I ground my teeth, my jaw so clenched the tendons almost snapped.

"What? You guys are so grumpy and moody, all serious with your better-than-thou attitudes. It's a turnoff." She made a sour face to emphasize her thoughts.

"I find it sexy," Harmony chimed in, and I couldn't stop myself from throwing her a lopsided grin. She was definitely my girl.

"That's because you're half Shadow. Normal Torch want nothing to do with our moody counterparts."

"And we want nothing to do with your cheerful, gratingly optimistic dispositions," I countered.

"So there you have it," Triana said with a shrug. "None of us could figure out why she and Landon were fated, but in the grand scheme of things, it didn't hurt anyone. We could have cared less, except the few guys who wanted my sister for themselves."

"You more than made up for that, Tri," Helios teased.

"Mmm, yes I did."

"Get to the point," Belkair said, looking perplexed.

"My point is, we didn't begin having doubts or to question until they killed her. Only then did we worry about our standing and our place in the world of the gods. If they could easily kill a Torch for loving someone, what else could they kill us for? There was an undercurrent of fear and talk of rebellion for some time before it died down."

"It was the same with the Shadow," I said. "It started the moment they made us hunt for Landon. When he turned himself in, we thought maybe the gods would grant him some leniency, allow him to live out what remained of his life before his grief took him."

"The Goddess wouldn't have it," Belkair continued, his eyes hard, the Guard in him shielding his emotion. "She killed him within days of his capture. Although I think my brother died the minute they killed Trinity. He was hollow, too far gone to even plead for his life. He wanted to die."

"They both did," Harmony said, looking at the floor and pulling at the sweater she was wearing. "They died to protect me, to keep me from the gods until I could fade into mortal life and live. I'm sorry. You lost them because of me."

Fuck, that wasn't where I thought she was going and it definitely wasn't the intended direction of our conversation. Triana was out of her seat and to Harmony, pushing me out of the way before I could react. She folded Harmony in her arms and for the first time, I realized just how hard this had been on her. I'd pushed and pushed, never giving her time to process. She'd had a moment when she'd discovered the truth, but we'd both set it aside, burying her emotions in sex. There'd been no time for her to be anything but strong and since that was the part of her I loved the most, I hadn't questioned it. But she had a vulnerable side, one the Shadow in her likely kept hidden, one I'd yet to truly see.

Even Slate looked taken aback, and I thought perhaps he'd only seen the part of her I had, the one she wanted seen.

"We lost them because of the gods, because of a feud that is more ancient than even Belkair," Triana said.

"Hey, I'm not that old," he defended, rubbing his neck.

"You're older than the rest of us," she countered. "Harmony, you're here because my sister and your father loved each other and loved you enough to sacrifice themselves for you. They knew you were special, so special they took your secret to the grave. They died for you, not because of you."

Harmony still looked defeated, and I hated it. Her strength made her unique, and I didn't know what to do when she wasn't strong. I met her eyes. They were clear, open to me so that I could see into the depths of her soul. She didn't like this any more than I did; she hated looking weak. Hated that the others had seen her that way.

Her eyes were sparkling with the tears she was fighting, making me think about something Triana had said. They knew she was special. Landon had said something similar to Belkair. "We're missing something," I said.

Triana glanced at me, and I could feel the others do the same.

"We've covered a lot. How can there be any more?" she asked.

"Because Landon was smart. He was next in line to be leader of the Shadow. His brother was commander of the Guard. Trinity was one of the most calculating Torch leaders you've had. She was tough and just as sharp as Landon. Why not stay in hiding?"

"You thought they wanted me to have a life," Harmony said, her brows puckered in contemplation.

"True, but what life did you have without your parents? Thinking they'd abused you and deserted you? How many foster homes did you live in, Harmony?"

"Too many." I hated the sadness I heard in her voice.

"They could have survived, stayed underground, out of sight until the gods turned their attention to something else," I said.

288

"But they didn't," Belkair said. "In fact, about a month before they captured Trinity, they purposely exposed themselves, agitating the gods. By the time we captured Trinity, the hunt was in full swing again."

I'd forgotten they'd stayed hidden for several years before their capture. "You're right. The situation had died down," I said, remembering it clearly now. "The outbreak of demons in the Nilike province had the gods' attention diverted, and the gods sent us to deal with them."

"I remember that," Helios said. "The Torch were all called to the province to deal with it as well. Remember, Triana? It had our gods pissed."

"Wait, the Nilike province? Isn't that where the Wisent outbreak was?" Kanta asked. "I remember that when I was little, before Slate was born. The disease killed thousands."

"Disease?" Triana scoffed. "Damned mess of demons is what it was."

"And Torch," I grumbled. "Stupid shits kept getting in the way."

"I remember you hunting with a female Shadow who was more than friendly with you, Callum. Curvy blonde?"

If I'd wanted to kill Triana before, it had escalated. The desire to do so was tenfold now. Harmony's eyes narrowed, her jaw firmly set as she stared me down. "That was decades ago Harmony, before you were born. I never claimed to be innocent, but then again, neither did you." Her look hardened. "Thanks for the jab, Triana. I'll make sure to twist my dagger as I cleave it into your chest when we're done with this façade of niceties."

"Duly noted, Callum. I look forward to stirring your mate up further in the meantime."

If looks could have killed, I'd have had her flayed and strung across the room.

"Fucking Torch," I muttered, turning back to Harmony, who had flopped down on the couch next to Slate again.

He gave me a coy smile and slipped a hand on her thigh. My growl did nothing but raise his smile as Harmony sulked next to him.

"Can we get back to the story?" Kanta complained. "All this angst is getting me horny."

"I can help you with that," Triana said with a wink. Kanta's nipples hardened beneath her tight shirt, and I looked away, not caring to delve into their brief flirtations, not while my fated was pouting next to her ex-boyfriend.

"So the Wisent outbreak was really demons?" Slate asked, his arm now around Harmony's shoulders.

"I'm going to enjoy ripping your fingers off one by one before I move to your limbs," I threatened.

"I invite the challenge, Montrose. I haven't had a worthy opponent to fight in years."

"Can we get back to the conversation?" Belkair asked, rubbing his face in frustration. He looked like he was ready to go rabid on all of us. I was about to that stage as well.

Triana sat herself down in the seat next to Kanta, and I shook my head as they continued their flirting. There were many Shadow and Torch who found pleasure in any sex. It had never been my thing, but I'd reaped the benefits on more than one occasion of the females who did. Not that I would admit that to Harmony any time soon, given her current mood.

I shook my head as the two grew more comfortable, my eyes flicking to Belkair, who wore a grimace that enhanced his fearful presence as he watched them.

"You two want to take that to another room?" Helios asked with a laugh, and I wondered if this was a normal thing for his little sister. He'd clearly had no problem watching his niece get fucked, but I really didn't want to know if seeing his sister gave him a hard-on.

I glanced back at Harmony. Triana's room would see action tonight, but there was a possibility I'd be seeing no part of Harmony's body tonight. Not if she didn't stop stewing about my ex-lovers. Fated were notorious for their jealousy and possessiveness. And I had no doubt she was letting Slate touch her just to get back at me for Triana's comment about the past. That Shadow had been a brief fling, a good fuck when the adrenaline was running high. As if I'd known I had a fated out there. It wasn't like Harmony was so innocent. Nobody did the things she did without having plenty of sexual encounters. I didn't even want to think about how many times Slate had fucked her.

"If you don't stop thinking whatever you're thinking, Montrose, this room is going to go up in flames," Slate teased.

"Your ass is about to go up in flames if you don't get your hands off of her."

Harmony threw me a look, pursing her lips at me.

"Good gods, enough already. Callum, what were you saying about there being something we missed with the situation?" Belkair groused.

His words brought my attention back. "Not with the situation, with Harmony. Trinity and Landon saw something in her, and that's why they drew attention to themselves again, why they needed the gods to kill them. They wanted them to think it was over. We missed something about Harmony that we haven't discovered."

"Oh, I think you've discovered every inch of her," Helios joked, and I threw a punch, hitting him square in the jaw. Relieving my tension felt good, and I flexed my muscles.

"Enough, you two. What are we missing?" Triana had turned serious, her eyes cold and calculating as she leaned forward and studied Harmony.

I walked over to Harmony and pulled her from Slate's grip, hearing him grumble. The man was going to be the death of himself if he kept pushing me. And I was planning to make sure Harmony understood that no matter how angry she was about something that happened in my past, no man, not even Slate, could touch her. The grin I had at the thought was hard to suppress and she gave me a curious look, her eyes dancing with that curiosity.

"They layered the spell in the markings on her back," I said, lifting her shirt.

She pushed it down. "What are you doing?"

"Are we doing this again? Because you scolded me the last time I got enjoyment from watching you two," Helios said.

"We're not doing anything. Not in front of you, at least." I turned my attention back to Harmony. "Let me see your back again."

"But you already studied my back. That's how my wings released. And now my healing power—"

"Healing that lags," Belkair mused.

"And magic that doesn't sit in your aura when your wings are out," Triana added, rising from the chair.

"Do you trust me, Harmony?" I asked her.

"Of course."

"Then take your shirt off."

She lifted her sweater the rest of the way, throwing it aside.

"Damn, I forgot how nice those tits are," Slate said.

Kanta tossed a pillow at him. "Shut up, Slate, and let them figure this out. Her tits aren't for you, anyway."

I turned Harmony all the way around so we could all see her back, giving Slate a warning. "If your eyes even drop from her face, I'll slash your neck and splatter her skin with your blood. Then I'll fuck her with it drying on the very tits you died looking at."

"Damn, you're sick, Montrose," he muttered.

"I'm a Shadow. I don't fuck around and you're lucky you weren't dead the minute I found out you had a history with her."

"Stop it, both of you," Harmony hissed.

Triana touched Harmony's back, and Harmony jumped forward. "Your hands are cold."

"Cold on the outside and the inside," I muttered, receiving a sharp jab in the ribs from Triana.

"What are these markings?" she asked, tracing them.

Helios and Belkair had gathered behind us.

"Shadow language, from the time of the first Shadow," I answered. "It's an incantation, a spell Landon inked her with, Torch magic sat within the spell, binding her wings and her magic."

"I know that. She showed us her back earlier. I'm talking about these." She ran her finger over the black pattern again. "There are markings below the Shadow language. I'd know my sister's shaky handwriting anywhere, and she sucked at making out the symbols of the early Torch language. She barely passed her classes in it."

I looked closer, my breath catching. Below the black letters sat a fine dusting of gold, Torch magic that hadn't lifted when the original spell had broken. "I didn't see those before."

"No, you wouldn't have," Helios said. "You needed a Torch present for them to appear."

"Not just present," Belkair said. "That wasn't there earlier. You needed the touch of a Torch."

"It seems Landon and my sister were hiding much more than wings in Harmony," Helios mumbled. "That spell is the only thing keeping what I suspect is the thing the gods really want kept secret."

"And what is that?" Harmony asked, a tremble going through her.

"The weapon you hold within you," Helios said, the gravity of his words hanging in the air. "The weapon that will change the course of Shadow and Torch, Guard and Sentinel, even the gods themselves."

CHAPTER 24
HARMONY

The words Helios uttered vibrated through my chest, gripping it like a vise so that I struggled to breathe. I turned and backed away, not wanting to be any more than what I was.

"Harmony," Callum's voice broke through the chaos that was howling through my mind: doubt, confusion, fear.

I met his eyes, the hazel in them shadowed with concern.

"I…I can't be anything like that. I can't be any more than this."

He took me by the arms, his touch strengthening me immediately. "You're already more."

"No," I said, shaking my head. "I don't want to be more. This is insane. I can handle the wings, the healing, the magic, even being hunted, but this? A weapon manipulated into existence by the gods, gods who are deceiving the other gods and dragging me into their cause? I can't be what they want me to be."

He drew me closer. "Then don't."

The others erupted, but he silenced them, his voice a force

through the storm of dissension. "She doesn't have to be anything right now but my girl. That's all. Give her time to digest—"

"We don't have time," Belkair argued.

But Callum was right. I needed time. So much had happened over the past few days that I felt like I'd splintered into pieces. My identity was being reshaped, the edges of those pieces morphing with each minute that passed. I was strong, but this was enough to crush the strongest of people and they were expecting me to carry on as though all of this was normal. And it wasn't. None of it was, and all of it left me scrambling to reconnect the pieces that each new revelation was fracturing. The only thing that gave me even a semblance of being whole was Callum. His presence, his touch, his love fortified me.

"Yes, we do," Callum said with a certainty that strengthened me. "The gods aren't searching yet, or we'd all be dead. Whatever is hidden behind that Torch writing hasn't been invoked. She doesn't have to do anything or be anything more right now. Everyone back to your rounds, she needs to rest before we unleash whatever it is her parents locked in her."

With each word he spoke, I could see the frustration in their eyes. They were immortal warriors and hunters whose one job was to protect, and Callum was preventing them from doing their job. They needed to continue figuring out what it was about me that had the gods hunting me and how to unleash it. Unless it was something they shouldn't unleash. Whatever it was, they needed answers…and so did I. My fear of the truth, this overwhelming feeling that everything was out of control, and the mere fact that my existence was a manipulation of the gods were not as important as discovering what my parents had locked inside of me.

"Since when do you give the orders?" Helios asked Callum as my determination to stay focused on my markings grew.

"I've always been in charge. It's my girl in danger," Callum sneered.

He took my arm and started leading me out.

Dragging my feet, I said, "Callum, I don't think—"

He turned to me, frowning, a dark threat behind his eyes before he flung me over his shoulder. A scream escaped me at the suddenness of the move.

"She's not getting any rest," Triana scoffed. "I think it's Callum that's had enough of this conversation."

"Fuck you, Triana," he muttered.

She snickered and shook her head as the room faded from my view.

"Callum, put me down," I protested, hitting his back as he continued to stomp away.

He ignored me and slapped me on the ass, the crack echoing through the stairway.

"Ouch!" It had stung, but it had also given me a rush of stimulation that lingered between my legs.

When we were partway down the hall that led to our room, he dropped me, shoving me against the wall. His kisses were powerful, stealing my breath and as they lowered to my breast, my resolve to fight him faded. Maybe this was what I needed, what we both needed because while danger had tainted our love before, that danger was now an ominous cloud that was slowly suffocating us. And I wanted to escape that pressure, to have him free me from it. I clawed at his hair, encouraging his mouth to take more of my breast. When he scooped my ass into his hand, it forced my pelvis against his hardness, and a moan slipped from me. I hadn't realized just how much I wanted him. The sexual tension that had built while we'd been with the others sat coiled within me, ready to explode.

"We leave it all aside for now," he muttered against my breast. "Everything we discussed, everything that was brought to light. We put it away like we did last time." He stopped his kisses, taking my face in his hands. "It's just us, understand?"

I nodded, knowing exactly what he meant. It was the exact thing I wanted, to not think about what the future held, what tomorrow would bring. To experience only the pleasure his touches brought me. "Yes, only us." I kissed him, my tongue bursting through his lips to tease his until he picked me up, his hand under my ass, my legs wrapping around him. He walked me the rest of the way, never stopping our kisses as my arms laced around his neck in a hold I never wanted to break.

He threw the door open and tossed me on the bed, removing his shirt as I watched him. His tattooed chest was taut with tension that I wanted to release. The way his eyes flared with desire as they perused my body had me so wet I didn't think I could wait for him to take me, so I tugged my sweater over my head. He took my pants off within seconds, his own falling to the floor as he dropped over me, nudging his knee between my legs.

"Fill me, Callum," I rasped, my fingers running the length of his chest. He ignored me as I moved my pelvis, rubbing against his leg while his tongue drew circles around my nipple. I arched my back, my breast filling his mouth, the sucking motion he made maddening me.

He kissed his way back up my neck, his lips brushing my skin so that I was squirming for more of his touch.

"I don't care who you are, Harmony," he murmured, making his way to my lips, his tongue licking along them. "I don't care if the gods brought us together, if they manipulated it so we would fall in love. I don't care who's in your past or who's in mine. I don't care what you did, I only care what you do now. Because I was only existing before you, and now…now I'm alive."

His words tugged at the heart he owned, sending electricity shooting through my core, and I pulled his face to mine. "You are my life, my everything, Callum."

"And you're mine, sweetheart. Now," he forced his thigh higher, and my breath hitched at the change in his tone, "spread those luscious legs for me. I want to sink my tongue into that soaked pussy before I sink my cock into it."

He laughed at the ragged breath I drew, then slid his tongue down my body. My stomach muscles quivered as he hovered over them, his lips brushing along my skin.

"Are you going to come for me, sweetheart?" he said, his voice hoarse. Sweetheart was becoming my second favorite word next to baby and the way either word fell from his mouth stoked the fire in my belly.

"Yes," I answered, lifting my pelvis as he spread my legs further, his hand grazing my inner thigh before he drove his fingers into my depths. I threw my head back and released the cry that had been clamoring to be freed.

He pulled his fingers out, replacing them with his tongue, and I pushed my body further into his face, the heat in me building so that it was almost intolerable.

"I want to hear you scream again." His breath was warm against me, causing me to lift my left leg. He hooked his arm under it, bringing my other leg up and doing the same thing as he dove back into me. "Scream my name, sweetheart," he murmured in a muffled tone as I writhed beneath his mouth.

The fire built until it was burning through my core and coating my body, every part of me trembling with the oncoming blast that was building. I bucked, tipping my head back and pressing into his face. His tongue tormented my clit, applying an exquisite pressure that sent me tumbling into the flames. I screamed his name, my body nearly lifting from the bed as my climax gripped me so hard I couldn't breathe. He continued to assail me until I was building again, the need for release battering every nerve in my body.

The touch of his tongue disappeared, and he flipped me,

yanking my hips up and plunging into me with a thrust that sent another scream tearing through me. His finger slid along my ass, delving in as his other hand gripped my hip, giving me a delectable mix of pain and pleasure.

"Gods, baby, you're so tight," he moaned, and I noticed a slight tremble in his grasp. He slowed his pace, removing his finger and grabbing my waist. "Fuck, you need to come again before I'm ready, but you feel so good."

"Then come for me, Callum," I said, taking the power from him only to have him strip me of it.

He stopped moving, bending over me and dropping his head to my back. "I don't think so, baby. I still need to teach you a lesson."

"A lesson?" I said, lifting my head. He slammed me back into the bed, sending my face flat against the sheets.

"That letting another man touch you while I was out of the room, and again right in front of me, has consequences." His finger ran circles around my ass, and I clenched in anticipation. "No one touches my girl."

I quivered, hearing the dominating tone and knowing he was going to give me a lesson that would take me over the edge. He pulled out of me, leaving me empty, and I bit back my frustrated whine.

His fingers slid to my clit as he pushed my back down, sending his fingers deep inside of me. I cried out as he leaned over me and said, "Who's girl are you, Harmony?"

The shiver that cascaded through my body was uncontrollable.

"Yours," I breathed, knowing there was no trying to assert my dominance. The Shadow in him was in control again. His breath was warm on my neck as he removed his fingers and focused on my clit again. The sensations he was summoning were soaring through me, seeking the release his movements were inviting. But he stopped his touches just as my body was ready to give in and I moaned into the mattress.

"Who's the only one who gets to touch this body?" His hand slid over my back and wrapped around my neck, sending tingles of excitement through me.

"You, Callum."

He squeezed his fingers, bringing his body against me and pressing at my entrance.

"You know what I want to hear, Harmony. Now be a good girl and beg me to rip that climax from you."

My entire body convulsed at his words, my release so close to barreling through me I didn't think I could speak. "Gods, Callum…"

He pushed his hardness further into me, teasing with every inch he moved.

"Harmony." My name was a hoarse murmur, and I knew he was tormenting himself with his need for me to know there were repercussions to what I'd done.

I hadn't done it purposely until Triana had mentioned the Shadow he'd been fucking. The envy that had taken hold of me was irrational, but it scorched through me like hot embers, turning my vision to red. I'd enjoyed seeing his reactions to Slate's hands on me. And now I was paying the price for punishing him.

His fingers threaded through my hair and pulled, his dick twitching as it moved a little deeper into me.

"I don't like begging, Callum," I dared, needing to take some control back even though what he was doing was about to send my climax toppling.

He pulled out of me, and I gritted my teeth, annoyed that I'd spoken up and lost the sensation of his touch. Dropping his head next to my ear, he said, "And I don't like other men touching my girl."

Fuck. He was going to destroy me because I may have hated the possessiveness in that statement, but I also loved it. And I realized then that it was the mate in me that needed to hear those words, to know he owned me just as much as I owned him. That side of me didn't care if I had control because the other half of my soul belonged to him. Now wasn't the time for me to assert my dominance because I wanted to submit to Callum and have him touch me until he destroyed me.

"My climax is yours," I said. "My body is yours. My heart and my soul are yours. You have ruined me for any other man, and I only want your touch for eternity, Callum."

He shuddered, and my body responded, trembling below him. His fingers loosened in my hair, and he draped his hand down my body, lifting my pelvis.

"I'll accept that, sweetheart."

He plunged into me, and I cried out, my scream muffled by the mattress as he yanked my hips back to meet his thrust. My body exploded, my release coursing through me in waves.

His growl only intensified my orgasm, and I felt him jerk inside of me.

"Shit," he muttered as I thrust my hips back. The residual spasms of my climax tore through me, leaving me shaken and weak.

Callum clung to my waist as he thrust into me so deep, another orgasm was soon mounting. But he drew from me, holding my hips tight, his breathing loud and shaky. My body craved more of him, and I pushed back, but he stopped my movement, flipping me before he hovered over me, his hazel eyes slowly shifting to a deep amber as their darkness dissipated. I brought my shaky hand to his face and pulled him down to kiss him. The depth of emotion in that kiss was so different from the commanding aggression that had just torn my orgasm from me. I didn't know what to make of the change, but Callum had two sides to him, and I didn't stop to question it. Instead, I returned his kiss, sending every bit of love I had for him into it.

His hand came around my back, pulling me against his chest, and I sensed the shift from demanding sex to love making. And I welcomed it. If everything that had come to light this evening was true, then we were facing separation and likely death. It seemed the crux of our fated love, that with it came the ever-lingering threat of loss.

He moved his hand further down and tilted my pelvis, entering me again, but this time filling me with a slow gentleness. I gave over to it, knowing I could have taken control back and turned this into more dirty fucking, dominating him as he'd just done to me. But I didn't want that. I wanted this, the lover who was the other half of my heart and soul. I wanted his strength and his power because I knew what faced us and I knew what awaited me—the decision I'd made as they'd talked about the weapon inside of me. The destiny that remained undiscovered.

So, I took his love and let him make love to me, relishing the touches and kisses as our bodies moved in unison. And when we came together, both of us plummeting to the depths of rapture, I held on tight, afraid to let go of him even when he drifted off to sleep. The firm hold of his arm around me confirmed he was just as afraid to let me go. A feeling of contentment washed over me. If this was our last night, then it had been another wonderful night, filled with Callum and the pleasure he brought to me.

He'd taken me to heights that left me dizzy. It was always like that, his touch stirring some part of me that was only for him, that had lain dormant until he'd claimed me. And gods, how he'd claimed me again tonight. It didn't seem like we'd just had each other only hours before. No, it felt like we hadn't touched each other in decades. Each lick, each touch, each squeeze, every damn time he'd commanded me to come or called me baby, had seemed like the first. He'd set my body and soul ablaze so that there was no extinguishing it.

With each steady breath he took, that contentment deepened until I knew it was time. Time to face whatever lay ahead of us, of me. I was in the arms of the man who held the other half of my heart and my soul. My fated. I accepted that perhaps fate hadn't intended us to be anything more than a flame that raged unhinged until the wick disappeared, and its time was up.

I kissed his cheek and gently shifted from his arms, making sure not to wake him. My breath caught at the beauty of him. At the man who belonged to me in ways no other man had, nor would ever again. Quietly, I dressed and left the room, leaning against the door at the searing sense of loss that cut through my core with his absence. Then I made my way from him, ready to face the destiny the gods had in store for me.

"TRIANA." I nudged her sleeping form, trying not to wake Kanta, who was sprawled naked next to her.

I smiled, glad Kanta had found someone up to her speed. She had come out as bisexual when Slate and I were in high school and, as was typical with her mother and with Slate, they'd embraced it. I was hoping Triana was just a fling. Mortals didn't seem to fit into the scheme of Torch or Shadow, even though I knew Callum had indulged in quite a few in the past. I didn't want Kanta to be hurt.

I nudged Triana again, trying to calm the envy that had slithered through me at the thought of Callum with other women. It was just the fated thing, and after what he'd told me earlier that evening, I needed to let his past go, just as he was letting mine go. We were all that mattered now, no matter that our time together was short.

"Harmony?" Triana rolled over and stared wide-eyed at me. I tried not to look at her nude body, which looked remarkably similar to mine, but it was hard not to. Callum had said the gods had built all Shadow women like me and it must have been the same with Torch women because Triana had breasts almost as big as mine and hips with thighs that were made for men to crave.

I put my finger to my lips, gesturing for her to stay quiet. I didn't want to wake Kanta and have her talk me out of this. Triana was going to be hard enough to convince. I threw her clothes at her and nodded to the door to give her the hint that I wanted to talk to her outside, away from Kanta.

"What in the gods' names are you doing, Harmony?" Triana closed the door behind her a few minutes later, pulling her shirt over her head and tugging her hair out from below it. I hadn't noticed how similar she and Helios had dressed. But now, as she tucked her white t-shirt into her black leather pants, I realized how distinct the two were from Callum and Belkair.

"I need your help." I took her arm and moved her further down the hall to where no one else was sleeping. The room Callum and I had was on the other end of the hall, so I didn't think he would wake, but I didn't want to take a chance. I led her down the stairs, thankful Slate had finally turned in.

As one of his men rounded the corner, I dragged Triana into a room and silently closed the door. I turned to find her with her hands on her hips, frowning at me. "This had better be good because right now, it looks like you're up to something that I want no part of."

"I need you to take me to The Sect."

Her mouth fell open. "Are you mad? You can't be serious. Have you told Callum about this?"

"No," I said hurriedly, "and you won't tell him either."

"The fuck I won't. I'm not taking you anywhere."

"Please, Triana. I think this is what I need to do, and Callum will only stop me."

"Of course he'll stop you because this is idiotic. And why my realm? Why not Callum's?"

"Because the last spell is Torch and either you or Helios are the only ones who can invoke it."

She stepped back, her hands up defensively. "Oh no, you're not doing this to me."

"If whatever I am is necessary for whatever purpose Seranik and Marinasta have in mind, then I need to be in the realm of the gods."

"They'll kill you, Harmony."

"I don't think they will. If Marinasta has anything to do with it and if what the four of you think is true, they won't kill me. But if I stay here, if I don't do something, they will, and they'll kill all of you because of me. I can't risk that."

Her face softened, the blue of her eyes dimming. "Harmony, you need to tell Callum."

"No. He'll only stop me, and I can't lose him." Even voicing it hurt like one of Callum's daggers slicing through my heart.

"But he'll lose you. We all will."

"Please. I think it needs to be The Sect. My mother's spell is below the other for a reason. Maybe she had faith you would see it and unlock whatever it is she bound in me."

Her eyes grew watery, and she grimaced. I could see she was forcing back her emotion.

"Fine," she said with a sigh. "I'm guessing you want to go right now?"

"Yes."

"Damn, you're as stubborn as your mother. She irritated the crap out of me when she was like this. Are you ready?"

Taking a shaky breath, I nodded.

"Then let me see your back. I need to memorize the spell. I don't know if we'll have time to lift your shirt when we get there. They may bind you." I lifted my shirt, feeling her fingers trace the patterns on my back. "You're brave, Harmony. I'll give you that. No one voluntarily faces the gods…not unless they're looking to die."

THE TRIP to the realm of the Galere gods was not anything like I imagined. I would have thrown up if not for the sudden rush of Torch surrounding me the moment my feet hit land again. My eyes took everything in at once. Land sprawled before me, a field of long grass to my left where the world seemed to disappear. A strange wall of opaque cloud-like substance stopped my sight. Before me was a series of buildings that looked like barracks and beyond in the distance, nestled within a span of mountains, sat what had to be the palace of the gods, towering and intimidating.

We'd interrupted a fighting match, and all eyes turned to us as the fight stopped.

"Triana, what is the meaning of this?" The Torch who approached looked familiar, and I thought he might be the one who had chased me in the air. Krinle. His small eyes evaluated me, contemplating something I couldn't read.

"I've brought the mark to face the gods."

We'd put a game plan together, one Triana and I hoped would buy us time to get me in the presence of the gods. My stomach was in knots over the thought.

"Our orders were to kill the mark, not bring her here," he argued. Creasing his brow, he shot her a look. One I could only gather was due to his confusion about why she would bring me in after he'd gone to lengths to tell her who I might be.

"The gods need to see her," Triana told him.

"Farinthion wants her dead," another Torch said.

I suddenly felt exceedingly small. A mere one against an army of Torch. I hadn't even gotten to the Sentinel yet, never mind the gods. I remained a quiet observer to the politics of the Torch, my fingers and toes crossed that we could manage this, and that I hadn't just guaranteed my execution. A sudden desperate need to be with Callum overcame me and it took everything in me to keep my panic at bay.

"She's special. They need to see her," she argued, a hinting tone in her voice as she looked at her leader.

Arguing broke out among them. Another Torch grabbed my arm, dragging me away as he pulled a dagger out. Triana yelled, about to attack him, when my wings burst free. The Torch stumbled back, the rest stepping away from me. This was my moment. There would not be another or they would bind my wings and I would be dead.

"I am the daughter of Trinity and Landon!" I stood to my full height, the words empowering me. I was owning my past, the parents whom the gods had stolen from me, and my place within this grand realm, a realm that didn't seem complete, as though something had torn it in two. My body sensed that I didn't completely belong here, that something was missing. "Fated to Callum of the Shadows, niece to Triana, Helios, and Belkair, and I demand to see the gods!"

"No one demands to see the gods," Krinle said. The others were slowly recovering from their shock, but he had seen my wings before. His keen eyes only evaluated me.

I looked to the sky, not really sure why when a palace the size of my entire province stood in the distance. My gut told me our plan wouldn't work, that taking the time to get through the Torch, then the Sentinel, to stop and explain at each hinderance, would only give the gods warning of my presence. That Farinthion would take the opening and kill me before I could get to Marinasta. Following instinct, I decided to catch him off guard and summon him as well as the other gods.

Nerves ricocheted through me, my hands shaking so badly I had to squeeze them to hide the movement. "I do," I said to Krinle, gathering up my courage before I turned my eyes back to the palace and screamed, "I summon you Farinthion, god of dominion. I summon your brothers and sisters. Marinasta, come to my aid and finish what you started!"

"What are you doing?" Triana hissed. "This wasn't the plan."

But I didn't have time to explain. A rush of wings hummed through the air, and the Sentinel appeared. A moment passed when they took me in, with wide eyes and stunned expressions.

"Help me protect her," Triana pleaded with the other Torch. "We stood by and let them kill Trinity. They stole her from me, from us. Don't let them kill her daughter."

I held my breath as time seemed to still, everything moving in a slow motion that had each pound of my heart echoing in my ears.

Krinle turned his attention to the Sentinel, moving to stand in front of me. The Torch followed his lead and assembled before me, in a move that stole my breath with its beauty and solidarity.

"We've lost enough," Krinle said. "Yemir, you are not commander of the Sentinel. Stand down."

"My commander is not here," Yemir answered, and I assumed he was referring to Helios, who was likely still oblivious to the fact that we'd left him in the mortal world. "As his second, it is my duty to take this spawn of treachery to Farinthion, just like she wants."

No, no, no. That was not what I wanted because only Farinthion would see me then and I needed the other gods to witness. I needed Marinasta. That's why she had interfered, why my parents were dead, and I existed.

"Farinthion, I demand you appear to me!" I yelled in a desperate attempt to save myself. The thought that I'd made a mistake, that coming here had been suicide and the cleaving of Callum's soul at my death would wake him, threatened to drown me. "I will have my voice heard! Every god in The Sect will witness what Farinthion does not wish them to see!" My voice was raw. Triana was so tense next to me her fingers were digging into the flesh of my arm.

The sky rumbled, turning a rich mauve, the clouds turning gray, and I suddenly understood why Helios had said this realm didn't hold the good guys. I suspected neither realm did. Below my feet, the ground shook as the Sentinel took form, dividing their rank to form two lines. They stood at attention, stiff and unyielding.

"You wanted to speak to the gods. Well, you're going to get your wish," Krinle murmured. "I sure hope you two know what you're doing."

A blistering wind swept through us, pushing me back. I blocked the sting from my eyes and when I lowered my hand, the god of dominion, the most powerful of the Galere gods, stood before us.

My wings had retreated, but he knew exactly who I was. "Spawn of the betrayer, how dare you summon me!"

My bones shook with the power of his voice, and I nearly peed my pants. What was I doing? Fear and doubt crept in as I surveyed the god. He was massive, towering over even the Sentinel. His thick brown hair fell in waves to his shoulders and his piercing blue eyes seemed to see straight into my soul. His clothing was ornate, lined with gold. It reminded me of the clothes men wore in the history books. The ivory shirt he wore was unbuttoned and untucked so that his chiseled abs were visible for all to see his strength. He was beautiful and terrifying at once.

"Bring her forth, now!" he bellowed.

Except for Krinle and Triana, the Torch were on their knees, making it easy for two Sentinel to grab me from Triana's grip.

"How dare you think to even speak my name, you insolent mutt!" he snarled, the handsome features morphing to disgust.

"Kill me if you must, but I deserve answers."

"Yes, she does, brother." A jaw-dropping woman draped over his shoulder, her green eyes like a tiger's, shining and inquisitive. I didn't need to be told who she was. The knowledge of her screamed through my being. Marinasta, goddess of seasons. The reason for my existence.

"She deserves nothing. She is a mongrel who needs to be killed. And these traitors need to be punished. Triana, you brought an outsider into my realm. You will die with her."

"My lord—" Triana started.

"Silence!"

"This is the most excitement I've seen in eons, Farinthion. Why is it this insignificant mortal is in our realm and that she still lives?" another god asked. I glanced around, seeing that six of them now stood before us.

This was what I'd wanted, but now that I faced the gods, I wasn't so sure I hadn't made the wrong decision.

"Because she is no mere mortal," Marinasta said. I looked at her, pleading with my eyes that she do something.

Her red silk dress swayed languidly with her movements as she sauntered to me. She wore her long black hair piled atop her head, long curls of red through it, some cascading down, having freed from the rest.

"She is a masterpiece."

With her words, my wings burst open. The gasp among the gods was audible, but I couldn't tear my eyes from her. "Do what you came here to do, child." She brushed her lips across my ear. "Free us."

"Marinasta, what is the meaning of this?" Farinthion boomed.

She swiveled toward him.

"You did this, didn't you?" he accused, the veins on his forehead standing out.

"I did," she snarled. "I am tired of being torn from my brothers and sisters! You and Harperia forced us here, ripping us from them. She is my solution."

Her words confirmed Callum's suspicions, leaving me with mixed emotions. Anger that she had indeed used me, but pity for the pain I'd heard in her voice when she'd spoken of the other gods.

"And she will die!"

I heard Triana behind me, her voice in a whisper as she recited the spell. My back itched, the itch turning to a burn as the gods argued. With their escalating tempers, the realm became unstable, or perhaps it was the spell, or even a combination of both. I couldn't tell. My body was ablaze with pain that wracked my every cell. A scream tore from me, the argument stopping as the gods turned to me. The Sentinel stepped back, and power coursed through my body like electricity that needed an outlet to escape.

"That's it my child," Marinasta cooed.

"What have you done, sister?" Farinthion roared.

"Righted a wrong and united enemies."

I looked at Farinthion, unafraid. "My parents did not die in vain, and you will no longer punish Torch and Shadow for your own misgivings." The power fled my body, taking over my senses as he lifted his hand to strike me.

I whispered a goodbye to Callum in my mind, closing my eyes as the power engulfed me and the magic of the gods barreled toward me.

CHAPTER 25
CALLUM

Something jarred me awake, and I reached for Harmony, only to find her side of the bed empty. Sitting up quickly, I looked around the room for her.

"Callum!" Helios burst in before I could figure out where she'd gone. "Something's happening. The gods have summoned the Sentinel. My internal alarms are going off, and I can't find Triana."

I scrambled up, snatching my clothes and dressing as I ran to the window. The sky looked like it was bleeding, trails of mauve cutting through the moon's beams. The clouds were so black I couldn't see them.

"And there's that."

"Triana took Harmony to The Sect," I said, my heart twisting into a million pieces. "Harmony is facing the gods."

"I think so," he answered.

"Fuck!"

I stormed past him, slamming into Slate as he ran down the hall.

"What's going on?"

"Harmony. That's what's going on." I was angry and devastated at once, my hands trembling at the thought of losing her.

Belkair rushed down the hall. "Callum!"

"I know." I turned to Helios. "I need you to take me to The Sect."

"You know I can't do that. Shadow don't cross the realm veil, neither do Torch. It's forbidden."

"It's forbidden for Harmony to exist, yet she does," I argued. "It's forbidden to take an outsider into either realm, yet Triana just did that."

"I can't take you into The Sect."

"No," Belkair said. "You'll take both of us."

The hall shook as thunder echoed through the land. I glanced over at Belkair.

"You go, I go," he said. "I didn't get to fight for Landon. I'll fight for his daughter."

"Can I go?" Slate asked, and we all shot him a look. "It was worth the ask. Can I do anything to help?"

I thought about it. Mortals were no help with the dealings of the gods, but there was one thing they did well. One thing the gods listened to. "Pray. Pray to the gods, especially to Marinasta and Seranik, pray they protect Harmony. Get your sister and every person on this property to pray to them. Call everyone you know. Pray like the gods are raining their terror down upon you because that's what they'll do to her." I grabbed Helios by the shirt. "Take me to my girl, Helios."

"Fuck, I can't believe I'm doing this. Hold on." He reached out and took both our arms. Unfurling his wings, he took us to the realm of the Galere gods. Enemy territory. Discomfort washed through me, and I shrugged the strange sensation from me as we landed in a storm that battered us from every angle. At the center stood Harmony. Her wings were wide behind her, and power spilled from her. She looked like a prism of magic, gold and ebony streams of it flickering around her. And across from her stood the Galere gods.

"We're too late," Helios said.

I'd never seen the other gods, but I recognized Farinthion instantly. He had his hand out, his power drawn and aimed at Harmony. As it fled his hand, a goddess jumped between them, the power hitting her and sending her tumbling past Harmony. It could only have been Marinasta. She landed among the Torch. Chaos ensued, the other gods screaming at Farinthion, the Torch and Sentinel breaking rank and backing from the madness. Marinasta slowly picked herself up, her green eyes falling on me. She gave me a breathtaking smile, her voice filling my mind.

Watch how magnificent she can be.

Wrenching my gaze from her, I looked at Harmony. So much light and shadow encased her that I could barely see her, but I sensed her presence in the very air that filled my lungs, her touch in the way it sat on my skin. There was a quiver in the air, followed by a series of cracks.

"No!" Farinthion bellowed.

Marinasta had made her way back to them, her eyes beaming with excitement. "Yes, brother. It's time."

Anger disfigured his face, the veins in his neck prominent with it. He was every bit as terrifying as Harperia was. "I will not face her!"

"You will! And you will make amends and stop stewing in this half of what was once a united realm."

As they fought, the sky behind them fractured, splintering into too many pieces to count, the pieces exploding in one final massive boom. Marinasta's voice seeped into my head again.

Go to her.

Harmony was teetering. The magic had slammed back into her, causing her wings to coil in pain. I ran, shoving everyone aside until I reached her just as her body went limp. I caught her, folding her into my arms.

"Callum," she rasped, clinging to my chest.

"Shhh, I'm here. What have you done, sweetheart?" I asked as the Goddess' shrill shriek cut through the fray.

"Farinthion!" she screamed from where the veil that separated the realms had shattered. The veil was indestructible, or so I'd always been told. A wall of impenetrable magic that separated this realm from ours. A second veil stood as a barrier between the land of the gods and that of the mortals. Nothing had ever breached a veil since the time the gods had erected them, but now the sheer volume of Harmony's power had shattered our veil, making me doubt it was as strong as the one that kept the realms of the gods from the mortals.

"Harperia!" Farinthion boomed back.

Harmony leaned into me, and I held her tight, terrified of the repercussions of what she'd done. To my left, Belkair stood. To our right, Helios and Triana. The other Torch followed their lead. The Sentinel looked at us warily, questioning their commander's new allegiance.

Harperia disappeared, then reappeared closer to us, the ground quaking as sparkles of gold penetrated the air at the impact. She left a distance between her and Farinthion. The animosity between the two was palpable. It sat like a thick cloud in the air. "You have brought down the barrier I erected so I would no longer have to see your ugly, cheating face again!" I'd never seen the Goddess so angry. Anger distorted her features, her usual beauty hidden behind the ire she spouted. The blood-red dress she wore accentuated it. The color seemed to seep into the ground below her feet.

"I have done nothing!" He pointed to Harmony. "This spawn has destroyed it."

The Goddess honed her sharp eyes on Harmony before they

flickered to me and to Belkair. "You will all suffer for your betrayal. And you," she sneered at Harmony, "you die now!"

I shoved Harmony behind me, seeing the other Shadow behind the gods, the Guard gathering as well.

I knew I had one chance to keep Harmony from Harperia's grasp, and it was a slim one. "You won't kill her," I said, my arm behind me and wrapped tightly around Harmony, pressing her body into mine. "You killed Landon, and we stayed silent in fear. They killed Trinity, and the Torch remained silent with that same fear. Harmony is not to blame for being anything more than she is—the true beauty of what you have created. The blend of Shadow and Torch, bound as it should be. No longer enemies, no longer adversaries, but alive in Harmony."

"He's right, sister," Seranik said, stepping forward. I tried not to react as the odd sensation of his power skirted over my spine. Harmony shivered behind me, pushing herself further into my back. As terrifying as Harperia and Farinthion were, there were a few others, like Seranik, who even the bravest of us avoided. "You and Farinthion started this, dividing our family, splitting us, and for a long time, that was fine. We sided with you, they sided with him. But it's been eons." He moved toward Marinasta and took her hand. The dichotomy between the two was striking. She was like a light to his darkness, and I wondered how the two had found themselves in love.

"We want peace again," Marinasta continued for him. "This child is an example of what it looks like when all of us are one. Just as the mortal world is. We created something amazing, a world, a people, and yet this feud has corrupted that beauty. It has turned what should have been celebration into something rancid, festering for all this time, spawning demons from that corruption."

"Marinasta and I love each other," Seranik said. The gasp from those around us was loud. What he had admitted went against everything Harperia and Farinthion had built with the factions of warriors they'd created. We were enemies, as were the gods in each realm. Two gods from enemy realms could not be in love. "We want to bond, and we cannot when you keep us separated, your dispute a constant gulf between us."

"Bond?" Harperia said, her expression softening. I had to catch my reaction, afraid she would notice and turn her attention back to Harmony. My jaw clenched as I kept it from dropping. Bonding was the ultimate show of love between two gods. It was rare and something I'd only read about. The word held as much power to the gods as fated held for us.

Seranik nodded, squeezing Marinasta's hand. "Yes."

"You've been sneaking behind our backs?" Farinthion groused.

"What other choice did we have?" Marinasta said. "We tried breaking through with fating the Shadow and the Torch, but you killed them. This child was our last hope."

"You had a child do what you were not brave enough to do?" the Goddess snapped, her tone acidic and matching the sour expression on her face.

Harmony moved from behind me, but I kept my hand around her waist, fearful of letting go. "I'm not a child," she grumbled, and I squeezed her closer.

"You are to them," I whispered to her. "Even to me, you're still young."

She glanced at me, trickles of power still flittering in her blue eyes.

"You would not have listened to us. She, however, caught your attention," Seranik replied.

They'd used her, used her parents, even used me for their own gain. Such was the way of the gods, and there was no questioning them, no matter how angry it made me. They were selfish and too powerful to question. Harmony's life still hung in the balance, and we were all walking a tightrope, waiting to see if the meddling Seranik and Marinasta had done would make any difference. And even if it did, there was no guarantee Harmony would live. All I could do was hold my breath and pray they would protect us now that Harmony had broken the veil. They hadn't protected Landon and Trinity, so there were no guarantees.

Harperia looked at Farinthion and I could see the emotion in her eyes, eyes that had been emotionless and cold since the day she'd first granted me an audience with her. I clutched Harmony tighter as Farinthion's stance softened.

Harmony drew in a sharp breath, and I glanced at her, searching for something wrong. Her mouth formed a subtle *oh* as her eyes moved between the two, her mind piecing together what the rest of us knew.

"You were in love," Harmony said, and my grip on her increased, unsure of what Harperia's reaction would be.

There were uncomfortable coughs, and the other gods backed away. All of us knew the truth of the feud between the gods. The reason Blight and Sect existed. The feud between Harperia and Farinthion. The mortals, however, remained in the dark, and that included Harmony.

The Goddess looked around. With the wave of her hand, we were no longer in the open. We were in a larger version of the hall where the gods met. Dust covered the stone chairs which showed the wear and tear of eons of neglect. She'd left the other gods, the Shadow, Torch, Sentinel, and Guard. Everyone but me and Harmony.

"There was a time," Harperia said, her fingers drifting over the back of a chair, "when we ruled the world in peace, one united front." Her eyes grew dark, power spilling from her and I held Harmony close against me, not liking where this was going. Our advocates were no longer with us. We were prey, sitting in the open for a vicious predator who could turn on us at any moment. "That time lasted well into the first centuries of the mortals," she continued. "We relished the lives we'd created, the world that flourished below us."

I wasn't certain that gaining insight into the way of the gods boded well for our fates, but I didn't want to interrupt.

"But that time was short," she said, her expression souring. "My happiness shredded, my bliss obliterated, until I erected the new veil separating the other half of our family from us. Two new realms created, two sets of gods, one ruling The Blight, the other The Sect. And do you know why?"

I did: a falling out between Harperia and Farinthion, a violent one that sparked a war between the gods, the world below thrown into chaos until the gods divided. They had created Shadow and Torch to clean up the mess.

"Because Farinthion couldn't keep his dick in his pants, finding favor in a whore goddess who should have kept her hands on the gods in her world instead of stealing mine!" Her roar shook the room. Shards of stone from the ceiling above rained down on us.

Harmony let out a muted cry, and I pulled her into my arms, protecting her from the falling debris and from the wrath I knew was coming. As much as she was trying to put on a brave face, her body was trembling. I needed to get her anywhere but here. The Goddess was unstable on most days, and this was pushing her even further over the edge.

I didn't know what to say in response to her admission. We'd known of the falling out, but none of us had known the impetus. That her anger at Farinthion had started a war that divided the gods showed just how unhinged she could be.

"She wasn't a whore, Harperia." Farinthion stepped from the shadows and Harmony jumped. I moved us back a few steps, not sure what was about to happen, but certain it wasn't something good.

"You bastard," the Goddess hissed, forgetting we were present.

I took the moment to usher Harmony into a corner, as the two gods began a heated argument about whatever goddess had dared seduce Farinthion. It didn't give me confidence to hear Harperia say she'd chased the goddess from our world and hunted her to this day. She was vengeful, and that didn't help our cause.

"I need you to stick with me, stay close and follow my lead, understand?" I whispered to Harmony.

She looked up at me, her blue eyes holding confusion amid the fear. "Callum—"

"We need to get out of here. Her temper is unstoppable. I've seen her in action. You know those storms that wipe out entire cities? Tsunamis, tornados, hurricanes? That's Harperia. We need to flee now," I said, my tone commanding. An argument between two gods was dangerous enough. One between the Goddess and Farinthion could lead to another war and most certainly to our deaths.

My need to get Harmony to safety screamed through me, but my options were limited. I couldn't use my power. Harperia would turn on us the moment I drew it. We would have to run. But I didn't know where we were. The gods only gave Shadow access to part of the realm. The Guard had more, but none of us knew the true depths of the realm.

I rushed to a door, squeezing through a crack and dragging Harmony through it as Harperia and Farinthion grew more heated. There was a boom that sounded like stone crashing against the wall, and I wondered if one of them had thrown one of the massive chairs. If they were getting physically violent, we stood no chance.

"Callum, what are we doing?"

"Escaping." I ran, keeping her hand in mine, too fearful of losing her to let go.

We were several minutes out when the ground shook, walls rising on each side of us, guiding the direction in which we were running. I continued forward, my instinct howling at each corner I came to until we reached a dead end.

"Fuck!" I screamed, slamming my fist against a wall. "It's a maze. She knows we ran."

"Then we go back," Harmony said, snatching my hand as she turned. I snagged her back. She hit the wall, and I pinned her in.

"No, we don't. There is no going back. The Goddess loves torture, and we are now in her maze. Whatever way we go, there will be no way out."

Her eyes grew fearful, the blue in them turning a darker shade. I took a moment to hover over her, resting both hands above her head.

"You left me, Harmony." My tone was terse, the hurt at her leaving clear in it. "You snuck off and landed us in this mess."

"You landed yourself in this mess. I had it handled."

"Did you? Starting another war between the gods after you decimated the veil separating Blight from Sect? That doesn't seem like you were handling it."

She tried to push away, but I leaned in closer. "If we get out of this, I'm going to spank you so hard you'll have my hand-prints on your ass for days."

She drew in a ragged breath, causing my pants to become uncomfortably tight. It wasn't the right time for either of us to get turned on, but the image of her ass below my hand was an instant stimulant.

"I don't like to be spanked," she replied, calming some. Maybe this diversion was a needed one after all. The tension that sat on my shoulders was dissipating.

"Oh, you'll learn to like it, baby, because when I'm fucking that pussy of yours, I'm going to be smacking that ass until it's bright red."

"Is that supposed to be incentive to survive this?"

"Fuck yeah it is. It's incentive for me." I pressed my body against hers. "How many times do you think you'll come for me while you learn to take your spanking like a good girl?"

"Enough times," she purred.

I dug my fingers into her hip, my cock straining to reach her as her pelvis tipped toward it.

"Callum, we should move before something kills us."

"That's probably a good idea, but if something did, at least I'd die happy buried deep inside of you."

She rolled her eyes and pushed at my chest. "Gods, Callum." No matter how pissed she was that I was playing, I could hear the desire in her tone.

"Don't invoke their name, sweetheart. You did that before and look at the trouble we're in."

She shoved my mouth from her neck and frowned. It was a cute look that didn't nearly convey the irritation she had toward my comment.

"And don't try to be angry," I said, slipping my hand up her bra to touch her tit. "It's much too adorable and will only encourage me."

"Fuck you," she sneered with an even cuter look.

"I plan to, hard and dirty." The walls shook, and I knew my time of play was over. "Once we get out of here and calm a pissed-off goddess."

The wall next to us crumbled, shriveling my hard-on as panic took hold of me. I moved in front of Harmony as the stone rose, taking form. Within seconds, a ten-foot beast stood before us. Its mouth opened, pieces of stone falling from it like saliva dripping through its massive teeth. It reared up on its back legs, bringing its enormous body back down with a force that made me stumble. The stone hide shifted, no longer smooth but now jagged and deadly.

"Shit," I muttered. "Run!"

I pushed her back and turned, slapping her ass to make her move faster as the stone trelark lunged for me.

"What is that?" she screamed as she ran.

"A trelark. The Goddess' pets. She uses them to torment Guard and Shadow who make her unhappy. They're usually made of flesh so we can kill them. I don't think this one's going down so easily!"

We ran as the trelark grew closer, and I tried to think of a solution. Trelarks were like massive wolves with the head of a lion and the tail of a scorpion. Their fur, although soft, would clump into pointed spikes when they attacked. They were difficult to kill and a pain to deal with, but one made of stone seemed impossible to take down. Daggers wouldn't cut through the stone, and I didn't have a sword like I would in practice. All I had were my wings and the power that came with them, one designed for killing demons, not stone trelark.

But Harmony's magic was different. A blend of Torch and Shadow. She'd broken through a barrier created by the gods themselves. As we rounded another corner, the trelark right at my heels, I yelled to her.

"I'm going to attack it. I want you to release your magic when I do!"

"My magic?" she asked, glancing over at me. I could see the fear in her eyes, and I hated seeing it there. It was my job to protect her, and I couldn't.

"Do that shit you did to bring down the veil."

"I don't really know what I did!"

"Figure it out, fast!" I released my wings and lifted myself, turning quickly as I drew my daggers, imbuing them with my power so they twisted into the beast's eyes. It reeled back, lurching and trying to shake itself free from my hold. I was relentless, my hands gripped so tight to the daggers that the veins bulged against my skin.

"Now, Harmony!"

I couldn't see her. My focus was on keeping the beast occupied. But I heard the ripple of her wings as they expanded. She was learning to release them faster.

"Gods be damned," she cursed.

"Any day now, sweetheart!" My hold was slipping, the handles of my daggers growing damp with my perspiration. And the pointed shards of stone on the beast were repeatedly ripping into my skin.

"Fuck you, Callum, I'm trying!"

"Try harder so I can fuck that attitude out of you!"

"Dammit," she groused, but I could hear the strain in her voice. She was trying, and I wasn't helping.

The trelark snapped its head forward, the motion throwing me, its fangs dangerously close to clamping down on me. A gold and black spear flung into its mouth, piercing it with a flash of magic and shattering its head. The beast crumbled as I rolled to the ground with a heavy thud.

Harmony stood over me, hands on her hips, a smug look on her face. "Any more orders, asshole?"

"Only when you're on your knees, sweetheart. You continue to do stunts like that, and I'll be taking your commands like an obedient puppy."

She laughed, tucking her wings in and sticking her hand out to help me up. I took it, pulling her on top of me and kissing her.

"Damn, you're sexy. Can you do some of those tricks while you're riding me?"

Sitting back on the erection that had shot up at witnessing her power, she clawed at my chest, saying, "Only if you promise to be a good boy."

The laugh I released thundered through my chest, and I pulled her back down, wrapping my arm around her neck. "I'm a naughty boy, baby. You should know that by now. It's you who needs to be the good girl to keep that bad boy contented."

"Hmm, then we may be at an impasse because I'm feeling very naughty with all that power stirring in me."

"Shit, we need to get out of this fast or you're gonna be running around this maze with my cum leaking out of you."

"Don't make promises you can't keep." She worked herself from my grasp and rose, standing over me. The temptation to yank her pants down and pull her body over my face was screaming to me, but we needed to keep moving. Just because we'd defeated one of Harperia's minions didn't mean there weren't deadlier ones waiting to strike.

I hopped up, brushing myself off, and pulled my daggers from the rubble. The spear she'd created was gone, and I looked back at her, puzzling over how she'd even summoned something like that. We had the power to imbue our weapons with magic, to strengthen them, or to influence the force of our physical moves to overwhelm a mark, but we couldn't make things from thin air.

"What?" she asked, scratching her arm self-consciously.

I shook my head and moved us forward. "How did you do that?"

"I don't really know. I thought it was going to eat you and I reacted."

"You reacted and made a spear?" I glanced at her, catching her gnawing at her bottom lip.

"I reacted, and the spear appeared, then flew at that thing."

Stopping, I halted her steps, turning her to me. "You didn't touch it?"

"Nope."

"Harmony, tell me exactly what happened."

"I told you. I saw you in trouble and I thought of how I could stop the thing. I guess I thought a spear would work. I remembered seeing movies where they stopped creatures by shoving a weapon in their throats, and that's what happened."

I stared at her, not comprehending how she had such an ability. An ability that was closer to the gods than to any of ours. But then, she wasn't like any of us, not really. She was half Shadow, half Torch, her birth spurred by the gods themselves to serve a purpose.

"Callum, what's wrong?" Her eyes had narrowed in concern, small worry lines forming around the corners of them.

"Nothing, it's just…we don't have that ability. I think Marinasta and Seranik did some tampering with you to ensure you could do what they needed you to do." And by doing so, they'd made her incredibly powerful. The thought was both a turn on and terrifying. While I loved that my girl was strong enough to fend for herself and easily decimate beasts that would take me three times as long to kill, it made her even more of a target. Harperia wouldn't hesitate to execute her now.

"Break the veil?" she asked, before sucking her bottom lip in to chew it. She was processing the fact that Helios had been right, and she truly was a weapon of the gods. The reality of it sent an urgency through me that was escalated from where it had been. But I didn't want to frighten her any more than she was, no matter how she was trying to hide it from me.

"Yes," I answered. "Something they apparently couldn't do, so they gave you the ability and with it, a strange magic that none of us has." Power even the gods didn't have.

A roar came from behind me, accompanied by a warm breeze, and distracting me from my thoughts.

"Damn you, Harperia," I muttered, grimacing at what I knew lay behind that roar.

"What was that?" Harmony said, looking around nervously.

I didn't want to tell her things had just gotten worse. That the beast Harperia had sent after us this time was worse than the last. "A dragon-demon."

"A what?" Her voice shook, her lips quivering. I was trying to keep myself from doing the same. Dragon-demons were the most lethal of her minions.

"A dragon spawned from the demons Harperia keeps prisoner," I said, throwing a glance toward the roar as I grasped her waist to bring her closer to me "They spew flames of blue that burn with an everlasting heat, incapacitating their victims in a tormenting pain that never ceases until the dragon is hungry and eats it."

She let out a squeak of fear, her face growing pale. The ground shook with each step closer the dragon came.

"Did I tell you they're massive?" I added, having nothing comforting to tell her because there was nothing about this situation I could find to reassure her.

Her lips thinned. "No, that's a big help. Thanks."

"No problem," I muttered.

The beast let out another roar that nearly deafened me, and Harmony opened her mouth to scream. I slammed my hand over her mouth.

"Don't make a sound," I said, trying my best to figure a way out of this that didn't involve us dying.

"Shouldn't we be running?" The size of her eyes had grown two-fold, and she clutched my arm.

"No, they move even faster if they sense fear."

I could almost hear the pounding of her heart. The fear etched in her expression almost destroyed me because I couldn't keep her safe against this beast.

"I'm terrified, Callum," she mumbled, stepping against me.

I brought my arm around her, keeping my movement slow so the beast wouldn't notice and hoping it wouldn't sense how frightened she was.

"I know." I had fought enough dragon-demons during training to know how they worked and how to defeat them, but I'd never had to worry about someone else while I fought. Harmony was a target, and the dragon would sense her fear, aiming its venomous fire at her. In normal times, we would whisk a wounded fighter away to the infirmary, where they would fight the venom for days until their healing abilities flushed it out. This wasn't one of those times. "But you can't be terrified."

"How am I supposed to not be terrified?" Her voice was taking on a shrill quality, and the dragon was growing closer.

"Relax," I said, rubbing her arms. Her entire body was shaking, so I pulled her to me, doing the only thing I could think of to help calm her. I kissed her. She melted into me immediately. The world always fell away when we were touching each other, like nothing else existing. I was hoping I could use that sensation to my advantage. It was a ridiculous idea, one that would likely kill us both. I slipped both hands down her pants, disregarding the way the ground was shaking more violently. I gave her ass a squeeze, trying to ignore how ridiculous this idea was. With my other hand, I dipped my fingers between her legs, sinking into the dampness which still lingered from our earlier play.

"Callum, I don't think—"

"Close your eyes and just concentrate on how good it feels, Harmony," I said, dropping my mouth to her neck. I released her ass, shoving her shirt and bra up, her tit bursting out and filling my mouth while I plunged my fingers into her. She relaxed into me as she pulled at my shirt. Another roar made the hairs on my neck stand, adding a complexity of terror to the arousal that was assailing me. Part of me questioned my sanity, and my decision to not stand guard and fight the beast that was only a few steps around the corner from us aggravated the Shadow in me.

She tensed, and I dragged my teeth over her nipple. "Be a good girl and ignore everything else."

Harmony whimpered but dug her fingers into my chest and began moving against my fingers, pushing them further into her with each thrust they made. My cock throbbed with the movement, my mind screaming for me to stop this madness.

"Come for me, baby," I murmured against her skin, knowing how my nickname for her made her hot.

She moaned, the sound like hands stroking me until the roar halted the sensation and nearly burst my eardrums.

"Shut up," she complained at the dragon, her nails digging further into me.

"Shut it up, sweetheart, so I can continue to please you until you're clenching around my fingers."

She let out a cry, her wings bursting free as the warmth increased, the magic of the dragon nipping at my back.

"Now, baby," I said, thrusting harder and tugging her nipple between my teeth.

She screamed, her power flaring around us as the dragon let out another roar, one that was cut short and replaced by a frenzied whine. Harmony's muscles tightened, her legs squeezing around my hand. She shoved my face further into her breast as she came undone, her orgasm hitting her with an intensity that matched the explosion behind us. I ignored it, reveling in her body's response to my touch and knowing that whatever she'd done, the beast was dead.

I was so hard by this time I was aching. Her legs were still quivering as she loosened her hold on me, my fingers sliding through the wetness that surrounded them. I licked her nipple, my tongue drawing circles around it before I glanced over my shoulder. The dragon had collapsed, a steel muzzle around its mouth. Its stomach had exploded, and guts covered in blue blood layered the ground, stopping in a circle at my feet.

I looked back at her, raising my brow.

"It wouldn't stop that incessant roaring and I wanted to come so badly," she said, giving me a wicked grin.

"I thought you were sexy before, sweetheart, but there's no describing how hot I think you are now. Would it be disturbing if I tried to take some semblance of power back and make you drop to your knees to relieve this massive erection?"

She threw her head back and laughed, then dropped to her knees. I hadn't expected her to, and my cock jumped in anticipation.

"Fuck, that's naughty, baby."

"You promise there are no more of those blasted things coming for me?"

"Nothing coming for the next few minutes but me," I said as she drew me out.

It was not the place for a blow job, nor had it been the place to finger fuck her, but I was so hard, I didn't think I could walk. And I knew I wouldn't last long, not with that power play she'd just displayed. I wasn't sure if her coming on my fingers or killing the dragon had turned me on more. Whatever it was, I needed release.

Her mouth enveloped me, and I licked my fingers clean. Savoring the taste of her, I brought my other hand to her head and grabbed a fistful of her hair. It didn't matter to me that death lingered on the fringes or that I stood in the middle of a dragon-demon's guts. Only the velvety feel of Harmony's tongue mattered.

Her tits were still hanging loose, and I watched how they jiggled with the movements of her head. I reached down and played with one before I brought my other hand to her head and directed her movements.

"That's it, baby. Take me all the way like a good girl. I want to hit the back of that throat while my cum is spilling down it."

The delicious nastiness of what we were doing heightened my craving for her, my words causing me to twitch in her mouth. She took me deeper, and I shoved her head forward. The sounds she began making on top of thoughts of how soaked she was took me over the edge within minutes. My legs quivered as my climax washed through me with wave after wave that left me breathless.

The groan she gave as she ran her tongue down my length, swirling in taunting circles before licking away the remaining drops of my release, pulsed through my body. She was so sexy, it threatened to make me firm again. Peeking up at me, she gave me a devious smile while gently tucking me away.

"I'll kill a thousand dragons if that's the reward I get each time," she said, standing.

She was something, and I couldn't help bringing her to me and kissing her, ignoring the taste of myself on her tongue as I tackled it. "I love you, Harmony."

"You love my mouth, Callum. Don't lie to me."

I chuckled and helped her fix her shirt. "I do love that mouth, but I also love these tits, and that pussy, and fuck, I could go on all day, but I think we've delayed all we can."

"We delayed? You're the one who had the massive hard-on," she teased, looking over at the mess she'd caused with her magic.

"One brought on by you coming on my fingers."

"And whose fault was that?"

"It saved us, didn't it?" I asked as she examined the departed dragon closer. "Do I need to finger you each time you face a demon or a creature?"

She glanced over her shoulder at me. "Only the terrifying ones, although I won't turn it down if you make me come each time."

"I bet you won't," I mumbled, looking over the beast and

studying the steel gag she'd created. Her magic differed from ours, but it still encompassed the same things—weapons and the materials which comprised them. The spear had been magical, but it was still a weapon. The muzzle consisted of the same steel as my daggers. Her magic centered on weapons and the ways of a warrior. "So, a gag, huh?"

She shrugged, trying to kick the muck from her boots.

"I'm not really into bondage, but if that's your thing, I'm always willing."

She shot me a look intended to be menacing, but the twitch of her lip lessened its impact.

"You two are sexy."

I turned quickly, pulling my daggers out. Shenala, goddess of enchantment, stood behind us, an amused expression on her face.

"And I've tried the gag thing. Not my speed, but it can be a turn on when done with the right person." Her eyes twinkled as her tongue drifted over her top lip. She oozed sexuality, and it was difficult not to let my eyes wander over her exposed curves.

"Are you here to kill us, or flirt with my mate?" Harmony said with an acidic tone.

I shook my head to clear the hold Shenala had on me. She was a goddess I'd only seen in passing and, thankfully, had never had the pleasure of fucking. I steered clear of the goddesses. And since they were very particular, few played with the ranks of the Shadows, although I had heard tell of a few Guard who'd warmed their beds occasionally.

"Tsk, tsk. Is that any way to great a goddess, Harmony Decker, daughter of Landon and Trinity?" Shenala sashayed her way closer to us. Her hips moved in a mesmerizing way that I found entrancing until Harmony elbowed me hard in the ribs.

"He can't help it, child. All men succumb to me if I want them and if I'd known this one was among the Shadow, I would have had him in my bed centuries ago."

Shit, this wasn't good. Harmony stepped in front of me, breaking the hold Shenala had on me. "You're not touching my Shadow. What do you want and who are you?"

Shenala scowled before her lips formed a seductive smile. "Oh, I like you." She pulled a strand of Harmony's hair forward. "Quite the beauty, but it's that attitude he loves you for. Sharp, witty, able to hold your own, and…" she looked over Harmony's shoulder at the dragon "…a fighter. That's what he loves about you. That and how deliciously you come."

I tensed. She'd seen us, watched as the dragon-demon had steadily gained on us, yet she'd done nothing. Her hand drifted from Harmony and onto my arm, her power nudging its way back into me. Fighting against it, I lifted her hand from my arm. The Shadow in me had its hackles up and didn't like the unknown this goddess offered.

"Callum, son of Riliek and Velia, second to Gerrand and soon to be leader of the Shadow…. Well, you were until you stumbled onto a woman who matches you in every way." She leaned closer to me. I heard Harmony hiss, felt the sensation of her wings unfurling as that possessive side took hold. "Don't bare your teeth at me, child. If I wanted him, I could have him in an instant and from what I just saw, it would be worth risking your wrath."

"What do you want, Shenala?" I asked, gritting my teeth.

"Besides a go at you? I want to teach Harperia a lesson." Her other hand dropped dangerously close to my dick, which I was trying hard to control, but her power was slithering into me, making the fight a challenging one.

Steel chains appeared, encasing her hands and yanking her back. Harmony snarled, "Get your hands off my Shadow before I show you just how dangerous I can be."

Power poured from Shenala, but it didn't touch Harmony. Instead, it billowed past her as if a shield protected her.

"Sister, stop playing. That's not why I sent you here." Marinasta stepped from behind her and Shenala's power stopped, the chains around her hands disappearing. A lilac hue encased Harmony where Marinasta's power had protected her from Shenala's temper.

"Your pet threatened me, sister."

"Good. Now stop flirting with her mate before I let her show you exactly what she is."

Shenala sneered at Marinasta. "Why don't you do this yourself, then? You made the mess, clean it up."

"There's no going back. Now take them to the mortal world until I can talk some sense into Harperia."

"And what of Farinthion?" Shenala snapped. "The two of them are tearing the old hall apart with their fighting. There's no way you'll make either of them conform to what you and Seranik want. You should have just fled to another world."

Marinasta glowered at her. "You know we can't do that. Now shut up and take them. The further they are from her temper, the better. I'm not ready for the ultimate play yet."

"What ultimate play?" I asked, irritated that the gods were making a game out of our lives.

Marinasta turned her attention to me. "Your mate."

"Harmony? What's that supposed to mean?" My temper flared. I was tired of them using Harmony for their selfish purposes, for some agenda that had nothing to do with her. "She brought down the divide between the realms, your secret affair is out, Harperia and Farinthion are..." My words faded as more pieces of the puzzle clicked into place.

"Are what?" Harmony asked, stepping beside me.

I looked over at her, then back at Marinasta. "Harperia still loves him, doesn't she?"

"She always will," Shenala said. I continued looking at her

sister, not wanting to risk the chance of falling under her spell again.

"And he still loves her," Harmony added, and I could detect the surprise in her tone.

"When gods love, we love hard, especially those who bond. Harperia and Farinthion had made the pledge to bond their souls. Before they could make it complete, she found out that he'd had an affair with a goddess from another world," Marinasta explained with a deep sigh. "It wasn't the goddess's fault. Farinthion can be extremely seductive when he wants to be. Harperia went on a rampage. She had the goddess hunted, she had to leave her world, and Harperia's scouts still hunt her to this day. It's been millennia, and she still hasn't forgiven him."

"Which is why she's such a bitch," Shenala said. "We're tired of it."

"I'm confused. Why me?" Harmony asked. "Why any of this? What am I supposed to do to fix some ancient vendetta she has against her old lover?"

I was just as confused, but I'd been around the gods my entire life. I knew they worked in ways that weren't clear to others, in ways that seemed counter-intuitive to what we would think. Sometimes I wondered if they did it to ease their boredom, to make the eons of their lives seem less monotonous.

"Because that's what they do," I answered her. "They influence and manipulate for their own greedy reasons."

"Not exactly," Marinasta griped. "And just because you have my favor, Shadow, don't push my kindness. I can easily manipulate that fated love when this is over and give her to another."

The threat was like a punch to my gut, and given the power that flickered in her eyes, I knew it was possible.

Harmony inhaled so sharply I could feel the pull of the air in her lungs.

"Understood," I said, my jaw going rigid at having to

concede and bite my tongue. I wanted to give her a piece of my mind for dragging us both into this, but I knew if they hadn't, Harmony would never have been my fated. "Tell us why Harmony is necessary to whatever plan you've concocted and what it is you expect her to do?"

"Harmony is necessary because she embodies precisely what her name implies," Marinasta explained.

"And that implication reaches beyond the veil and to the two who started this feud in the first place," Shenala said, slinking behind me, her hand brushing along my muscles and distracting me from her words. Her power teased me, taking me unawares, and I clenched my jaw at my body's reaction.

"Do you ever stop?" Harmony asked her.

"No, I don't. I am the goddess of enchantment, dear. If you'd like, I can enchant you as well and all three of us could have an unforgettable time."

My cock throbbed at the thought. I'd heard that sex with a goddess was an experience like no other. The idea of Harmony and a goddess at once was tantalizing.

"I've had the commander of the Guard. Now I'd like a taste of the leader of the Shadow."

"Too bad he's not the leader," Harmony snapped, shredding any possibility of that fantasy.

"You had sex with Belkair?" I asked Shenala, still fighting the urge to forget everything else and fuck her. It was her magic, and my mind knew it, but she had my body enthralled, no matter how I fought. No matter how strong my tie to Harmony was.

"All brawn and muscle. By the Creator, that man can fuck and when those wings came out..." The memory left her distracted, her spell on me slipping. I moved closer to Harmony and further from her reach. Harmony took my arm and pulled me even closer.

"Are you done, sister? Don't mess with them and get your power out of his body. He's off limits, and he's hers."

"Never stopped me before."

Marinasta grew brighter, her power surrounding her in shades of violet and black.

"All right, all right." Shenala threw her arms in the air.

The aura of power faded from Marinasta. "I want them out of here before Harperia sends another of her creatures after them."

"What about the others?" I asked, thinking of Triana and Helios. Belkair was another, but after hearing Shenala's confession, I wasn't sure what to think of him right now.

"Safe. They're with our brothers and sisters, those who aren't fighting. Most of us want to be one again," Marinasta said, her voice softer. A flash of sadness crossed her eyes, revealing the toll the centuries of hatred had taken on her. "We miss being a family." And in those words, I realized just how devastating the fight between the Goddess and Farinthion had been to the other gods.

"And what of the Shadow and Torch?" I asked, wondering where we would fit in if this all worked out.

"Well, that's where your fated comes in," Marinasta said with a wink, her demeanor shifting and reflecting a different goddess from the one she'd been moments before.

And that's when all of it fell into place—the pieces I'd been trying to make fit, why Landon and Trinity had been fated, why Harmony and I were fated, the reason for her existence, for her powers. This was more than just reuniting the realms and the gods. So much more.

Marinasta didn't give me time to confront her about it. "Shenala, get them out of here. I'm going with Seranik to calm Harperia and Farinthion. If it doesn't work and she finds you,"— she stepped to Harmony, taking her face in her hands—"you need to reach further than you have. Your destiny is still in there.

The veil, the magic, those are only the beginning. You'll know what to do if Harperia finds you."

She disappeared, leaving my heart hammering. Her words had confirmed my revelation, and I had no way of changing the course Harmony was on. Within seconds, Shenala whisked us away with her magic, landing us back in Slate's safe house.

"What the fuck?" I said, looking around.

"This is where Belkair said you'd been. It seemed an okay place to return you."

I stared at her as she began looking around, picking things up that were distinctly mortal and looking at them like they were some kind of toy. She'd dropped us back to the one place I knew the Goddess would find us. The magic was gone from around the house. Even if I replaced it, the trace was still there, leading from The Blight to here. A magical trail from when Triana and Harmony had broken through the protection spell and the rest of us had followed. Shenala had led us straight into a corner, one we couldn't escape, and one I thought might not have been a miscalculation.

CHAPTER 26
HARMONY

I wanted to slam that goddess' perfect face into the wall. She had beguiling eyes and a sexy body that her dress exposed in all the right places, but she was playing with fire if she expected me to stand by and let her flirt with Callum. The annoying part was how her magic affected him. He looked like a puppy, his eyes big, his mouth hanging open. Only when I spoke up did he snap out of it. Thankfully, I could see him fighting her spell, although his dick wasn't doing that good of a job. I'd make him suffer for it later.

While she was distractedly wandering around Slate's living room, playing with random objects, I took a chunk of Callum's shirt in my hand and yanked him to me. His eyes had grown guarded, and I could see the worry in the lines that sat around them. Something was bothering him, and I suspected it had to do with more than the fact that we were standing in Slate's safe house with a goddess who clearly didn't know boundaries.

"If your cock reacts to that goddess one more time, I'll bite next time it's down my throat."

The worry faded, a wicked grin lighting his face. "I think I promised you a spanking that would leave you red for days. You sink those teeth into me any further than to graze me, and I'll spank you so hard I'll have to carry you around."

The surge of wetness that filled my panties was sudden, and I clenched my legs to stop it.

"Stop your jealousy. I don't want anyone coming around me except you, baby. Although the idea of eating you out while a goddess rides me is tempting." I smacked his chest, and he grabbed my hand, pinning my arm behind me. "Tempting, but not worth the wrath of my mate."

"It might be," Shenala purred, but Callum's eyes didn't leave mine. He was showing me who he belonged to, that he was mine, and only mine. My heart soared.

"You two are no fun," she muttered.

"Harm?" Slate's voice came from behind me, and Callum let my arm go. I turned just as Slate took me in his arms and picked me up in a bear hug. Callum's growl did not go unnoticed.

"Oh my, what do we have here? Two men for our special child? I underestimated you, Harmony."

"She's not his," Callum snapped, pulling me from Slate's arms.

"No?" Shenala said. "Then he's free game, and he looks tasty."

"That's because I am," Slate said without skipping a beat. If he noticed he was in the presence of a goddess, he didn't let it show, giving her a confident playboy grin.

Shenala tipped her head, her eyes reaching every part of Slate's body before they returned to his eyes. "That might be worth exploring. I don't normally touch mortals. They aren't up to my standards or my abilities, but you look like you could handle me in ways most men can't fathom."

Slate's lips curved into a playful smile. "That I could."

"Well, that's disturbing," Callum muttered. "Shenala, why are we here?"

"So I could meet this—"

"No, why are we *here*? There's no protection for Harmony here."

"There doesn't need to be protection for her, Shadow. You haven't figured that out yet?"

I puckered my brows, trying to think of why I wouldn't need protection.

"Yes, she does. She can barely call her magic or her wings."

Shenala huffed. "They came out beautifully when she thought I was seducing you. You're a tough one, too, I'll give you that. Most men would have caved as soon as I touched them, regardless of whether their woman was there. You put up a fight."

"You tried to steal him from Harm?" Slate asked, chuckling. "That was bold. She's not one to be tested when it comes to her men, especially that one. And don't even get me started on him. Talk about possessive."

"Do you know who I am?" she asked, slithering up to Slate. I could sense her power in the air and Callum must have as well because his arm curved around my waist. Gods, I loved this man. He was holding on to me and fighting the seduction in the air, fighting against a sexy goddess to stay true to me.

But it wasn't Callum who was the target this time, it was Slate. "Hmmm, let's see, great tits, lips that give Harmony's a run for their money, hair made for pulling, and a body made for fucking. I'm guessing goddess and if I'm wrong," he stepped against her, his hand threading in her hair, "I can make you one."

For the first time since I'd seen her, Shenala looked unsettled. Her eyes stayed locked on Slate's, full of wonder as her mouth parted.

"Yeah, that mouth would fit perfectly around my hard cock, goddess."

I could see the hitch in her chest as she struggled to breathe. Leave it to Slate to break a goddess.

"As enlightening as this is, what do you mean Harmony doesn't need protection?" Callum said, interrupting the moment.

Shenala pushed Slate away and I could see her trying to regain her poise. He'd left her shaken, and I found it amusing. Head held high, she smoothed her hands down her dress and turned from Slate. I had a suspicion she didn't like how Slate had unraveled her, or that we'd witnessed it.

"Marinasta designed her to bring Harperia to her knees," she replied nonchalantly, running her fingers through her hair like she was wiping Slate's touch from her. I glanced at him. The smirk he wore faded at her words, his eyes flicking from her ass up to me.

"What?" I asked, my heart tightening so badly that it hurt. The tension had returned to the room and this time it came from all three of us. Callum's hold on me was so firm I could barely move.

"You're a weapon," she said, putting her hands on her hips.

"Weapon is a pretty strong word," Slate commented with a gruffness that told me he didn't like what she was saying any more than we did.

It wasn't the first time I'd heard the word used in reference to me. But hearing it from Shenala confirmed that everything Callum and the others suspected was true. Callum's entire arm encased my waist. I didn't think he could hold me any closer, and I was fine with that because I needed him there to hold me up.

She shrugged, moving further from Slate, and if I wasn't so fixated on what she was saying, I would have suspected she was moving away to avoid the reaction he'd caused in her.

"But it's the truth," she said, picking up the television remote and randomly pushing buttons. "Marinasta specifically created her to make my sister see that she's too wrapped up in hating Farinthion to lead us the way she said she would when we put her in charge." The television turned on just as my knees went weak, and if Callum hadn't been holding me, I would have fallen over. Slate snatched the remote from her hand and turned the television off, giving her a menacing glare.

"Get to the point. What do you mean Marinasta created her to prove something to Harperia?" Slate growled. "Shit, I can't believe you guys have me talking about the gods now. This is insane."

"Mortals are so easily flustered," Shenala said. She tiptoed her fingers up Slate's chest. "Don't growl at me unless you want me to show you just what my power can do."

"I invite it, goddess."

Shenala shivered, and I rolled my eyes.

"Would you two fucking focus?" The muscles in Callum's arms were so tight I knew he was on the edge of killing them both. "Shenala, finish what you were saying."

With a huff, she moved from Slate and walked over to us. "Harmony is the weapon that will end this nonsense of Harperia's. Marinasta and Seranik want to bond, and the rest of us want peace." Her features softened, a melancholy overcoming her demeanor. She dropped her eyes momentarily, and I wondered if she was thinking about the damage Harperia's fight with Farinthion had wreaked on their family. "As fun as pitting the Shadow and Torch against each other has been, it's getting boring. There's so much potential in them and in this world, and we stopped because of Harperia and her jealousy." Her features hardened again as she looked back up. "So what if Farinthion fucked Derina? She didn't know Harperia was with him, and it wasn't like they had bonded yet."

"He still cheated on her," I grumbled, feeling badly for Harperia.

"Sure, but there were circumstances, and my sister can be a bitch." The moment of vulnerability was gone, her power touching my skin once more. Callum's other arm encircled my waist so that he now had me caged in, but I didn't think it was for my protection. Her magic was at it again.

"That's still not a reason to cheat," I argued, hearing the bite to my voice.

"It doesn't matter, anyway," she said with a wave of her hand. "It's time for the ultimate battle and you're the star."

She pranced to the sliding glass door, struggling to figure out how to open it before she gave up and shattered the glass with her magic.

"Hey!" Slate yelled.

"Don't worry, mortal. I'll fix it if you're a good boy…no, a naughty boy for me."

Slate's jaw dropped before he pulled himself together, rolling his neck and flexing his tattooed arms. "I'm already a naughty boy, goddess. Just you wait until I show you how naughty I am."

"You two really need to shut the fuck up. And what the fuck are you doing with the window?" The tension was rolling from Callum in waves.

"Preparing for the battle," Shenala said.

"Battle?" I asked. The word weapon had been frightening enough.

"We're supposed to be protecting Harmony," Callum said, ignoring my question. I tried to throw an irritated look at him, but his hold on me was too firm.

Shenala picked at a shard of glass that hung from the broken window, not bothering to look our way as she said, "She's never needed your protection, Shadow. She needed what you do to her, what you bring out in her. She's the solution to this, and she's about to show my sister that."

Callum's entire body went rigid. "I don't think so. She's staying far away from the Goddess."

Shenala hissed. "I hate how you fools reserve that title only for her. We're all goddesses. The snarky bitch can be one of us again." She peered out into the darkness. "She should be here any minute."

Callum squeezed my waist so tight I thought a rib broke. "Dammit, I was right. This wasn't a run to save Harmony. This was a trap."

Shenala looked over her shoulder. "Of course it was. Marinasta wanted Harperia lured from the realm. She never leaves, never sets foot beyond her precious border. It's time she leaves the safety of the realm and sees the world we built. She needs to enjoy the fruits of it instead of hiding behind veils of hatred."

My jaw dropped. Harperia, the most powerful goddess, the same one who had sent her Shadow and Guard to kill me, then her beasts, was coming to kill me herself.

Callum released me and I teetered before he steadied me.

"No, I can't face her," I said as Callum stalked toward her, his muscles bulging with the anger I could see wrenched on his face.

"You have no choice," she said, paying Callum no heed. The sky turned a violent shade of black, wind whipping through the open doorway as thunder cracked the sky so loud I covered my ears. Every nerve in my body pulsed, and fear streaked through me like a bolt of lightning. Callum stopped and looked at me, understanding in his eyes. The same understanding that was pounding through me. There was no escape, no hiding me this time, no running. Whatever the other gods wanted me to do, I was at their whim. I was nothing more than a device for them to get what they wanted. They'd created me to deal with their shit, so they didn't have to face Harperia on their own.

"There she is." Shenala turned back to Slate. "Keep that sexy body primed for me, mortal. I'll be back for a taste when this is over."

She disappeared as Slate murmured, "Fuck, now that's a woman who might actually tame me."

"Mind off the goddess and onto the death sentence building outside. I need weapons," Callum said, determination etched in his features and overtaking the moment of defeat I'd shared with him. Slate's face morphed, the ruthless man replacing the horny playboy. "Every piece of metal you have. Leave the guns. I want knives, swords, whatever the fuck you have handy."

I tuned them out, my eyes going beyond to the storm and the sound of Harperia's vengeance thundering through it. Marinasta's words went through my mind, telling me there was more that I hadn't tapped into. I thought about the differences in my abilities, my wings, even the way I saw things, not the black and white that Shadow and Torch saw, but the gray in between. I was a weapon of the gods, designed to change the course of their lives and even our world. It was a terrifying place to be, but everything had led to this moment. My parents' love, my birth, their sacrifice, the markings, Callum. All of it building to bring me before Harperia.

I looked back at Callum as acceptance settled through me. He met my eyes, seeing my thoughts in that one look.

"Harmony, don't."

Giving him a smile, I said, "This is my fight, Callum, not yours. It never was yours. It's always been mine, and this won't stop until I face Harperia. You heard Shenala and Marinasta. I am the weapon, the piece that will change the course of their imprisonment in their separate realms, healing the divide between their family. It's me."

"You can't go out there," he said, grabbing my arm and pulling me to him, clutching me like he never wanted to let me go.

"I need to. Otherwise, I lose everything. You, Slate, and Kanta, the family I've found, the world I've discovered with a history I want to learn." I brought my hand to his cheek, brushing my thumb along the stubble that sat upon it. "You need to let me go."

"Never." He pressed his forehead to mine. "I will never let you go, Harmony. I spent a lifetime blind to what you could bring me and now that I've found you, I won't lose that. I won't lose you."

"Then trust me," I said, raising my head and passing my lips over his. "This is my fight."

He tightened his grip on me, then slowly loosened it as the ground shook so hard the house swayed. His eyes were heavy with emotion as he let his hands fall from me.

"I love you, Callum Montrose. I've never loved anyone the way I love you."

"Harmony." His voice broke, and I turned from him, knowing if I stayed, I wouldn't have the strength to face what lay beyond those doors.

"Go get her, Harm," Slate said, and I nodded, afraid to look back at him, at either of them. I ran, knowing if I walked, Callum would change his mind. My hand fell from his and losing his touch was like one of his daggers twisting deep in my core. Tears threatened to fall, but I couldn't let them. I needed my strength because what I found waiting for me was the most terrifying creature I'd faced yet. An angry goddess whose power shrouded the world around me so that all I could see was the color of her pain.

HARPERIA WAS a goddess to whom I had never prayed. Maybe it was instinct, but I'd always hesitated to invoke her name. She was a brutal goddess whose powers lay in warfare and discontent. Standing before her, seeing her wrapped in her power, she seemed more like a goddess of vengeance than anything else.

"You will die today, spawn," she snarled at me, her face so engulfed in hatred that it morphed her true beauty.

From my periphery I saw the other gods watching from afar, witnesses to the punishment Harperia would dole out on me. Small, inconsequential me who had gone through life living as a mortal, loving as a mortal until a Shadow had passed over her and changed her entire being. Unlocking something that had been bound in me for thirty-three years and embracing it, embracing me.

I glanced at Farinthion, the god who had caused this mess. He didn't look so godlike now. Whatever fight he'd had when Harperia had been throwing her tantrum in The Blight had faded. He looked sad, worn down, remorseful. I'd never been one to believe in second chances for men who cheated, but that was looking at it from the eyes of a mortal. Shenala had said there had been circumstances to his transgression, and perhaps there were. If fated love was anything near to the love gods experienced, I couldn't imagine being separated from my other half, especially for eons.

"No, I won't," I said, straightening my back.

"How dare you!"

"How long has it been?" I asked her, ignoring the fact that she had drawn her hand to strike me with her power. "How long has that grudge been weighing on you? Eating at your soul, at your heart?"

She stared at me, and I couldn't tell what she was thinking. Not that I thought reading a god's mind would be easy.

"The eons that have passed have only made your pain fester, but it has changed him."

My purpose was becoming clearer with each word, my confidence growing.

"You know nothing," she said, her lips pursing.

But I did know because I could sense her pain sitting like a heavy fog over my skin. "I know you walled yourself off in The Blight and with each passing day, your anger grew. You built a wall with that anger, and he accepted it with his guilt." Her eyes stayed steady on me, unyielding, and I didn't know if my words were doing anything more than further stirring her ire. "You created the Shadow with that anger, and he created the Torch with his guilt, you made the Guard with that anger, he made the Sentinel with his guilt. But over time, that guilt returned to love while your anger continued to hide the pain you never let heal."

The storm abated some as she stepped back, glancing over at Farinthion, who held her gaze. I could see the love he had for her, the one he'd tried to show her all this time, the one her hurt had blinded her to, leaving her too broken to accept, to forgive. Her face was soft for a moment and her true beauty shone. The blonde hair with streaks of black and purple shimmered in her power, her green eyes sparkling. But too quickly, the softness fled, transforming her back to the wrathful goddess.

"I sentence you to death. My Shadow will return you to my realm where my Guard will torture you until I am ready to give you mercy and take your soul."

"No!" I heard Callum yell, but I continued to look at her, tilting my head as I saw the other part of my purpose. I let the air flee my lungs as I touched the center of my power, my wings unfurling behind me.

"The Shadow will not obey you, nor will the Guard. The Torch will not obey your lover, nor will the Sentinel."

I let my command go, perceiving the connection to both sides of my power, the reason behind my parent's fated love, and the weapon they had created through it. I called to both sides of my identity, uniting them for the first time since their creation.

Harmony? I perceived the touch of Callum's thought as my mind touched his.

Shhh.

Within seconds, the current around me stirred with the power of wings. The Shadow filed in to my left, the Torch to my right, the Guard and Sentinel behind me. All heeding my call, recognizing my power. Callum, Belkair, Triana, and Helios stood beside me, joined by Krinle and Gerrand.

"They were the product of your anger and his guilt, but together they forged the product of your love—me."

She backed up further, her defenses lowering as her face contorted with a myriad of emotions. I dared to walk closer to her, taking the moment to take her hand in mine.

"I know he hurt you and I hate him for that, too. But the love you share has touched every fated pairing, bursting forth when it could because nothing could contain it. Each one of those pairings was beautiful."

Her eyes searched mine, and I drew my hand back, knowing I had lowered her standing in front of the other gods and all her troops. I needed to raise it back before she turned on me. Dropping to my knee, I lowered my head in deference. I had one chance to save myself, to save us all now that the factions stood behind me, defying her order. If I misjudged, we'd all die.

"I have never prayed to you, goddess of discontent, but I

pray to you today. I pray to make peace between the gods. I pray to bring your gifts forth so the mortals can see how divine you are. I pray to let love in once more and move past the pain that has held you prisoner for too long." I paused, thinking of all I knew about Harperia. She wasn't a goddess mortals favored. Her power wasn't elegant or calming. It was harsh and driven, just like the Shadow and Guard she had created. But there was a side to her she didn't show. Under the power and the anger was a woman who had once loved. And maybe it was time the world saw her as more. Taking a deep breath, I continued, "And I pray to ask that you be my patron goddess. That you allow me to spread the word of your power throughout the provinces and return the eyes of the mortals back to you."

I heard the gasps, the pained inhales as they all realized what I'd done. I understood the balance of power. There was a reason Callum and I played that dichotomy between power and submission so well. It was part of me. And I'd just handed the power back to Harperia, giving her the chance to rise again to the standing she'd had when her heart had shattered. Knowing that with each passing century, the mortals had turned from her to Farinthion and the other gods.

The storm calmed, leaving nothing but silence, which sat upon my ears like a deafening emptiness. I fought the nerves that were trickling in, the fear that I'd misunderstood my purpose, that I'd needed to fight and not kneel. Worry that I hadn't broken through to a goddess who had hardened her heart long before I'd been born. I didn't want to imagine what was going through Callum's mind; he had to be a wreck. I knew him well enough to know it was killing him not to come to my rescue, but I loved him even more for trusting that I could handle this myself.

You think I still love him? Harperia's voice was soft now, like the touch of silk on my mind. She was talking only to me.

I wasn't sure how to respond, so I sent my answer back in a thought like when I'd responded to Callum earlier.

I see it.

How so? There was only curiosity to the question, no anger.

I was afraid to look up at her and break the calm of her storm.

In the fated that have come through the centuries, I replied. *In the pain you carry that won't abate, and...and within me.*

Within you? You are not my child. You are the result of Marinasta and Seranik's meddling.

The muscles in my legs were shaking, and I didn't know if it was from her terse tone or from being on my knees in this position for too long. I decided it was the latter and fortified myself with the knowledge that she hadn't killed me yet. *Yes, but Shadow are your children, Torch are Farinthion's. I am a blend of both, and the touch of you both stirs inside of me. It makes my love for Callum deeper, my soul freer when I'm with him. It strengthens me. Shadow and Torch hold a part of you both, and those pieces now live in me, bonded as they should have been.*

As I finished, I understood the truth of those words. I may have been Marinasta and Seranik's creation, but in creating me, they'd made me an example of what Harperia and Farinthion's love could be when combined. I dared to peek up at her, seeing the gentleness in her.

"I am not a benevolent goddess," she said aloud, her gaze still penetrating as she held my own.

"No, you are a warrior, a hunter, a fighter. You are the strength that fills our blood, the call of courage that whispers on the wind. The mortals have forgotten this. Let me remind them of it."

She narrowed her piercing eyes, and I saw the recognition. She knew the game I had played. The corner of her mouth lifted.

"You would be my messenger?"

"If you would have me."

"No, I think not," she replied, and I couldn't help the sting of dread that touched my soul until she continued. "You will lead Shadow and Torch as your heritage has shown you should. Guard and Sentinel shall fall beneath your reign, and, through them, the mortals will know of me."

"Torch and Sentinel?" Farinthion said.

Her head turned to him quickly, and I held my breath.

"Yes. If our realms are to unite again, we need one united front with our hunters and our warriors. Harmony will lead them. Do you take issue with that?"

"No," he answered.

I wanted to jump for joy, but I was still too nervous to move. Harperia looked at the other gods, who all shook their heads. Marinasta had a huge grin on her face, and I could see the pride in her eyes.

"Rise, Harmony. You will acclimate yourself to the realms. Have your troops work to finish clearing the barrier between them. You…and Callum will report to me at the next rising of the sun." My heart was racing, and a sense of disbelief sank its claws into me. It had worked, and she was putting me in charge. That hadn't been my intention, and the disbelief turned to horror as I realized I would now lead all four factions. I barely knew how to fly. She didn't seem aware of my internal conflict as she looked up at the sky, her lips pursing. "Since it appears we've already made it to this sunrise, the rest of you return home. Farinthion and I have some discussing to do about how his groveling will begin."

Farinthion looked like he wanted to say something but held back, shaking his head, a coy smile playing on his lips.

The gods disappeared, Harperia giving me one last appraising look before she left as well. I remained where I was, the factions behind me. I was at a loss as to what to do and terrified that if I turned, they'd see me for the bundle of nerves I was. I felt Callum's hand in mine, and I turned to him, seeing the army of winged hunters and warriors, none of whom I knew what to do with, behind him.. He leaned in and whispered, "Dismiss your troops, commander, so I can devour your amazing body until the morning is upon us."

CHAPTER 27
CALLUM

Leaving Harperia's chambers, I couldn't help but think in wonder about the woman walking next to me. Harmony Decker had stolen my heart the moment I'd seen her, and she'd only continued to steal pieces of me. I didn't think there was any part of me left she didn't own.

Watching as she'd stood in the storm of Harperia's fury had been the most terrifying thing I'd ever had to witness. Every part of me had screamed to run and take her from there, but she'd asked me to trust her. I'd had no idea where that trust would lead, but as she'd summoned the hunters and warriors of both realms, her call weaving through me like a beacon none of us could ignore, my faith was completely in her hands. I'd hated seeing her kneeling, swearing her fealty to the goddess who had been ready to kill her. But she'd known exactly what to say and do to win Harperia over. My pride for Harmony had been hard to contain.

Now, after a day of dismantling what remained of the barrier between The Blight and The Sect, hours of acclimating Harmony to our world, acclimating the Shadow to The Sect and Torch to

The Blight, and of grueling meetings with Belkair, Helios, Gerrand, Krinle, and Triana, we'd spent the morning with Harperia.

Amazingly, she had taken a liking to Harmony. The goddess we'd met today was nothing like the one I'd known, weighed down by vengeance and hatred, her features marred from it, her power corrupted with it. This goddess was light and cheerful, a far cry from what she'd been only days before. She was now a goddess who no longer distinguished herself from the other gods with a title they had always shared.

And Harmony…. Well, Harmony had been the turn-on she always was. Something about how powerful she was, the authority she held, the balls she had turned me on so intensely I was rock hard the entire time we'd been there. All I could think about was pounding that curvaceous ass, as though I hadn't just had her right before we'd left to see Harperia.

"That went well, right?" she asked, interrupting the dirty thoughts that were stewing.

I tried to convince my dick to quiet down so I could reply without sounding like a dirty old man. "Yeah."

She halted her path down the hallway that led back out to the barracks and lifted her brow, a knowing look in her blue eyes.

"That cock of yours hungry again?"

"Fuck, yeah. It's famished," I replied, pushing her against the wall.

"I thought I did a pretty good job of satisfying you, Callum."

"That you did, baby, but you're too tasty to resist. I didn't get to sink my tongue between those legs this morning, and I don't think that ass got as much attention as it deserves."

She laughed, her head tilting back and giving me the perfect angle to kiss her neck. I loved her laugh, how it tingled in my ears and worked its way through my body.

"I have a lot of work to do today, as do you, Shadow." Her

new thing was to call me Shadow in a commanding tone, and it never failed to have my pulse thudding.

"It can wait while I ravage you."

She pushed me back, her eyes intense, her face serious.

"What?" I asked, pushing against her hand.

"How about you make love to me this time and we leave the naughty play for later?"

My heart thumped, her words changing our dynamic like the flick of a switch. Leaving the dirty talk and aggressiveness we both loved aside, and welcoming the romantic, heart-stopping lovemaking we occasionally gave ourselves over to.

Brushing my lips over hers, I said, "I can deal with that, but I get that pussy on my face later and that ass in my hands."

"I promise, you'll have both," she replied with a gorgeous smile that melted my heart, reminding me how much I loved that she was mine.

I pulled her to me, bringing my mouth to hers and setting my heart free as her arms embraced me. The pounding of her heart sang in unison with mine as I folded my wings around her and brought us to my quarters, where I made love to her just as promised. And as my climax took me, her body responded, waking my soul and reminding me she was my everything—my fated, my other half, and the only woman to whom I would ever obey.

Thank you for reading **Mark of the Shadow**. Love the Shadow and Torch world? Be sure to pick up **Touch of the Torch** for Belkair and Triana's story. When two Guard and two Torch are stranded in the mortal world, the lines between enemies and lovers blur quickly.

Read on for a sneak peek at the first chapter.

TOUCH OF THE TORCH
CHAPTER ONE

BELKAIR

The strike of steel against steel split the air as my sword met Brigan's. With a quick step back and a swing to my left, I disarmed him, the tip of my sword slicing his neck just enough to draw blood. His blue eyes danced with humor despite the blood that remained above the now healed wound.

"Guess I owe you a mug of ale," he said, pushing my sword down.

I wiped his blood from it and sheathed it as he retrieved his sword from the ground.

"Guess you do. Given how fast I took you down, I'd say you owe me two."

"Fast?" he said, raising his brow. "We've been at this for an hour."

I slapped his back and walked past him. "Should have been two. You're my second, not some rookie from the lower ranks." I turned, walking backwards as I continued talking. "Maybe I should send you back to the bottom and let Sert take your spot."

The humor vanished from his eyes. "Just because you're irritated that you have to take orders from your niece now, don't take it out on me."

"If you had put up a better fight, you would have distracted me from that irritation." He shook his head, and I turned back around. "Head to the barracks and shower. You reek."

"Fuck you, Belk," he yelled. The humor was back in his voice. It didn't take long for Brigan to get over things. He was too laid back, and he knew me well enough to know when to take me seriously. "Where are you heading?"

"To take Leck's watch."

"More distraction?"

"Something like that," I replied, passing the path to the barracks and gesturing for him to go in that direction.

"It won't help. You need to accept that things are different now." His voice faded the more distance I put between us, and I didn't bother to turn back around.

Torchlight flickered in the hall that led to the dwelling of the gods, casting shadows that darkened my path. I gestured for Leck to go, telling him I'd take his watch for the rest of the night. Too on edge, I knew sleep wouldn't come easily. It hadn't since Harmony's arrival.

I settled into my guard pose, pulling my dagger out and keeping my sword close, ready to defend the gods if a threat arose. Things were happening too fast, and it made me nervous. The changes were too monumental, and I couldn't help thinking they were only the beginning.

The Blight as I'd known it was now merged into The Sect, the two realms of the gods now one. Our gods were still reconciling, still figuring out how to run the world, their realms, and their warriors and hunters as one combined front. We were navigating fresh waters—Guard and Sentinel, Shadow and Torch—and we were no longer what we used to be.

I was no longer who I once was. My reputation had always been that of the hard and cruel commander of the Guard, relentless and unbending. Now change faced me at every turn. A constant need to bend, to yield to transformation and to Harmony. My brother's daughter, my niece, and the most powerful of us. A blend of Shadow and Torch.

Where did that leave us? For eons we had lived in stasis, ruled by the gods of each realm. Lived as enemies. To turn us into allies went against everything we stood for, everything the gods had ingrained in us from the day they created our factions.

"If you stare any harder at that wall, it might shatter."

I scowled at Callum, my jaw straining and tension lining my muscles.

"What do you want, Callum?"

He stared me down, his observant eyes seeing what I didn't want him to see, knowing he'd take it back to Harmony. They were inseparable now. Callum led the Shadow, Gerrand stepping down just like he'd planned, and Callum taking the lead as had been his path since my brother's death moved him to second. I remained leader of the Guard, but Harmony oversaw us all and what Callum knew and observed, he would report to her.

"I'm wondering why the leader of the Guard is staring at a wall while he grips his dagger as if it might run from him." He gestured toward my hand. "You may want to clean up that puddle of blood."

I looked down, seeing that the dagger was slicing into my hand, the skin repairing, then ripping repeatedly. Rolling my neck, I put the dagger in my belt.

"What else?" I grumbled.

"You're going to the mortal realm—"

"I'm what?"

He grimaced, the veins in his neck becoming more prominent. "Don't interrupt—"

"I'll interrupt when I want. You're not my commander."

Moving so that he stood in my face, he snarled. "I may not be, but my mate is. Now shut the fuck up and let me give you her orders."

I shoved him, and a deep rumble came from his chest. "Fucking Shadow. I don't take orders from you. Have her deliver them herself."

"Fuck off, Belkair. She's busy kissing ass to the Goddess, trying to talk her out of merging your precious Guard with the Sentinel."

That caught my attention. "She what? Who put that idea in her head?"

"Farinthion."

"Oh, fuck me, I'm not working with the Sentinel." Farinthion was an ass, and the Goddess was a bitch. But at least I respected her. Farinthion hadn't earned my respect, no matter that she'd forgiven him for cheating on her. This entire debacle with merging the realms had resulted from their reconciliation. That didn't make me like Farinthion or any of the Galere gods from The Sect. "Those shitheads are pussies who do nothing but sit around all day on their lazy asses."

He rolled his eyes at me and folded his arms. "As much as I hate Torch and Sentinel, even I know that's not true. Look, Belkair, none of us like this, but we need to get along. The realms and the gods have united. Shadow and Torch are communicating. It's time for the Guard to get on board. Even the Sentinel have been working with the other factions. You and your Guard are the stubborn holdouts on this unity thing."

And that was the way I liked it.

"You don't have a choice, Callum. You're a sellout who won't get laid if he doesn't cooperate and make his mate happy."

His jaw clenched, and I knew I'd gotten him. He was a

commanding prick, but Harmony was just as tough. The two of them were a pair to be feared…by anyone but me.

"I won't stand here and bicker with you because that's what you want," he said, the torchlight touching his eyes but making them no lighter.

"No, what I want is to punch you, but it will piss my niece off if I fuck you up the way I really want to right now."

I loved goading him. Shadow and Guard had always been bitter toward each other. We weren't rivals like we were with Torch and Sentinel, but we didn't particularly like each other. I suspected it stemmed from the gods pitting us against each other for fun at some point, but I had no proof of that.

"I'd like to see you try, old man."

"Fuck," I muttered. "Had to go there?"

He gave me a crooked grin, the tension relaxing in his shoulders. "Of course. Now stand down and listen to Harmony's plan."

With crossed arms, I stood my ground. "I'll listen, but that doesn't mean I'll obey. I give the commands around here."

That grin turned to a smirk. "I'm the only one who gives Harmony commands, and the only one she takes them from."

"You two are twisted. I've told you before, keep that shit to yourselves. That's my niece you're talking about."

His laughter echoed through the room. After that stunt he'd pulled in the mortal world, staking his claim on her in the window for everyone to see, I'd made it clear he needed to keep their sex life behind closed doors or I'd tear the wings from him.

"Calm down, Belkair. Save your irritation for what I'm about to tell you."

Wonderful, that didn't make me want to hear what Harmony was up to any more than before.

"If it has anything to do with those fucking Sentinel, I'm walking away."

"You can't walk away. You're on duty."

I regretted taking watch duty because I had no way of leaving my post and him. I wished I had Harmony's ability to talk to us in our minds. Then I could call Leck back and leave Callum and his news here.

My eyes narrowing, I said, "Did you plan this, knowing I was down here? Knowing I couldn't leave my post?"

"Of course. I'm not an idiot, Belkair. I was planning to ambush you in the morning, but when I heard you were on duty, my job became easier." Again, I regretted the decision. "Tomorrow your duties change. Harmony wants the Guard to experience hunting."

"She what?" I pushed from the stone wall, getting in his face. "Is she mad? Guard don't hunt. We are warriors, not fucking hound dogs like your lot." Just the thought had my blood boiling. There was no way she was sending my Guard to do the dirty work of the gods. That's what Shadow were for.

Callum bristled, and his fists clenched so tightly I wondered if he'd dare punch me. I would invite it. The amount of pent-up angst I had from all the commotion over the past few weeks was clamoring to escape, and beating the shit out of Callum would be a welcome relief. The spar with Brigan hadn't helped.

"You call me or my Shadow 'hound dogs' again and I won't give a fuck if you're Harmony's uncle."

I snorted. "Idle threats. Tell her my Guard don't leave the realm."

"Then you'll want to tell the Goddess that because she agreed."

My mouth dropped so far it nearly hit the ground.

"That one shut you up, didn't it?" he taunted. "You and your second will team with Krinle and Triana."

I grabbed him, shoving him so hard against the wall that it shook. To his credit, he didn't fight back, but the look on his face was enough to make any other man crumble. I, however, wasn't any other man.

"I'm not working with the Torch."

"Yes, you are," he said, his teeth clenched so that he emphasized each word. "Harmony has already spoken with Krinle and me about it. We think the Guard can teach our ranks and we can teach yours. There's no reason we shouldn't all be as strong as we can. The Guard fight differently, you train differently. The same with the Shadow."

"Then why aren't we teaming with you and your second? Why those blasted Torch?"

He shrugged free of my hold. "You will be. We're starting with the leaders of opposing factions. You'll be the first to test it out, to see if it can work."

That gave me even more reason to dislike this idea.

"I'm on an assignment for the Goddess tonight," he continued, "so we're pairing you with the Torch leaders first. The Sentinel will pair with me and my second on the next run if you four don't kill each other."

I walked back to my spot, mumbling curses under my breath. The cold stone against my back did nothing to cool the fire in me.

"Torch and Sentinel are an unknown to us, Belkair. We've never fought side by side with them. We can learn from them and they from us. Harmony thought it best to have the top ranks start then work our way down."

"So, she's testing this out with us? Not the other way around?"

"With you. She trusts you, you're her uncle—"

"So is Helios." Although, after his reaction to Callum's stunt with the window, I preferred him as far from Harmony as possible.

"I trust you, and I know your ways. I don't know Helios any

more than you do, and I certainly don't trust him. We want you to lead this, Belkair, and the Goddess agrees." Which meant I had no choice. I could fight Harmony on this, but not the Goddess. "Guard are fiercer than Sentinel, Torch not as disciplined as Shadow. The factions are now expected to work together, and you're the test to see if that's possible or if we're stuck with divided factions within the realm."

I ran my hands through my hair. "What do you and Harmony expect me to do?"

"Observe and learn but show them what Guard can bring to a fight. Torch may grate on our nerves, but they are hunters. They have their own way of hunting, but that doesn't mean it's any less lethal." He absently played with the hilt of the knife tucked in his belt as he paced. "You and your second need to know how hunters work, how we move in the mortal world, how we seek out demons, and destroy them." I followed his pacing, wondering if he was aware he was doing it. "The Torch need to see the strengths of the Guard—your precision, your discipline. To see what makes you different from their Sentinel. And all of you need to learn from each other." He stopped and faced me.

I eyed him, uncertain if that answer held the truth. "Why not pair us with Shadow and Sentinel with Torch then?" He tipped his head, and I knew I had him. There was something more to this. "Callum?"

"Because you'll report back to me with what you find."

"Shit, this was your idea?"

His lip tilted like he was hiding a grin. "It was Harmony's…I just tweaked it a little."

Raising my brow, I couldn't help but ask, "And does she know you tweaked it?"

"She will," he replied with a shrug.

I shook my head. "Will that be before or after you've fucked her? Because if you say before, I can guarantee she won't be satisfying that hungry dick of yours."

"I can handle my mate and my dick, Belkair," he said, the grin turning to a smirk. "Go hunting with Krinle and Triana. Watch them and watch how they work. I want to know what makes the Torch so special to the Galere gods."

I leaned against the wall, seeing the side of Callum that made him leader of the Shadow.

"You want to know if the Shadow have competition. If Torch will come to be favored by the Goddess." He didn't reply. "It's smart, Callum. Tactical. But if I do this, I expect the same when you hunt with the Sentinel."

"Done. Remember, Belkair, we're all one big family now. No killing either of them, especially Triana. You don't want to piss Harmony off."

I tried not to roll my eyes. Considering anyone other than my Guard as family rubbed me the wrong way, especially Torch and Sentinel.

"Like she won't already be pissed that you've twisted around her reasons for this excursion. Let me guess, she thinks we'll start fucking Torches like my brother did?" The thought turned my stomach. I still didn't understand how Landon had even stomached touching Trinity. It made more sense now that I knew the gods orchestrated their fates, but it still made me sick if I stopped to think about it.

"I wouldn't go that far, but she expects that we'll all get along and work together."

"Thousands of years of groomed animosity is a hard thing to break, Callum. She's got her work cut out for her." I pushed from the wall and stepped closer to him, and he continued to stare me down like an unmoving mountain. Not that I thought getting into his space would bother him. Callum was not someone who backed down, no matter who was in his face. The gods had chosen well when they'd made him Harmony's mate. He was the toughest Shadow and the only one who had the balls to defy the gods like he had. "Especially if she can't even convince you that it should happen. You better hope your commands are enough to take her attention from that fact."

"She always heeds my commands, Belkair," he replied, ignoring my grimace. "Leave Harmony to me. I'm not saying I don't believe it will happen, look what she did with the gods."

"We're not the gods. We're pricks and assholes who loathe each other because that's the way the gods designed us."

He dropped his defensive stance and walked away, saying, "It might be time to change that."

About the Author

J. L. Jackola is a writer of love stories with morally gray men and the feisty women they adore. She's an admitted sugar addict with a penchant for anything with salted caramel. When she's not weaving tales, snacking on sweets, or downing her morning cup of tea, you can find her logging miles in her running shoes, watching movies with her family, or curled up with a book.

She resides in Delaware with her husband and three children.

To learn more, visit her website at www.jljackola.com and be sure to sign up for J L's newsletter to keep up with all the latest release news.